MIAMI NOIR
THE CLASSICS

MIAMI NOIR
THE CLASSICS

EDITED BY LES STANDIFORD

AKASHIC
BOOKS

BROOKLYN, NEW YORK

Published by Akashic Books
©2020 Akashic Books

Series concept by Tim McLoughlin and Johnny Temple
Miami map by Sohrab Habibion

ISBN: 978-1-61775-806-5
Library of Congress Control Number: 2020936147

First printing

Grateful acknowledgment is made for permission to reprint the stories in this anthology. See page 404 for details.

Akashic Books
Brooklyn, New York
Twitter: @AkashicBooks
Facebook: AkashicBooks
E-mail: info@akashicbooks.com
Website: www.akashicbooks.com

ALSO IN THE AKASHIC NOIR SERIES

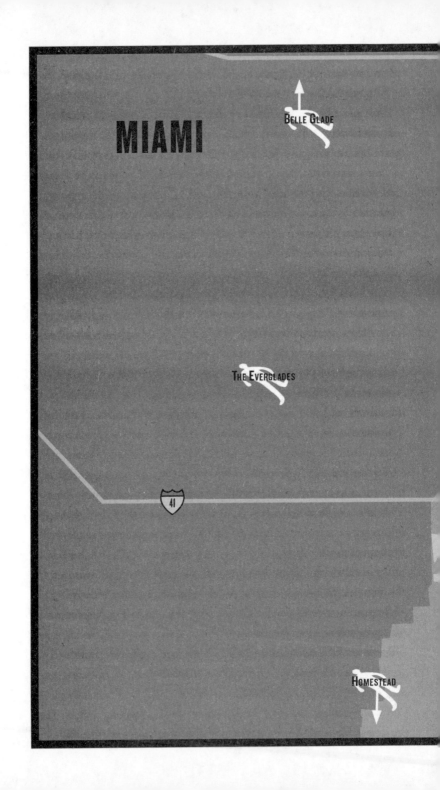

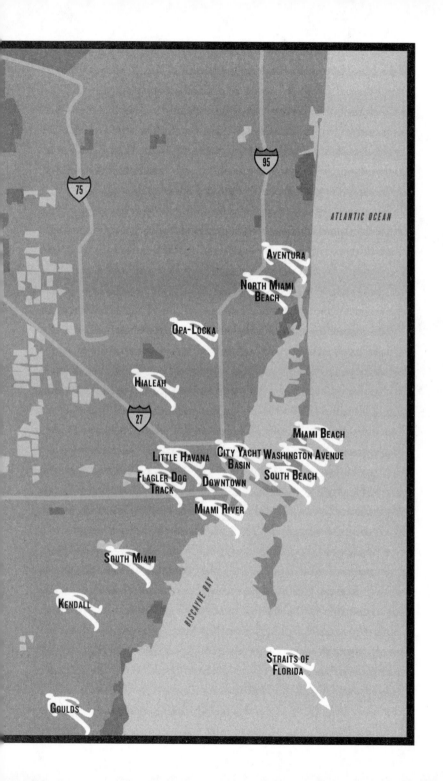

TABLE OF CONTENTS

INTRODUCTION
LONG ON BEAUTY, SHORT ON RECTITUDE

W hen I wrote the introduction to the original *Miami Noir* in 2007, I spoke of the relative youth of the city, barely more than one century and one decade old at the time, and of the appropriate fact of the irascible crime story as its reigning literary emblem. There might come a day, I theorized, when Miami—having acquired its art and science museums, and its thriving opera house and shimmering performing arts centers—would have developed the ease and the multifaceted cultural and historical backdrop from which reserved and careful works exhibiting the decorum of literature some purists denote with a capital "L" might be spawned.

But, said I, Miami remained at the time essentially a frontier town, a city on the edge of the continent, inviting all comers, full of fractious delight, where nothing of import had been settled, where no special interest group could yet claim control of politics or culture, and every day brought a new melee between some subset of those on the make and destined for collision. The perfect literary medium to give voice to such a place, I ventured, was the story of crime and punishment.

As I write today, despite the fact that Miami has in the past decade-plus added a downtown performing arts complex to outdo all but the Kennedy Center in DC, a jaw-dropping art museum by the Biscayne Bay, an exemplary science museum, the establishment of the world-renowned Art Basel festival on Miami Beach, and so much more, I am sticking to my metaphorical guns: the operative literary form to portray Miami—the essential aria of the Magic City—is spun from threads of mystery and yearning and darkness.

The lure of Miami remains to this day essentially what it was when Ponce de León and his men crossed the Atlantic in search of streets paved with gold and glistening with waters that spilled over from a fountain of youth. By the thousands, each year, they still come—immigrants, retirees, high rollers, jokers and midnight tokers, by yacht, by raft, by RV, by thumb—all in search of one or another version of the same impossible promise. Who would expect a series of drawing room comedies to emerge from such a scene?

And here is one more consideration: when terrible things threaten in some ominous neighborhoods, in some tough cities, a reader of a story set in those locales might be forgiven for expecting the worst; but when calamity takes place against the backdrop of paradise, as we have here in Miami, the impact is all the greater.

And yet with all that said, when Johnny Temple from Akashic Books first proposed a second volume of *Miami Noir*, I was doubtful. The sequel was to be subtitled "The Classics," Johnny explained. Unlike the first collection, which invited original stories from a set of working Miami writers, this was to be a collection of previously published stories in the genre, one to give a sense of how the story of crime and punishment had developed along with the history of the place.

"But we don't *have* a history," I protested to Johnny. "At least not one that includes much story publishing, let alone *noir* publishing."

"I don't believe it," was the essence of Johnny's response. "Go to work and get back to me when you've got something."

Though I thought there was about as much possibility as me coming up with a volume of *Des Moines Noir*, I took Johnny at his word and began the search. Having penned a series of crime thrillers of my own featuring the travails of honest (!) Miami building contractor John Deal, I was familiar with the work of the so-called "Miami School" of crime writers who came to attention in the eighties and nineties, including Charles Willeford, Elmore Leonard, Carl Hiaasen, James W. Hall, James Grippando, Barbara Parker, and so many others. But most of us were writing novels, the paying markets for short crime and mystery fiction having shrunk to relatively nothing by the time.

Furthermore, prior to that great flowering that came with such titles as *Miami Blues* and *Stick* and *Strip Tease*, Miami was simply not much of a writer's town, let alone a *mystery* writer's town. John D. MacDonald had of course immortalized fictional South Florida detective Travis McGee in a series of twenty-one novels published from 1964 to 1985, but McGee operated out of his houseboat *The Busted Flush*, docked thirty miles up the road at the Bahia Mar marina in Fort Lauderdale, and while MacDonald produced a few short stories set in various South Florida locations, none were set in Miami.

I by chance learned of the work of Douglas Fairbairn back in the early 1980s shortly after I arrived in Miami, when his niece, playwright Susan Westfall, put me onto his matchless thriller, *Street 8*, which tells the story of used-car dealer Bobby Mead and his ill-fated run-in with a group of Cuban expatriates looking for a warehouse in which to store munitions destined for a Bay of Pigs–styled invasion. I found the book astonishing—in my view the very prototype of nearly all the best Miami crime novels that have followed—and even though Fairbairn, who fell victim to early onset dementia, never wrote another piece of Miami-based fiction, much of *Street 8* (Fairbairn's original title was *Calle Ocho* but his publishers complained that English-speaking readers would be puzzled and leaned on the author to come up with an alternate title) is told episodically, enabling me to convince Johnny to include an excerpt of this very important work.

In fact, it was that decision which came to form the philosophical cornerstone for this collection, something of the opposite of the original intention. Here is what I mean: while there may be something of an overview of the development of the Miami crime story over the past century to be found in these pages, I think there is a much greater cogency to be found in the overview of the history of a most unusual and distinctive place reflected here. Furthermore, that sense of history is delivered with none of the typically dusty overtones of an all-too-often dry and arcane subject, given that at the forefront of nearly all the tales are questions of life or death.

The Fairbairn material would be the perfect linchpin between the past and the contemporary crime writers, I reasoned, as I set out in earnest on my search for what had come before. I could only hope that there were short stories to be found to illustrate the point.

As I detailed in the introduction to the original *Miami Noir,* there have been a number of early crime novels set in Miami, including *Kid Galahad* (1936) by Francis Wallace, about mob-influenced boxing; Leslie Charteris's *The Saint in Miami* (1940), an installment in the British series; and several Brett Halliday–penned Mike Shayne novels of the forties and fifties, with Shayne operating as pretty much the lone capable moral force in a tropical landscape long on beauty but short on rectitude.

The Brett Halliday moniker was in fact only one pen name employed by Davis Dresser, who (while spending much of his time in Santa Barbara) wrote dozens of novels of all stripes, but, as it turns out, nary a single short story to be found set in Miami, with the exception of the bordering-on-novella-length piece included in this volume, "A Taste for Cognac," originally published in *Black Mask* magazine in 1944. In fact, the story was later published as a stand-alone "dime novel" in 1951 and bundled with another story/novella, "Dead Man's Diary," as a kind of omnibus in 1959. While it may test the limit of what can be termed a "short" story, the piece is not only relatively compact, it contains the usual tropes and carries the blunt force typical of a Shayne novel.

Another author high on the wish list was the master of the wise guy form, Damon Runyon. While much of Runyon's short story work was of course set in New York, he was a widely traveled reporter and correspondent not averse to the occasional Florida trip to inspect how the ponies might be running during the winter and to escape the snowdrifts for a bit. "A Job for the Macarone," published originally in a 1937 issue of the *Saturday Evening Post*, is proof of the latter and perhaps the only Miami-based story to be penned by Runyon.

Lester Dent may be best remembered today as the creator of the long-running Doc Savage series, but in the mid-1930s, as that phenomenon was gathering steam, Dent was exploring other possibilities, including a series based around the exploits of a Miami-based detective named Oscar Sail living aboard a schooner anchored in Biscayne Bay. That series never came to fruition, but tantalizing hints of what it might have become are found in two stories published by Dent in *Black Mask* magazine. "Luck," included here, was Dent's original version of the story finally published in 1936 as "Sail," the latter somewhat diminished by changes demanded of the author by the magazine's editors. There are some who contend that Oscar Sail came to live on as the prototype for that other live-aboard private investigator just up A1A a few miles, but if John D. MacDonald found Oscar Sail a viable model for Travis McGee, he never said so.

A somewhat anomalous addition to this volume is the segment from the later pages of *Their Eyes Were Watching God*, the tough-about-the-edges novel published by Zora Neale Hurston in 1937. While an excerpt, it is nonetheless a self-contained one, detailing the dark and tragic end of narrator Janie's third marriage in the aftermath of a powerful hurricane that sweeps through the Everglades, one very likely modeled after the real-life monster storm of 1928. Given the vivid detailing of an often-overlooked segment of South Florida's population, the theme-appropriate nature of the book's climax, and the ever-growing critical stature and influence that Ms. Hurston's work has gained over the past half century, it seemed to this writer a crime *not* to include the passage.

The earliest publication in the volume—and perhaps the first piece of Miami crime fiction to be published—comes from the pen of a writer seldom associated with the genre: Marjory Stoneman Douglas, more commonly lionized by conservationists for her classic 1947 work of nonfiction, *The Everglades: River of Grass*, a book generally given credit for the eventual establishment of Everglades National Park. From 1915 to 1923, however, she was a hardworking reporter for the *Miami Herald*, which her father had helped establish, and she was also submitting poetry, plays, and fiction to outlets across the country. One of her first big scores was *White Midnight*, a novella about sunken treasure in the West Indies, for which *Black Mask* paid her six hundred dollars in 1924. "Pineland," included here, was originally published by the *Saturday Evening Post* in August of 1925 and, along with the work of Zora Neale Hurston, provides ample evidence that tough, capable women have populated South Florida for a good long time.

There were a few other short stories from the pre-Fairbairn years that surfaced, but not many, and none, in the opinion of this writer, with a great deal to recommend them. In fact, the efforts of Douglas, Dent, Hurston, Runyon, and Halliday exhibit collectively the archetypal trove for just about everything that has appeared in the genre ever after, including literary excellence.

And while it has seemed to me to be appropriate and even necessary to lend a few words of context to those works penned by those who are no longer with us, I am not so sure I want to put myself in the position of interloper between readers and the still-working colleagues collected here. Better to let the work of these fine and able practitioners do the talking, with the only presumption of the editor being this: I would not have included any of these works if I did not find them captivating, well-wrought, and in one way or another, exemplary.

Which of course leads me to a few last words, given that two of the modern masters included have in fact passed on. It seems impossible that Charles Willeford has been gone for more than thirty years, for the legacy of his work continues to burn bright for all of us in the field and for anyone who has read it. Many in fact refer to Willeford as the godfather of the Miami School, and his in-your-face approach continues to inspire young writers who might have been a bit too cautious before reading *Sideswipe* or *Kiss Your Ass Goodbye*. Charles once proudly showed me a copy of one of his novels, sent back to him by a fan, accompanied by a terse note: *Just thought you'd like to see what I thought of your new book*, it said. The book had been punctured dead center by what must have been a .45 slug, shards of its innards blown out and curled against the back cover in perfect symmetry. He thought it one of the funniest things he'd ever seen.

There were a number of Willeford stories to choose from, but I thought it would be a disservice to an old pal if I were to pick something that lacked an outrageous component. As a promotional line for a film adaptation of the Terry Southern novel *Candy* once stated: "This movie has something in it to offend almost anyone." So, included in this volume is "Saturday Night Special." I'll add only this: Willeford did not write in order to present models of decent behavior. He simply saw us for what we truly are, and he wrote accordingly.

The last I'll single out is Elmore Leonard, sometimes referred to as the Dickens of Detroit—but "Dutch," as he was known to his friends, was also the Maestro of the Miami Academy of Crime. Leonard could effortlessly propel a story almost entirely via dialogue, yet there was never any mistaking that the fuel for his characters' repartee came from the streets where they lived, whether they be those of the Motor City or of South Beach. And like Willeford, humor played a large part in most of the darkest of Leonard's Miami proceedings, though in Willeford's case the guffaws grew out of the macabre, while the humor in the latter's was more of the eye-rolling type derived from Runyon. The sole Miami-based short story penned by Leonard was not available for this volume, but included here is his chapter created for the peerless pass-along novel of Miami, *Naked Came the Manatee*, where each author did her or his best to keep a steadily compounding tale going, adding an episode to whatever stage the yarn was at when it landed on the desk. In fact, Leonard's so-called chapter "The Odyssey," included here, strikes this writer as a fully self-contained piece that Leonard had already on hand when the invitation to participate in *Naked Came the Manatee* arrived.

All the above, then, will have to serve as the companion notes for the enjoyment of this volume, though I might offer one final observation. Some of the older stories contain language that, though used as part of the popular parlance of the time, are frankly racist and deeply offensive today. A character in the Douglas story refers to *nigras* working and living as field hands in close proximity to her home, and in the Dent story there is an offhand reference to a *darkie* working as a service person in a restaurant. Even the Hurston excerpt uses phonetic reproduction of dialect spoken by the characters that might raise an eyebrow. Yet it has been the editorial decision for this volume to reproduce the stories exactly as they were originally published. This does not constitute endorsement of any failings of an earlier time in history, by any means, but it does permit the contemporary reader the opportunity to consider the shortcomings of another era, and allows for each reader to make independent judgments as to the impact of such upon the whole and upon the continuing value of the works at hand.

Go ye forward, then.

Les Standiford
Miami, Florida
August 2020

PART I

ORIGINAL GANGSTERS

PINELAND

BY MARJORY STONEMAN DOUGLAS

Goulds

(Originally published in 1925)

L arry Gibbs was thankful that the roughness of the road
took all his attention, because he had no idea what to say
to a woman whose son has just been hanged. She sat like a
stone beside him in the front seat of the car. Out of the corner of
his eye he could see her cheap black skirt covering her bony knees
and the worn toes of her shoes to which still clung some particles
of sand from around Joe McDevitt's grave. The heavy black veil
which muffled her hat and her face gave off the acid smell of black
dye. Her hands in black cotton gloves with flabby tips that were
too long for her fumbled with a clean folded handkerchief in her
lap.

All around them the white brilliance of the Florida noon
poured down upon the uneven road from the burial place, caught
on the bright spear points of palmettos and struck into nakedness
the shabby houses among stumps of pine trees of this outskirt of
Miami. The light and the hot wind seemed whiter and hotter for
the figure of Sarah McDevitt in her mourning.

It was Jack Kelley, the man who had turned state's evidence
on the Pardee gang case, who had told Larry he would loan him
an automobile if he would take Sarah McDevitt home. It was the
same Jack Kelley who had started the fund to provide Joe Mc-
Devitt's body with decent burial. He had seen to it that his own
figure had a prominent place in the newspaper photographs of the
grave, which next morning would assure all Dade County that

the Pardee gang, including the McDevitts, was at last broken up, either by being driven from Florida or doing endless terms in prison camps, like George McDevitt; or like Joe here, made safe for Southern progress with a stretch of rope, a pine coffin and a few feet of Florida marl.

"Go on now," Jack Kelley had said, pushing at Larry with large, firm pushes. "There's a story in Sarah McDevitt yet. The last of her boys gone and she going home to sit and listen to her pine trees, see? A nice little front-page story, see? And you might just mention the canned goods I've put in the back of the car for her. Enough to last her a month. Here you are, Sarah McDevitt. Larry Gibbs will take you home, see?"

Larry wondered miserably if she were crying behind that stuffy veil. He had not seen her face yet. He had never seen her before.

She had not come to the trial, although he wondered a little why Joe McDevitt's lawyer had not brought her in for her effect on the jury. He thought of Joe McDevitt as he had been then, lounging, copper-haired, a sleek reddish animal, his veins crammed with healthy life. He had not shown much interest even when the facts about the bank robbery and the cashier's death were made damningly evident.

Now Joe McDevitt was dead. It had made a tremendous impression on Larry. It was his first big court case since he had been on the paper. He had written home to his mother that he was seeing the real bedrock of life at last. He pictured his mother reading it in her breakfast room in Brookline, turning the pages of his letter with that little look of amused horror on her distinguished face. She would hope he would not be obliged to come in close contact with miserable creatures in jails.

He had written with affected carelessness about interviewing McDevitt the man-killer, but secretly he was thankful that he had not had to cover the hanging this morning. The other court reporter had done that. But this business of taking home the mother was almost as bad. It made him feel perfectly rotten. She was so quiet.

"That road," she said to him suddenly, and he flushed and jerked the car around on the way she had pointed. He was taken completely by surprise that her voice could be so clear and firm.

"This is—this is the Larkins Road, isn't it?" he asked hastily to prevent the silence from forming again. "I didn't know it was surfaced yet."

But she said nothing, and he continued to stare forward at the road paralleling the shine of tracks, the shine and glitter of palmettos on the other side. The sky ahead was steely and remote, and it made his eyes ache. A corner of her veil snapped outside the car. Every once in so often her hat joggled forward over her forehead and she pushed it back and wiped her face with the wad of her handkerchief. He was somehow sure that it was not tears she wiped.

He turned to ask her if she would not like to have him stop somewhere and get her a glass of water, and saw for the first time that her skin was pale and clammy with heat. Her mouth, with the deep soft wrinkles on it of an old woman, was half open and panting. But as he spoke she closed her lips in a tight line and looked at him straight out of faded gray eyes within faded lashes. There was nothing feeble in her glance. She pulled off her hat abruptly and her thin gray hair blew against the brown skin of her forehead.

When they had passed by the stores and railway station of Larkins she began slowly to take off her black gloves. She rolled them into hard balls, working and working at them sightlessly until he thought she would never let them alone. Her hands were curiously like the look in her eyes, vigorous in spite of the blotched brown skin stretched over the large-boned knuckles.

"What did Jack Kelley think he was going to get out of sending me home with a lot of canned goods?" she asked suddenly.

"Why—I don't know," Larry said. "He—I think he was just—I

mean I imagine he wanted to show you he was sorry that you—that your—"

"Huh!" she said, and her voice was dryly deliberate. "Any time Jack Kelley spends money you can bet he knows right well where he's going to get something for it. I guess maybe he figured you'd put something in the paper about it."

Larry was always sharply conscious when his fair skin reddened. "But, Mrs. McDevitt, I wouldn't write anything you wouldn't want me to write. I—"

"I could tell you to write something Jack Kelley wouldn't want you to write, about the time he tried to do me out of my homestead. I guess he wouldn't relish that much."

"When was that?" Larry leaped eagerly to the question. He felt easier, now that she was talking. The only sense of strain of which he was aware was the slow dry way she talked, as if her tongue were swollen and sticky. "Tell me about that, won't you?"

"Oh—it wasn't much. Nothing to put in the paper. He just wasn't so smart's he thought he was. It was one time about two years after I come down on my land here. McDevitt's mother up in Vermont wrote me that George was awful sick. I'd been working in Miami, waiting on table like I did in the six months they let you live off your homestead, and it was time I went back on it, but I got permission from the land agent to leave long enough to go north and look after my children.

"In Jacksonville I met this Jack Kelley between trains, that I'd seen coming into the restaurant time and again, and the minute he saw me he knew I was supposed to be on my land. 'Well, Sarah McDevitt,' he says to me. 'So the pineland was too much for you, was it?'

"'When you see me giving up my pineland you can have it yourself, Jack Kelley,' I says to him, and thought no more of it. But don't you believe it but that man turned right around and come back to Miami and started to file a counterclaim against my property. And now he thinks he can fool me with canned goods. Jack Kelley. Huh!"

"But he didn't get your land, did he?"

"Of course he didn't, the big fool. He didn't have a chance. I had my permission right enough, and the day after he'd filed the claim he come down to look at my house, and a good neighbor of mine that see him coming fired off a six-shooter in the air, and he said Jack Kelley ran like a whitehead. And up in Miami Mr. Barnes that owned the restaurant told me he'd go to court himself to see I kept my place. He said Jack Kelley'd ought to be run out of the county for trying to take a woman's land from her. I don't mean you should put that in the paper, though."

Larry pondered regretfully the news value of that story. But she was quite right that he couldn't print it. The paper wouldn't stand for it, and besides it was libel.

They were running past pineland now, and he turned and stared at the passing ranks. They were like no pine trees he had ever seen in his life, these Caribbean pine. Their high bare trunks, set among palmetto fans that softened all the ground beneath them, rose up so near the road that he could see the soft flakes of color of their scaly bark, red and brown and cream, as if patted on with a thick brush. Their high tops mingled gray-green branches, twisted and distorted as if by great winds or something stern and implacable in their own natures. Their long green needles were scant, letting the sky through. They were strange trees, strange but beautiful. The brilliance of the sun penetrated through their endless ranks in a swimming mist of light. They were endlessly alike, endlessly monotonous, and yet with an endless charm and variety.

Every tree held its own twist and pattern; every tree, even to the distant intermingled brown of trunks too far away to distinguish, was infinitely itself. Sometimes the pine woods came so near the road he could smell their sunny resinous breath. Sometimes they retreated like a long, smoky, green-frothed wall beyond

house lots and grapefruit groves or open swales of sawgrass or beyond cleared fields where raw stumps of those already destroyed
stood amid the blackness of a recent burning. Against the horizon
their ranks rushed cometlike and immobile into the untouched
west. He felt the comprehension of them growing upon him—
the silence of their trunks, the loveliness of their tossed branches,
the virginity of their hushed places, in retreat before the surfaced
roads and filling stations, the barbecue stands and signboards of
the new Florida.

"They're wonderful, aren't they, the pines?" he said abruptly.
"There's something beautiful and fresh about them, different from
any trees I've ever seen."

The woman beside him took a great deep breath, as if what he
said had released something in her.

"I remember the first time I went to see my place," she said.
"Twenty years ago. In those days the nearest road was six miles
away. You could take a horse and carriage from Miami to a place
near Goulds where the road branched. Then you'd have to walk
across country to where my land began. It wasn't my land then,
though. The land agent had it surveyed and told me where the
boundary stob was. The palmetto was deeper than it is now, but I
was younger and nothing was too much for me. When I'd walked
a ways through the palmetto under those pines and come to the
place where they said would be good for a clearing, I just stood still
and listened, I don't know how long. It was so still you could hear
little noises a long ways off, like a bird rustling up on a branch or
an insect buzzing.

"The tops of the trees were higher up than these here, and
they didn't move any. The light was all soft and kind of bright, and
yet green and dim too. Those trees were the quietest things I ever
see. It did you good just to feel them so quiet, as if you'd come to
the place where everything began. I couldn't hardly believe there
was places outside where people were afraid and worried. I just—I
tell you I just started crying, but not to hurt. I never was one for

crying, but this was just good easy tears, the way you cry when you're so happy you don't believe it's true."

Larry hardly dared to speak, keeping his hands tight on the wheel and his eyes on the road. Yet when she continued to maintain the silence into which she had fallen he ventured, "What made you come down here homesteading in the first place, Mrs. McDevitt?"

"I was in the freeze years ago, up in Orange County." Her reply came with a little effort, as if she had lost her present self in a sturdy dark-haired woman, wiping her eyes all alone among silent acres of pineland. "Eh, law!" she sighed. "That was a long time. McDevitt bought an orange grove and we were froze out."

"Tell me about that," Larry insisted.

Presently she went on speaking, with her chin on her breast and her eyes staring forward at the road racing and racing toward them, between the straight gleaming rails and the dusty palmettos, the few pines, half dying, with patent-medicine signs tacked to them, that followed this part of the road. She talked as if it were as easy as thinking—easier. "McDevitt would have it that we mustn't sell the oranges until the season was later and the prices better, although I told him to sell. The fruit was coloring wonderful that winter. 'Ninety-four and five. In those days in Orange County the orange trees were tall and dark and glossy, on strong thick trunks. When you walked in an orange grove the dark leaves met overhead and you walked on bare brown earth in a kind of solid shadow, not like the pines that strain the light through clear and airy. Up in the dark branches you could see the oranges in clusters, growing gold color like there was sun on them. I never saw fruit like ours that winter. It seemed like the branches would break with it. Then came the big freeze. There never was one like it before and there never has been since.

"That was about the last difference McDevitt and I had."

Larry felt a pricking in the back of his neck at the even depth of hatred in her voice, the first naked emotion she had shown.

"He was a smooth one, a smooth, smiling, hateful man, with easy ways and eyes boring in for the weak place in you. It was what made him furious, not finding mine. 'I'll be stronger than you are,' I'd say to myself often and often. 'And stiller and more of a man. You see if I won't.' That was even as soon as after George was born. I'd grit my teeth and bear that look in his eyes until he'd fling off and leave me a week or two for spite. We come down to Orange County from Vermont state, where his mother was. He got this orange grove with money my own mother left me, but I knew he'd never be one for holding it. So I held it."

The car dipped and rose on the swinging levels of the road. The sun was beginning to crawl down from its zenith and the burning white of the sky was turning a faint flower-petal blue. The wind from the invisible sea to eastward came to them in steady, freshening gusts.

"Turn here," she said. "That winter he had a great beard that was the color of the oranges, and he'd sit around barefooted on the porch of the shack we had and comb it. Joe was—Joe was a year old then." Her tongue thickened as she spoke the name for the first time. Larry heard the sticky parting of her lips. The car was running almost silently on a dirt road in the shadow of pines that seemed stronger and more dense than those by the main highway.

"I was a thick stumpy woman then, and the heat behind all those trees there in the middle of Florida was like a tight hand over your lungs. But I'd leave the baby and little George on a mattress in the breeze-way between the two rooms of the house and go out to see that the nigras were working. McDevitt wouldn't ever. He'd sit there smiling, with those eyes over his beard and never sweated. The heat was terrible. That's what made the fruit ripen early. I was wild with nerves at it, but I wouldn't let McDevitt know. Only when he come home from Orlando and said he'd got an offer to sell the crop on the trees for ten thousand, only he'd decided not to, that night I had to go out and walk up and down the road that had a place where there wasn't any orange trees. That night I thought I'd choke with orange trees.

"Up around the house the shadow of them was black and thick, and the smell of the new bloom that was coming here and there up among the yellowing fruit sickened you. There was a starlight that fell wet and glittery like knives on the leaf edges. The next day McDevitt went off somewhere to spite me because I wanted him to sell, and left me alone. I'd never let him guess how afraid I was to be alone. I guess that's why I married him when he come along when Ma died. Or maybe he guessed and thought I'd beg him to take me away.

"He would have liked me to beg him to. But I never let on that my knees were like string to see him go. He turned at the gate and smiled at me over that orange-colored beard with his stone-white teeth and his eyes that were like wires boring into you, and I shut my mouth tight and let him look. So he stopped smiling and went, and I was there with the two children and four nigras living down a ways in a shack in the grove, and the days got hotter. I would of sold the crop, only I couldn't find the man that made the offer. But everybody in Orlando, at the bank and everywhere, said to hold on, because prices were going up. Then one day it begun to get cold.

"It came on in the morning, and by afternoon it was so cold the children shivered, and I had to put two-three extra shirts on them. In all the groves up and down the road they began to light fire pots and start bonfires to keep the oranges from feeling it. You could smell the smoke and the blossoms in the chilly air. The sky was heavy and gray-looking and there wasn't any wind, and the smoke drifted and hung between the long dark rows of trees. But still it kept getting colder. Late that afternoon I went out and stopped the nigras from lighting any more fire pots. I could see it wasn't going to do any good. I told them to cut down a couple of old trees to keep themselves warm in their houses that night and had them bring me some of the wood too.

"Then it got dark sudden and I gave the children some bread and milk and put them to bed with all the bedclothes over them, and I put a shawl around my knees and one over my shoulders and sat close to the stove and fed it with orange wood. All night long I sat there and it kept getting colder. About midnight I could tell it was freezing outside, because the trees begun to crack and snap. Then pretty soon you could hear thumps on the ground where the oranges were freezing and falling off. I set there and heard them and knew that every cent I had in the world but two dollars was being frozen up. Then some more oranges would thump down.

"Next morning when I unbolted my front door and looked out the ground was all covered with frost that was melting in the sun, and everywhere you looked the edges of the leaves were blackened, and on the ground carloads and carloads of oranges were scattered. The crop was ruined. Every orange was hurt. And all the way into Orlando and all over Orange County and all the way up to Jacksonville it was the same way. It wasn't just me that was ruined. The whole state was. I've often wondered why we had to get caught in the one big freeze Orange County ever had.

"Well, when McDevitt heard how things were, he told a man that was coming to Orlando to tell me that I could have the grove. He said he was tired of oranges anyway and thought he would go to Texas and I prob'ly wouldn't see him anymore. So there I was. I was scared so when the crop went I didn't hardly know what to do, but what McDevitt did, put the ginger in me I needed.

"Maybe he thought he'd find the weak place in me that way, but it made me mad enough to do anything. So then I found that the trees weren't dead, only the fruit. There was maybe a chance to save next year's bloom. So I went into the bank at Orlando and borrowed some money to keep going on, and almost everybody else that wasn't too discouraged done the same thing. Things looked bad, but they weren't too bad.

"Until along in February when the second freeze came. The sap had begun to come back with the heat that shut down again and the bloom was forced beyond its time. People were getting real cheerful, like people get in a fruit country, living on next year's promise, and Orlando looked prosperous. And then the second freeze came. I sat up all night again and listened to the crackling of the boughs. There wasn't any oranges to thump down, but some-how now it made it all the worse. You couldn't hear anything but the crackling and snapping of wood, but you could feel the chill that meant that next year's hopes were dying.

"My fire went out and I was chilled through, and yet even when it come daylight and the sun straggled in the window I kept sitting there by the stove, not daring to go and look. There wasn't a sound outside, nobody going by in the road, and the nigras not making any noise at all. I just sat there all huddled up until little George woke up and ran and opened the door and told me to look.

"You never saw anything like it in your life. It was the abomi-nation of desolation. It wasn't only that the leaves were black and shriveled and fallen and the new bloom gone. The trees them-selves were frozen stiff and the sap had frozen and then split the trees down to the roots; and there they lay, looking like an earth-quake or a tornado had hit them. Every tree was killed, every one of them, down to the roots. And when the sun was hot and the warmth was coming back all the country smelled of rottenness. People went around with mouths that spoke but couldn't smile, and they could look with their eyes, but it was like they weren't looking at anything.

"It was like death. Business was stopped. All the banks were ruined. Then the people begun to go away. They could have stood it without money, but they couldn't stand it without the hope of their trees that they'd worked so hard over and put their last cent in. They went away from the blackened rotting groves and they left their houses wide open and maybe food on the table and bread in the oven, and in a week it was like everybody had died. Some went back to places they'd come from in the North or the old South, and some went to Texas and Oklahoma.

"But some of the young men that didn't have all the spirit taken out of them were talking about going farther south, way down in South Florida that nobody thought was fit to live in on account of swamps, down to this new place Miami on the coast where they were bringing the railroad. These men said that maybe down there they could start new orange groves, and there was gov'ment land you could homestead.

"If I hadn't been so mad with McDevitt I don't see how I could have done it, but I begun to think if a man could take up a homestead maybe I could, and then I'd put a grove in and show him I was a smarter man than he was, if I was a woman. So I wrote to his mother that lived in Vermont state and told her just how it was, and she wrote back she was sorry McDevitt had been so mean and she'd take the children for a while. She was a good, kind woman and I guess McDevitt took after his father. There was some people going back to Vermont state from Orlando that could take the children to her. So that's how I took up the land. Perhaps I made a mistake. There's plenty of people has made good money growing oranges in Orange County since then. Go slow here. We're coming to my gate."

There was a straggling grove of grapefruit at the left, which presently revealed a road more like a path. Up this, in answer to her hand, Larry turned. The weeds were long under the trees. Beyond that was unused cleared land that may have been used to grow vegetables. But beyond that still the pines began again, pressing down almost into the faint roadway, rising endlessly to each side and ahead, larger and more stately than any Larry had yet noticed. The palmetto around their roots was all untouched. Between their ranks the distance was smoky with crowding trunks. Superb trees, they seemed to be the very ancestors and originals of all the others they had passed. The house stood in a small clearing, perhaps the half acre prescribed by the government for homesteaders. It was made of pine logs and there was a well beside it and a small garden. When he stopped the car Larry found himself listening intently. It was as she had said. You could hear only little noises faint and far away. When she was walking from the car to the house steps, stiffly, with her black hat and veil trailing from her hand and her heavy black skirt bunched up as she had been sitting on it, Larry asked, "Where do you want me to put these canned goods, Mrs. McDevitt?"

At first he thought she had not heard him, but at the top step she turned and looked back at him and her thin lips stretched in a mirthless smile. "You take those things back to Jack Kelley," she said, and stood eyeing him. Something in the flush on his face must have reached to her, for she said, "Come and set down, don't you want to? I'm going to have me a cup of coffee. You've been— you're a right kind young man and it's a long ways back."

When she came out again with a pot of coffee in her hand, and cups, Larry had been sitting on the porch steps, thinking of the pine trees. Their airy quiet was a healing and a blessing. He had had a moment of feeling sure that if he could only be still enough himself, hands still, eyes still, heart still, perhaps he would enter into the knowledge of something deep and hidden and wonderful, as if he were standing on the threshold of a slow moment of revelation, a moment for which being had been created. The feeling went when he heard her behind him, and he stretched and looked about him with a feeling of good happiness. The long light of afternoon slanted through brown trunks across the grass of the clearing. Beyond the tossing green of pine tops the sky was glowing with a blue at once misty and intense, and a great cloud mass, as if carved from a soft creamy marble, was lifting up and up into unimaginable free heights, where the great clean wind ran westward from the sea.

She gave him a cup of coffee, and he took it absently, noticing that she had changed her heavy black for a shapeless dress of some gray cotton stuff that made her look thinner and smaller. She sat in a rocking chair at his shoulder and creaked it softly now and then.

"But you must have had a terrible time clearing all this, Mrs. McDevitt. And living here all by yourself. How did you ever do it?"

She creaked reflectively. "I had a six-shooter," she said, and then stopped again. "And it's wonderful how you toughen up to using a grubbing hoe. I grubbed all that out myself, after the men cut the trees. I made them leave all those pine trees, though. I didn't mind being alone here. It got so I didn't like to be anywhere else. Once when the rains were bad I waded in from Goulds with water up to my waist and a sack of Irish potatoes on my shoulder. Mr. Barnes didn't want me to go.

"I was up in Miami, waiting on table to make enough money to put grapefruit in. A man come in and said all this part of the country was swept away with a cloudburst, and I couldn't rest until I'd come to see. My house hadn't been finished long. But when I got here, sopping wet to my armpits, the house was all high and dry. This land is higher'n anything around here. So I stayed here for a week until the water went down, and worked around and lived on Irish potatoes. I was glad to get back here from town. It was getting too crowded to like it. I finished clearing my half acre and an old nigra that was around here then showed me how to put in sweet potatoes."

The chair creaked. "That was kind of funny. I wasn't afraid of much of anything by that time but snakes and McDevitt. Staying out here by myself nights somehow I got to hating him worse and worse, and every once in a while if I'd hear somebody coming up that road I'd think what I'd do if it was him. Well, this morning—just about when my house was finished and the well was dug, it was early in the morning. I always got up at the peak of day, and it wasn't hardly light when I thought I heard McDevitt stumbling around the well. I don't know what got into me. I was all of a-tremble, and I went to the door and fired all six shots up in the air over the man I could see down by the well.

"All he did was kind of crouch down, and when I went over to look, it was this old nigra, and he was so scared he was as white as I was. 'Law, Miss Sarah,' he says to me. 'No man's goin' to ever steal up on you in the nighttime,' and he would of run when he got his breath, but I started laughing and I told him he needn't to be scared. All he wanted was a drink of water, anyway. Uncle Joseph, they used to call him, and when he showed me about the sweet potatoes I put a lot in just over there where the soil's good, and I sold them to Mr. Barnes in Miami. Then I put in tomatoes for a while, and did right well with them, so I didn't have to work in town the six months they allow you off your land. I did all the work myself, so it didn't cost much."

Larry had leaned back against the post so that he could look up at her and at the soft sky too. The morning and what had happened to Joe McDevitt seemed very far off to him. He thought perhaps they began to seem so to her, too, for suddenly her face wrinkled into a network of silent laughter. Her narrowed eyes were brightly vigorous and all the lines of her face were pleasantly relaxed. Her hands were relaxed on her knee.

"Talk about funny, though. I have to laugh every time I think of it. It shows what a fool I was in those days. When I'd made enough money in Miami to get my house built down here I was crazy to get into it. I wanted my own roof and my own pine trees. Well, it was all done but the front door, and that had to come down from Miami special on a wagon. I'd been sleeping over to the Marshs', those good neighbors I told you about ten miles up the road, and I'd got my furniture in, a stove and a bedstead and one-two things McDevitt's mother sent down to me, and I made up my mind I wasn't going to wait any longer for that front door.

"I was just going ahead and live in my house, anyway. So when night come I put on my six-shooter, with the belt over my nightgown, and I shoved the headboard of the bed right up against the open door. It's one of those high wooden headboards. I went to sleep and slept like a log, not thinking of anything. Well, 'long about three-four o'clock in the morning I woke up with a jump and lay there listening to how still it was and thinking how far I was from anything and how dark it was, and me all alone in the middle of it. Well, it come over me all of a sudden that anybody could crawl right through that door in the space under the bed. I never thought of that before. And while I was laying there thinking that, something screamed way out in the woods.

"Well, say—scared? I was so scared I was cold and stiff, and I could see things moving in the dark all around me and things crawling and creeping out of the dark under that bed. I didn't dare to move or creak the bed springs, and there was my six-shooter that had worked around under my hip and was boring a hole right through me. When that thing screamed I thought I'd just die right there. You could hear wild cats sometimes in those days, only then I didn't know what it was. And the next morning I went over to Marshs' and stayed there until that door got there, and I had three bolts put on, and you bet I used them. But I can laugh over that now any time I think of it.

"And two days later was the time I shot all the snakes I ever see around here. That was another funny thing. I can't bear snakes. I was sitting in this chair inside my door, with the door open—that was before this porch was built. I was sewing something and I had my six-shooter in my lap. And all of a sudden I just kind of saw something on the floor out of the tail of my eye, and before I ever turned to see what it was, a kind of cold feeling went all over me and, thinks I, 'That's a snake.' Before I knew exactly what I was doing I grabbed my gun and I shot all six shots at that thing I saw, and it was a rattlesnake as thick as your wrist, and not two feet from my foot.

"The first time I got a good look at it, it was as dead as a piece of string, and there was bullet holes through it and around it right into my new floor. You can go in and see where they are right now. And that afternoon there was a man here and we were planting some orange trees, for I thought I'd see how they'd do here. He says, 'Look, there's a snake,' and I turned around, and sure enough there was another one. I guess maybe two snakes in one day was too much for me, for everything went all kind of black and I didn't know what I was doing until I see the man looking and laughing at me. I was killing that snake with a stick and then stamping and dancing on its head like I was crazy, with my six-shooter bumping on my hip. He says he never see anything so funny in his life the way I looked, but I didn't remember much of anything, I was so blind mad. I always did hate a snake. But that was about all I ever saw on my place. Though that time I told you about when it rained so hard and I waded in from Goulds there were moccasins on some of the stumps. You don't see them hardly any now, except out in the deep Glades."

The chair creaked. The high great pillar of cloud was turning a soft pink. A mockingbird, tail and wings all a-cock, landed on the ground before the steps with a flirt and stared at them first out of one eye and then the other, and flew off as suddenly as he had come, with a flash of white wing bars and three or four notes of song like sweet impertinent words.

Larry fumbled in his mind for the right question. "Were you— did you stay here all alone, always?" he asked cautiously. "You were very brave, I think."

Her profile in the softening light was bold and bony, he saw as he stared up at her. The gray hair blew straight back from her forehead and the scanty knob of it behind hardly altered the shape of her head. The skin over the cheekbones was smooth in spite of the soft wrinkles about the mouth and eyes. Her body was a bony shapelessness under the cotton dress, but her head, from the angle at which he gazed, seemed fine and distinguished. There was about it that sexless look which approaching age sometimes takes on, in which men seem like old women and old women like delicate, bony old men. She looked like a worn old statesman, wise, weary, patient.

He found himself thrilling to all this she had been telling him, as if the courage and drama of it had stirred deeply his sensitive imagination. She was indeed a better man than McDevitt, this shapeless old woman. She was unique, she was magnificent. Staring at her he saw what it was really to be a pioneer, a woman, lonely, afraid of snakes, sustained by no dream of empire, but only by a six-shooter and the enduring force of her own will. He felt at once humbled and exalted at this glimpse of the dumb, inevitable thrust forward of the human spirit. Her name was Sarah McDevitt and her sons were—

As if in the brooding into which she had fallen she had come to a similar place in her thoughts, she turned her bright gray eyes on him slowly, and he remembered that he had asked her a question.

"I sent for the boys as soon as I could," she said. "George was big for his age and Joe was—Joe wasn't a baby anymore. They come down with some people that were coming to Miami, and I met them there. I was afraid they wouldn't recognize me. I was sunburned more than they had ever seen me and I guess I was a lot heavier. George said I was taller, and maybe I was. Carrying boxes of tomatoes makes you stand straight, and grubbing palmettos and planting and hoeing and picking kind of stretches your spine. I couldn't seem to sleep much the night the boys got here. I'd have to keep getting up and light the lamp to look at them all over again. Sleeping that heavy way children have, they looked beautiful. George was black-haired and heavy, like my father, and Joe was all kind of gold color then. He used to—he used to wrinkle up his nose and laugh right out loud in his sleep."

Larry studied carefully the nearest knot hole. He felt a stinging behind his eyes at the careful monotony of her voice. Her words were labored. And yet when he looked up again there was only on her eyelids that look of a worn, distinguished old statesman with silence lying heavy upon her mouth.

"It didn't seem—I guess it was pretty lonely here for the boys after a while," she went on slowly. "They'd been to school in Vermont state and there wasn't any school here nearer than Coconut Grove. They were used to playing with children, and I was busy from daylight to dark. George liked to help with the tomatoes sometimes, but Joe was too little at first. They got to like to roam around the pine woods. Once George shot a wild cat. I gave them the orange trees if they'd take care of them, but they didn't take to that much, and anyway, oranges aren't so good here as in Orange County. I saw that right off, and besides, I didn't want to bother with them.

"Times when my tomatoes failed or the crop was short I could always go over to Goulds or Peters and work in the tomato-packing house. It was easier money than waiting on table in Miami, and I could walk home nights. Sometimes the boys liked to pack a little when the season was good and I saved up money for them. I knew they'd have to go to school sometime, but I kind of kept putting it off. There's a lot of company in a couple of kids fighting and hollering and yoo-hooing around. I'd got used to baking big batches of bread and pies and having to patch trousers. And besides, I was afraid of McDevitt.

"It didn't seem any time at all before they was big. Time goes fast down here, with the pine trees. There isn't much difference, summer or winter. In the winter the warm dark comes early and there's maybe cool nights, and once in two-three years maybe a slight touch of frost, and there isn't any rain, and the grass and leaves are yellow-green and brittle. In the summer you can hear the rains come booming and hissing in from the sea way out beyond and trampling down the dry grass. And afterward everything springs up juicy and green and the palmetto blossoms are sweeter than orange bloom, and little yellow and purple wildflowers grow up around the pines, and on a west wind the mosquitoes come. The nights are like pieces of black-and-white velvet laid on the earth, and the mockers go crazy, and all kinds of little birds that come from hot countries farther south sing all night in the moonlight.

"The old leaves fall off the trees and the next day the new leaves are rich and glossy and the young pine trees carry long white candles on their tips. But summer and winter smooth into each other so you don't notice how time goes creeping, except by watching young trees grow taller and boys grow big and try to act like men. Springs they would get excited to see the fires that start in the dry time leaping and roaring off in the pines. Falls, when the big rains filled up the roads, and the swales and all low places and everything was sopping, they'd run around splashing in it and having fun with plank boats. But all the time I knew they ought to be in school.

"The country around here was changing too. When they'd put the railroad through, gangs of men camped out not ten miles from here, and the boys liked to hang around the camps. That was what started me to send them to school. I was afraid they'd learn things that wouldn't be good for them, and I guess they did. Then the railroad was being finished way to Key West and the roads were better and people begun to come through and buy up land and talk of grapefruit groves and the tomato prairies.

"So I sold some of my land nearest to the main highway and sent the boys to Miami, where a woman I knew that used to cook for Mr. Barnes promised she'd board and room them and darn their stockings and look out for them. Sometimes Saturdays and Sundays they'd come down here or I'd go in and see them there. But they didn't like school so well as they thought they would and George was crazy to go to work. I didn't like him to. All my people in Massachusetts were educated and I wanted my boys to have all the learning they could. But the next two years my tomato crop failed, once with too much wet and the next year with nail-head rust, and I had to get a job cooking for a woman over to Perrine.

"So George worked awhile and then Joe wanted to go to work too. They worked around at different things, so I could give up cooking and next year put in another crop of tomatoes. That was about all we thought about raising down here then. And that crop was fine. It was a big year and I got George and Joe down here to help me picking and carrying to the packing house, and I paid them the same wages as anybody, and it was real nice. They were big strapping boys then and it seemed like everything was coming all right at last. We'd get home and light the lamp and I'd cook them a good hot supper and see them lean over the table and eat hearty.

"Then McDevitt come back. I can see it just as plain as if it was yesterday. After supper the boys were setting on the porch with their shoes off and smoking and I come to the door after the dishes was done, and just as I stood there McDevitt walked out of the dark into the patch of lamplight by the steps. I knew it was him even before he looked up at me and smiled with his teeth shining under a long red mustache and his eyes gleaming like hot wires. His beard was gone and he had a good suit of clothes on and a white collar. He put a leather bag on the step and stood looking at me, and then the house and at the big boys staring at him, and my knees begun to shake with the cold that come over me.

"'Well, Sarah McDevitt,' he said, 'I see you've done pretty well here,' and he started to come up the steps.

"I couldn't say anything at all at first, and then all of a sudden I called out to him, 'Don't you dare to set foot on this porch, Peter McDevitt, or I'll shoot off my gun at you. This is my land and my house, and I got made a free dealer right and proper under the Florida law so's you couldn't get any of it. You've got no more right here than a dog has, and you can just go back the way you came.'

"He stood there and looked at me, with his nose coming down over his mustache and the veins standing out in his forehead where he'd taken his hat off, and I could see he was older than he used to be and not so smooth. Because now he couldn't cover up how mad he was. But he stood still in his tracks, with his head and shoulder held careful and stiff, the way a tomcat stands that hasn't made up his mind how to jump, except he'd turn his eyes and look at the boys standing there with their mouths open, and then back at me, a hateful, sliding sort of look. If he'd been a snake I couldn't have hated him worse.

"'Well, well, Sarah,' he says at last, changing his feet easy, 'I see you know how to take care of yourself all right. But it's a long ways back to Miami and I haven't seen my boys since they was little, and any father has a right to talk to his own children. You haven't got the heart to keep me from doing that just a minute, have you?'

"I had, though, and I would of if I could. But when he smiled at me like that I knew I couldn't do anything more with him than what I had, so I slammed the door and walked up and down the kitchen, trying not to listen to the sound of their men voices talking easy on the porch, and trying to hear what they said, and trying to make myself think I didn't care and that it would be all right anyhow as long as he couldn't get my property away from me. I remember I stood at the sink and kept wiping and wiping the same clean plate over and over again until I couldn't stand it any longer.

"But when I opened the door again McDevitt and the two boys were standing out in front with just their feet in the patch of light from the door, and he was talking to them and they were laughing. Pretty soon he went away and George carried his bag for him, and they must have stood awhile talking down by the gate, for the boys didn't come back for a while. It seemed like hours. When they did come they walked and acted real careless, joking and talking loud and cutting up with each other. But when they stood at the foot of the steps and looked up at me, standing stiff in the doorway, their eyes were shining and hard and they wouldn't quite look at me, the way men act when they think their womenfolks are standing in their way. If I'd been cold before, I went frozen all over then, for I see that McDevitt had turned their minds away from me a little so that there was something hard and cold come between them and me. They didn't want to talk to me much, and after they went to bed I heard them talking low and laughing to themselves at something.

"The next day they said they wanted to go to Miami, and I gave them some money and let them go. I couldn't have said anything to them against it, any more than I could have begged Mc-Devitt to come back that time. It felt as if something inside of me was a hard lump that wouldn't let me feel anything. I wasn't going to have McDevitt say I'd kept them from seeing him. It was just as it used to be when he'd try to find out if I had a weak place he could get hold of, and I gritted my teeth to keep from showing it to the boys.

"They didn't come back for two days, and I didn't expect them to. I had a couple of nigras working for me then and I made them cut down all the orange trees I had and burn them. I couldn't stand the look of them. I had them drag the trees down to a cleared space at the edge of my land and the fire showed red through the pine trees. That night the boys came back as if nothing had happened, walking up the path, with the glare through the pines showing faint and McDevitt walking between them.

"I wouldn't let him set foot on the porch. 'I told you once and I tell you again, Peter McDevitt,' I says, 'that I won't have you on my place. The boys can do what they like. They're old enough to know better. But you, I don't have to have, and I won't have, and you can make up your mind to it.'

"George come up to me and put his arm around me and his black head, like my father's, was way taller than mine. 'Aw, Ma,' he said to me, 'Grammer McDevitt used to say you were too hard. Dad never done as much harm to you as you thought. Joe and I think you'd ought to let him come and talk things over with you. He's had a hard time, too, and it would be nice to let bygones be bygones.'

"I didn't feel his arm around me no more than if it was a piece of iron, and I looked down at Joe standing there beside McDevitt, and he was as tall as McDevitt. For the first time I see that his hair that had been gold color when he was a baby had turned to be copper-colored like his father's, and his eyes were the same red-brown when he narrowed them. The two of them stood and looked at me, and George dropped his arm and looked at me, and

McDevitt's eyes begun to shine and his nose came down over his mustache and his teeth under it were white and shining like gravestones, and he smiled as if at last he'd found the place where I was weak, and I knew it.

"That was when it seemed as if I didn't know what I was doing, except that I heard somebody telling them they could all three go away and never let me see them again as long as they'd rather have him than me. Then I saw them walking back down the road, all of them, as if they were hurrying, and I ran in and got my six-shooter and ran down the path after them, and I was shooting over their heads. When I'd shot all six shots I threw my gun away and went on stumbling in the dark after them, down through the pine woods where there was a reddish light from the bonfire still flickering.

"At the gate I saw McDevitt go on down to a car he had there, but Joe turned around and started to come back toward me, and George stopped and watched him, and then he began to walk toward me too. I stopped and watched them come, with their backs to McDevitt, and it seemed as if the hard thing in me was melting and softening and warming me all over. I come to myself all of a sudden and I could see Joe's face and George's, just as clear, without any kind of dark mist over them, and it seemed to me that it didn't really matter how weak anybody thought I was as long as I had my boys. I started to walk to them, too, almost crying, and I was just going to beg them to come back anyway, that I'd do anything they wanted me to. That was when Henry Marsh drove up and turned in my gate, passed the boys and leaned out and shouted at me that the pine woods in back of the place where the orange-tree fire was had caught and it was threatening the rest of my pines and on his side clear up to his grapefruit grove. I didn't understand him at first, until he kept saying that the fire was creeping toward the pines. And I looked, and sure enough all that light wasn't just the bonfire but the palmetto flaring up and popping and flying and the flames climbing like ragged ribbons all the way up one dead tree that stood nearest. If I hadn't been so taken up with McDevitt I would have known the difference long ago.

"Well, there wasn't anything else to do but go and fight the fire. I guess George and Joe must have turned around and gone back with McDevitt, because I didn't see them anymore that night. I rushed up to the house for some burlap bags, and then Henry Marsh and I drove as near the fire as we could get. I could see Marsh's men black against the flames thrashing at it. A fire in the pines down here isn't the same as a forest fire anywhere else. The fire clings to the woody soil and the oily palmettos and once in a while it gets up into a tree. If there's a dead branch or a rotten place the whole tree burns up then. The bark is made tough and heavy like scales, so that the fire can't hurt it if the tree is sound, and even young pines, if there isn't anything the matter with them, will burn only a little and not be killed. But where there's an old tree with its insides dead and rotted the fire leaps at it and the whole tree bursts into flame like it was tinder and the light of it brightens everything all around. Before you know it the tree crashes down and throws burning branches and ends of fire clear across a road or a fire path, and a new patch of palmetto will crackle up and blaze as if it was covered with kerosene.

"Through the smoke we could see the ground covered with blazing stumps and little edges of fire and an outer ring of flames where the fire was running toward my pine. Then a big tree that was burning fell like a fiery flag, falling straight toward the finest stand of them between there and the house, and I just went crazy. What I'd been with snakes or with McDevitt wasn't anything to that, I was so scared the pines would go. Henry Marsh said I snatched a wet burlap out of his hand and went at that burning tree single-handed, stamping and beating, with my skirts and my shoes in the flying embers, until he said it was a miracle I didn't catch fire myself. But all I remember was the heat on my face and a kind of wildness in me to get that fire out, no matter what happened or what it cost.

"And then suddenly that tree was out and there wasn't any more creeping ring of flame, but only black stumps and branches and the ground hot and smoking underfoot. The men had stopped the fire up on the other side next to Henry Marsh's grove and there was only some palmettos still burning in the middle and the smoldering earth where the fire had crept down into the peat and would smolder that way for days until it burned itself out. They got me back to my house and fixed up my burned hands and legs and feet, and I slept that night as if I was dead.

"The next day I sent word up to George and Joe that they could come back and see me when they wanted to, but I never said anything about McDevitt. And although they come back sometimes, it wasn't any use. I guess I knew it all along. Something had changed in them. McDevitt hung around Miami and I knew the boys saw him and were with him, although he never tried to come out here again himself. That night finished something for me. I knew I'd never dare to say his name to them again or ask them what they were doing. I never did. They got jobs in town, I guess, and when they come to see me I was glad to see them, but I never treated them like I'd used to, and they weren't the same with me.

"They brought me money sometimes, and I wouldn't take it and I wouldn't ask them how they got it, although they seemed to have plenty and dressed real nice. But I guessed things. They got to act more and more like McDevitt, smile like he did and not move their heads when they'd look at things, but only their eyes, and talk smooth and shifty. But sometimes they'd come back, or one of them alone, all tired out, and stay for a while, and all that would slip off them and they'd be just like my boys again, laughing and joking. I'd go in nights when they were asleep and look at them, great long heavy boys, the black one and the red one, sprawled over the bed."

The quick tropic twilight was driving the yellow light of the sun out of the clearing between the pine trees. The sky overhead was lifting and receding into a high thin dome of green quivering light into which the prickle of a star came suddenly.

Larry Gibbs did not dare to turn his head to look at her, stone-still in her chair. Her chair itself did not creak anymore. But when she spoke again, except for the stiffness of her lips, her voice was deliberate and clear and dry.

"So I never let them or McDevitt see that I had a weak place, never once. I never said anything to them or pleaded with them. I never let them see me cry. I didn't cry. McDevitt went away finally, I guess. I guess maybe he got driven out of town. And the things that happened then—happened."

There was a long silence. Her voice said at last, in a breathless murmur, "And they can tell McDevitt—I haven't—cried—yet."

There was a man coming up the roadway to the house. Larry turned and watched him come. He was glad he would not have to say anything now. The man was thin and aimless-looking, and as he came up to the steps Larry saw he fumbled with his hat and had red rims to his blue eyes.

"Evenin', Mis' McDevitt," he said uncomfortably. "Mis' Marsh wanted I should step over and see if you needed anything, or if you wouldn't like to sleep to our house tonight."

Larry stood up slowly and turned to look at her. She was rocking again, but her profile was white parchment stretched tight over the boldness of her mouth and chin and her eyes were like smudges deep within their sockets.

"You're a right good neighbor, Henry Marsh," she said. "Tell Lizzie I don't want anything, thank you, and I wouldn't be comfortable anywheres else but here. I want to be up early in the morning. There's a man coming with some avocado seedlings. I thought I'd see how they'd do here. This young man is going back now. Maybe he'd give you a ride back as far as your house. I'm much obliged to you, I'm sure."

Her chair creaked slowly as the two men went toward Larry's car. Driving back along the dark road Larry spoke only occasionally to the thin man, who seemed much affected. He told himself it was ridiculous to be affected so much himself, and yet he could not forget her sitting there on that dark porch. He found he had dreaded, in leaving her, to see some evidence of the defeat and dissolution of what in her he had found splendid, that spirit which by repeated and hard-won victories had strengthened itself, had learned to do without all the ordinary happinesses. He saw now that he had had nothing to dread. She had maintained herself, like an old pine through many burnings, by the enduring soundness of its own wood. That, Larry saw, was his story, if he could put into English his feeling of so important and so abiding a thing.

LUCK

BY LESTER DENT

City Yacht Basin
(Originally published in 1936)

Threw fish trembled its tail as the knife cut off its head, then
red ran out of it and made a mess on the planks and
spread enough to cover the wet red marks where two human hands had tried to hold to the dock edge.

Sail put the palm of his own hand in the mess.

The small policeman came from shore. He had shoved through
the small green gate with the discreet sign, *Private Yachts—No Ad-
mittance,* at the shore end of the swanky pier, and was under the
neat green canopy, tramping in the rear edge of the glare from his
flashlight. His leather and brass glistened in the light. He was cautious enough to walk in the middle of the narrow long pier, but did
enough stamping with his feet to show he was the law.

When he reached Sail, he stopped. His cap had a cock. His
lower lip was loose on the left side, as if depressed by a pipe stem
that wasn't there. He was young, bony and brown.

He asked, "That you give that yell?"

Sail picked up the hook and wet line. He held the hook close
to his left palm. He grimaced at the small oozing rip in the brown
callus of the palm. It was about the kind of a hole the fishhook
would have made.

"Yeah?" the cop said vaguely. "You snagged the hand on a
hook, eh? Made you yell?" The policeman toed the fish head's
open mouthful of snake-fang teeth.

"Barracuda," he said, but not as if that was on his mind.

Red drops came out of the ripped palm, fattened on the lower edge, came loose and fell on the dock. Sail picked the fish up with his other hand. When he stood his straightest, he was still shorter than the small cocky policeman.

The officer splashed light on Sail. He saw the round jolly brown features of a thirtyish man who probably liked his food, who would put weight on until he was forty, and spend the rest of his life secretly trying to take it off. Sail's hair might have been unraveled rope, and looked as if it had been finger-combed. Some of the black had been scrubbed out of his black polo shirt. Washings had bleached his black dungarees; they fitted his small hips tightly and stopped halfway below the knees. Bare feet had squarish toes. Weather had gotten to all of the man a lot.

The officer hocked to clear his throat. "They don't eat barracuda in Miami. Not when you catch the damn things in the harbor, anyhow."

He didn't sound as if that was the thing bothering him, either. Sail asked, "You the health department?"

The little policeman filled Sail's eyes with light. He said, "If that was a crack—" and changed to, "Was it you yelled?"

"Any law against a yell when you get a hook in your hand?"

The policeman popped his light into Sail's face again. Derision was around Sail's blue eyes and in the warp of his lips.

Loud music was coming from the moonlight excursion boat at the south end of the City Yacht Basin, but a barker spoiled the effect of the music, if any. Two slot machines alongside the lunch stand at Pier Six ate sailor nickels and chugged away.

A hundred million dollars' worth of yachts within a half-mile radius, the Miami publicity bureau said. Little Egyptian-silk-sail racing cutters that had cost a thousand a foot. A big three-hundred-foot Britisher, owned by Lady Something-or-other who only had officers with beards. And in-between sizes. Teak, mahogany, chromium, brass. Efficiency. Jap stewards as quiet as spooks. Blond Swede sailors. Skippers with leather faces, big hands and great calm.

The policeman pointed his flashlight beam at the boat tied to the end of the dock. The light showed the sloping masts, the black canvas covers over the sails, the black, neat, new-looking hull. Life preservers tied to the mainstays had *Sail* on them in gold leaf.

"What you call that kind of a boat?" the cop asked.

"Chesapeake five-log bugeye," Sail said. "Her bottom is made out of five logs drifted together with Swedish iron rods. The masts on bugeyes always rake back like that. She's thirty-four feet long in the water. You'll have trouble beating a bugeye for knocking around shallow water, and they're pretty fair sea—"

"Could it cross the ocean?"

"She has."

"Yeah? My old man's got the crazy idea he wants to go to the South Seas. He's nuts about boats."

"It gets you."

"This one yours?"

"Yes," Sail said.

"How old is it?"

"Sixty-eight years old."

"T'hell it is! That's older'n my old man. I don't think he'd want it."

"She'll take you anywhere," Sail defended.

"What's she worth?"

"Seventy-five thousand dollars," Sail said.

The policeman whistled. Then he laughed. He did not say anything.

Sail said, "There are some panels in the cabin, genuine hand carvings by Samuel McIntire of Salem. Probably they were once on a clipper ship. That's what makes her price stiff."

The cop did not answer. He switched off his light.

"All I can say is you let out a hell of a funny yell when you catch a fish," he said.

He took pains to stamp his feet while he walked away. By the time Sail got the effects of the flashlight out of his eyes, the officer was out of sight.

Sail held his hands close to his chest, fingers spread, palms in. There was barely enough breeze to make coolness against one side of his face. The music on the moonlit sailboat stopped. The barker was silent. Over in the Bayfront Park outdoor auditorium a political speaker was viewing something with alarm. After he had felt his hands tremble for a while, Sail went to his boat.

The boat, *Sail,* rode spring lines at the dock end. She had a thirty-four-foot waterline. Twelve-foot beam, two-foot draft with centerboard up, seven with it down. She was rigged to be sailed by one man, all lines coming aft.

The interior was teak, with inset panels of red sanders, fustic and green ebony, all hand-carved by a man who had died in 1811. How Samuel McIntire panels came to be in the bugeye, Sail did not know, but he had been offered a thousand dollars for each year of age for the boat and was hungry broke when he turned it down. It was not a money matter. Some men love dogs.

Sail slapped the fish into a kettle in the galley and, hurrying, put most of his right arm through a porthole, grasped a line, took half hitches off a cleat, and let the line go. The line snaked quietly down into the water, following a sinking live-box and its contents of live fish and crawfish.

Sail looked out of the hatch.

The young policeman had come quietly back to where the fish had bled and was using his flashlight. He squatted. After a while, he approached the dock end, moseying. Too carefully. When his flashlight brightened the bugeye's black masts and black sail covers, Sail was in the galley, making enough noise cutting up the fish to let the cop know where he was and what he was doing.

Sail waited four or five minutes before putting his head out of the hatch. The cop had gone somewhere silently.

Sail was still looking and listening for the policeman when he heard the man's curse and the woman's cry, short, sharp. The man's curse was something of a bray of surprise. The sounds came out of Bayfront Park, between the waterfront yacht basin and Biscayne Boulevard. Sail, not stirring, but watching the park, saw a man running among the palms. Then the young policeman and his flashlight were also moving among the palms.

During the next five minutes, the policeman and his flash were not still long enough for him to have found anything.

Sail stripped naked, working fast once more. His body was rounding, the hair on it golden and long, but not thick. He looked at his belly as if he didn't like it, slapped it and sucked it in. The act was more a habit than a thought. He put on black jersey swim trunks.

Standing in the companion looking around, Sail scratched his chest and tugged the hair on it. His fingers twisted a little rattail of the chest hair. No one was in sight. He got over the side without being too conspicuous about it.

The water had odor and the usual things floated in it. He swam under the dock, searching. The tide was high slack, almost, but still coming in just a little, so things in the water were not moving away.

The pier had been built stout because of the hurricanes. There was a net of cross timbers underneath, and anything falling off the south side of the dock would drift against them. Sail found what he was seeking on the third dive.

He kept in the dark places as he swam away with it.

The little island—artificial, put there when they dredged the harbor—was darkly silent when Sail swam laboriously toward it. Pine trees on the island had been bent by the hurricanes, and some torn up. The weeds did not seem to have been affected.

Sail tried not to splash as he shoved through the shallows to the sand beach. He towed the Greek underwater. Half a dozen crabs and some seaweed clung to the Greek when Sail carried him into the pines and weeds. The knife sticking in the Greek, and what it had done, did not help. The pines scratched and the weeds crunched under the Greek when Sail laid him down. It was very dark.

Pulpy skins in a billfold were probably greenbacks, and stiffer, smaller rectangles, business cards. Silver coins, a pocketknife, two clips for an automatic. The automatic holster empty under the Greek's left armpit. From inside the Greek's coat lining, another rectangle, four inches wide, five times as long, a quarter of an inch thick. It felt like hardwood. The Greek's wristwatch still ticked.

Sail put the business cards and the object from the coat lining inside his swim trunks, and was down on his knees cleaning his hands in the sand when the situation got the best of him. By the time he finished being sick, he had sweated profusely.

The water felt cold as he swam back the way he had come—under the docks and close to the seawall—with the Greek.

Sail clung to *Sail*'s chain bobstay until all the water had run off him that wanted to run off, then swung aboard and moved along the deck, keeping below the wharf level, and dropped down the hatch. He started to take the bathing suit off, and the girl said, "Puh-lease."

She swung her legs off the forward bunk. Light from the kerosene gimbal lamp did not reach all of her. The feet were small in dark blue sandals which showed red-enameled toenails. Her legs had not been shaved recently, but were nice.

Pink starting on Sail's chest and spreading made his tan look dark and uncomfortable, and he chewed an imaginary something between his large white front teeth as he squinted at the girl. He seemed about to say something two or three different times, but didn't, and went into the stateroom and got out of the swim trunks. The shadow-wrapped rest of her did not look bad as he passed. He tied a fish sinker to the trunks and dropped them through a porthole into the bay, which was dredged three fathoms deep here. He put on his scrubbed black clothes.

The girl had moved into the light. The rest of her was interesting.

"You probably think I'm a tart," she said. "I'm not, and I wish you'd let me stay here awhile longer. I have a good reason."

Sail scratched behind his right ear, raised and lowered his eyebrows at her, stalked self-consciously into the galley, pumped freshwater in a glass and threw it on the galley floor, then stepped in it. His feet now left wet tracks such as they had made when he came aboard. He seemed acutely conscious that his efforts to make this seem a perfectly sensible procedure were exaggerated. His hands upset a round bottle, but he caught it. He set it down, picked it up again, asked:

"Drink?"

She had crossed her legs. Her skirt was split. "That would be nice," she said.

Sail, his back to her, made more noise than necessary in rattling bottles and glasses and pinking an opener into a can of condensed milk. He mixed two parts of gin, one of crème de cacao, one of condensed milk. He put four drops from a small green bottle in one drink and gave that one to the girl, holding it out a full arm length, as if he didn't feel well-acquainted enough to get closer, or didn't want to frighten her away.

They sipped.

She said, "It's not bad without ice, really."

"I did have an electric ice box," he told her, as if excusing the lack of ice. "But it and this salt air didn't mix so well."

Her skirt matched her blue pumps, and her yellow jersey was a contrast. Her long hair was mahogany, and done in a bun over each ear, so that her long oval face had a pure, sweet look. She drank again. Her blue leather handbag started to slip out of the hollow of her crossed legs and she caught it quickly.

Sail put his glass down and went around straightening things which really didn't need it. He picked up the *News* off the engine box. It was in two parts. He handed one part to the girl. That seemed to press the button. She threw the paper down and grabbed her blue purse with both hands.

"You don't need to be so goddamn smart about it!" she said through her teeth.

She started to get up, but her knee joints did not have strength, and she slid off the bench and sat hard on the black battleship linoleum. Sail moved fast and got his plump hands on the blue purse as she clawed it open. A small bright revolver fell out of the purse as they had a tug-of-war over it.

"Blick!" the girl squealed.

Blick and a revolver came out of the oilskin locker. The gun was a small bright twin to the girl's. Blick's Panama fell off slick mahogany hair, and disarranged oilskins fell down in the locker behind him. Blick had his lips rolled in until he seemed to have no lips. He looked about old enough to have fought in the last war.

"Want it shot off?" he gritted.

Sail jerked his hand away from the girl's purse as if a bullet was already headed for it. He put his hands up as high as the cabin carlins and ceiling would allow. His mouth and eyes were round and uneasy, and the upper part of his stomach jumped a little with each beat of his heart, moving the polo shirt fabric.

Blick gave Sail a quick search. He was rough. His lips were still rolled in, and a sleeve was still jammed up on one arm, above a drop of blood that was not yet dry.

The girl started to get up, couldn't. She said, "Blick!" weakly.

Blick, watching Sail, threw at her, "You hadda be a sucker and drink with him!"

The girl's lips worked over some words before sounds started coming. ". . . was . . . I . . . know he . . . it doped."

Blick gritted at Sail, "Bud, she's my sis, and if she don't come out of that, I wouldn't wanta be you. Help me get her goin'!"

Blick dropped his sister's purse and gun in his coat pocket, got his Panama, then took the girl's right arm, letting Sail look into the little gun's muzzle all the while. "Help me, bud!"

Sail took his hands down. Sweat wetness was coming through his washed black polo shirt. He watched Blick's eyes and face instead of watching the gun. They walked the girl up the companion and onto the dock. Blick put his hand and small revolver into a trouser pocket.

"We're tight. Stagger!"

They staggered.

The orchestra on the moonlit excursion boat was still trying to entice customers for the moonlight sail. Yacht sailors, some of them with a load, stood in a knot at the end of the lunch stand, and out of the knot came the chug of the slot machines. Blick was tall enough to glare over his sister's head at Sail. His glare was not bright.

"What'd you give her?"

Sail wet his lips. The sweat had come out on his forehead enough to start running.

"Truth serum."

"You louse!"

Two sailors, one without his shirt, went past, headed for the slot machines.

Blick said, "Bud, I think I got you figured. You're a guy Andopolis rung in. He'd still try to get a boat and another guy."

Sail squinted out of one eye. Perspiration was stinging the other.

"Andopolis was the one who didn't digest the knife?"

"You ain't that dumb!"

"Was he?"

"You know that was Abel!"

Sail said, "Believe it or not, I'm guessing right across the board. Abel was to do the dirty work while you and the girl hung around on shore. Abel tried to take something from Andopolis on the dock. Abel had something that had something to do with whatever he wanted. He tapped it inside his coat as he talked. Abel got knifed, let out a bellow, and went off the dock into the drink. Andopolis ran after he knifed Abel. You headed him off in the park. He got away and ran some more. You did a sneak to my hooker while the cop looked around."

"Did you guess all that?" Blick sneered.

They were nearing Biscayne Boulevard and traffic. On the *News* building tower, the neon sign alternately spelled *WIOD* and *NEWS*. Sail took a deep breath and tried to watch Blick's face.

"I'd like to know what Abel wanted."

Blick said nothing. They scuffed over the sidewalk, and Blick, walking as if he did not feel as if he weighed much, seemed to think to a conclusion which pleased him.

"Hell, Nola. Maybe Andopolis didn't spill to our bud, here."

Nola did not answer. She seemed about asleep. Blick pinched her, slapped her, and that awakened her somewhat.

A police radio car was parked at the corner of Biscayne and Blick did not see it in time. He said, as if he didn't give a damn, "Stagger, bud! This should be good."

Sail shoved a little to steer the girl to the side of the walk farthest from the prowl car. Blick shoved back to straighten them up. The result was that they passed close enough to the police machine to reach it with one good jump. Sail shoved Blick and Nola as hard as he could, using the force of the shove to propel himself toward the car. He grabbed the spare tire at the back and used it to help himself around the machine to shelter.

Blick's revolver went off three times about as rapidly as a revolver could fire. Both cops in the car brayed, and fell out of the car onto Sail.

Blick carried Nola to a taxicab forty feet down the street, and dumped her in. He stood beside the hack, aimed, and air began leaving the left front tire of the police car. The cops started shooting in a rattled way. Blick leaped into the taxi. An instant later, the hack driver fell out of his own machine, holding his head. The taxi took off. The two cops sprang up, and piled into their machine, one yelling:

"What about this one in the street?"

"Hell, he's dead."

The cops drove after the taxi, one shooting, his partner having trouble steering with the flat tire.

Sail, for a fat man, ran away from there very fast.

* * *

Sail planted his heaving chest against the lunch stand counter, held on to the edge with both hands, and stood there a while, twice looking down at his knees and moving them experimentally, as if suspecting something was wrong with them. The young man, who looked as youths in lunch stands somehow always manage to look, came over and swiped the counter with his towel.

"What've you got in cans?" Sail asked him, then stopped the answering recital on the third name. Beer suds overflowed the can before it hit the counter. Sail drank the first can and most of the next in big gulps, but slowed down on the third and seemed tied up in thought. He scraped at the tartar on a tooth with a finger-nail, then started chewing the nail and got it down to the quick, then looked at it as if surprised. He absently put three dimes on the counter.

"Forty-five," the youth corrected.

Sail added a half and said, "Some nickels out of that."

He carried the nickels over to the mob around the slot machines. He stood around with his hands in his pockets. He tried whistling, and on the second attempt got a good result, after which he looked more satisfied with himself. His mouth warped wryly as he watched the play at the two machines. He took his nickels out, looked at them, firmly put them back, but took them out a bit later. When there was a lull, he shoved up to the slot machines.

The one-armed bandit gave him a lemon and two bars, with another bar just showing.

"You almost made it," someone said. "A little more and you'd have made the jackpot."

"Brother," Sail said, "you must be a mind reader."

He backed up, waited, still giving some attention to his private thoughts, until he got a chance at the other machine. It showed a bar, a lemon, a bar. Sail rubbed his forearms, looked thoughtful and walked off.

A telephone booth was housed at the end of Pier Four. Sail,

when a nickel got a dial tone, dialed the 0, said, "Operator, I believe in giving all telephone operators possible employment, so I never dial a number. Give me police headquarters, please." He waited for a while after the operator laughed, said, "I want to report an attempted robbery," then told someone else, "This is Captain Sail of the yacht *Sail*. A few minutes ago, a man and a woman boarded my boat and marched me away at the point of a gun. I do not know why, except that the man was a drug user. I feel he intended to kill me. There was a police car parked at the corner of Biscayne, and when I broke away and got behind it, the man tried to shoot me, then drove off with the woman in a taxi, and two officers chased them. I want to know what to do now."

"It would help if you described the pair."

The man and woman Sail described would hardly be recognized as Blick and Nola.

"Could you come up to headquarters and look over our gallery?" asked the voice.

"Where is it?"

"Turn left off Flagler just as you reach the railroad."

When Sail left the telephone booth, the youth with the hot-dog-stand look was jerking the handle of one slot machine, then the other, and swearing.

"Funny both damn things blew up!" he complained.

Sail walked off wearing a small secret grin.

Two hours later, Sail pushed back a stack of gallery photographs in police headquarters and said in a tired, wondering voice, "There sure seem to be a lot of crooks in this world. But I don't see my two."

The captain at his elbow said heartily, "You don't, eh? That's tough. One of the boys in the radio car got it in the leg. We found the taxi. And we'll find them two. You can bet on that." He was a big brown captain with the kind of jaw and eyes that went with his job. He had said his name was Rader.

Sail rode back to the City Yacht Basin in a taxi, and looked around before he got out. He walked to *Sail*. While adjusting a spring line, he saw a head shape through the skylight. By craning, he saw the head shape was finished out by a police cap. Sail walked back and forth, changing the spring lines, which did not need changing, and otherwise putting off what might come. Finally, he pulled down his coat sleeves, put on an innocent look and went down.

One policeman waiting in the cabin was using his tongue to lather a new cigar with saliva. The tongue was coated. He was shaking, not very much, but shaking. His face had some loose red skin on it, and his neck was wattled.

The second policeman was the young bony cop with the warp in the end of his mouth. He still had his flashlight.

The third man was putting bottles and test tubes in a scuffed brown leather bag which held more of the same stuff and a microscope off which some of the enamel was worn. He wore a fuzzy gray flannel suit, had rimless, hookless glasses pinched tight on his nose, and had chewed up about half of the cigar in his mouth without lighting it. The cigar was the same kind the other policeman was licking.

Sail said, "I just talked to Captain Rader."

The warp got deeper in the end of the young cop's mouth. He switched his flashlight on and off in Sail's eyes, then hung it from the hook on his belt.

"What about?"

Sail told them what he had talked to Captain Rader about—the kidnapping, which he said he could not understand. In describing Nola and Blick, whom he did not name—he made no mention of having heard their names—he repeated the words he had used over the telephone.

When it was over, the young cop stepped forward, jaw first.

"All right, by God! *Now you can tell us the truth!*"

The shaking policeman got up slowly, holding his shiny damp

cigar and looking miserable. "Now, Joey, that way won't do it."

Joey grabbed Sail's right wrist and squeezed it. "The hell it won't! Lewis says there was human blood on the dock along with the fish blood!"

The shaking policeman said, "Now, Joey."

Joey shouted, "A lot of people heard somebody let out a yip. Even over in the park where I was doing the vice squad's work, I heard it."

Sail held out his left hand to show the tear in the brown callus of the palm.

"A fishhook made that," he said. "You saw it bleed. There's your human blood on the dock."

Joey yelled, "Mister sailor, we've been checking on you by radio. You cleared from Bimini, the customs tells us. We radioed Bimini. You know what? You were asked to get out of Bimini. A gambling joint went broke in Bimini because one of their wheels had been wired and a lot of lads in the know made a cleaning. It ended up in a brawl and the gambling joint owner went to the hospital."

Joey shook his finger at Sail's throat. "The British police asked around and it began to look as if you had tipped the winners how to play. The joint owner claimed he didn't know his wheel was wired. It ended up with you being asked to clear out. The only reason you're not in the Bimini jug is because they couldn't figure any motive. You didn't get a cut. You hadn't lost any jack on the wheel. You didn't have a grudge against the owner. It was a screwy business, the British said, from beginning to end. But that's what they think. I think different. You know what I think?"

"I doubt if it would be interesting," Sail said dryly.

"I think you outfoxed 'em. You're a smooth article. That's what you think. But you can't pull this stuff here."

The shaking policeman said, "You haven't got a leg, Joey," between teeth clicks.

"I'll sweat the so-and-so until I got a thousand legs!"

The freezing policeman groaned, "You should have your behind kicked, Joey."

Joey released Sail's right wrist to frown at the other officer. "Listen, Mister Homicide—"

The shaking policeman got between Joey and Sail and stood there, saying nothing. Joey frowned at him, then sucked at his lower lip, pulling it out of shape.

"Hell, if you gotta run this, run it!" he said.

He turned and stamped up the companion, across the deck and, judging from the sounds, had some kind of an accident and nearly fell overboard getting from the boat to the dock, but finally made it safely.

The other policeman, grinning without much meaning in it, extended a hand which, when Sail took it, was hot and unnatural. After he held the hand a moment, Sail could feel it trembling.

"I'm Captain Chris of homicide," the officer said. "I want to thank you for reporting your trouble to Captain Rader, and I want to congratulate you on your narrow escape from those two. But next time, don't take such chances. Never fool with hop and guns. We'll let you know as soon as we hear anything of your attacker and his girlfriend or sister, whichever she was. I hope you have a good time in Miami in the meantime. We have a wonderful city. Florida has a wonderful climate." He shook with his chill.

The rabbity man, Lewis, who had not said anything, finished putting things in his bag, picked up a camera with a photoflash attachment which had been unnoticed on a bunk, and went up the companion, stepping carefully, as one who was not used to boats. He got onto the dock carefully with bag and camera. Captain Chris followed.

Sail said, "Quinine and whiskey is supposed to be good for malaria. But only certain quinines."

"Thanks," said Captain Chris. "But I think whiskey gave it to me."

They walked away, and young Joey was the only one who looked back.

The tide stood at flood slack, the water still, so that things did not float away. Something bright was bobbing on the water, and Sail got a light. He found five of the bright things when he hunted. Used photographic flashlight bulbs, with brass bases not corroded enough by the salt water for them to have been in long. Sail went below and looked around. Enough things were out of place to show the hooker had been searched. Fingerprint powder had not been wiped off quite well enough.

Sail catnapped all night, sleeping no more than a half hour soundly at any one time. He spent long periods with a mirror which he rigged to look out of the companion without showing himself.

On a big Matthews cruiser tied across the slip, somebody was ostensibly standing anchor watch. Boats lying at a slip do not usually stand on anchor. The watcher did not smoke and did not otherwise allow any light to get to his features. It was dark enough that he might have been tall or short, wide or narrow. The small things he did were what any man would do during a long, tiresome job, with one exception.

He frequently put a finger deep in his mouth and felt around.

Party fish boats making noise on their way out of Pier Five furnished Sail with an excuse to go on deck at about six bells. He stood there yawning, rubbing his head with his palms and making faces. He rubbed a finger across his chest and rolled up little twists and balls of dirt or old skin, after which he took a shower with the dock hose.

The watcher was not around the Matthews in the morning sun. Sail went below to don a pair of black shorts which washing had faded.

Sail's dinky rode in stern davits, bugeye fashion, at enough of a tilt not to hold seas or spray, and Sail lowered it. He got a brush and the dock hose and washed down the topsides, taking off dried salt that seawater had deposited on the hull. He dropped his brush in the water three different times; it sank, and he had to reach under for it.

The third time he reached under for the brush, he retrieved the stuff which the Greek's clothing had yielded the night before. The articles had not worked out of the nook between the dock cross braces underwater where Sail had jammed them after swimming back from the island where he had taken the dead Greek.

Sail finished washing down, hauled the dink up on the davits, and during the business of coiling the dock hose around the faucet in the middle of the dock, he worked his eyes. Any one of a dozen staring persons within view might have been the watcher from the Matthews. The other eleven would be tourists down for a gawk at the yachts.

Sail took the Greek's stuff out of the dink when he got the scrub brush. He went below. Picking the business cards apart was a job because they were soaked to pulp. He examined both sides of each card as he got it separated. One card said Captain Santorin Gura Andopolis of the yacht *Athens Girl* chartered for Gulf Stream fishing and that nobody caught more fish. The address was Pier Five. *I live aboard,* was written in pencil on the back.

The other twenty-six cards said the Lignum Vitae Towing Company had a president named Captain Abel Dokomos. The address was on the Miami River, and there was a telephone number for after six.

The piece of board was four by twenty by a quarter inches, mahogany, with screw holes in the four corners. Most of the varnish was gone, peeled rather than worn off, and so was some of the gold leaf. There were a letter and four figures in gold leaf: *K9420.*

Sail burned all of the stuff in the galley Shipmate.

A man was taking two slot machines away from the lunch stand as Sail passed on his way uptown. Later, he passed four places which had slot machines, and there was a play around all of them. Sail loafed around each crowd, but not as if he wanted to. He walked off from one crowd, then came back. In all, he managed to play three machines. The third paid four nickels and he played two back without getting anything. The slot in a dial telephone got one of the surviving nickels.

He told the operator he didn't dial as a matter of principle and asked for Pier Five, and when he got Pier Five, asked for Captain Santorin Gura Andopolis of the *Athens Girl*. It took them five minutes to decide they couldn't find Captain Andopolis.

After the telephone clanked its metal throat around the fourth nickel, Sail repeated the refusal to dial and asked for the number of Captain Abel Dokomos' Lignum Vitae Towing Company.

When he heard the answer, he made his voice as different as he could. "Cap'n Abel handy?"

"He hasn't come down this morning. Anything we can do?"

"Call later," Sail said.

The woman on the other end of the wire had been Blick's sister Nola, visitor aboard *Sail* the night before.

Sail selected a cafeteria which was a little overdone in chromium. The darkie who carried his tray got a dime. There was a small dab of oatmeal on the first chair Sail started to sit on. He broke his egg yolks and watched them run with an intent air. The fifth lump made his coffee cup overflow. He put almost a whole egg down with the first gulp from the force of habit of a man who eats his own cooking and eats it in solitude.

A boy wandered among the tables, selling newspapers and racing tip sheets. He carried and sold more tip sheets than newspapers. Sail took the coffee slowly with the spoon, getting a little undissolved sugar out of the bottom of the cup with each spoonful, seeming to enjoy it. The sugar lumps were wrapped in paper carrying the cafeteria's advertisement, and he unwrapped one and ate it after he finished everything before him. He put the papers in the coffee cup.

The man in a stiff straw hat eating near the door did not put syrup or anything sweet on his pancakes or in his coffee. And when he finished eating, he poked the back of his cheek absently with a finger, then put the finger in the back of his mouth to feel.

Sail got up and took a slow walk until he came to a U-Drive-It. There was a slot machine in the U-Drive-It. He tried it, and it paid off only in noise. He made a deposit and got a light six sedan. For three blocks, he drove slowly, looking out and appraising buildings for height. He picked one much taller than the others and parked in front of it. After starting into the building, he came back to look over an upright dingus, one of a row of the things along the curb. Small print said motorists could park there half an hour if they put a nickel in the dingus and turned the handle.

"The whole town's got it," he complained, and shook the device to see if it would start working without a nickel. It wouldn't and he put one in.

He said loudly, just before entering one of the tall building elevators, "Five!"

The fifth-floor corridor was not much different from other office building corridors. There were three real estate and one law office and some more.

The man who had felt his bad tooth in the cafeteria came sneaking up the stairs from the fourth floor and put his head around the corner. Sail was set. The man's straw hat sounded surprisingly like glass when it collapsed, and the man got down on all fours to mew in pain. Sail hit again, then unwrapped his belt from his fist. He blew on the fist, working the fingers.

"I've got to rush my friend to a place for treatment," he told the operator when the elevator cage came.

He thanked the operator and half a dozen other volunteer assistants while he started the rented car. He drove past the U-Drive-It. The proprietor was fussing with his machine.

Sail drove five or six miles by guess before he found a lonesome spot and got out. He hauled the man out. Sail's breathing was regular and deeper than usual; his eyes were wide with excitement, and he perspired. He wiped his palms on his clerical black shorts and bent over his victim.

The man with the bad tooth began big at the top and tapered. His small hands were callused, dirt was ground into the calluses, and the nails were broken. He had dark hair and a dark face, but got lighter as he went down, finishing off with feet in a pair of white shoes. He smelled a little as men smell who live on small boats with no baths.

His pockets held three hundred in nothing smaller than tens, all new bills, in a plain envelope. There was a dollar sixty-one in silver mixed up with the cashier's slip for his cafeteria breakfast. In ten or so minutes, he was scowling at Sail.

He said something in Greek. It sounded like his personal opinion of Sail or the situation.

Sail said, "Andopolis?"

"You know my name, so whatcha askin' for?" the man growled without much accent.

"You're here because I been getting too much attention," Sail said. "That oughta be clear, hadn't it?"

Andopolis felt his head, that part of his cheek over his bad tooth, then got to his feet. Sail took his belt out of his pocket and started threading it through the loops. Andopolis clutched his head, groaned, started to sit down, but jumped at Sail instead. Sail moved to one side, but not enough, and Andopolis hit his shoulder and the impact turned him around and around. Andopolis hit him somewhere else, and the whole front of his body went numb and something against his back was the ground.

"I'll stomp ya!" Andopolis yelled.

He jumped on Sail with both feet, and Sail was still numb enough to feel only the dull shock. His rounded body rolled under the impact, and Andopolis waved his arms to keep erect. Sail had his belt unthreaded. He laid it like a whip across Andopolis' face. Andopolis grabbed his face, and was wide open when he sat down heavily beside Sail.

When Andopolis came to, his wrists were fastened with the belt. Sail had his shirt unbuttoned and was examining the damage the other's feet had done. There was one purple print of the entire bottom of Andopolis' right foot, and a skinned patch where the other had slid off, with loosened skin tangled in the long golden hairs, but not much blood. He put back his head and shoulders and started to take a full breath, but broke it off in coughing. He sat down coughing, holding his chest, and sweated.

"Yah!" Andopolis gloated. "I stomp your guts good if you don't lay off me! What you been follerin' me for?"

Sail looked up sickly. "Followin' you?"

"Yah."

Sail, still sitting, said, "My Christian friend, you stood anchor watch on me last night. You haunted me this morning. But still I was following you, was I?"

"Before that, I'm talk about," Andopolis growled. "You follow me to Bimini in that black bugeye. I make the run from Bimini here yesterday. You make it too. What kinda blind fool you take me for? You followin' me, and don't you think I don't know him."

"It must have been coincidence."

"Don't feed me, mister."

"It just might be that nobody will have to feed you for long."

"Whatcha mean?"

"You were walking down the dock toward my boat last night when Abel jumped you. You sort of ruined Abel, and I covered up for you, but that's not the point. The point is, why were you coming to see me?"

"Aw, hell, I was gonna tell you about follerin' me."

Sail coughed some, deep and low, trying to keep it from moving his ribs, then got up on his feet carefully.

"All right, now we're being honest with each other, and I'll tell you a true story about a yacht named *Lady Luck*."

Andopolis crowded his lips into a bunch and pushed the bunch out as far as he could, but didn't say anything.

Sail said, "The *Lady Luck*, Department of Commerce registration number K9420. She belonged to Bill Lord of Tulsa. Oil. Out in Tulsa, they call Bill the Osage Magician on account of what he's got that it seems to take to find oil. Missus Bill likes jewelry, and Bill likes her, so he buys her plenty. Because Missus Bill really likes her rocks, she carries them around with her. You following me?"

Andopolis was. He still had his lips pooched.

"Bill Lord had his *Lady Luck* anchored off the vet camp on Lower Matecumbe last November," Sail continued. "Bill and the missus were ashore, looking over the camp. Bill was in the trenches himself, and is some kind of a shot with the American Legion and the Democrats, so he was interested. The missus left her pretties on the yacht. Remember that. Everybody has read about the hurricane that hit that afternoon, and maybe some noticed that Bill and his missus were among those who hung on behind that tank car. But the *Lady Luck* wasn't so lucky, and she dragged her pick off somewhere and sank. For a while, nobody knew where."

Sail stopped to cough. He had to lie down on his back before he could stop, and he was very careful getting erect. Perspiration had most of him wet.

"A couple of weeks ago, a guy asked the Department of Commerce lads to check and give him the name of the boat, and the owner, that carried number K9420," Sail said, keeping his voice down now. "The word got to me. Never mind how. And it was easy to find you had had a fishing party down around the Matecumbes and Long Key a few days before you got curious about K9420. It was a little harder to locate your party. Two guys. They said you anchored off Lower Matecumbe to bottom-fish, and your anchor fouled something, and you had a time, and finally, when you got the anchor up, you brought aboard some bow planking off a sunken boat. From the strain, it was pretty evident the anchor had pulled this planking off the rest of the boat, which was still down there. You checked up as a matter of course to learn what boat you had found."

Andopolis looked as if more than his tooth hurt him.

Sail kept his voice even lower to keep his ribs from moving.

"Tough you didn't get in touch with the insurance people instead of contacting Captain Abel Dokomos, a countryman who had a towing and salvage outfit and no rep to speak of. You needed help to get the *Lady Luck*. Cap Abel tried to make you cough up the exact location. You got scared and lit out for Bimini. You discovered I was following you, and that scared you back to Miami. You wanted a showdown, and when Cap Abel collared you on the dock as you were coming to see me, you took care of that part of your troubles with a knife. But that left Abel's lady friend, or whatever she is, and her brother, Blick. They were in the know, too. They tried to grab you last night in the park after you fixed Abel up, and you outran them. Now, that's a very complete story, or do you think?"

Andopolis was a man who did his thinking with the help of his face, and there was more disgust than anything else on his features.

"You tryin' to cut in?" he snarled.

"Not trying."

"Then what—"

"Have."

The sun was comfortable, but mosquitoes were coming out of the swamp around the road to investigate.

"Yeah," Andopolis said. "I guess you have, maybe."

Sail put his shirt on, favoring his chest. "We've got to watch the insurance outfit. They paid off on Missus Bill's stuff. Over a hundred thousand. They'll have wires out."

Andopolis got up and held out his hands for the belt to be taken off, and Sail took it off. Andopolis said, "I thought of the insurance when I got Cap Abel. We used to run rum. The Macedonian tramp!"

"There's shoal-water diving stuff aboard my bugeye," Sail said.

"You don't get me in no water! Shark, barracuda, moray, sting rays. Hell of a place. If I hadn't been afraid, I'd have done the diving myself. I thought of that, believe me."

"That's my worry. It's not too bad, once you get a system." Sail felt his chest. "I guess maybe these ribs will knit in a while."

Andopolis looked much better, almost as if he had forgotten his tooth. "It's your neck. Okay if you say so."

"Then let's get going."

Andopolis was feeling his tooth when he got into the car. Sail had driven no more than half a mile when both front tires let go their air. The car was in the canal beside the road before anything could be done about it.

The car broke its windows going down the canal bank. The canal must have been six feet deep, and its tea-colored water filled the machine at once. Sail had both arms over his middle where the steering wheel had hit. So much air had been knocked out of him, and his middle hurt so, that he had to take something into his lungs, and there was only water. He began to drown.

The water seemed to be rushing around inside the car, although there was room for no more to come in. Sail couldn't find the door handles. The broken windows he did find were too small to crawl out of, but after exploring three, he got desperate and tried a small one. There was not enough hole. He pushed and worked around with the jagged glass, his head out of the car, the rest of him inside, until strange feelings of something running out of his neck made him know he was cutting his throat.

He pulled his head in, and pummeled the car roof with blows that did not have strength enough to knock him away from what he was hitting. It came to his mind to try the jagged glass again as being better than drowning, but he couldn't find it, and clawed and felt with growing madness until he began to get fistfuls of air. He sank twice before he clutched a weed on shore, after which the spasms he was having kept him at first from hearing the shots.

Yells were mixed in with the shot sounds. Andopolis was on the canal bank, running madly. Blick and his sister were on the same bank, running after Andopolis, shooting at him, and having, for such short range, bad luck. They were shooting at Andopolis' legs. All three ran out of sight. Sound alone told Sail when they winged Andopolis and grabbed him.

Sail had some of the water out of his lungs. He swam to a clump of brush which hung down into the water, got under it, and managed to get his coughing stopped by the time Blick and Nola came up hauling Andopolis. Andopolis sobbed at the top of his voice.

"Shoot his other leg off if he acts up, Nola," Blick yelled. "I'll get our little fat bud."

Sail wanted to cough until it was almost worth getting shot just to do so. Red from his neck was spreading through the water under the brush.

"He must be a submarine," Blick said. He got a stick and poked around. "Hell, Nola, this water is eight feet deep anyhow."

Andopolis babbled something in Greek.

Blick screamed, "Shut up, or we'll put bullets into you like we put 'em into your car tires!"

Andopolis went on babbling.

"His leg is pretty bad, Blick," Nola said.

"Hell, let 'im bleed."

Air kept coming up from the submerged car. Sail tried to keep his mind off wanting to cough. It seemed that Blick was going to stand for hours on the bank with his bright little pistol.

"He musta drowned," Blick said. "Get that other leg to workin', Andopolis. You didn't know we been on your trail all night and all mornin', did ya? We didn't lose it when this Sail got you, either."

Andopolis whimpered as they hazed him away. Car sound departed.

Captain Chris, wide-eyed and hearty and with no sign of a chill, exclaimed, "Well, well, we began to think something had happened to you."

Sail looked at him with eyes that appeared drained, then stumbled the other two steps down the companion into the main cabin of *Sail* and let himself down on the starboard seat. Pads of cotton under gauze made Sail's neck and wrists three times normal thickness. Tape stuck to his face in four places, and iodine had run out from under one of the pieces and dried.

Young bony Joey looked Sail over and his big grin took the warp out of the corner of his mouth.

"Tsk, tsk," he said cheerfully. "Somebody beat me to it."

Sail gave them a look of bile. "This is a private boat, in case you forgot."

"He's mussed up and now he's tough!" Joey said. "Swell!"

"Now, now, let's keep things on an amiable footing," Captain Chris murmured.

Sail said, "Drag it!"

Joey popped his palms together, aimed a finger at Sail. "You got told about Lewis finding human blood in that fish mess on the dock last night. But try to alibi the rest. There was wet tracks in this boat. That was all right, maybe, only some of the tracks were salt water and the water spilled on the galley floor was fresh. We got the harbor squad diver down this morning. He found a box on the bottom below this boat with live fish in it. He found a bathing suit with a sinker tied to it. And this morning, a yachtsman beached his dink on the little island by Pier One and found a dead Greek. We sat down with all that and done our arithmetic, and here we are."

Sail's face began changing from red and tan to cream and tan, although the bandages took away some of the effect.

Captain Chris said, "Joey, you'd make a lousy gambler, on account of you show your cards."

Sail said in a low voice, "You're gonna get your snouts busted if you keep this up!"

Captain Chris looked unconvincingly injured. "I didn't think we'd have any trouble with you, Mister Sail. I hoped we wouldn't. You acted like a gentleman last night."

Sail had been seated. He got up, bending over first to get the center of gravity right. He pointed a thumb at the companion. "Don't fall overboard on your way out."

"I bet he thinks we're leaving!" Joey jeered.

A string of red crawled out from under one of the bandages on Sail's neck. His face was more cream than any other color. He reached behind himself into the tackle locker and got a gaff hook, a four-foot haft of varnished oak with a bright tempered-steel hook with a needle point. He showed Joey the hook and his front teeth.

He said violently, "I've got a six-aspirin headache and things to go with it! I feel too lousy to shy at cops. You two public servants get the hell out before I go fishing for kidneys."

Joey yelled happily, "Damn me, he's resisting arrest and threatening an officer!"

Sail said, "Arrest?"

"I forgot to tell you." Joey grinned. "We're going to—"

Sail asked Captain Chris, "Is this on the level?"

"I regret that it is," Captain Chris said. "After all, evidence is evidence, and while Miami is noted for her hospitality, we do draw lines, and when our visitors go so far as to use knives on—"

"I'm gonna hate to break your heart, you windbag!" Sail said angrily.

He took short steps, and not very fast ones, into the galley, and took the rearmost can of beer out of the icebox. He cut off the top instead of using the patent opener. When the beer had filled the sink with suds, he got a glass tube which had been waxed inside the can. He held out the two sheets of paper which the tube contained.

Joey raked his eyes over the print and penned signatures, then spelled them out, lips moving.

"This don't make a damn bit of difference!"

Captain Chris complained, "My glasses fell off yesterday during one of them infernal chills. What does it say, Joey?"

"He's a private dick assigned to locate some stuff that sank on a yacht. The insurance people hired him."

Captain Chris buttoned his coat, pulled it down over his hips, set his cap by patting the top of it.

"I'm afraid this makes it different, Joey."

Joey snorted. "I say it don't."

Captain Chris walked to the companion. "Beauty before age, Joey."

"Listen, if you think—"

"Out, Joey."

"Mister Homicide, any day—"

"Out!" Captain Chris roared. "You're as big a goddamn fool as your mother."

Joey licked his lips while he kept a malevolent eye on Sail, then took a step forward, but changed his mind and climbed the companion steps. When he was outside, he complained, "Paw, you and your ideas give me an ache."

Captain Chris sighed wearily while he looked at Sail. "He's my son, the spoiled whelp." He hesitated. "You wouldn't want to cooperate?"

"I wouldn't."

"If you get yourself in a sling, it'd be better if you had a reason for refusing to help the police."

Sail said, "All I get out of this is a commission for recovering the stuff. Right now, I need that money like hell."

"You'd still get it if we helped each other."

"Maybe. But I've cooperated before."

Captain Chris shrugged, climbed three of the companion's five steps, and stopped. "This malaria is sure something. I could sing like a lark today, only I keep thinking about the chills due tomorrow. Did you say a special quinine went in that whiskey?"

"Bullards. It's English."

"Thanks." Captain Chris climbed the rest of the way out.

When the two policemen reached the dock, Sail came slowly

on deck and handed Captain Chris a bottle. "You can't buy Bullards here."

"Say, I appreciate this!"

"If my day's run of luck keeps on the way it has, you'll probably
find your knife man in a canal somewhere," Sail said slowly.

"I'll look," Captain Chris promised.

The two cops went away with Joey kicking his feet down hard
on the dock boards.

There was a rip in the nervous old man's canvas apron, and he
mixed his words with waves of a pipe off which most of the stem
had been bitten. He waved the pipe and said, "My, mister, you
must've had a car accident."

Sail, holding to the counter, said, "What about the charts?"

"Yeah, there's one other place sells the government charts
besides us. Hopkins Carter. But if you're going down in the keys,
we got everything you need here. If you go on the inside, you'll
want thirty-two-sixty and sixty-one. They're the strip charts. But
if you take Hawk Channel, you'll need harbor chart five-eighty-
three, and charts twelve-forty-nine, fifty and fifty-one. Here, I'll
show—"

Sail squinted his eyes, swallowed and said, "I don't want to
buy a chart. I want you to slip out and telephone me if either of
certain two persons comes in here and asks for chart twelve-fifty,
the one which has Lower Matecumbe."

"Huh?"

Sail said patiently, "It's simple. You just tell the party you got
to get the chart, and go telephone me, then stall around three or
four minutes before you deliver the chart, giving me time to get
over here and pick up their trail."

The nervous old man put his pipe in his mouth and immediately took it out.

"What kind of shenanigans is this?"

Sail showed him a license to operate in Florida.

"One of them private detectives, huh?" the old man said, impressed.

Sail put a ten-dollar bill on the counter.

"That one's got twins. How about it?"

"Mister, if you'll just describe your parties. That's all!"

Sail made a word picture of Blick and Nola, putting the salient points down on a piece of paper. He added a telephone number.

"The phone's a booth in a cigar store on the corner. I'll be there. How far is this Hopkins Carter?"

"Two blocks."

"I'll probably be there for the next ten minutes."

Sail, walking off, was not as pale as he had been on the boat. He had put on a serge suit more black than blue and a new black polo. When he was standing in front of the elevator, taking a pull at a flat amber bottle which had a crown and a figure 5 on the label, the old man yelled.

"Hey, mister!"

Sail lowered the bottle, started coughing, and called between coughs, "Now"—*cough*—"what?"

"Lemme look at this again and see if you said anything about the way he talked."

Sail moved back to where he could see the old man peering at the paper which held the descriptions. The old man took his pipe out of his teeth.

"Mister, what does that feller talk like?"

"Well, about like the rest of these crackers. No, wait. He'll call you bud two or three times."

The old man pointed his pipe at the floor. "I already sold that man a twelve-fifty. 'Bout half hour ago."

Sail pumped air out of his lungs in a short laugh which had no sound except the sound made by the air passing his teeth and nostrils. He said, "That's swell. They would probably want a late chart for their X-marks-the-spot. And so they've got it, and they're off to the wars, and me, I'm out ten percent on better than a hundred thousand."

He had taken two slow steps toward the elevator when the old man said, "The chart was delivered."

Sail came around. "Eh?"

"He ordered it over the telephone. We delivered. I got the address somewhere." He thumbed an order book. "*Whileaway.* A houseboat on the river below the Twelfth Street causeway."

Sail put a ten on the counter. "The brother."

He was a fat man trying to hide a big face behind two hands, a match and a cigar. He said, "Oof!" and his dropping hands dragged cigar ashes down his vest when Sail prodded him in the upper belly with a fingertip.

Sail said, "I just didn't want you to think you were getting away with it."

The fat man turned his cigar down at an injured angle. "With what?"

"Whatever you call what you've been doing."

"There must be some mistake, brother."

"There's been several. It'll be another if you keep on trying to tail me."

"Me, tailing you! Why should I do that?"

"Because you're a cop. You've got it all over you. And probably because Captain Chris ordered me trailed."

The plainclothesman sent his cigar between two pedestrians, across the sidewalk and into the gutter. "Mind telling me what you can do about it?"

Sail had started away. He came back, pounding his heels. "What was that?"

"I've heard all about you, small-fat-and-tough. You're due to learn that with the Miami Police Department, you can't horse—"

Sail put his hand on the fat man's face. The fingers were spread, and against the hand's two longest fingers, the fat man's eyeballs felt wet. Sail shoved out and up a little. The cop did not yell or curse. He swung a vicious uppercut. He kicked with his right foot, then his left. The kicks would have lifted a hound dog over a roof. He held his eyes. The third kick upset a stack of gallon cans of paint.

Sail got out of there. He changed cabs four times as rapidly as one cab could find another.

Whileaway was built for rivers, and not very wide rivers. She was a hooker that couldn't take a sea. A houseboat about sixty feet waterline, she had three decks that put her up like a skyscraper. She should never have been built. She was white, or had been.

Scattered onshore near the houseboat was a gravel pile, two trucks with nobody near them, a shed, junk left by the hurricane, a trailer with both tires flat, windows broken, and two rowboats in as bad shape as the trailer. Sail was behind most of them at one time or another on his way to the riverbank. There was a concrete seawall. Between Sail and the houseboat, two gigs, a yawl, a cruiser and another houseboat were tied to dolphins along the concrete river bulkhead. Nobody seemed to be on any of the boats.

Sail wore dark blue silk underwear shorts. He hid everything else under the hurricane junk. The water had a little more smell and floating things than in the harbor. He kept behind the moored boats after he got over the seawall, and let the tide carry him. He was just coming under the *Whileaway* bow when one of the square window ports opened almost overhead.

Sail sank. He thought somebody was going to shoot or use a harpoon.

Something large and heavy fell into the water and sank, colliding with him, pushing him out of the way and going on sinking. He had enough contact with it to tell the first part of it was a navy-type anchor. He swam down after it. The river had two fathoms here, and he found the anchor and what was tied to it. The tide stretched his legs out behind as he clung to what he had found.

Whoever had tied the knots was a sailor, and sailor knots, while they hold, are made to be easily untied. Sail got them loose.

It would have been better to swim under the houseboat and come up on the other side, away from the port from which the anchor and Nola had been thrown, but Sail didn't feel equal to anything but straight up. His air capacity was low because of his near drowning earlier in the day.

He put his head out of the water with his eyes open and fixed in the direction of the square port. No head was sticking out of the port. No weapon appeared. The tide had taken Sail near the stern of the *Whileaway* and still carried him.

He got Nola's head out. Water leaked from her nose and mouth. Sail got an arm up as high as he could, clutching. He missed the first sagging spring line, got the second. The rope with which the anchor had been attached to Nola still clung to her ankles. He tied one of her arms to the spring line so that her head was out.

Sail went up the spring line with his hands until one foot would reach the windowsills. From there to the first deck was simpler.

Nola began to gag and cough. It made a racket.

Sail opened his mouth to yell at her to be quiet. She couldn't hear him yet, or understand. He wheeled and sloped into the houseboat cabin.

The furnishings might have been something once, but that had been fifteen years ago. Varnish everywhere had alligatored.

Sail angled into the galley when he saw it. He came out with a quart brass fire extinguisher which needed polishing, and a rusted ice pick. There had been nothing else in sight.

Nola got enough water out to start screeching.

Beyond the galley was a dining room. Sail had half crossed it when Captain Santorin Gura Andopolis came in the opposite door with a rusty butcher knife.

Andopolis was using a chair for a crutch, riding its bottom with the knee of the leg which Blick and Nola had put a bullet through. Around his eyes—on the lids more than elsewhere—were puffy gray blisters about a size which burning cigarettes would make.

Three fingernails were off each hand. Red ran from the three mutilated tips on the right hand down over the rusty butcher knife.

Sail had time to throw the fire extinguisher and made use of the time, but the best he did was bounce the extinguisher off the bulkhead behind Andopolis.

Andopolis said thickly, "I feex you up, mine fran!" and deliberately reversed the butcher knife for throwing.

Sail threw his ice pick. It stuck into Andopolis' chest over his heart. It did not go in deep enough to bother Andopolis. He did not even bother to jerk it out.

Sail jumped for the door, wanting to go back the way he had come. His wet feet slipped, let him down flat on his face.

Feet came pounding through the door and went overhead. Sail looked up. The feet belonged to the plainclothes detective who had been in the hardware store which sold marine charts.

Andopolis threw his knife. He was good at it, or lucky. The detective put his hands over his middle and looked foolish. He changed his course and ran to the wall. His last steps were spraddling. He leaned against the bulkhead. His hands did not quite cover the handle of the butcher knife.

Andopolis hobbled to Sail on his chair. He stood on one leg and clubbed the chair. Sail rolled. The chair became two pieces and some splinters on the floor. Sail, still lying on the floor, kicked Andopolis' good leg. Andopolis fell down.

As if that had given him an idea, the detective fell. He kept both hands over the knife handle.

Andopolis used the two largest parts of the chair and flailed at Sail. On all fours, Sail got away. His throat wound was running again. He got up, but there was no weapon except the bent fire extinguisher. He got that. Andopolis hit him with the chair leg and his left side went numb from the belt down. He retreated, as lopsided on his feet as Andopolis, and passed into the main cabin.

Nola was still screaming. A man was swearing at her with

young cocky Joey's voice. Men were jumping around on the decks and in the houseboat rooms.

Blick sat on the main cabin floor, getting his head untangled from the remains of a chair. His face was a mess. It was also smeared with blue ink. The ink bottle was upside down under a table on which a new chart was spread open. A common pen lay on the chart.

Andopolis came in following Sail. Andopolis crawled on one knee and two hands.

Blick squawked, "What's Nola yellin' for?"

Andopolis crawled as if he did not see Sail or Blick, had not heard Blick. A tattered divan stood against the starboard bulkhead. Andopolis lay down and put an arm under that. He brought out a little bright pistol, either Blick's or his sister's.

Captain Chris jumped in through the door.

Andopolis' small pistol made the noise of a big one. Blick, sitting on the floor, jumped a foot when there seemed no possible way of his jumping, no muscles to propel him upward. He came down with his head forward between his knees, and remained that way, even after drops began coming out of the center of his forehead.

Captain Chris had trouble with his coattails and his gun. Andopolis' little gun made its noise again. Captain Chris turned around faster than he could have without some help from lead, and ran out, still having trouble with his gun.

Sail worked the handle of the fire extinguisher. The plunger made *ink-sick!* noises going up and down. No tetrachloride came out. There was nothing to show it ever would. Then the first squirt ran out about a foot. The second was longer, and the third wet Andopolis' chest. Sail raised the stream and pumped. He got Andopolis's eyes full and rolled.

Andopolis fired once at where Sail had been. Then he got up on one foot and hopped for the door. His directions were a little confused. He hopped against a bulkhead.

Andopolis went down on the floor and began having a fit. It was a brief fit, ending by Andopolis turning over on his back and relaxing.

The wall had driven the ice pick the rest of the way into his chest.

Outside, Nola still screamed, but now she made words, scatteredly.

"Andopolis . . . killing Blick . . . tried . . . me . . . Andopolis . . . last night . . . Abel . . . knife . . . we . . . him . . . tell . . . broke loose . . . me . . . anchor . . . Blick . . ."

Sail ran to the table. The chart on the table had two ink lines forming a V with arms that ran to landmarks on Lower Matecumbe, and compass bearings were inked beside each arm, with the point where the lines came together ringed.

Sail left with the chart by the door opposite the one which he had come in by, taking the chart. He found a cabin. He tore the V out of the chart, folded it flat and tucked it under his neck bandages, using the stateroom mirror to adjust the bandages to hide the paper. He threw the rest of the chart out of a port on the river side.

Captain Chris was standing near dead Andopolis. Torn coat lining was hanging from under the right tail of his coat, but he had his gun in his hand.

"Where'd you go to?" he wanted to know.

"Was I supposed to stick around while you drew that gun?"

"The fireworks over?"

"I hope so."

Captain Chris put his gun in his pants pocket. "You're pinched. Don't say I didn't warn you."

Young Joey came in, not as cocky and not stamping his feet. Two plainclothesmen followed him, then two uniformed officers walking ahead of and behind the old man who sold the charts in the hardware store.

The old man pointed at Sail and said, "He's the one who

asked about the feller who ordered the chart. Like I told you, I gave him—"

"Save it." Joey glared at Captain Chris. "We still ain't got nothing on this fat sailor, Paw. The girl says Andopolis is a party fisherman whose anchor pulled up part of a boat."

The girl had told about everything. Joey kept telling the story until he got to, "So Sail yanked the dame out, and now what've we got to hold him on?"

Captain Chris, looking mysterious and satisfied, told Sail, "Get your clothes on or we'll book you for indecent exposure along with the rest."

"What rest?"

"Get your clothes on."

Sail dressed sitting on the hurricane wreckage, brushed off the bottoms of his feet and put on socks and shoes. He looked up at Captain Chris as he tied the shoestrings.

"Kidding, aren't you?"

"Sure, sure!"

Sail bristled. "You've got to have a charge. Just try running me in on an INV and see what it gets you."

"I've got a charge."

"In a gnat's eye."

Captain Chris said with relish, "You've been playing the slot machines which are so popular in our fair city. You used a slug made of two hollow halves that fit together and hold muriatic or something that eats the works of the machines and puts them on the fritz. We found a box of the slugs on your boat. We have witnesses who saw you play machines before they went bad."

Sail wore a dark look toward the squad car. "This is a piker trick."

Captain Chris tooled the car over a bad street. "You put that gambling joint in Bimini on the bum, too. What's the idea?"

"Nuts."

"Now, don't get that way. I'm jugging you, yes. But it's the principle. It's to show you that it ain't a nice idea to football the cops around. Not in Miami, anyway. You'll get ten days or ten bucks is all. It's the principle. That, and a bet I made with Joey that if he'd let me handle this and keep his mouth shut, and you beat me to the kill, I'd jug you on this slot machine thing. Joey wanted you jugged. Now, what's this between you and slot machines and wheels?"

Sail considered for a while, then took in breath.

"I even went to an institution where they cure things, once," he said. "Kind of a bughouse."

"Huh?"

"One psychologist called it a fixation. I've always had it. Can't help it. Some people can't stand being alone, and some can't stand being shut up in a room, and some can't take mice. With me, it's gambling. Can't stand it. I can't stand the thought of taking chances to make money."

"Just a lad who gets his dough the safe and sane method."

"That's the idea," Sail agreed, "in a general way."

THEIR EYES WERE
WATCHING GOD (EXCERPT)

BY ZORA NEALE HURSTON
Belle Glade
(Originally published in 1937)

Tea Cake had two bad attacks that night. Janie saw a changing look come in his face. Tea Cake was gone. Something else was looking out of his face. She made up her mind to be off after the doctor with the first glow of day. So she was up and dressed when Tea Cake awoke from the fitful sleep that had come to him just before day. He almost snarled when he saw her dressed to go.

"Where are you goin', Janie?"

"After de doctor, Tea Cake. You'se too sick tuh be heah in dis house 'thout de doctah. Maybe we oughta git yuh tuh de hospital."

"Ah ain't goin' tuh no hospital no where. Put dat in yo' pipe and smoke it. Guess you tired uh waitin' on me and doing fuh me. Dat ain't de way Ah been wid *you*. Ah never is been able tuh do enough fuh yuh."

"Tea Cake, you'se sick. You'se takin' everything in de way Ah don't mean it. Ah couldn't never be tired uh waitin' on you. Ah'm just skeered you'se too sick fuh me tuh handle. Ah wants yuh tuh git well, honey. Dat's all."

He gave her a look full of blank ferocity and gurgled in his throat. She saw him sitting up in bed and moving about so that he could watch her every move. And she was beginning to feel fear of this strange thing in Tea Cake's body. So when he went out to the outhouse she rushed to see if the pistol was loaded. It was a six-shooter and three of the chambers were full. She started to unload it but she feared he might break it and find out she knew. That might urge his disordered mind to action. If that medicine would only come! She whirled the cylinder so that if he even did draw the gun on her it would snap three times before it would fire. She would at least have warning. She could either run or try to take it away before it was too late. Anyway Tea Cake wouldn't hurt *her*. He was jealous and wanted to scare her. She'd just be in the kitchen as usual and never let on. They'd laugh over it when he got well. She found the box of cartridges, however, and emptied it. Just as well to take the rifle from back of the head of the bed. She broke it and put the shell in her apron pocket and put it in a corner in the kitchen almost behind the stove where it was hard to see. She could outrun his knife if it came to that. Of course she was too fussy, but it did no harm to play safe. She ought not to let poor sick Tea Cake do something that would run him crazy when he found out what he had done.

She saw him coming from the outhouse with a queer loping gait, swinging his head from side to side and his jaws clenched in a funny way. This was too awful! Where was Dr. Simmons with that medicine? She was glad she was here to look after him. Folks would do such mean things to her Tea Cake if they saw him in such a fix. Treat Tea Cake like he was some mad dog when nobody in the world had more kindness about them. All he needed was for the doctor to come on with that medicine. He came back into the house without speaking, in fact, he did not seem to notice she was there and fell heavily into the bed and slept. Janie was standing by the stove washing up the dishes when he spoke to her in a queer cold voice.

"Janie, how come you can't sleep in de same bed wid me no mo'?"

"De doctah told you tuh sleep by yo'self, Tea Cake. Don't yuh remember him tellin' you dat yistiddy?"

"How come you ruther sleep on uh pallet than tuh sleep in de bed wid me?" Janie saw then that he had the gun in his hand that was hanging to his side. "Answer me when Ah speak."

"Tea Cake, Tea Cake, honey! Go lay down! Ah'll be too glad tuh be in dere wid yuh de minute de doctor say so. Go lay back down. He'll be heah wid some new medicine right away."

"Janie, Ah done went through everything tuh be good tuh you and it hurt me tuh mah heart tuh be ill treated lak Ah is."

The gun came up unsteadily but quickly and leveled at Janie's breast. She noted that even in his delirium he took good aim. Maybe he would point to scare her, that was all.

The pistol snapped once. Instinctively Janie's hand flew behind her on the rifle and brought it around. Most likely this would scare him off. If only the doctor would come! If anybody at all would come! She broke the rifle deftly and shoved in the shell as the second click told her that Tea Cake's suffering brain was urging him on to kill.

"Tea Cake, put down dat gun and go back tuh bed!" Janie yelled at him as the gun wavered weakly in his hand.

He steadied himself against the jamb of the door and Janie thought to run into him and grab his arm, but she saw the quick motion of taking aim and heard the click. Saw the ferocious look in his eyes and went mad with fear as she had done in the water that time. She threw up the barrel of the rifle in frenzied hope and fear. Hope that he'd see it and run, desperate fear for her life. But if Tea Cake could have counted costs he would not have been there with the pistol in his hands. No knowledge of fear nor rifles nor anything else was there. He paid no more attention to the pointing gun than if it were Janie's dog finger. She saw him stiffen himself all over as he leveled and took aim. The fiend in him must kill and Janie was the only thing living he saw.

The pistol and the rifle rang out almost together. The pistol just enough after the rifle to seem its echo. Tea Cake crumpled as his bullet buried itself in the joist over Janie's head. Janie saw the look on his face and leaped forward as he crashed forward in her arms. She was trying to hover him as he closed his teeth in the flesh of her forearm. They came down heavily like that. Janie struggled to a sitting position and pried the dead Tea Cake's teeth from her arm.

It was the meanest moment of eternity. A minute before she was just a scared human being fighting for its life. Now she was her sacrificing self with Tea Cake's head in her lap. She had wanted him to live so much and he was dead. No hour is ever eternity, but it has its right to weep. Janie held his head tightly to her breast and wept and thanked him wordlessly for giving her the chance for loving service. She had to hug him tight for soon he would be gone, and she had to tell him for the last time. Then the grief of outer darkness descended.

A JOB FOR THE MACARONE

BY DAMON RUNYON

Miami River

(Originally published in 1937)

When the last race meeting of the winter season closes in Miami and it is time for one and all to move on to Maryland, I take a swivel at the weather reports one day and I observe that it is still down around freezing in those parts.

So thinks I to myself, I will remain in the sunny southland a while longer and continue enjoying the balmy breezes, and the ocean bathing, and all this and that, until the weather settles up yonder, and also until I acquire a blow stake, for at this time my bank-roll is worn down to a nubbin and, in fact, I do not have enough ready to get myself as far as Jax, even by walking.

Well, while waiting around Miami, trying to think of some way of making a scratch, I spend my evenings in the Shark Fin Grill, which is a little scatter on Biscayne Boulevard near the docks that is conducted by a friend of mine by the name of Chesty Charles.

He is called by this name because he has a chest like a tub and he walks with it stuck out in front of him, and the reason Charles keeps his chest out is because if he pulls it in, his stomach will take its place, only farther down, and Charles does not wish his stomach to show in this manner, as he likes to think he has a nice shape.

At the time I am speaking of, Chesty Charles is not as young as he used to be, and he wishes to go along very quiet and avoiding undue excitement, but anybody can see that he is such a character as observes a few things in his time. In fact, anybody can see that he is such a character as is around and about no little and quite some before he settles down to conducting the Shark Fin Grill.

The reason Charles calls his place the Shark Fin Grill is because it sounds nice, although, of course, Charles does not really grill anything there, and, personally, I think the name is somewhat confusing to strangers.

In fact, one night a character with a beard, from Rumson, New Jersey, comes in and orders a grilled porterhouse; and when he learns he cannot get same, he lets out a chirp that Charles has no right to call his place a grill when he does not grill anything and claims that Charles is obtaining money under false pretences.

It finally becomes necessary for Charles to tap him on the pimple with a beer mallet, and afterward the constables come around, saying what is going on here, and what do you mean by tapping people with beer mallets, and the only way Charles can wiggle out of it is by stating that the character with the beard claims that Mae West has no sex appeal. So the constables go away saying Charles does quite right and one of them has half a mind to tap the character himself with something.

Well, anyway, one night I am in the Shark Fin Grill playing rummy with Charles and there is nobody else whatever in the joint, because, by this time, the quiet season is on in Miami and Charles's business thins out more than somewhat; and just as I beat Charles a pretty good score, who comes in but two characters in sport shirts, and one of them has that thing in his hand and he says to us like this:

"Reach," he says. "This is a stick-up. No beefs, now," he says.

Well, Chesty Charles and me raise our hands as high as possible, and, in fact, I am only sorry I cannot raise mine higher than possible, and Chesty Charles says: "No beefs," he says. "But," he says, "boys, you are on an awful bust. All you are liable to get around this drum is fleas. If there is any dough here I will be using it myself," Chesty says.

"Well," one of the characters says, "we will have a look at your damper, anyway. Maybe you overlook a few coarse notes here and there."

So one character keeps that thing pointed at Chesty Charles and me, and the other goes through the cash register, but, just as Charles says, there is nothing in it. Then the character comes over and gives Charles and me a fanning, but all he finds is eighty cents on Charles, and he seems inclined to be a little vexed at the scarcity of ready between us and he acts as if he is thinking of clouting us around some for our shortage, as these git-'em-up characters will sometimes do if they are vexed, when all of a sudden Charles looks at one of the characters and speaks as follows:

"Why," Chesty Charles says, "do my eyes deceive me, or do I behold The Macarone, out of Kansas City?"

"Why, yes," the character says. "Why, hello, Chesty," he says. "Meet my friend Willie," he says. "He is out of Kansas City too. Why, I never expect to find you in such a joint as this, Chesty," he says. "Especially a joint where there is so little dough."

"Well," Chesty Charles says, "you ought to drop around when the season is on. Things are livelier then. But," he says, "sit down and let's have a talk. I am glad to see you, Mac," he says.

So they sit down and Chesty Charles puts out a bottle of Scotch and some glasses and we become quite sociable, to be sure, and presently The Macarone is explaining that Willie and him have been over in Havana all winter, working with a pay-off mob out of Indianapolis, Indiana, that has a store there, but that business is rotten, and they are now en route north and just stop over in Miami to pick up a few dibs, if possible, for walk-about money.

The Macarone seems to be quite an interesting character in many respects and I can see that he and Charles know each other from several places. The Macarone is maybe around forty and he is tall and black-looking, but the character he calls Willie is younger and by no means gabby, and, in fact, he scarcely has a word to say.

We sit there quite a while drinking Scotches and speaking of this and that, and finally Chesty Charles says to The Macarone:

"Mac," he says, "come to think of it, I may be able to drop something in your lap, at that. Only last night a character is in here with a right nice proposition, but," Chesty says, "it is not in my line, so it does not interest me."

"Chesty," The Macarone says, "any proposition that is not in your line must be a very unusual proposition indeed. Let me hear this one," he says.

"Well," Chesty says, "it is a trifle unusual, but," he says, "it seems quite sound, and I only regret that I cannot handle it in person. I am froze in here with this business and I do not feel free to engage in any outside enterprises. The character I refer to," he says, "is Mr. Cleeburn T. Box, who lives on a big estate over here on the bay front with his nephew. Mr. Cleeburn T. Box wishes to quit these earthly scenes," Chesty says. "He is sick and tired of living. His nerves are shot to pieces. He cannot eat. He is in tough shape.

"But," Chesty says, "he finds he does not have the nerve to push himself off. So he wishes to find some good reliable party to push him off, for which service he will pay five thousand dollars cash money. He will deposit the dough with me," Chesty says. "He realizes that I am quite trustworthy. It is a soft touch, Mac," he says. "Of course," he says, "I am entitled to the usual twenty-five percent commission for finding the plant."

"Well," The Macarone says, "this Mr. Box must be quite an eccentric character. But," he says, "I can understand his reluctance about pushing himself off. Personally, I will not care to push myself off. However," he says, "the proposition seems to have complications. I hear it is against the law in Florida to push people off, even if they wish to be pushed."

"Well," Chesty says, "Mr. Box thinks of this too. His idea is that the party who is to do this service for him will slip into his house over on the bay front some night and push him off while he is asleep, so he will never know what happens to him. You understand, he wishes this matter to be as unexpected and painless as possible. Then," Chesty says, "the party can leave that thing with which he does the pushing on the premises and it will look as if Mr. Box does the pushing in person."

"What about a club?" The Macarone says. "Or maybe a shiv? That thing makes a lot of racket."

"Why," Chesty says, "how can you make a club or shiv look like anything but something illegal if you use them to push anybody? You need not be afraid of making a racket, because," he says, "no one lives within hearing distance of the joint, and Mr. Box will see that all his servants and everybody else are away from the place every night, once I give him the word the deal is on. He will place the dough at my disposal when he gets this word. Of course he does not wish to know what night it is to happen, but it must be some night soon after the transaction is agreed to."

"Well," The Macarone says, "this is one of the most interesting and unusual propositions ever presented to me. Personally," he says, "I do not see why Mr. Box does not get somebody to put something in his tea. Anybody will be glad to do him such a favour."

"He is afraid of suffering," Chesty Charles says. "He is one of the most nervous characters I ever encounter in my life. Look, Mac," he says, "this is a job that scarcely requires human intelligence. I have here a diagram that shows the layout of the joint."

And with this, Chesty Charles outs with a sheet of paper and spreads it out on the table, and begins explaining it to The Macarone with his finger.

"Now," he says, "this shows every door and window on the ground floor. Here is a wing of the house. Here is Mr. Cleeburn T. Box's room on the ground floor overlooking the bay. Here is a French window that is never locked," he says. "Here is his bed against the wall, not two steps from the window. Why," Chesty says, "it is as simple as WPA."

"Well," The Macarone says, "you are dead sure Mr. Box will

not mind being pushed? Because, after all, I do not have any reason to push him on my own account, and I am doing my best at
this time to lead a clean life and keep out of unpleasant situations."

"He will love it," Chesty says.

So The Macarone finally says he will give the matter his earnest consideration and will let Chesty Charles have his answer in
a couple of days. Then we all have some more Scotches, and it is
now past closing time, and The Macarone and Willie take their
departure, and I say to Chesty like this:

"Chesty," I say, "all this sounds to me like a very strange proposition, and I do not believe anybody in this world is dumb enough
to accept same."

"Well," Chesty says, "I always hear The Macarone is the
dumbest character in the Middle West. Maybe he will wind up
taking in the South too," he says, and then Chesty laughs and we
have another Scotch by ourselves before we leave.

Now, the next afternoon I am over on South Beach, taking a
little dip in the ocean, and who do I run into engaged in the same
pastime but The Macarone and Willie. There are also numerous
other parties along the beach, splashing about in the water in their
bathing suits or stretched out on the sand, and The Macarone
speaks of Chesty Charles's proposition like this:

"It sounds all right," The Macarone says. "In fact," he says, "it
sounds so all right that the only thing that bothers me is I cannot
figure out why Chesty does not take it over one hundred percent.
But," he says, "I can see Chesty is getting old, and maybe he loses
his nerve. Well," The Macarone says, "that is the way it always is
with old folks. They lose their nerve."

Then The Macarone starts swimming towards a float pretty
well out in the water, and what happens when he is about halfway
to the float but he starts flapping around in the water no little, and
it is plain to be seen that he is in some difficulty and seems about
to drown. In fact, The Macarone issues loud cries for help, but,
personally, I do not see where it is any of my put-in to help him,

as he is just a chance acquaintance of mine and, furthermore, I cannot swim.

Well, it seems that Willie cannot swim either, and he is saying it is too bad that The Macarone has to go in such a fashion, and he is also saying he better go and get The Macarone's clothes before someone else thinks of it. But about this time a little Judy with about as much bathing suit on as will make a boxing glove for a mosquito jumps off the float and swims to The Macarone and seizes him by one ear and holds his head above the water until a lifeguard with hair on his chest gets out there and takes The Macarone off her hands.

Well, the lifeguard tows The Macarone ashore and rolls him over a barrel and gets enough water out of him to float the *Queen Mary*, and by and by The Macarone is as good as new, and he starts looking around for the little Judy who holds him up in the water.

"She almost pulls my ear out by the roots," The Macarone says. "But," he says, "I will forgive this torture because she saves my life. Who is she, and where is she?"

Well, the lifeguard, who turns out to be a character by the name of Dorgan, says she is Miss Mary Peering and that she works in the evening in a barbecue stand over on Fifth Street, and what is more, she is a right nifty little swimmer, but, of course, The Macarone already knows this. But now nothing will do but we must go to the barbecue stand and find Miss Mary Peering, and there she is in a blue linen uniform and with a Southern accent, dealing hot dogs and hamburger sandwiches and one thing and another, to the customers.

She is a pretty little Judy who is maybe nineteen years of age, and when The Macarone steps forward and thanks her for saving his life, she laughs and says it is nothing whatever, and at first The Macarone figures that this crack is by no means complimentary, and is disposed to chide her for same, especially when he gets to thinking about his ear. But he can see that the little Judy has no idea of getting out of line with him, and he becomes very friendly towards her.

We sit there quite a while with The Macarone talking to her between customers, and finally he asks her if she has a sweet-pea anywhere in the background of her career, and at this she bursts into tears and almost drops an order of pork and beans.

"Yes," she says, "I am in love with a wonderful young character by the name of Lionel Box. He is a nephew of Mr. Cleeburn T. Box, and Mr. Cleeburn T. Box is greatly opposed to our friendship. Lionel wishes to marry me, but," she says, "Mr. Cleeburn T. Box is his guardian and says he will not hear of Lionel marrying beneath his station. Lionel will be very rich when he is of age, a year from now, and then he can do as he pleases, but just at present his Uncle Cleeburn keeps him from even seeing me. Oh," she says, "I am heartbroken."

"Where is this Lionel now?" The Macarone says.

"That is just it," Miss Mary Peering says. "He is home, sick with the grippe or some such, and his Uncle Cleeburn will not as much as let him answer the telephone. His Uncle Cleeburn acts awful crazy, if you ask me. But," she says, "just wait until Lionel is of age and we can be married. Then we will go so far away from his Uncle Cleeburn he can never catch up with us again."

Well, at this news The Macarone seems to become very thoughtful, and at first I think it is because he is disappointed to find Miss Mary Peering has a sweet-pea in the background, but after a little more talk, he thanks her again for saving his life and pats her hand and tells her not to worry about nothing, not even about what she does to his ear.

Then we go to the Shark Fin Grill and find Chesty Charles sitting out in front with his chair tilted up against the wall, and The Macarone says to him like this:

"Chesty," he says, "have the dough on call for me from now on. I will take care of this matter for Mr. Cleeburn T. Box. I study it over carefully," The Macarone says, "and I can see how I will render Mr. Box a service and at the same time do a new friend of mine a favor.

"In the meantime," The Macarone says, "you keep Willie here amused. It is a one-handed job, and I do not care to use him on it in any manner, shape or form. He is a nice character, but," The Macarone says, "he sometimes makes wrong moves. He is too handy with that thing to suit me. By the way, Chesty," he says, "what does Mr. Cleeburn T. Box look like?"

"Well," Chesty says, "he will be the only one you find in the room indicated on the diagram, so his looks do not make any difference, but," he says, "he is smooth-shaved and has thick black hair."

Now, several nights pass away, and every night I drop into the Shark Fin Grill to visit with Chesty Charles, but The Macarone does not show up but once, and this is to personally view the five thousand dollars that Charles now has in his safe, although Willie comes in now and then and sits around a while. But Willie is a most restless character, and he does not seem to be able to hold still more than a few minutes at a time, and he is always wandering around and about the city.

Finally, along towards four bells one morning, when Chesty Charles is getting ready to close the Shark Fin Grill, in walks The Macarone, and it is plain to be seen that he has something on his mind.

A couple of customers are still in the joint and The Macarone waits until they depart, and then he steps over to the bar, where Chesty Charles is working, and gazes at Chesty for quite a spell without saying as much as aye, yes, or no.

"Well?" Chesty says.

"Well, Chesty," The Macarone says, "I go to the home of your Mr. Cleeburn T. Box a little while ago. It is a nice place. A little more shrubbery than we like in Kansas City, but still a nice place. It must stand somebody maybe half a million. I follow your diagram, Chesty," he says. "I find the wing marked X and I make my way through plenty of cactus and Spanish bayonets, and I do not know what all else, and enter the house by way of an open French window.

"I find myself in a room in which there are no lights, but," The Macarone says, "as soon as my eyes become accustomed to the darkness, I can see that is all just as the diagram shows. There is a bed within a few steps of the window and there is a character asleep on the bed. He is snoring pretty good too. In fact," The Macarone says, "he is snoring about as good as anybody I ever hear, and I do not bar Willie, who is a wonderful snorer."

"All right," Chesty Charles says.

"Show me the dough again, Chesty," The Macarone says.

So Chesty goes to his safe and opens it and outs with a nice package of the soft and places it on the back bar where The Macarone can see it, and the sight of the money seems to please The Macarone no little.

"All right," Chesty says. "Then what?"

"Well, Chesty," The Macarone says, "there I am with that thing in my hand, and there is this character on the bed asleep, and there is no sound except his snoring and the wind in some palm trees outside. Chesty," he says, "are you ever in a strange house at night with the wind working on the palm trees outside?"

"No," Chesty says. "I do not care for palm trees."

"It is a lonesome sound," The Macarone says. "Well," he says, "I step over to the bed, and I can see by the outline of the character on the bed that he is sleeping on his back, which is a good thing, as it saves me the trouble of turning him over and maybe waking him up. You see, Chesty," he says, "I give this matter some scientific study beforehand. I figure that the right idea in this case is to push this character in such a manner that there can be no doubt that he pushes himself, so it must be done from in front, and from close up.

"Well," The Macarone says, "I wait right over this character on the bed until my eyes make out the outline of his face in the dark, and I put that thing down close to his nose, and just as I am about to give it to him, the moon comes out from behind a cloud over the bay and spills plenty of light through the open French window and over the character on the bed.

"And," The Macarone says, "I observe that this character on the bed is holding some object clasped to his breast, and that he has a large smile on his face, as if he is dreaming very pleasant dreams, indeed; and when I gently remove the object from his fingers, thinking it may be something of value to me, and hold it up to the light, what is it but a framed stand photograph of a young friend of mine by the name of Miss Mary Peering.

"But," The Macarone says, "I hope and trust that no one will ever relate to Miss Mary Peering the story of me finding this character asleep with her picture, and snoring, because," he says, "snoring is without doubt a great knock to romance."

"So?" Chesty Charles says.

"So," The Macarone says, "I come away as quietly as possible without disturbing the character on the bed, and here I am, Chesty, and there you are, and it comes to my mind that somebody tries to drop me in on a great piece of skullduggery."

And all of a sudden, The Macarone outs with that thing and jams the nozzle of it into Chesty Charles's chest, and says:

"Hand over that dough, Chesty," he says. "A nice thing you are trying to get a respectable character like me into, because you know very well it cannot be your Mr. Cleeburn T. Box on the bed in that room with Miss Mary Peering's photograph clasped to his breast and smiling so. Chesty," he says, "I fear you almost make a criminal of me, and for two cents I will give you a pushing for your own self, right here and now."

"Why, Mac," Chesty says, "you are a trifle hasty. If it is not Mr. Cleeburn T. Box in that bed, I cannot think who it can be, but," he says, "maybe some last-minute switch comes up in the occupant of the bed by accident. Maybe it is something Mr. Cleeburn T. Box will easily explain when I see him again. Why," Chesty says,

"I cannot believe Mr. Cleeburn T. Box means any fraud in this matter. He seems to me to be a nice, honest character, and very sincere in his wish to be pushed."

Then Chesty Charles goes on to state that if there is any fraud in this matter, he is also a victim of same, and he says he will surely speak harshly to Mr. Cleeburn T. Box about it the first time he gets a chance. In fact, Chesty Charles becomes quite indignant when he gets to thinking that maybe Mr. Cleeburn T. Box may be deceiving him, and finally The Macarone says:

"Well, all right," he says. "Maybe you are not in on anything, at that, and, in fact, I do not see what it is all about, anyway; but," he says, "it is my opinion that your Mr. Cleeburn T. Box is without doubt nothing but a great scalawag somewhere. Anyway, hand over the dough, Chesty," he says. "I am going to collect on my good intentions."

So Chesty Charles takes the package off the back bar and hands it over to The Macarone, and as The Macarone is disposing of it in his pants' pocket, Chesty says to him like this: "But look, Mac," he says, "I am entitled to my twenty-five percent for finding the plant, just the same."

Well, The Macarone seems to be thinking this over, and, personally, I figure there is much justice in what Chesty Charles says, and while The Macarone is thinking, there is a noise at the door of somebody coming in, and The Macarone hides that thing under his coat, though I notice he keeps his hand under there, too, until it turns out that the party coming in is nobody but Willie.

"Well," Willie says, "I have quite an interesting experience just now while I am taking a stroll away out on the Boulevard. It is right pretty out that way, to be sure," he says. "I meet a cop and get to talking to him about this and that, and while we are talking the cop says, "Good evening, Mr. Box," to a character who goes walking past.

"The cop says this character is Mr. Cleeburn T. Box," Willie says. "I say Mr. Box looks worried, and the cop says yes, his nephew is sick, and maybe he is worrying about him. But," Willie says, "the cop says, 'If I am Mr. Box, I will not be worrying about such a thing, because if the nephew dies before he comes of age, Mr. Box is the sole heir to his brother's estate of maybe ten million dollars, and the nephew is not yet of age.'

"'Well, cop,' I say," Willie says, "'are you sure this is Mr. Cleeburn T. Box?' and the cop says yes, he knows him for over ten years, and that he meets up with him every night on the Boulevard for the past week, just the same as tonight, because it seems Mr. Cleeburn T. Box takes to strolling that way quite some lately.

"So," Willie says, "I figure to save everybody a lot of bother, and I follow Mr. Cleeburn T. Box away out the Boulevard after I leave the cop, and when I get to a spot that seems nice and quiet and with nobody around, I step close enough for powder marks to show good and give it to Mr. Cleeburn T. Box between the eyes. Then," Willie says, "I leave that thing in his right hand, and if they do not say it is a clear case of him pushing himself when they find him, I will eat my hat."

"Willie," The Macarone says, "is your Mr. Cleeburn T. Box clean-shaved and does he have thick black hair?"

"Why, no," Willie says. "He has a big mouser on his upper lip and no hair whatsoever on his head. In fact," he says, "he is as bald as a biscuit, and maybe balder."

Now, at this The Macarone turns to Chesty Charles, but by the time he is half turned, Chesty is out the back door of the Shark Fin Grill and is taking it on the Jesse Owens up the street, and The Macarone seems greatly surprised and somewhat disappointed, and says to me like this:

"Well," he says, "Willie and me cannot wait for Chesty to return, but," he says, "you can tell him for me that, under the circumstances, I am compelled to reject his request for twenty-five percent for finding the plant. And," The Macarone says, "if ever you hear of the nephew of the late Mr. Cleeburn T. Box beefing about a missing photograph of Miss Mary Peering, you can tell him that it is in good hands."

A TASTE FOR COGNAC

BY BRETT HALLIDAY

Homestead

(Originally published in 1944)

Chapter One: "This is Murder!"

Michael Shayne hesitated inside the swinging doors, looked down the row of men at the bar, and then strolled past the wooden booths lining the wall, glancing in each one as he went by.

Timothy Rourke wasn't at the bar and he wasn't in any of the booths.

Shayne frowned and turned impatiently toward the swinging doors.

A voice called, "Mr. Shayne?" when he reached the third booth from the end.

He stopped and looked down at the girl alone in the booth. She was about twenty, smartly dressed, with coppery hair parted in the middle and lying in smooth waves on either side of her head. She didn't wear any makeup, and her small face had a pinched look. Her eyes were brown and shone with alert intelligence. Her left hand clasped a glass half filled with dead beer as she smiled at Shayne.

Shayne took off his hat and stood flat-footed looking down at her. Lights above the bar behind him cast shadows on his gaunt cheeks. He lifted his shaggy left eyebrow and asked, "Do I know you?"

"You're going to." The girl tilted her head sideways and looked wistful. "I'll buy a drink."

"Why didn't you say so?" Shayne slid into the bench opposite her.

A waiter hurried over and the girl said, "Cognac," happily, watching Shayne for approval.

The Miami detective said, "Make it a sidecar, Joe." The waiter nodded and went away.

"But Tim said cognac was your password," the girl protested. "He said you never drank anything else."

"Tim?" Shayne said, surprised.

"Tim Rourke. He thought you might tell me about some of your cases. I do feature stuff for a New York syndicate. Tim couldn't make it tonight. He's been promising to introduce me to you, so I came on to meet you here. I'm Myrna Hastings."

Shayne said bitterly, "When you order cognac these days you get lousy grape brandy. California '44. It's drinkable mixed into a sidecar. This damned war . . ."

"It's a shame your drinking habits have been upset by the war. Tragic, in fact." Myrna Hastings took a sip of her flat beer and made a little grimace.

Shayne lit a cigarette and tossed the pack on the table be-tween them. Joe brought his sidecar and he watched Myrna take a dollar bill from her purse and lay it on the table. Shayne lifted the slender cocktail glass to his lips and said, "Thanks." He drank half of the mixture and his gray eyes grew speculative. Holding it close to his nose, he inhaled deeply and a frown rumpled his forehead.

Joe was standing at the table when Shayne drained his glass. "I've changed my mind, Joe. Bring me a straight cognac—a double shot in a beer glass."

Joe grinned slyly and went away.

Sixty cents in change from Myrna's dollar bill lay on the table. She poked at the silver and asked dubiously, "Will that be enough for a double shot?"

"It'll be eighty cents," Shayne told her.

She smiled and took a quarter from her purse. "Tim says

you've always avoided publicity, but it'll be a wonderful break for me if I can write up a few of your best cases."

The waiter brought the beer glass with two ounces of amber fluid in it, took Myrna Hastings's eighty-five cents, and went away.

Shayne lifted the beer glass to his nose, closed his eyes and breathed deeply of the bouquet, then began to warm the glass in his big palms.

"Tim thinks you should let yourself in on some publicity," the girl continued. "He thinks it's a shame you don't ever take the credit for solving so many cases."

Shayne looked at her for a moment, then slowly emptied his glass and set it down. He picked up his cigarette and hat and said, "Thanks for the drinks. I never give out any stories. Tim Rourke knows that." He got up and strode to the rear of the bar.

Joe sidled down to join him and Shayne said, "I could use another shot of that. And I'll pour my own."

Joe got a clean beer glass and set a tall bottle on the bar before Shayne. He glanced past the detective at the girl sitting alone in the booth, but didn't say anything.

The label on the bottle read: Monterrey Grape Brandy, *Guaranteed 14 months old.*

Shayne pulled out the cork and passed the open neck of the bottle back and forth under his nose. He asked Joe, "Got any more of this same brand?"

"Jeez, I dunno. I'll see, Mr. Shayne." He turned away and returned presently with a sealed bottle bearing the same label.

Shayne broke the seal and pulled the cork. He made a wry face as the smell of raw grape brandy assailed his nostrils. He said angrily, "This isn't the same stuff."

"Says so right on the bottle," Joe argued.

"I don't give a damn what the label says," Shayne growled. He reached for the first bottle and poured a drink into the empty beer glass. Keeping a firm grip on the bottle with his left hand he drank from the mug, rolling the liquor around his tongue. His gray eyes shone with dreamy contentment as he lingeringly swallowed the brandy, while a frown of curiosity and confusion formed between them. "Any more of the bar bottles already open?" he asked.

"I don't think so. We don't open 'em but one at a time nowadays. I'll ask the barkeep." Plainly mystified by Shayne's request, Joe went to the front of the bar and held a low-voiced conversation with a bald-headed man wearing a dirty apron that bulged over a potbelly.

The bartender glanced at Shayne, then waddled toward him. He looked at the two bottles and asked, "Whassa trouble here?"

Shayne shrugged his wide shoulders. "No trouble. Your bar bottle hasn't got the same stuff that's in the sealed one."

The hulking man looked troubled. "You know how 'tis these days. A label don't mean nothin' no more. We're lucky to stay open at all."

Shayne said, "I know it's rough trying to keep a supply."

The bartender regarded Shayne for a moment with his pale, puffed eyes. "You're private, huh? Ain't I seen you 'round?"

"I'm private. This hasn't anything to do with the law."

"If you got a kick about the drink, it'll be on the house," the bartender said magnanimously.

"I'm not kicking," Shayne told him earnestly. "I'd like to buy what's left in this bottle." He indicated the partially empty one which he had moved out of the bartender's reach.

The man shook his head slowly. "No can do. Our license says we gotta sell it by the drink."

Shayne held the bottle up and squinted through it. "There's maybe twenty ounces left," he calculated. "It's worth ten bucks to me."

The big man continued to shake his head. "You can drink it here. Forty cents a shot."

"Maybe I could make a deal with the boss," suggested Shayne.

"Maybe. I'll find out." He waddled around the end of the bar and preceded Shayne to an unmarked door to the left of the ladies' room. Shayne saw Myrna Hastings still sitting in the booth, watching him.

The bartender rapped lightly on the door, turned the knob, and motioned Shayne inside.

Henry Renaldo was seated at a desk facing the doorway. He was a big, flabby man with a florid face. He wore a black derby tilted back on his bullet head and an open gray vest revealed the sleeves and front of a shirt violently striped with reddish purple. He was eating a frayed black cigar that had spilled ashes down the front of his vest.

The bartender stood in the doorway behind Shayne. He said heavily, "This shamus is kickin' about the service, boss. I figured you might wanna handle it."

Renaldo's black eyes took in the brandy bottle dangling from Shayne's fingers. He wet his lips and said, "Okay, Tiny," and the bartender went out.

Renaldo leaned over the desk to push out his right hand. "Long time no see, Mike."

Shayne disregarded the proffered hand. "I didn't know you were in this racket, Renaldo."

"Sure. I went legal when prohibition went out."

Shayne moved forward, set the bottle down with a thump, and said mildly, "This is a new angle on me."

"How's that?"

"Prewar cognac under a cheap domestic label. Monnet, isn't it?"

"You must be nuts," Renaldo ejaculated.

"Either you or me," Shayne agreed. "Forty cents a throw, when it would easily bring a dollar a slug in the original bottle."

Henry Renaldo was beginning to wheeze heavily. "What's it to you, Shayne? Stooging for the Feds?"

Shayne shook his head. He lifted the bottle to his lips, let the cognac gurgle down his throat, then murmured reverently, "Monnet. Vintage of '26."

Renaldo started. Fear showed in his bulging eyes. "How'd

you—" He paused, taking the sodden cigar carefully from his lips. "Who sent you here?"

"I followed my nose."

Renaldo shook his head. He said huskily, "I don't know how you got onto it, but why jump me?" His voice rose passionately. "If I pass it out for cheap stuff, is that a crime?"

"You could make more selling it by the bottle to a guy like me," Shayne told him casually.

Renaldo spread out his hands. "I gotta stay in business," he wheezed. "I gotta have something to sell over the bar to keep my customers. If I can hang on till after the war—"

Comprehension shone in Shayne's eyes. "That's why you're refilling legal bottles?"

"What other out is there?" demanded Renaldo. "Government inspectors checking my stock—"

"All right," Shayne interrupted, "but let me in on it. A case or two for my private stock."

"I only got a few bottles left," the big man said.

"But you know where there's more."

"Go make your own deals," Renaldo said sullenly.

"Sure. I will. All I want is the tip-off."

"Who sent you here?"

"No one. I dropped in for a drink and got slugged with Monnet when I ordered domestic brandy."

"Nuts," sneered Renaldo. "You couldn't pull the year of that vintage stuff. I don't know what the gimmick is, but—"

A rear door opened and two men came in hastily. They stopped dead in their tracks and stared at the redheaded detective seated on one corner of Renaldo's desk. One of them was short and squarish with a swarthy face and a whiskered mole on his chin. He wore fawn-colored slacks and a canary-yellow sweater that was tight over bulging muscles.

His companion was tall and lean with a pallid face and the humid eyes of a cokie. He was bareheaded, and wore a tightly belted suit. He thinned his lips against sharp teeth and tilted his head to study Shayne.

Renaldo snarled, "You took long enough. How'd you make out, Blackie?"

"It wasn't no soap, boss. He ain't talkin'."

"Hell, you followed him out of here."

"Sure we did, boss," Blackie said, whining earnestly. "Just like you said. To a little shack on the beach at Eighteenth. But he had comp'ny when he got there. There was this car parked in front, see? So Lennie and me waited half an hour, maybe. Then a guy come out an' drove away, an' we goes in. But we're too late. He's croaked."

"Croaked?"

"S'help me, boss. He was croaked. Lennie an' me beats it straight back."

Renaldo said sourly to Shayne, "Looks like that fixes it for both of us."

Shayne said, "Give me all of it, Renaldo."

"Can't hurt now," Renaldo muttered after a brief hesitation. "This bird comes in with a suitcase this evening. It's loaded with twenty-four bottles of Monnet 1926, like you said. It's prewar," he went on defensively, "sealed with no revenue stamps on it. All he wants is a hundred, so what can I lose? I can't put it out here where an inspector will see it, but I can refill legal bottles and keep my customers happy. So I give him a C and try to pry loose where there's more, but he swears that's all there is and beats it. So I send Blackie and Lennie to see can they make a deal. You heard the rest."

"Why yuh spillin' your guts to this shamus?" Lennie rasped. "Ain't he the law?"

"Shayne's private," Renaldo told him. "He was trying to horn in—" He paused suddenly and shot a suspicious look at the detective, his heavy jaw dropping. "Maybe you know more about it than I do, Shayne."

"Mebbe he does." Lennie's voice rose excitedly. "Looks to me like the mug what come out an' drove away, don't he, Blackie?"

Blackie said, "Sorta. We didn't get to see him good," he explained to Renaldo. "But he was dressed like that—and big."

All three of the men looked at Shayne, studied him closely.

"So that's how—" said Renaldo slowly and harshly. He jerked the cigar from his mouth and asked angrily, "What'd you get out of him before he kicked off? Maybe we can make a deal, huh? You're plenty on the spot with him dead."

Shayne said, "You're crazy. I don't know anything."

"How'd you know about the 1926 Monnet?" Renaldo demanded.

"Like I told you. I dropped in for a drink and knew it wasn't domestic stuff as soon as I tasted it."

"Maybe." Renaldo rubbed his pudgy hands together, went on suspiciously and deliberately: "But that didn't spell out Monnet '26. Now, my boys'll keep quiet if—"

Shayne interrupted dispassionately, "You're a fool, Renaldo." He slid off the desk and his gray eyes were very bright. "Your boys are feeding you a line. It's my hunch they messed things up and are afraid to admit it to you. So they make up a fairy tale about someone else getting there first, and you swallow it." He laughed indulgently. "Think it over, and you'll see who is really on the spot." He turned toward the door.

Blackie got in front of him. He stood lightly on the balls of his feet and a blackjack swung from his right hand. Behind him Lennie crouched with his gun bunched in his coat pocket. His pallid face was contorted and he panted, "You don't listen to him, boss. Blackie and me both can identify him."

Shayne turned and said to Renaldo, "You'd better call them off. I've a friend waiting outside, and if anything happens to me in here you'll have a lot of explaining to do."

Renaldo said smugly, "If I turn you over for murder—"

"Try it," Shayne snapped. He turned toward the door again, the open bottle of cognac clutched laxly in his left hand.

Blackie remained poised with the blackjack between Shayne and the door. He appealed to Renaldo, "If it was this shamus out there an' the old guy talked before he passed out—"

A sharp rapping on the door interrupted Blackie.

A grin pulled Shayne's lips away from his teeth. He said, "My friend is getting impatient."

Renaldo said, "Skip it, Blackie."

Shayne moved past the swarthy man to the door and opened it. Myrna Hastings stood outside.

"If you think—" she began.

Shayne said, "Sh-h-h," close to her ear, took her arm firmly, and pulled the door shut. He slid the uncorked bottle of Monnet into his coat pocket and started toward the front with her.

She twisted her head to look back at the closed door and said uncertainly, "Those men inside—didn't one of them have a weapon?"

"You're an angel," Shayne said softly, "and I was a louse to treat you the way I did." They went out through the swinging front doors of the saloon. He stopped on the sidewalk. "Keep on going and beat it," he told her harshly. "I have things to do."

Myrna looked up into his face and seemed frightened at what she saw there. "Something is wrong."

Shayne shrugged and said, "Maybe this will be a case you can write up." He looked into her eyes briefly, then turned and strode to his sedan parked at the curb and started to get in.

He didn't hear her light footsteps following him, but he turned when she asked breathlessly, "Can't I go with you, Mr. Shayne? I promise not to be in the way."

Shayne caught her elbows in his big hands and turned her about. "Run along, kid. This is murder. I'll tell you about it tomorrow."

Chapter Two: Evidence of Torture

Shayne drove out Biscayne Boulevard and turned right on Eighteenth Street. A thin crescent moon rode high in the cloudless sky overhead, and the night was humidly warm. He drove slowly to the end of the street and stopped his car against a low stone barrier overlooking the bay front, turned off his motor, and sat for a moment gripping the steering wheel. Light glowed through two round and heavily glassed windows in a squatty, square stone structure at his left. It perched boldly on the very edge of the bluff overlooking the bay, and a neat shell-lined walk led up to the front door. He got out and walked up the walk.

The little house was built solidly of porous limestone, and its only windows were round, metal-framed portholes that looked as though they had been taken from a ship. The door had a heavy bronze knocker and the hinges and lock were also of bronze.

He tried the knob and the door opened inward. The narrow hallway disclosed a ship's lantern with an electric bulb hanging from a hand-hewn beam of cypress. An open door to the right showed the interior of a tidy and tiny kitchen.

Shayne went down the hall to another door opening off to the right. The room was dark, and he fumbled along the wall until he found a light switch. When he flipped the switch, it lighted two wrought-iron ship's lanterns similar to the one in the hall. He stood in the doorway and tugged at his left earlobe, looking down at the man lying huddled in the middle of the bare floor.

He was dead.

A big-framed man, his face bony and emaciated. His eyes were wide open and glazed, bulging from deep sockets. He wore a double-breasted uniform of shiny blue serge. The buttons were of brass and recently polished. His ankles were wired together, and the wire had cut deeply into his bound wrists.

Shayne went in and knelt beside the body.

Three fingernails had been torn from his right hand. This appeared to be the only mark of violence on his body, which was warm enough to indicate that death had occurred only half an hour or so before. Shayne judged that shock and pain had brought on a heart attack, causing death. The man was about sixty, and there was no padding or flesh on his bony frame.

Rocking back on his heels and wiping sweat from his face, Shayne went through the dead man's pockets. He found nothing but a newspaper clipping and the torn stub of a bus ticket. The ticket had been issued the previous day, round trip from Miami to Homestead, a small town on the Florida Keys.

The clipping was a week old, from the Miami *Herald*. It was headed: PAROLE GRANTED.

Before reading the clipping, he raised his eyes and looked around the room. It was bare of furniture except for a built-in padded settee along one wall. Bare, and scrupulously clean, the room had the appearance of a cell.

As he turned his eyes again to the newspaper clipping he stiffened. He heard a car stopping outside. He thrust the clipping and the ticket stub in his pocket and waited.

Footsteps sounded on the walk, and the voices of men outside. Shayne lit a cigarette and blew out the match, then turned to look up at the bulky figure of Detective Chief Will Gentry in the doorway.

Shayne grinned and said, "Doctor Livingstone?"

Gentry snorted. He was a big man with heavy features, a permanent worry frown between his eyes, and a solid, forthright manner. He was an old friend of Shayne's, and he said scathingly, "I thought I smelled something."

Gentry walked heavily forward and scowled down at the body. A tall, white-haired man hurried in behind Chief Gentry. He wore an immaculate white linen suit and his features were sharp and clear-cut. He stopped at sight of the body and groaned, "My God! Oh, my God! Is he—"

"Dead." Gentry grunted as he kneeled beside the dead man and asked Shayne in a tone of casual interest, "Why'd you pull out his fingernails, Mike?"

The tall, white-haired man exclaimed in a choked voice, "Good God, has he been tortured?"

"Who is he?" Shayne interposed sharply, turning toward the tall man.

"Who is he?" the man said excitedly. "Why, that's Captain Samuels! I knew something must have happened to him." He turned to Chief Gentry. "I knew something must have happened to him," he repeated, "when he wasn't here to keep his appointment with me. If only I'd called earlier!"

Gentry apparently ignored the man's excitement and turned to Shayne. He asked calmly, his rumpled eyelids half raised, "What are you doing here?"

"Nothing much. I was driving by and saw the lights. Something just smelled wrong. I stopped by to take a look, and that's what I found."

Gentry said, "I suppose you can prove all that?" in a scoffing tone.

"Can you disprove it?" asked Shayne.

"Maybe not, but you're holding out plenty. Damn it, Mike, this is murder. What do you know about it?"

"Not a thing, Will. I've told you how I just drove by—"

Will Gentry raised his voice to call, "Jones . . . you and Rafferty bring in the cuffs."

Jones's voice rumbled, "Okay, Chief," and heavy footsteps sounded in the hall.

At the same time there was the light click of heels outside and Myrna Hastings came in. She said, "You don't need to cover for me, Mike," and stopped to catch her breath. There was a sob in her voice as she cried out, "You don't need to cover up for me. Go ahead and tell them I asked you to stop here." She turned toward the stalwart chief of detectives, as though seeing him for the first time, and said, "Oh! This is Chief Gentry, isn't it?"

Gentry rumbled, "I don't think—"

"Don't you remember me, Chief?" Myrna laughed uncertainly. "Timothy Rourke introduced me to you in your office today. I do feature stories for a New York syndicate. I'm to blame for Mike coming here tonight. I'd heard about Captain Samuels and about his shipwreck and all—years ago, so I thought he might be material for a story. I asked Mike to stop here for a minute tonight, and that's how it was."

Gentry turned his bulky body toward Shayne and asked gruffly, "Why didn't you tell me that, Mike?"

Myrna laughed merrily. "He had some idea of protecting me, Chief. You see I didn't want to tell *why* I wanted to stop here. Then, when he found the man dead—well—I guess maybe Mike thought I knew something about it. Wasn't that it, Mike?" She whirled toward Shayne.

"Yeah. Something like that," said Shayne stiffly.

Gentry turned away from them and said, "Put your bracelets away, Jones, and go over the place," to one of the two dicks hovering in the doorway.

"Now that you've got me cleared up," Shayne suggested, "why not tell me about it?"

"I don't know any more than you do," Gentry admitted. "Mr. Guildford called a while ago and asked me to come out here with him. Seems he had a hunch something had happened to Captain Samuels."

"I felt sure of it after I had time to think things over," the white-haired man said. "I had a definite appointment here with the captain for nine o'clock tonight and I waited almost half an hour for him."

Shayne said, "It's almost eleven now. Why did you wait so long before calling the police?"

"I had a flat tire just as I reached the boulevard driving away," Guildford explained. "I had it changed at the filling station there and was delayed. I called as soon as I reached home."

Shayne asked, "Were the lights burning while you waited?"

"No. I'm quite sure they weren't. The house was dark and apparently empty."

"What was your appointment for?" Shayne pressed him.

Guildford hesitated. He glanced at Will Gentry. "I don't mind answering official questions, but what is this man's connection with the case? And the young lady?"

"None," Gentry rumbled. "You can beat it, Mike, unless you feel like telling the truth."

"But we have told the truth," Myrna asserted, her eyes wide and childlike. "We were just—"

Shayne took her arm tightly. He said, "Come on," and led her out the door.

Neither of them said anything until they were in Shayne's car and headed for the boulevard. Then Myrna leaned her head against his shoulder and asked in a small voice, "Are you terribly angry with me, Mike?"

"How did you get in that house?" he countered angrily.

"You brought me. I hid in the trunk compartment of your car. Then I slipped into the house while you were searching the body. I was in the rear bedroom all the time, and when I heard you getting the third degree I knew you didn't want to tell the truth and I thought I'd better stick my oar in. Didn't I do all right?"

"How did you know the Captain's name and about him being shipwrecked?"

Myrna chuckled softly. "I found an old logbook by his bed. I had my flashlight, and found a clipping that was in the book." She patted a large suède handbag in her lap. "I've got the book in here. It made a pretty good story even if I did think of it on the spur of the moment—the one I told Chief Gentry, I mean," she amended, and chuckled again.

"Why did you hide in the back of my car?" Shayne snapped.

"Because you were trying to get rid of me and I wanted to see the famous Michael Shayne in action," she said. "But I must say you didn't do much detecting out there."

Shayne stopped the car suddenly in front of an apartment building on the river front. "I live here," he told her. He got out and went toward a side entrance.

Myrna Hastings tripped along with him, trying to keep pace with his long-legged strides. She said hopefully, "I'm dying to taste whatever is in that bottle you've got in your coat pocket."

She waited quietly behind him in the doorway while he unlocked his apartment door. He went inside and switched on the lights, and she followed him into a square living room with windows on the east side. There was a studio couch against one wall, and a door on the right opened into a kitchenette. Another door on the left led into the bedroom and bath.

Shayne tossed his hat on a wall hook and went into the kitchen without a word or glance for Myrna. He returned presently with two four-ounce wineglasses and two tumblers filled with ice water. He walked past her, ranged the four glasses in a row on the table, and filled the wineglasses nearly to the brim with cognac. He pushed one of the tumblers toward Myrna, set one wineglass within easy reach of her hand, then pulled another chair to the table and sat down, half facing her.

It was very quiet in the apartment, and very restful. Shayne sighed when he drained the last drop from his glass of Monnet. He frowned at the portion remaining in Myrna's glass. "Don't you appreciate good liquor?"

She smiled and said, "It's so good I'm making it last."

Shayne lit a cigarette and spun the match away, then got the purloined clipping and bus ticket stub from his pocket. He laid the stub on the table and read the short clipping aloud. It was an AP dispatch from Atlanta, Georgia.

It stated that John Grossman, suspected prohibition-era racketeer, sentenced to federal prison in 1930 on income tax charges from Miami, Florida, had been released that day on parole. Grossman announced his intention to take a long vacation at his fishing lodge on the Florida Keys.

When Shayne finished reading the clipping aloud he placed it beside the ticket stub and said to Myrna, "These two items were the only things I found in the dead man's pockets."

"You didn't tell Chief Gentry about them?"

He shook his red head in slow negation.

"Isn't that against the law? Concealing murder evidence?

Who's John Grossman and why was the old sea captain interested in the clipping about his parole?"

Shayne said, "I remember Grossman. He was one of our big-time bootleggers with a clientele willing to pay plenty for high-class imported stuff. Like Monnet. I don't know why the Captain was interested in Grossman's release."

"What's it all about, Mike?" Myrna leaned forward eagerly. "It began back in the tavern with something odd about those drinks, didn't it? Why did you go back to the proprietor's office and come out with a bottle, and then drive straight out to the scene of the murder?"

Shayne said softly, "You've done me two good turns tonight. One, when you knocked on the door of Renaldo's office, then out at the Captain's house when I didn't see how in hell I was going to explain my presence there without telling the truth." He hesitated, then admitted, "You deserve a break. You're in it now because you lied to Gentry and he'll probably discover you lied."

He began at the beginning and related what had happened in Renaldo's office. "You know what happened after I drove out to the house."

"Then this is real prewar cognac?" Myrna lifted her glass to study it, and her voice was incredulous.

"Monnet 1926," Shayne stated flatly. "The Captain sold Renaldo a case of it for a hundred dollars, and was tortured to death immediately afterward. Renaldo admits he had his men follow the Captain to try to persuade him to tell them where they could get more, but they claim he was dead before they got to him."

"Do you believe them?"

Shayne shook his head. "It doesn't do to believe anything when murder is involved. Their story sounded all right, but that wire and those torn fingernails could very well be their idea of gentle persuasion. And if the Captain did fool them by dying before they got the information they wanted, they'd hate to admit it to Renaldo and might have made up that story about his being murdered by an unknown visitor.

"And there's another angle. Maybe Blackie and Lennie are playing it smart and did get the information before the Captain croaked. If they decided to use it themselves and cut Renaldo out—" He paused and shrugged expressively.

"What makes you and Renaldo so sure there's more cognac where that first came from?"

"I imagine it was just a hopeful hunch on Renaldo's part. And I wasn't sure until I found this clipping indicating a connection between the Captain and an ex-bootlegger."

"Would that be sufficient motive for murder? At a hundred dollars a case?"

Shayne made a derisive gesture. "A C-note for two dozen bottles of Monnet is peanuts today. That's what got Renaldo so excited. It shows that the Captain knew nothing about the present liquor shortage and market prices. It could retail for twenty or twenty-five dollars a bottle if properly handled today."

Myrna Hastings's eyes widened. "That would be about five hundred dollars a case!"

Shayne's eyes were morose. "If Grossman had a pile of it cached away when he was sent up in '30," he mused, "that would explain why it stayed off the market all this time. But Grossman would know what the stuff is worth today." He shook his head angrily. "It still doesn't add up. And if the Captain knew about the cache and had access to it all the time, why wait until a week after Grossman's parole to put it on the market? Did you notice the condition of the Captain's body?" he asked abruptly.

Myrna shuddered. "I'll never forget it," she vowed.

"He looked like an advanced case of malnutrition," said Shayne harshly.

"Who was the white-haired man who brought the police—that Mr. Guildford?"

"He's a lawyer here. Very respectable."

Myrna said hesitantly, "His story about waiting at the house half an hour for Captain Samuels to keep an appointment—do you think *he* could be the man the gangsters saw drive away from the house just before they went in and found the Captain dead?"

"Could be. If there was any such man. The timing is screwy and hard to figure out. Guildford claims his appointment was for nine, and he waited half an hour. It was well past ten when the mugs got back to Renaldo's office. That leaves it open either way. Guildford could have waited until nine thirty and then driven away just before the Captain returned with Blackie and Lennie trailing him. Or Guildford may have deliberately pushed the time up a little. Until we know why Guildford went there—" Shayne threw out his hands in a futile gesture.

He poured himself another drink and demanded, "Where's that logbook you mentioned, and the clipping about the shipwreck?"

She reached for her handbag and unsnapped the heavy gold clasp. She drew out an aged, brass-hinged, and leatherbound book with *Ship's Log* stamped on the front in gilt letters.

Shayne opened it and looked at the flyleaf. It was inscribed: *Property of Captain Thomas Anthony Samuels. April 2, 1902.*

"The clipping is in the back," Myrna told him. "Lucky I saw it and made up a story that Chief Gentry would swallow."

Shayne said, "Don't kid yourself that he swallowed it. He knows damned well it wasn't coincidence that put me at the scene of the murder." He turned the logbook upside down and shook out a yellowed and brittle newspaper clipping from the Miami *Daily News* dated June 17, 1930. There was a picture of a big man in a nautical uniform with the caption: SAVED AT SEA.

Shayne read the news item swiftly. It gave a dramatic account of the sea rescue of Captain Samuels, owner, master, and sole survivor of the auxiliary launch *Mermaid* which was lost in a tropical hurricane off the Florida coast three days before the Captain was rescued by a fishing craft. He had heroically stayed afloat in a life preserver for three days and nights.

"Where," asked Shayne, "was the book when you found it?"

"In a small recess in the rock wall at the head of his bed. The bedding was all mussed up as though the room had been hastily searched, and the bed was pulled away from the wall. That's how I saw the logbook. Normally, the wooden headboard must have stood against the wall, hiding the recess."

Shayne began thoughtfully flipping the pages of the log. "This seems to be a complete account of Captain Samuels's voyages from—"

The ringing of the telephone interrupted him. He got up and answered it. The voice of the night clerk came over the wire:

"The law is on its way up to your apartment, Mr. Shayne. You told me once I was to call you—"

"Thanks, Dick." Shayne hung up and directed Myrna tersely: "You'd better get out—through the kitchen door and down the fire escape. Take your two glasses to the kitchen and close the door behind you. The key's on a nail by the outside door."

Myrna jumped up. "What—?"

"I don't know." Shayne heard the elevator stop down the hall. "Better if Gentry doesn't find you here. He's already suspicious. Go home and go to bed and be careful. Call me tomorrow."

Chapter Three: Into the Trap

Shayne breathed a sigh of relief when Myrna went out quietly. Most women would have argued and asked questions. He opened a drawer and thrust the logbook, clipping, and ticket stub inside. A loud knock sounded on the outer door of his apartment and Will Gentry's voice rumbled, "Shayne."

Shayne darted a quick glance behind him and saw that Myrna had closed the door as she went into the kitchen. He sauntered to the outer door and opened it, rubbed his chin with a show of surprise when he saw Gentry and the tall figure of Mr. Guildford waiting in the hallway. He said, "It's a hell of a time to come visiting," and stepped aside to let them enter.

Will Gentry moved slowly and steadily past him to the center table to look with suspicion on the two glasses. He went to the bedroom door, opened it, and stepped inside, turned on the light, then looked in the bathroom.

Shayne grinned as Gentry doggedly went on to the kitchen door, opened it, and turned on the light. He stalked heavily back and sat down across the table from Shayne.

"Where is she, Mike?"

"I told her she'd better go home and get some sleep. She was quite upset, you know. Seems she was rather fond of the old sea captain—though she'd known him only a couple of days," he added hastily.

"She isn't in her room. Hasn't been all evening."

"How did you know where to look for her?" Shayne asked.

"I called Tim Rourke. He told me she was stopping at the Crestwood, but she's not in."

Shayne said, "You know how these New York dames are. Why come to me?"

"I hoped I'd find her here," Gentry admitted, "knowing how New York dames are, and knowing you."

"Sorry to disappoint you, Will."

Mr. Guildford said, "May I?" He cleared his throat and looked at Gentry.

The Chief nodded. "Go ahead."

"Knowing your reputation, Mr. Shayne," Guildford said in a professional tone, "I suspect you withheld certain information tonight."

Shayne said, "It's illegal to conceal murder evidence."

"To hell with that stuff," Gentry put in impatiently. "What did you and Miss Hastings find before we got there?"

"You know I wouldn't hold out on you, Will, unless there was something in it for me. And who could possibly profit by the death of an old man like that? He looked to me as though he'd gone hungry for weeks."

"That's true," Guildford said. "I happen to know he was in dire straits. Our appointment tonight was to discuss a payment long overdue on his mortgaged house."

"But the poor devil was obviously tortured," Gentry said.

"Death resulted from shock due to his poor physical condition. Torture generally means extortion."

"Which makes us wonder if he harbored some secret worth money to someone," Guildford explained. "We found none of his private papers, but we did find evidence that the house had been burgled."

"So you think I did it?" Shayne fumed.

"Wait a minute, Mike," Gentry rumbled soothingly. "You see we found that the bed had been pulled back and there was a sort of hiding place exposed. Mr. Guildford suggested that you may have discovered the cache and taken the papers away to examine them privately."

Shayne snarled, "The hell he did! What's his interest in it?"

"As Captain Samuels's attorney and now his executor, I have a natural interest in the affair," Guildford snapped.

"Come off it, Mike," said Gentry wearily. "If you'll tell me what you were doing there I won't be so sure you're holding out."

"I told you—rather Miss Hastings did."

"That doesn't wash, Mike. Rourke told me she didn't hit town till this afternoon. How could she have met Samuels and learned about the shipwreck story?"

"Ask her."

"I can't find her. I'm asking you. Did you get any stuff from the bedroom?"

"I didn't go in the bedroom."

"But Miss Hastings did," said Guildford triumphantly. "And I suggest *she* found his papers and looked through them while we were in the other room with you and the body. I further suggest that was how she learned about the shipwreck and her agile mind framed the excuse she gave us for your presence there."

Shayne stood up and balled his big hands into fists. "I suggest that you get out of that chair so I can knock you back into it."

"Lay off, Mike," Gentry groaned. "You've got to admit it's good reasoning."

Shayne swung around and faced Gentry. "I don't admit anything," he said angrily. "Is a two-bit shyster running your department now?"

Guildford said, "I resent that, Shayne."

Shayne laughed harshly. "*You* resent it?"

Gentry said, "I'm running my department, but I don't mind listening to advice. Are you willing to swear you and Miss Hastings just dropped in on the dead man by accident?"

Shayne said, "Put me on the witness stand if I'm going to be cross-examined."

Gentry compressed his lips. He started to say something, but instead, tightened his lips further and got up. He and Guildford went out of the room.

Shayne stood by the table until the door closed behind them, then strode to the telephone and asked for the Crestwood Hotel. He frowned, starting across the room, and tugged at his left earlobe while he waited. When the hotel answered he asked for Miss Myrna Hastings. Without hesitation the clerk said, "Miss Hastings is not in."

"How the hell do you know she isn't?" Shayne growled. "You haven't rung her room."

"But I saw her go out just a moment ago, sir," the clerk insisted.

Shayne said, "You must be mistaken. I happen to know she just went to her room."

"That's quite right, sir. She came in and got her key not more than five minutes ago, but she came downstairs almost immediately with two gentlemen and went out with them."

"Are you sure?"

"Positive, sir. I saw them cross the lobby from the elevator to the front door."

"Wait a minute. Did she go with them willingly?"

"Why, I certainly presumed so. She had her arms linked in theirs, and I didn't notice anything wrong."

"Can you describe them?"

"No. I'm afraid I didn't notice—"

"Was one of them short and the other one tall?"

"Why, now that you mention it, I think so. Is something wrong? Do you think—?"

Shayne banged up the receiver and stalked into the bedroom. He got a short-barreled .38 which he dropped in his coat pocket. Then he went to the kitchen and tried the back door. Myrna had locked it after she slipped out.

He turned out the kitchen light and strode across the living room, jammed his hat down on his bristly red hair, and went out.

Ten minutes later he parked in front of Henry Renaldo's tavern. He shouldered his way through the swinging doors and found half a dozen late tipplers still leaning on the bar. Joe was in the back with a mop bucket, turning chairs up over the tables, and the paunchy bartender was still on duty in front.

Shayne went up to the bar and said, "Give me a shot of cognac—Monnet."

The man shook his head. "We got grape brandy—"

Shayne said, "Monterrey will do."

The bartender set a bottle and glass in front of the detective, his eyes secretively low-lidded. Shayne poured a drink and lifted it to his nose. "This stuff is grape brandy," he said angrily.

"Sure. Says so right on the bottle." His tone was placating.

Shayne shoved the glass away from him and said, "I'll have a talk with Henry."

"The boss ain't in," the bartender told him hastily.

"How about his two ginzos?"

"I dunno."

Shayne turned and went along the bar to the back. Joe pulled the mop bucket out of his way and turned his head to stare wonderingly at the set look on Shayne's face.

He knocked on the door of Renaldo's office and then tried the door. It opened into darkness. He found the light switch and stood on the threshold looking around the empty office. He went to the rear door through which the two gunmen had entered earlier, and found it barred on the inside. It opened out directly onto the alley.

Back at the bar, he found the bartender lounging against the cash register. He said, "I tol' you," and backed away in alarm when Shayne bunched his hand in his coat pocket over the .38.

"Where," asked Shayne, "do Blackie and Lennie hang out?"

"I dunno. I swear to God I don't. I never seen 'em in here before tonight." He was frightened and he sounded truthful.

"Where will I find the boss?"

"Home, I reckon."

"Where?"

The bartender hesitated. He pouched his lower lip between thumb and forefinger and said sullenly, "Mr. Renaldo don't like—"

Shayne said, "Give it to me."

The bartender hesitated briefly, his eyes wary. Then he wilted and mumbled an address on West Sixtieth Street.

Shayne went out and got in his car, sat there for a moment, got out, and went back into the tavern. The bartender looked at him with naked fear in his eyes and put down the telephone hastily.

"Don't do it, Fatty. If Renaldo has been tipped off when I get there I'll come back and spill your guts all over the floor. The name is Shayne, if you think I'm kidding."

He went out again and swung away from the curb. He drove north a dozen blocks and stopped in front of a sign on Miami Avenue that read: CHUNKY'S CHILI. The place was crammed in between a pawnshop and a flophouse.

He went in and said, "Hi, Chunky," to the big man behind the empty counter.

Chunky said, "'Lo, Mike," without enthusiasm.

"Any of the boys in back?"

"Guess so."

Shayne got out his wallet, extracted a ten-dollar bill and folded it twice lengthwise, and held it toward him. "Blackie or Lennie in there?" he asked.

Chunky yawned. He took the bill and said, "Nope. Ain't seen either of 'em tonight."

"Working?"

"I wouldn' know. Gen'rally hang out back when they ain't."

Shayne nodded. He knew that Chunky's chili joint was a screen for a bookie establishment in the back that served as a sort of clubroom for the better-known members of Miami's underworld. He asked, "Seen John Grossman around since he was paroled?"

"A guy what's on parole don't hang out much with the old gang. Not if he's smart," Chunky told him.

"Have you seen him around?" Shayne persisted.

Chunky picked up a toothpick and chewed on it placidly. Shayne got out his wallet again and Chunky watched him fold another bill and hold it out. He took the bill and suggested, "Might ask Pug or Slim. They usta work for John some."

"Are they in back?"

Chunky shook his head. "Went out 'bout an hour ago."

Shayne said, "Tell them I'm passing out folding money." He went out and got in his car, drove north to Sixtieth and turned west.

Henry Renaldo's address was a modest one-story stucco house in the center of a block containing half a dozen such houses. It was the only one with lights showing through the front windows.

Shayne drove past it to the end of the block, swung around the corner, and parked. He got out and walked back, went up the concrete walk lined with a trim hedge on either side, and rang Renaldo's doorbell.

He took the gun out of his pocket while he waited.

He showed the weapon to Henry Renaldo when he opened the door. Renaldo was in his shirtsleeves, his vest hanging open. The cigar in his mouth looked like the same one he had been chewing on some hours previously. He blinked wrinkled lids down over his eyes when he saw the gun in Shayne's hand. He backed away, lifting his hands palms outward and mumbling, "You don't need to point that at me."

Shayne followed him in and heeled the door shut. The living room was small and crowded with heavy overstuffed furniture. There was no one else in the room.

Shayne gestured with his gun and asked, "Where's Miss Hastings?"

Renaldo rolled up his wrinkled lids and looked at him stupidly. "Who?"

"The girl who left your place with me."

"I sure don't know anything about a girl," Renaldo told him earnestly. "Look here—"

Shayne's eyes were dangerously bright. He palmed the gun and took a step forward, hit Renaldo in the face. Renaldo staggered back with blood oozing from a cut lip.

Shayne said coldly, "Maybe that'll help your memory."

Renaldo took another step backward and sank down on the red divan. He got a handkerchief from his hip pocket and wiped at his cut lip. He moaned, "Before God, Mike—"

Shayne rasped, "Where are your two gunmen?"

"Blackie and Lennie? How should I know?"

"They grabbed Miss Hastings from her hotel half an hour ago."

"I don't know anything about it." He looked at the blood on his handkerchief and shuddered. "I haven't seen them for two hours."

"Didn't you have them tail me when I left your place?"

"What if I did? But I didn't tell them to grab any girl."

Shayne narrowed his eyes. Renaldo sounded truthful. Shayne said, "I'll search this dump anyhow."

Renaldo got up slowly. There was a certain dignity in his bearing as he objected, "This is my house. If you haven't got a search warrant—"

Shayne said, "I'm not the police." He turned toward a passageway leading to the rear of the house.

Renaldo moved in front of him and folded his arms stubbornly. "My wife and kid are asleep back there."

Lennie's voice rapped out behind Shayne, "We'll take care of him, boss."

Renaldo's eyelids twitched and his eyes showed frantic terror. "I told you to stay in the kitchen, Lennie."

"To hell with that. Drop that gat, shamus," he rasped.

Shayne dropped the gun on the rug. He turned slowly and saw Lennie hunched forward and moving toward him from an open door. Blackie sauntered through the door after him.

Lennie had a heavy automatic in his right hand and his eyes glittered. His face was twisted and tiny bubbles of saliva oozed from between his tight lips. He was coked to the gills and as dangerous as a maddened snake. He glided soundlessly across the rug, the muzzle of his .45 in line with Shayne's belly.

Renaldo said, "Hold it, Lennie. We don't want any trouble here."

Lennie's hot eyes twitched toward the tavern proprietor. "He come here lookin' for trouble, didn't he? By the sweet God—"

"Hold it, Len," Blackie said coolly from behind him. "Stay far enough back so's you can blast him if he starts anything." He moved around Lennie on the balls of his feet, one hand swinging his blackjack in a short, lazy arc.

Shayne jerked his head back and it struck him on the side of the neck just above the collarbone. The blow was paralyzing, and he hit the floor before he knew he was falling. He heard Renaldo cry out, "Watch it, Blackie. Keep him so he can talk. If he croaked the old man he's maybe got some info."

Blackie said, "Sure. He'll talk." He drew back his foot and kicked Shayne in the face.

Shayne saw the kick coming but he couldn't move to avoid it. He closed his eyes and lay inert.

Blackie kicked him again in the face, and the pain brought knots in his belly. It also drove away the paralysis that had numbed him.

He sat up with blood streaming from his face and pulled his lips away from his teeth in a wolfish grin. He asked thickly, "Didn't you bring your pliers along this time, Blackie? I've got ten fingernails to work on."

Blackie hit him viciously with the blackjack again. Shayne toppled over and he heard Lennie laughing thinly as though from a far distance.

When he came to, water was being poured over his face. He lay quiescent and listened to Renaldo and Blackie arguing fiercely about him. Renaldo gave Blackie hell for knocking him out so that he couldn't talk, and Blackie angrily reminded Renaldo of Shayne's reputation for being tough. Lennie put in an aggrieved voice now and then, begging for permission to finish him off.

It was all foggy, but Shayne didn't hear any of them mention the girl. He gathered that they had followed him from the tavern to the little house on Eighteenth Street and had seen the police arrive. If they had followed him back to his hotel and tailed Myrna from the fire escape exit, it was evident that they were keeping that fact from Renaldo for reasons of their own.

"We gotta get him out of here," Renaldo said at last. "You boys've messed hell out of this whole thing, and the only way I see now is to finish him off."

"He pushed his face into it," Blackie muttered.

"Sure he did," Lennie said eagerly. "Don't worry about him none, boss."

"We'll take 'im out through the kitchen to our car." Blackie was placating now. They withdrew a short distance and began talking further in low voices. Shayne kept his eyes closed and gathered together the remnants of his strength.

They came back after a time and he heard Lennie saying happily, "Once in the heart to make sure is the best way. We don't wanna muff this."

Shayne saw the glitter of a knife in Lennie's hand as he un-coiled and rose from the floor. He saw Blackie's mouth drop open just before he hit him in the belly with his shoulder. They went to the floor together and Shayne kept on rolling toward the kitchen door. He stumbled through it just as Lennie's gun roared in the living room behind him.

Chapter Four: Pieces of a Puzzle

With a rush, Shayne jerked the back door open and staggered out into the night. He leaned against the side of the house and hoped Lennie or Blackie would follow him out. A light came on in the house next door and an irate voice bellowed, "What's going on over there? Was that a shot I heard?"

Shayne tried to call back, but his throat muscles were queerly knotted and he couldn't utter a sound. He shambled down the alley to the street where he had left his car and got in. He started the motor and drove away, made a circle back to Miami Avenue and drove to his apartment hotel. He didn't feel like tackling the side stairway, so he went in through the lobby to the elevator.

The clerk hurried out from behind the desk when he saw the detective's condition. He exclaimed, "Good God, Mr. Shayne! What happened? Here—lean on me."

Shayne put his arm gratefully around the clerk's shoulder and croaked, "It's okay, Dick. More blood than anything else."

Dick helped him into the elevator and rode up to his room with him. Shayne was an old and privileged client in the apart-ment hotel and the clerk had seen him in bad shape before, but never quite in this condition. He took Shayne's key ring and unlocked the door, then stared around in amazement when he turned on the light.

"Good Lord!" he ejaculated. "Did the fight start here in your room, Mr. Shayne?"

Shayne looked around the room with dazed and bleary eyes that refused to focus on any object. Things seemed to be in a sort of jumble but he didn't understand why the clerk was so excited. He let go of the clerk's steadying arm and staggered past him toward the center table and stared stupidly at the drawer that was pulled all the way out. He remembered having left it closed—with the things he and Myrna Hastings had brought from Captain Samuels's house.

His fingers closed around the neck of the brandy bottle which was still sitting where he had left it. He used both hands raising it to his mouth. He let the Monnet gurgle down his throat and felt his muscles relax and his eyes clear a little. He looked around the disordered room, and then at the clerk.

"Have I had any visitors since I went out, Dick?"

"Just that tall white-haired man who was with Chief Gentry. He came back right after you went out. He didn't stop at the desk, but went straight up. He came back almost immediately and went on out and I thought he'd come back hoping to catch you and found you'd already left."

Shayne took another slow drink of cognac. It brought warmth and relaxation to his tight belly muscles. "Was he up here long enough to do all this?" He motioned around the room.

Dick wrinkled his forehead. "I don't think so, but it would be hard to say for sure. You know how it is. Unless you watch, it's hard to judge time. Naturally I thought he was a friend of yours. It didn't seem as if he were up here more than a few minutes."

Shayne started to nod, but his sore neck muscles stopped him. He said, "Thanks for coming up with me," in a tone of dismissal.

"But couldn't I help—get you washed up—the blood off?" the clerk asked.

"No thanks, Dick."

He stood with the bottle in his hands until Dick went out and closed the door. Then he held it to his lips and drained it. He went out to the kitchen and set the empty bottle carefully on the sink beside the two glasses Myrna had put there on her way out. He tried the back door and found it unlocked.

He remembered distinctly that it had been locked and Myrna had had the key when he went away a short time before.

Going back to the bedroom he stripped off his clothes, turned water into the tub as hot as his hand could stand it. His face was pretty much of a mess, with both his lips puffed and bluish, lacerated flesh on his cheekbone clotted with blood, and streaks of dried blood on his chin.

He grimaced at his reflection in the mirror, testing two teeth that felt sore and a little loose. All in all, he was in pretty fair shape, considering the way he'd been knocked around.

He got a soft washcloth steaming hot and held it gently against his face while he waited for the tub to fill, loosened the dried blood, and cleaned the cuts carefully.

When he sank into the tub of hot water to soak his long frame, he continued the ministrations with the washcloth. He then let the water run cold on the cloth and splashed it over his face and neck. He stepped out of the tub and swabbed his face freely with peroxide, then dusted it with antiseptic powder. Carefully wiping around the worst cut, he put a Band-Aid over it, then vigorously toweled himself and put on clean clothes.

His neck throbbed with pain where the blackjack had struck. He went to a wall cabinet in the living room and got out a bottle of Portuguese brandy guaranteed to be at least five years old. He filled the wineglass on the table and got a fresh tumbler of ice water from the kitchen, then sank into a chair and lit a cigarette, letting it droop from an uninjured corner of his mouth.

He took a sip of brandy and began to go slowly over the events of the evening, dwelling upon each incident as he came to it in the light of later occurrences.

It started with his entering Renaldo's saloon expecting to meet Timothy Rourke. Myrna Hastings had been there instead. She had accosted him, and he had only her word for it that she was what she claimed to be and had been sent by Rourke. Yet,

Gentry had phoned Rourke to get her address, but at the Captain's house she had said Rourke introduced her to Will Gentry that afternoon.

Shayne went on from his meeting with Myrna Hastings. He carefully studied the scene in Renaldo's office, then jumped to Captain Samuels's home on the bay front. In secreting herself in the back of his car, slipping into the house without his knowledge, coming to his aid when Gentry questioned him, and finally stealing the logbook which she claimed to have found in a hiding place that another searcher had overlooked—

Had Myrna Hastings stepped out of character?

He took another long drink of brandy. It was difficult to say. Who could predict what a young girl feature writer from New York was likely to do? She had left his apartment willingly enough and had gone directly to her hotel room as he had told her to. Then she had been immediately escorted away by two men vaguely described as being short and tall. Had she gone willingly? Or had she been coerced, threatened?

He had immediately suspected Blackie and Lennie of her abduction, but after listening to them at Renaldo's house he was inclined to believe they were not responsible. It didn't quite add up. Now that he was thinking along logical lines, he realized they would have to have trailed him back to his hotel and somehow learned of her departure via the fire escape in order to have followed her to the Crestwood.

It was necessary to determine whether the two men who had accompanied her out had been there waiting for her return, or whether they had followed her in and up to her room. If they had been waiting, it could not have been Blackie and Lennie, unless Myrna was invloved in some way he knew nothing about.

That left the whole business of the missing murder clues up in the air. When she left his apartment, the clues had been lying on the table. If she had come back to get them she wouldn't have known to look in the drawer. She might have searched the rest of the room first. The table drawer was too obvious. She didn't, in fact, know the table had a drawer.

Shayne took another sip of brandy and settled more comfortably in his chair. The pain was gradually going away from his neck muscles. He switched his thoughts from Myrna to Guildford.

Had Guildford told the truth about waiting for the Captain to return? Or, granting that Blackie and Lennie had told Renaldo the truth about their venture, was Guildford the killer whom they had seen drive away after being closeted with the Captain for half an hour? If Guildford was the killer, why had he drawn attention to himself by calling Will Gentry? It would have been safer and more natural to say nothing about his visit and leave the body to be discovered by chance.

What about the paroled convict, John Grossman? This seemed to Shayne the crux of the affair. He was certainly mixed up in the possession of smuggled cognac somehow. Had Captain Samuels worked with him, or for him, in prohibition days? Did both men have knowledge of a cache of illicit cognac undisposed of at the time of Grossman's arrest? If so, why had Captain Samuels waited so many years to put a case of it on the market? Waited until he was weak from hunger and malnutrition?

It seemed likely that the Captain couldn't get his hands on it while Grossman was in prison, since the first case appeared soon after Grossman had supposedly returned to Miami.

Shayne's eyes were heavy with the swollen condition of his face. The throb in his neck was subsiding, but his mind was alert.

It seemed definitely unlikely that John Grossman was in on the deal with Renaldo. The ridiculously low price accepted by the starving Captain proved that it must have been his own idea. Grossman was smart enough to learn what the vintage stuff was worth in today's market. It looked more as though the Captain had put over a personal deal—one that for some reason he had been unable to put over while Grossman was in prison. One that Grossman might have resented even to the point of murder.

Shayne finished his glass of brandy and closed his mind against his musings. He needed more facts before he could do more than ask himself a lot of questions that, as yet, had no answers.

He heaved himself up painfully from his chair and gritted his teeth against a wave of physical weakness. He looked around for his hat, then remembered he had lost it in the fracas at Renaldo's. He went out bareheaded, thinking the cool night air would feel good on his head.

Dick frowned and shook his head, but his eyes showed admiration and amazement when Shayne crossed the lobby. Shayne pushed his swollen lips into the semblance of a grin and he waved a derisive hand at the clerk. He got in his car and drove to Second Avenue.

The Crestwood was a small, moderately priced hotel, and the night clerk was a thin-chested little man who tried to conceal his hostile amazement when Shayne showed his battered face at the desk. He shook a blond and scanty-haired head and said, "I'm afraid—"

"I don't want a room," Shayne assured him. He showed his badge and said, "It's about a guest of yours, Miss Myrna Hastings."

"Oh—yes," he stammered. "Room 305. She isn't in. There's been—"

"I'm the guy who telephoned you about an hour ago. Can you describe the men she went out with?"

"I'm afraid I can't, sir. You see, I didn't notice their faces."

"Could one of them have been holding a gun on her?" Shayne demanded harshly.

The clerk began to tremble, and his voice shook when he said, "I really don't know, sir. I—do you think something has happened to her?"

"Do you know whether they came in *after* she got her key and went up, or were they waiting?"

"I—really don't know. I didn't see them come in after she got her key, but I'm afraid I can't swear whether they were upstairs waiting for her or not."

Shayne turned away and went to the elevator. It was run by a young Negro boy who stood very stiff and straight, but he couldn't control his popping black eyes when they saw his face.

Shayne asked, "Do you remember the girl in three-o-five?"

"Yassuh. I knows the one you mean. Checked in jes' today."

"Do you remember her coming in late tonight and then going out again almost immediately?"

"Yassuh. That's what she done. I 'members it."

Shayne got out his wallet. "Now try to remember exactly what happened," he said quietly. "Did you bring her down in the elevator with two men?"

The boy's eyes rolled covetously toward the five-dollar bill. "Yassuh. I sho did. Ra't after I'd done taken her up."

"How long afterward?" Shayne prompted. "Did you make many trips in between?"

"Nosuh. Not none. I 'member how s'prised I was when I stopped at the thu'd floor on the way down an' foun' her waitin' with them two gen'mans, 'cause I'd jes' took her up to three on mah way up."

"Are you sure of that? You didn't take them up *after* you took her up?"

"Nosuh. How could I when I'd done taken 'em up pre'vous?"

"How much previous?"

"'Bout ten minutes, I reckon."

"Did you notice anything peculiar about the way either of them acted when they came down together?"

"How d'yuh mean peculiar?"

"I'm trying to find out whether she *wanted* to come down with them or whether they *made* her come."

The boy chuckled. "I reckon she liked comin', all right. She was sho all hugged up to one of 'em. The skinny one, that was."

"Can you describe them?"

"Wal, nosuh. Not much. One was skinny and t'other weren't. I reckon I didn't notice no more."

Shayne said, "You've earned this." The bill exchanged hands and he went out. He had learned something, but he didn't care much for it.

His next stop was at the Miami *Daily News* tower. The early hours of the morning were the busiest for the staff of the afternoon paper. Shayne found Timothy Rourke in one corner of the smoke-hazed city room pounding out copy with one rubber-tipped forefinger of his right hand, while the thumb of his left hand was poised and ready to shift for capital letters and shift lock.

Rourke looked up at Shayne and uttered a startled oath. He laughed raucously at the sight of Shayne's face and said, "I'm not the beauty contest editor. You just go down that hall there—"

"You go to hell," Shayne said bitterly.

"Michael!" Rourke drawled the name disapprovingly. "Such language in a newspaper office. Did he get his little face scratched?"

"It's all your God-damned fault for sicking that female onto me," Shayne rasped.

"My fault? My God, don't tell me a female did *that*."

Shayne lowered himself onto a corner of the desk and asked, "How well do you know Myrna Hastings?"

Rourke grinned up at him and said, "Not as well as I'd like to. Or, is she that sort of a gal? Of course, she's not a blonde, but maybe I'd want to—"

"Cut it, Tim," said Shayne wearily. "I'm up to my neck in murder, and God knows what-all. What do you know about the gal?"

Rourke looked into Shayne's somber eyes. "Not much, Mike," he said seriously. "She brought a note from a friend of mine on the *Telegram* in New York. I took her around and introduced her to a few people and places this afternoon. She found you at Renaldo's, huh? Sorry I couldn't make it."

"She found me, all right," said Shayne grimly.

"What's doing, Mike?" His eyes glittered and his nostrils began to twitch like a bloodhound's on the scent. "I wondered when Will Gentry called me about her tonight, but—"

"Do you know if she's known in Miami?" Shayne interrupted.

"I don't think so." Rourke leaned far back in his swivel chair and gazed excitedly into Shayne's puffed eyes. "She said it was her first trip, Mike."

"Has anyone else called you for her address, Tim?"

"Only Gentry. Is it a story, Mike?"

Shayne's gray eyes brooded, looking away from him, roaming around the room. He and the reporter had been friends for a long time, and he had given Rourke a lot of scoops in the past. He indicated the typewriter and asked, "Busy on something?"

Rourke pushed his chair back. "Nothing I can't give the go-by, Mike."

Shayne said, "I could use some help in your morgue."

Rourke sprang up and led the way back to a large filing room guarded by an elderly woman. She was knitting a pair of bootees, and her wrinkled mouth was tilted in a smile.

"I'm interested in John Grossman," Shayne told Rourke.

"The bootleg king?" They walked past the woman and Rourke stopped between a double row of filing cases. "He's the guy who is back in town on parole."

"When did he get back?" Shayne asked.

"Three or four days ago. I tried to interview him, but he wouldn't give out anything for publication. All he wanted was to go down to his lodge on the Keys and soak up some Florida sunshine."

Shayne said, "I want to go back to his arrest by the Feds in June, 1930."

"We've got a private file on him. It won't be hard to find." Rourke checked a card index eagerly and swiftly, then went to a file at the back of the room. He came back with a bulging Manila envelope and emptied it. He started pawing through it, Shayne close beside him and watching.

"Here's the trial," said Rourke. "It was a honey. With Leland and Parker representing him and not missing a trick. Here you are:

June 17, 1930. Federal agents nabbed him at Homestead on his way in from the lodge on the Keys." He spread out a large clipping.

"I remember it now," Rourke said. He chuckled. "They had the income tax case all set but had been holding off, hoping they could hang a real charge on him. They thought he used his lodge to receive contraband shipments from Cuba, and they raided it several times, but never found any evidence. This time they thought they had him for sure, with a red-hot tip that he was expecting a boatload of French stuff. They kept a revenue cutter patrolling that section of coastline day and night for a week.

"Here's the story on that." Rourke turned his burning slate-gray eyes on Shayne, then flipped the pages back to a clipping dated June 16. It was captioned: CUTTER SINKS BOOTLEG CARGO.

"I covered that story. I rode the cutter three nights and nothing happened. After I was pulled off on the night of the fifteenth they encountered a motor craft creeping along without lights just off the inlet leading to Grossman's lodge. They tried to make a run for the open sea, and bingo! the revenue boat cut loose with everything she had. There was a heavy sea running, the aftermath of a hurricane that blew hell out of things the day before, and they never found a trace of the boat, cargo, or crew. After that fiasco they gave up and decided they might as well take Grossman on the income tax charge."

"Wait a minute," Shayne said. "How bad was that hurricane?"

"Plenty bad. That's really the reason I missed the fun. The cutter had to run for anchorage on the thirteenth, and she couldn't put out again until the fifteenth on account of the storm."

"Then that strip of coast wasn't being patrolled the two nights before the sinking?" Shayne mused.

"Nope. Except by the elements."

"And that rum-runner might have been slipping out after discharging cargo, instead of being headed in."

Rourke stared at the redheaded detective. "If the captain was crazy enough to try and hit that inlet while the hurricane was blowing everything to hell."

Shayne said gravely, "I think I know the captain who was crazy enough to do just that—and succeeded."

Rourke raised his brows quizzically. "You've got something up your sleeve," he accused.

Shayne nodded. "It adds up. Tim, I'm willing to bet there was a boatload of 1926 Monnet unloaded at Grossman's lodge while the hurricane was raging. And it's still there someplace. Grossman was arrested the seventeenth, before he had a chance to get rid of any of it, and he left it there while he was doing time in Atlanta."

Timothy Rourke whistled shrilly. "It'd be worth as much now as it was during prohibition."

"More, with the country full of people earning more money than ever before in their lives."

"If your hunch is right—"

"It has to be right. How long do you think a man could stay alive floating around the ocean in a life preserver?"

"Couple of days, at the most."

"That's my hunch, too. From the fifteenth to the seventeenth might not be impossible. But the hurricane struck on the thirteenth and fourteenth. Take a look at your front page for June 17, and you'll see what I mean."

Rourke hurriedly brought out the *News* for June 17. On the front page, next to the story of Grossman's arrest, was the story of the sensational rescue of Captain Samuels which Shayne had already read in his apartment. Rourke put his finger on the picture and exclaimed, "I remember that now. I interviewed the Captain and thought it miraculous he had stayed alive that long. Captain Thomas Anthony Samuels. Why, damn it, Mike, he's the old coot who was found murdered tonight."

Shayne said soberly, "After selling a case of Monnet for a hundred bucks earlier in the evening."

"He was the only survivor of his ship," Rourke recalled excitedly. "Then he and Grossman must have been the only ones who knew the stuff was out there."

"And now Grossman is the only one left," Shayne said flatly. "Keep this stuff under your hat, Tim. When it's ready to break it'll be your baby." He turned and hurried out.

Chapter Five: Perfect Setting for Murder

Shayne didn't reach his apartment again until after three. He took a nightcap and went to bed, fell immediately into deep and dreamless slumber.

The ringing of his telephone awakened him. He started to yawn, and pain clawed at his facial muscles. He got into a robe and lurched to the telephone. It was a little after eight o'clock.

He lifted the receiver and said, "Shayne."

A thick voice replied, "This is John Grossman."

Shayne said, "I expected you to call sooner."

There was a brief silence as though his caller were taken aback by his reply. Then: "Well, I'm calling you now."

Shayne said, "That's quite evident."

"You're horning in on things that don't concern you."

"Cognac always concerns me."

"I'm wondering how much you found out from the Captain before he died last night," Grossman went on.

Shayne said, "Nuts. You killed him and you know exactly how much talking he didn't do."

"You can't prove I was near his place last night," said Grossman gruffly.

"I think I can. If you just called up to play ring-around-the-rosy, we're both wasting our time."

"I've been wondering how much real information you've got."

"I knew that would worry you," Shayne said impatiently. "And since you know Samuels was dead before I reached him, the source of information you're worried about is the logbook. Let's talk straight."

"Why should I worry about the logbook? I've got it now."

"I know you have. But you don't know how much I read about the *Mermaid*'s last trip before you got it."

"The girl says you didn't read it any."

Shayne laughed harshly. "You'd like to believe her, wouldn't you?"

"All right." The voice became resigned. "Maybe you did read more than she says. How about a deal?"

"What kind of deal?"

"You're pretty crazy about Monnet, aren't you?"

"Plenty."

"How does five cases sound? Delivered to your apartment tonight."

Shayne said, "It sounds like a joke—and a poor one."

"You'll take it and keep your mouth shut if you're smart."

Shayne said disgustedly, "You're rolling me in the aisle." He hung up and padded across the room in his bare feet to the table, where he poured a slug of Portuguese brandy. The telephone began ringing again. He drank some of the brandy, lit a cigarette, and went to the phone carrying the glass. He lifted the receiver and asked curtly, "Got any more jokes?"

The same voice answered plaintively, "What do you want?"

Shayne asked, "Why should I deal with you at all? I've got everything I need with Samuels's description of where the stuff is hidden."

"What can you do with it?" the murderer argued.

"The Internal Revenue boys could use my dope."

"And cut yourself out? Not if I know you."

"All right," Shayne said irritably. "You have to cut me in, and you know it. Fifty-fifty."

"Come out and we'll talk it over."

"Where?"

"My lodge on the Keys. First dirt road to the south after you pass Homestead, and then to your right after two miles."

Shayne said, "I know where it is."

"I'll expect you about ten o'clock."

Shayne said, "Make it eleven. I've got to get some breakfast."

"Eleven it is." A click broke the connection.

Shayne dressed swiftly, jammed a wide-brimmed Panama down over his head and pulled the brim low over his face, and went out. He hesitated a moment, then went back into the living room. He flipped the pages of the telephone directory until he found the number of Renaldo's tavern, lifted the receiver, and got a brisk "Good morning," from a masculine voice at the switchboard downstairs. A frown knitted his forehead, and instead of asking for Renaldo's number, he said, "Do you have the time?"

He was told, "It is eight twenty-two."

In the lobby, Shayne went across to the desk and leaned one elbow on it. He simulated astonishment and asked the day clerk, "Where's Mabel today?"

The clerk glanced around at the brown-suited, middle-aged man alertly handling the switchboard and said, "Mabel was ill, and the telephone company sent us a substitute."

Shayne went out, got in his car, and drove to a drugstore on Flagler. He called Renaldo's number and said briskly, "Mike Shayne talking."

"Mike?" Renaldo sounded relieved. "You're all right? God, I'm sorry about—"

Shayne laughed softly. "I'm okay. Your boys could be a little more gentle but I feel I owe them something for last night. I've got a line on that stuff you were after."

"Yeah? Well, I don't know . . ."

"I need some help to handle it," Shayne went on. "I figure Blackie and Lennie are just the boys—after seeing them in action."

"I don't know," Renaldo said again, more doubtfully.

"This is business," Shayne said sharply. "Big business for you and me both. Have them meet me at your place about nine thirty."

He hung up and drove out to a filling station on the corner of

Eighteenth and Biscayne. "Ten gallons," he said to the youth who hurried out.

Shayne strolled around to the back of his car and asked, "Were you on duty last night?"

"Until I closed up at ten. Just missed the excitement, I guess."

"You mean the murder?"

"Yeah. The old ship captain who lives down the street. And I was talking about the old coot just a little before that."

"Who with?"

"A lawyer fellow who'd been down to see him and got a flat tire just as he was coming back."

"What time was that?" asked Shayne.

"Pretty near ten. I closed up right after I finished with his tire. If that's all—" He took the bill Shayne offered him.

The detective swung away from the filling station and stopped on First Street east of Miami Avenue. He went into the lobby of an office building mostly occupied by lawyers and insurance men. He stopped to scan the building directory, then stepped into an elevator and said, "Six."

He got off on the sixth floor and went down the corridor to a door chastely lettered: LEROY P. GUILDFORD—ATTORNEY-AT-LAW.

There was a small reception room, and a tight-mouthed, middle-aged woman got up from a desk in the rear and came forward when Shayne entered. Her hair was pulled back from her face and tied in a tight knot at the back of her head. She wore rimless glasses and low-heeled shoes, and looked primly efficient.

"Mr. Giuldford hasn't come in yet," she said in response to Shayne's question. "He seldom gets down before ten."

Shayne said, "Perhaps you can tell me a few things. I'm from the police." He gave her a glimpse of his private badge.

She said, "From the police?" Her thin lips tightened. "I'm sure I don't know why you're here." Her gaze was fixed disapprovingly on his battered face.

He said easily. "It's about one of his clients who was murdered last night. Mr. Guildford gave us some help, but there are a few more details to be filled in."

"Oh, yes. You mean poor Captain Samuels. I know Mr. Guildford must feel terrible about it. Such an old client and so alone and helpless."

"Did you know him?"

"Only through seeing him here at the office. Mr. Guildford was trying to save his property, but it seemed hopeless."

"In what particular capacity did he need a lawyer?"

"It wasn't much," she said vaguely. "He was one of our first clients when Mr. Guildford opened up this office after resigning his position with the firm of Leland and Parker. There was something about the collection of insurance on a ship that had been lost at sea, and later Mr. Guildford handled the purchase of a property where Captain Samuels later built his little home."

"Do you know whether Guildford saw much of him lately?"

"Not a great deal. There was some difficulty about the mortgage and Mr. Guildford was trying to save him from foreclosure. He pitied the old man, you see, but there was little he could do."

"And this appointment last night. Do you know anything about that?"

"Oh, yes. I took the message early yesterday morning. Captain Samuels explicitly asked him to come at nine last night, promising to make a cash payment on the mortgage. I remember Mr. Guildford seemed so relieved when he received the message, and he didn't seem to mind the unusual hour."

Shayne thanked her and told her she had been of great assistance. He started out, then turned back to ask, "By the way, is Guildford generally in his office throughout the day?"

"Yes. Except when he's in court, of course."

"Was he in court last Tuesday?"

"Tuesday? I'm sure he wasn't."

"That's queer. I tried to phone him twice during the day and he was out both times."

The woman frowned uncertainly, then her face cleared. "Tuesday! Of course. How stupid of me. He was out all day with a client."

Shayne lifted his hat and went out. He drove north on Miami Avenue to Chunky's place and went in. A couple of men were seated halfway down the counter. Shayne took the stool by the cash register and Chunky drifted up to him after a few moments. He leaned his elbows on the counter, selected a toothpick from a bowl, and began picking at his teeth. He murmured, "Looks like somebody prettied you up las' night."

"Yeah. Some of the boys got playful," he said good-naturedly. "Look, I'm still hunting a line on John Grossman. Pug or Slim been in?"

"Ain't seen 'em. Grossman usta have a fishin' place south of Homestead."

"Think he went up there after he was paroled?"

"Good place to hole up," said Chunky. "I know he stayed in town just one night."

Shayne got up and went out, leaving a dollar at the place where he had been sitting. There was a public telephone in the cheap hotel next door. He called Timothy Rourke's home number and waited patiently until the ringing awoke the reporter. He said, "There's about be a Caesarean operation."

Rourke gurgled sleepily, "What the hell?"

"On that baby we were talking about in your morgue this morning."

"That you, Mike?"

"Doctor Shayne. Specializing in obstetrics."

"Hey! Is it due to break?"

"It's coming to a head fast. Get dressed and hunt up Will Gentry if you want some headlines. Don't, for God's sake, tell him I tipped you, but stick to him like a leech." Shayne hung up and drove to Renaldo's saloon.

Blackie jumped up nervously from his seat beside Renaldo's

desk when Shayne pushed the door open. He sucked in his breath and stared with bulging eyes at the result of his work on the detective's face, while his hand instinctively went to his hip pocket.

Behind him, Lennie leaned against the wall with his hand in his coat pocket. Lennie's features were lax and his eyes were filmed like a dead man's. The left side of his pallid face twitched uncontrollably as Shayne looked at him.

Seated behind the desk, chewing savagely on a cigar, Henry Renaldo looked fearfully from the boys to Shayne. He said, "I don't know what you're up to, Mike. The boys didn't much like the idea—"

Shayne closed the door and laughed heartily. He said, "Hell, there's no hard feelings. I'm still alive and kicking."

Blackie drew in another deep breath. He essayed a nervous smile. "We thought maybe you was sore."

Shayne said gently, "You got a pretty heavy foot, Blackie."

"Yeah." Blackie hung his head like a small boy being reprimanded. "But you come bustin' in with a gun, an' Jeez! what'd you expect?"

"That was my mistake," Shayne admitted. "I always run into trouble when I pack a rod. That's why I'm clean now." He lifted his arms away from his sides. "Want to shake me down?"

"That's all right." Renaldo laughed with false heartiness. "No harm done, I guess. The boys'll forget it if you will."

"Whatcha want with us?" Lennie demanded thinly.

"I need your help," Shayne said bluntly. "I've run into something too big for me to handle, and after seeing you guys in action last night I think you're the ones I need."

"That's white of you," Blackie mumbled.

"I never hold a grudge if it's going to cost me money," Shayne told them briskly. "Here's the lay." He spoke directly to Renaldo: "I can put my hands on plenty of French cognac—same as the case you bought last night. And this won't cost us a hundred a case. It won't cost us anything if we play it right."

Renaldo licked his lips. "So the old captain did talk before he died?"

"Not to me. I got onto it from another angle. Interested?"

"Why are you cutting us in?" Renaldo protested. "Sounds like some kind of come-on to me."

"I need help," Shayne said smoothly. "There's another mug in my way and he's got a couple of torpedoes gunning for me. I need a couple of lads like Blackie and Lennie to handle that angle. After that's cleared up, I still need somebody with the right connections like you, Renaldo. I haven't any setup for handling sales. You know all the angles from way back. And since you put me onto it in the first place I thought you might as well have part of the gravy. Hell, there's plenty for all of us," he added generously. "A whole shipload of that same stuff."

"Sounds all right," Renaldo admitted cautiously.

"I'm the only one standing in this other guy's way," Shayne explained. "So he plans to put me on the spot. I've got a date to meet him out in the country this morning, and I know he'll have a couple of quick-trigger boys on hand to blast me out of the picture." He turned to Blackie. "That's where you and Lennie come in. I'm not handing you anything on a platter. This is hot, and if you're scared of it just say so and I'll find someone else."

Blackie grunted contemptuously. "Lennie and me can take care of ourselves, I reckon."

"That's what I thought after last night. Both of you ironed?"

"Sure. When do we start?"

"Well, that's it," Shayne told Renaldo. "You sit tight until the shooting's over. If things work out right we'll do a four-way split and there should be plenty of grands to go around. I'm guessing at five hundred cases, but there may be more," he ended casually.

Renaldo took his cigar from his mouth and wet his lips. "Sounds plenty good to me. You boys willing to go along?"

Both of them nodded.

Shayne said briskly, "We'd better get started. I'm due south of

Homestead at eleven o'clock." He led the way out to his car and opened the back door. "Maybe both of you will feel better if you ride in back where you can keep an eye on me."

"We ain't worryin' none about you," Blackie assured him, but they both got in the back seat while Shayne settled himself under the wheel.

In the rearview mirror he could see the pair conferring together earnestly. Both sides of Lennie's face were getting the twitches and his hands trembled violently when he lit a cigarette. He took only a couple of drags on it, then screwed up his face in disgust and threw it out.

Shayne said sympathetically to Blackie, "Your pal doesn't seem to feel so hot this morning."

"He's all right," Blackie muttered. "Sorta got the shakes is all."

Shayne said, "He'd better get over them before the shooting starts."

Lennie caught Blackie's arm and whispered something in his ear. Blackie cleared his throat and admitted uneasily, "Tell you what. He could use somethin' to steady him all right. You know."

Shayne said, "Sure. I know. Anyplace around here we could pick up a bindle?"

"Sure thing," Lennie said, violently eager. "Couple of blocks ahead. If I had two bucks."

Shayne drove on two blocks and pulled up to the curb. He passed four one-dollar bills back to Lennie and suggested, "Get two bindles, why don't you? One to pick you up now and the other for just before the fun starts."

Lennie grabbed the money and scrambled out of the car. He hurried up the street and darted into a stairway entrance.

Blackie laughed indulgently as he watched him disappear. "You hadn't orta give him the price of two bindles," he reproved Shayne. "He'll be plenty high in an hour from now on one. 'Nother one on top of it will pull him tight as a fiddle string. Like he was last night," he added darkly.

Shayne said, "I want him in shape to throw lead fast. Those boy who'll be waiting for me may not waste much time getting acquainted." He lit a cigarette and slouched back in the seat.

Lennie came trotting back in about five minutes. His pinched face was alive and eager and his eyes glowed like live coals. He slid in beside Blackie and breathed exultantly, "Le's get goin'. Jeez, is my trigger finger itchin'."

Shayne drove swiftly south on Flagler, past Coral Gables and on to the village of South Miami, then along the Key West highway through the rich truck-farming section with its acres of tomatoes and bean fields stretching in every direction as far as the eye could see.

By the time they reached the sleepy village of Homestead with its quiet, tree-shadowed streets and its air of serene dignity, Shayne began to feel as though he were the one who had sniffed a bindle instead of Lennie. There was a driving, demanding tension within him. It was always this way when he played a hunch through to the finish. He had planned the best he could and it was up to the gods now. He couldn't turn back. He didn't want to turn back. The approach of personal danger keyed him to a high pitch, and he exulted in the gamble he was taking. Things like this were what made life worth living to Michael Shayne.

He drove decorously through Homestead and looked at his watch. It was a quarter to eleven. He stopped at a filling station on the outskirts of the village where the first dirt road turned off the paved highway to the left. He told Blackie and Lennie, "I'll be just a minute," and swung out of the car to speak to a smiling old man in faded overalls and a wide straw hat.

"Does the bus stop here, Pop?"

"Sometimes. Yep. If there's passengers to get on or off. 'Tain't a reg'lar stop."

"How about yesterday? Any passengers stop here?"

"Yestiddy? Yep. The old sailor feller got off here to go a-fishin'." The old man chuckled. "Right nice old feller, but seemed like he was turned around, sort of. Didn't know how far 'twas to the Keys. Had him a suitcase, too, full of fishin' tackle I reckon. Him an' me made a deal to rent my tin Lizzie for the day and he drove off fishin' as spry as you please. No luck though. Didn' have nary a fish when he came back."

Shayne thanked him and went back to his car. That was the last definite link. He didn't need it, but it was always good to have added confirmation. He wouldn't have bothered to stop if he hadn't had a few minutes to spare.

He got in and turned down the dirt road running straight and level between a wasteland of palmetto and pine on either side.

"This is it," he told the boys calmly. "Couple of miles to where I'm supposed to meet these birds, but they might be hiding out along the road waiting for me. You'd both better get down in the back where you can't be seen."

"We won't be no good to you that way," Blackie protested, "if they're hid out along the road to pick you off."

"They'll just pick all three of us off if you guys are in sight too," Shayne argued reasonably. "I don't think they'll try anything till we get there, and I want them to think I came alone so they'll be off guard. Get down and stay down until the shooting starts or until I yell or give you some signal. Then come out like firecrackers."

The two gunmen got down in the back. Shayne drove along at a moderate speed, watching his speedometer. It was lonely and quiet on this desolate road leading to the coast. There were no houses, no other cars on the road. It was a perfect setting for murder.

Chapter Six: Shayne Gets His Fee

A narrower and less-used road turned off to the right at the end of exactly two miles. A wooden arrow which had once been painted white, pointed west, and dingy black letters said: LODGE.

Shayne turned westward and slowed his car still more as it bumped along the uneven ruts. Sunlight lay hot and white on the narrow lane between the pines, and the smell of the sea told him he was approaching one of the salt-water inlets.

The car panted over a little rise and saw the weathered rock walls of John Grossman's fishing lodge through the pines on the left. It was a low, sprawling structure, and a pair of ruts turned off abruptly to lead up to it.

Two men stepped into the middle of the lane to block his way when he was fifty feet from the building. This was so exactly what Shayne had expected that he cut his motor and braked to an easy stop with the front bumper almost touching the men.

He leaned out of the window and asked, "This John Grossman's place?" then opened the door and stepped out quickly to show that he was unarmed and to prevent them from coming to the car where they would see Lennie and Blackie crouched in the back.

One of the men was very tall and thin, with cadaverous features and deep hollows for eye sockets. He wore a beautifully tailored suit of silk pongee with a tan shirt and shoes, and a light tan snap-brimmed felt hat. He had his arms folded across his thin chest. His right hand was inside the lapel of his unbuttoned coat close to a bulge just below his left shoulder. His face was darkly suntanned and he showed white teeth in a saturnine smile as he stood in the middle of the road without moving.

His companion was a head shorter than Slim. He had a broad, pugnacious face with a flat nose spread over a lot of it. He was hatless and coatless, wearing a shirt with loud yellow stripes, with elastic armbands making tucks in the full sleeves. He stood flat-footed with his hand openly gripping the butt of a revolver thrust down behind the waistband of his trousers.

Shayne stood beside the car and surveyed them coolly. He said, "I don't think we've met formally. I'm Shayne."

Pug said, "Yeah. We know. This here's Slim." He jerked the thumb of his left hand toward his tall companion.

Shayne said, "I thought this was a social call. Where's Grossman?"

"He sent us out to see you were clean before you come in." Slim's lips barely moved to utter the words. He sauntered around the front of the car toward Shayne, keeping his hand inside his coat. His deep-set eyes were cold and glittered like polished agate. His head was thrust forward on a long, thin neck.

Shayne took two backward steps. He said, "I'm clean. I came out to talk business. This is a hell of a way to greet a guy."

Pug moved behind Slim. He was obviously the slower witted and the less dangerous of the pair. He blinked in the bright sunlight and said, "Why don't we let 'im have it here?"

Slim said, "We do." He smiled, and Shayne knew he was a man who enjoyed watching his victims die.

Shayne pretended he didn't hear or didn't understand the byplay between the two killers. They had both moved to the side of the car now and were circling slowly toward him.

Shayne said, "I brought along some cold beer. It's here in the back." He reached for the handle of the rear door and turned it steadily until the latch was free. He flung himself to the ground, jerking the door wide open as he did so.

Slim's gun flashed at the same instant that fire blazed from the backseat. Slim staggered back and dropped to one knee, steadying his gun to return the fire.

Shayne lay flat on the ground and saw Pug spin around from the impact of a .45 slug in his thick shoulder, but Pug stayed on his feet and his own gun rained bullets into the tonneau.

Slim fired twice before a bullet smashed the saturnine grin back into his mouth. He crumpled slowly forward onto the sunlit pine needles and lay very still.

Pug went down at almost the same instant with a look of complete bewilderment on his broad face. He dropped his revolver and put both hands over his belly, lacing his stubby fingers together tightly. He sank to a sitting position with his legs doubled under him, and swayed there for a moment before toppling over on his side.

There was no more shooting. And there was no sound from the back of the car.

Shayne got up stiffly and began dusting the dirt from his clothes. He heard shouts and looked up to see excited men filtering through the trees and coming from behind the lodge to converge on the car.

He saw that both Blackie and Lennie were quite dead. Blackie lay with his body sprawled half out on the running-board, his gun hand trailing in the dirt. Blood trickled from two holes in his yellow polo shirt, and his mouth was open.

Lennie was crouched on the floor behind Blackie and there was a gaping hole where his right eye had been. His thin features were composed and he looked more at peace with the world than Shayne had ever seen him look before.

Will Gentry came puffing up behind Shayne, his red face suffused and perspiring. A tall, black-mustached man wearing the clothes of a farmer and carrying a rifle was close behind him. Other men were dressed like farmers, and Shayne recognized half a dozen of them as Gentry's plainclothes detectives. He saw Rourke's grinning face and had time to give the reporter a quick nod of recognition before Gentry caught his arm and pulled him around angrily, demanding, "What the bloody blazes are you pulling off here, Mike?"

"I? Nothing." Shayne arched his red brows at the Chief of Detectives. "Can I help it if some damned hoods choose this place to settle one of their feuds?" He stepped back and waved toward the rear of the car. "Couple of hitch-hikers I picked up. Why don't you ask them why they started shooting?"

"They're both dead," Gentry asserted angrily after a quick survey. "And the other two?" He started around the car.

"This one's still alive," Rourke called out cheerfully, kneeling beside Pug. "But I don't think he will be long."

Shayne sauntered around behind Gentry. Blood was seeping between Pug's fingers, but his eyes were open when Gentry shook him and demanded to know where Grossman was.

"Inside. Cellar." Pug's voice was low and hoarse.

"You—Yancy and Marks," Gentry directed two of his men. "Stay here and get a statement from him. Find out what this shooting is about. Everything. The rest of you fan out and surround the house. Take it careful and be ready to shoot. The real criminal is in there."

Shayne took Gentry's place beside Pug as Gentry moved away to direct the placing of his men around the lodge. He leaned close to the dying man and asked, "Where's the girl, Pug? The girl. Where is she?"

"Inside," the wounded man murmured.

Shayne got to his feet. Rourke got up beside him and grabbed his arm. "Sweet God, Mike! I don't know what any of this is about, but it's *some* Caesarean."

Shayne pulled away from him and stalked toward the fishing lodge. Rourke hurried after him, expostulating, "Hold it, Mike. Don't try to go in there. Didn't you hear the guy? Grossman's inside. Let Gentry and the Sheriff chase him out in the open."

Shayne didn't pay any attention to him. Unarmed, he strode on toward the sprawling stone house, his face set and hard.

Gentry was spacing his men around to cover all exits. He saw Shayne's intention and called out gruffly, "Don't, Mike. No need for anybody to get hurt now. We'll smoke him out."

Shayne continued steadily forward. He mounted the wide stone steps, his heels pounding loud in the sudden stillness, and went on to a sagging screen door. He pulled it open and went in, squinting his eyes in the dim interior.

There was a stale odor in the room. It was cool and quiet inside the thick rock walls. A wide arched opening led into a big room on the right.

Shayne went in and saw Myrna Hastings sitting upright in a heavy chair fashioned of twisted mangrove roots. Her legs and arms were tightly bound to the chair and her mouth was sealed with adhesive tape. Her eyes rolled up at him wildly as he strode across the room, taking his knife from his pocket.

He slashed the cords binding her arms and legs, pulled her upright, and put his left arm around her. "This is going to hurt," he warned. "Set your mouth as tight as you can."

She nodded, and he ripped the adhesive loose in one jerk, then put his other arm around her. She clung to him and cried softly, violent sobs shaking her slight frame.

Shayne was looking around the room as he held her close. He gave a grunt of satisfaction when he saw a square of water-soaked canvas on the floor with a pile of straw and bottles on top of it. An empty bottle lay on its side and another stood open.

Shayne said, "Try to walk a little. Use your arms and legs and they'll limber up." He began to move her slowly forward.

She sobbed, "I'm all right. I knew you'd come, Mike."

She steadied herself with a hand on his shoulder as he leaned down to pick up the open bottle. He studied the water-soaked label and his eyes glinted. It was Monnet, vintage of 1926, and the bottle was half full. He drew in a long breath of the bouquet, then tilted it to Myrna's lips.

"Take a good drink of this," he told her. "Everything is all right now."

She swallowed obediently when the liquor reached her lips. Shayne chuckled and took the bottle away. "It's my turn now." He took a long, gurgling drink, then led her over to a dusty rattan couch.

A flush came to her cheeks. She sat down limply and Shayne got out two cigarettes. He put one between her lips and the other in his mouth, thumbnailed a match and lit both.

Myrna started violently when Gentry's voice bellowed at him from outside. "Shayne! What's happening in there?"

Shayne called back, "A lady and I are having a drink. Leave us alone." He laughed down into Myrna's bewildered face. "We're surrounded by a posse of detectives and deputy sheriffs," he explained. "They're summoning their courage to storm the place."

"What happened?" she asked tensely. "All that shooting. They were laying a trap for you, weren't they? I heard them talking before they went out. They were going to kill you because they thought you'd read the logbook. I told them you hadn't, but they wouldn't believe me. I was so frightened when I heard the shooting. I was sure you had walked right into the trap." She began to tremble violently.

Shayne patted her hand reassuringly. "I practically never walk into a trap."

They heard cautious, shuffling footsteps on the porch outside and Gentry's voice rumbling, "Mike, where are you?"

"In here," Shayne called. He put the bottle to his swollen lips again and took a long drink. He lowered it and grinned as Gentry moved in quietly with drawn gun, followed closely by the mustached sheriff with his rifle cocked and ready.

"You look," Shayne chuckled, "like the last two of the Mohicans."

Gentry straightened his bulky body and glared across the dim room at Shayne and the girl.

"What the devil's going on? Who's this and how did she get here?"

Shayne said, "You met Miss Hastings last night, Will. Why don't you and Leatherstockings run along down to the cellar and look for Grossman? That's where Pug said he was."

Other men began to file cautiously into the room. Gentry turned to them and growled, "Find the cellar stairs. And take it easy. Grossman isn't the kind to be taken alive." He crossed the room heavily. "And you can start talking, Mike. What are you and this girl up to?"

"What can we do—with so many people prowling around?"

Gentry snorted, "What kind of a run-around am I getting?"

Shayne said, "You're giving it to yourself, whatever it is. I didn't invite you out here."

"No. You thought you were pulling a fast one—covering up for a murderer to get a rake-off on a bunch of smuggled liquor. By God, Shayne, you can't wiggle out of this one."

Shayne drank from the bottle again. "It's mighty good liquor. Next time you send a stool to cover the switchboard at my hotel don't use a guy with d-i-c-k written all over him."

Gentry swallowed his anger. "I wondered who sent Tim Rourke to me with a tip that there'd be fireworks. You can't deny you brought along a couple of gunmen to wipe out Grossman and his gang to keep the stuff for yourself. If I hadn't overheard the call and beat it out here you might have pulled it off."

Shayne chuckled and sank down on the couch beside Myrna. "How much of the deal do you know?" he asked Gentry.

"Plenty. I always suspected Captain Samuels was running stuff for Grossman when he lost his boat in 1930. That's why Grossman killed him last night. Fighting over division of the liquor that was cached here when Grossman was sent up."

"You're fairly close," Shayne admitted. "When you find Grossman—"

"He'll talk," Gentry promised.

"Want to bet on it?" Shayne's eyes were very bright.

"I never bet with you. With your damned shenanigans . . . What's this girl got to do with it? One of Grossman's little friends?"

"She wanted to see a detective in action," Shayne replied.

Shayne set the bottle on the floor and sat up straighter when the detective trotted in and reported excitedly, "We've searched the cellar and the whole house, Chief. Not another soul here."

Gentry began to curse luridly. Shayne stood up and interrupted him. "I don't think your men knew where to look in the cellar. Let's take another look."

When they reached the cellar stairs, Rourke was coming up with a flashlight in his hand. "No soap," he reported to Shayne. "Grossman must have made his getaway when we left the house uncovered to see what the shooting was about."

"Your fault," Gentry accused Shayne bitterly. "If we don't pick him up I'm slapping a charge of obstructing justice on you."

Shayne took the flashlight from Rourke. He led the way down

into a small dank furnace room with a dirt floor. He flashed the light around, then walked over to a small rectangular area where the ground showed signs of having recently been disturbed. "Try digging here, but don't blame me if Grossman doesn't talk when you find him."

"There?" Gentry gagged over the word. "You mean he's dead?"

"Hell, he had to be dead, Will. Nothing else made any sense."

"You mean nothing *makes* sense," Gentry said perplexedly.

Shayne sighed and said, "I'll draw you a few pictures. One question first, though. Did Guildford make a phone call between the time you checked for Miss Hastings at the Crestwood last night and before you came to my place looking for her?"

"Guildford? The lawyer?" Gentry's voice intoned his bewilderment. "What the hell has he got to do with it?"

"Did he?" Shayne persisted.

"Well, yes, I think he did, come to think of it. He called his home from the public booth in the Crestwood after we learned the girl wasn't in. I suggested that we see you, and he didn't want his wife to worry if he got home later than she expected."

Shayne nodded. "He said he called his wife. But you didn't go in the booth with him and listen in on his conversation?"

"Of course not," Gentry sputtered.

Shayne took his time about lighting a cigarette, then continued: "If you had, you would have heard him calling Pug or Slim at Chunky's joint and telling them to hang around the Crestwood until Myrna Hastings came in . . . then grab her. He was covering every angle," Shayne went on earnestly, "after he discovered that empty hiding place in the Captain's bedroom. He knew the Captain knew the location of the liquor cache after Samuels brought in a case and sold it for a hundred bucks to make a payment on the mortgage. And when the poor old guy died while he was torturing him, he must have been frantic for fear he'd never find the stuff."

"Are you talking about Mr. Guildford, the attorney?"

"Yeh." Shayne's eyes were bleak. "Leroy P. Guildford, once

a junior member of the firm of Leland and Parker. They special-
ized in criminal practice and defended John Grossman in 1930.
He must have known of the existence of the liquor cache all the
time, but it wasn't worth much until the recent liquor shortage,
and Captain Samuels wouldn't play ball with him. After he killed
Grossman, Samuels was his only chance to learn where the stuff
was hidden."

"Are you saying Guildford killed Grossman?"

"Sure. Or had Pug and Slim do the job for him. He brought
Grossman out here last Tuesday, then went to Samuels and told
him what had happened and suggested that with Grossman dead
they might as well split the liquor."

"But Grossman talked to you over the phone just this morning," Gentry argued.

Shayne shook his head. "I knew that couldn't be Grossman.
He *had* to be dead. The only person it could be was Guildford, dis-
guising his voice to lure me out here so he could get rid of the only
two people who knew about the logbook and the liquor."

"Why," asked Gentry with forced calm, "did Grossman *have*
to be dead?"

"Nothing else made sense." Shayne spread out his big hands.
"Captain Samuels knew where the liquor was all the time and
he was practically starving and in debt, yet he never touched it.
Why? Because he was an honorable man and it didn't belong to
him. Why, then, would he suddenly forget his scruples and sell a
case? Because Grossman was dead and it no longer belonged to
anybody."

Gentry said gruffly, "My head's going around. Maybe it's this
air down here."

Back in the big room upstairs, Shayne knelt beside the bottles
and straw. "Do you know where this came from, Myrna?"

"Certainly. Those men fished it up out of the lagoon this morning, all sewed up in canvas. They talked about it in front of me. I
think they planned to kill me, so they didn't care what I heard."

"What did they say about it?" Shayne was shaking the bottles free of their straw casings and lining them up on the floor.

"It's all in the bottom of the lagoon. A whole boatload. Just where Captain Samuels and his crew dumped it overboard as he described in his logbook. That's why the authorities could never find any liquor here when they raided the place, the men said."

Shayne got up with a bottle dangling from each knobby hand. He slipped them into the side pockets of his pants as Detective Yancy came hurrying in to tell Gentry excitedly: "We got the whole story from that man before he died. Grossman is dead, Chief. Buried in the cellar. And the real guy is—"

"I know," said Gentry wearily. "Get to a telephone and have Guildford rounded up right away."

"What are you doing?" Gentry demanded as he turned in time to see Shayne slide a third and fourth bottle into his hip pockets.

"Making hay while the sun shines," Shayne said, stooping to get two more bottles from the floor. "With you horning in I won't have any chance at all at that stuff under the water." He put two more bottles in his coat pockets and reached for two more, looking wistfully at the remaining bottles on the floor. "This is the only fee I can collect on this case."

Myrna Hastings laughed delightedly. "I can carry a few for you."

Gentry turned away and said gruffly, "There'd better be a couple of bottles left for evidence when the revenue men get here." He strode out, and Shayne began stacking bottles in Myrna's arms.

"You owe me something," he told her, "for the turn I got when I went back to my apartment and found the back door unlocked and the place burgled. I thought you were mixed up in it and your feature story was just a blind."

She laughed as she swayed slightly under the weight of eight bottles. "I wondered if you'd suspect me after they found the key and I admitted that it was to the back door of your apartment. I'm afraid they thought I was an immoral girl. I hated to have them take the key away from me," she ended gravely.

Shayne promised, "I'll give you another one," and they staggered out with as many bottles as both could carry.

PART II

PERILOUS STREETS, LETHAL CAUSEWAYS

STREET 8 (EXCERPT)

BY DOUGLAS FAIRBAIRN

Little Havana

(Originally published in 1977)

B obby lit a cigarette, then dialed the number.

"Hello?"

"Mrs. Pérez?"

"*Sí*—" She sounded terrified.

"Mrs. Pérez, this is Bobby Mead—"

"Señor Mead?"

"*Sí*. Mrs. Pérez, I have to talk to you for a minute about Oscar. Okay? When he first came to work for me he worked hard, he made deals for me, he sold *carros* for me, I was happy, he was happy. Now he don't make no deals no more, don't sell no *carros* no more. All he wants to do is argue with people and yell at people, and I'm not happy and he's not happy. I want you to tell me what's wrong with him."

The woman let out a weird sound, like a long low howl, and dropped the phone. In the background Bobby could hear a TV and some kids yelling. Mrs. Pérez came back. "Señor Mead!" she cried. "I tell you what's wrong with him! Pache! Pache! Pache!"

"Yeah," Bobby said. "Pache, Pache, Pache . . ."

"He hate Ramón Pache, Señor Mead!'"

"I know he hate Ramón Pache," Bobby said. "Why he hate him so much?"

"La Estrella bomb!"

"What?"

"La Estrella bomb!"

"La Estrella bomb?"

Mrs. Pérez was crying. "*Sí*, La Estrella bomb!"

"You mean the restaurant on Flagler Street that got bombed a few weeks ago?"

"*Sí*, La Estrella bomb! La Estrella owner Juan y Ricardo Azuela. Juan y Ricardo Azuela my Oscar best friend since long time. Since Cuba time. Since Havana time. Then La Estrella bomb. Ricardo die. Juan no legs no more, no eyes no more. Oscar know Ramón Pache done it, want to tell everybody Ramón Pache done it—"

How he know Ramón Pache done it?" Bobby said.

"Ah, Señor Mead, he know, he know! And now he don't feel good no more. He's problem come back. No sleep no more, no eat no more. Same 1968. Chicago. Dr. Martinez give him pills. No good. Still no eat no more, no sleep no more. One year with pills no good. St. Louis hospital one year. Then feel good. No pills. Work Pepsi, Texaco, Sears, feel good. Then he's problem come back again. Get fire. Go to work Kentucky Fry Chicken. Get fire. Hospital one year more. Come to Miami. Feel good. Work Walgreen, Suave Shoe, Firestone, Dixie Ford. Work you. Feel good. No pills. Work hard. Make money. Then La Estrella bomb! He's problem come back! Make trouble you! Make trouble Dixie Ford! No sleep! No eat! Talk, talk, talk! Pache, Pache, Pache! I think Dixie Ford gonna fire him! You gonna fire him?"

"I don't know," Bobby said. "Maybe."

"Señor Mead, no fire him!" Mrs. Pérez wailed. "Please no fire him!"

"I don't need this," Bobby said. "*Entiende?* I don't need no more trouble than I already got. *Entiende?*"

"Please no fire my Oscar, Señor Mead!"

Bobby listened to her sobbing for a minute. "Okay, okay, I no fire him," he said.

In the office there was a cluttered desk, a swivel chair behind the desk, file cabinets, miscellaneous junk everywhere, four arm-chairs, all different, two straight-backed chairs, a battered sofa. In one corner there was a small black-and-white TV with the sound off but on the screen a game show. The walls were covered with old calendars, framed city, county and state licenses and permits and a big photomural of the "Grand Opening" of the lot seven years ago. Tacked to the wall behind the swivel chair was a front page of the *Miami Herald* with a big color picture of a young girl, tanned almost black, barefoot, with dark blond hair hanging down to her hips, wearing cutoff Levi's shorts, a white T-shirt that was much too small for her and showed off her perfect braless breasts and her flat tanned belly. She stood on the narrow median in the midst of six lanes of traffic on the Dixie Highway, smiling, in the classic flower-girl's pose, her legs wide apart, one hand on her hip, the other holding a bunch of carnations high over her head.

Bobby sat at his desk, gazing through the open doors at the lot. After a while he took a bottle of Bacardi out of the bottom drawer of the desk and went out and got a Coke from the machine and made himself a rum and Coke. Then he picked up the phone and dialed a number. The number rang ten times before a guy answered it.

"Is Sara Mead around?" Bobby asked.

"No, she ain't here," the guy said.

"Do you know where she is?" Bobby said.

The guy made him repeat the question twice. There was a lot of music in the background.

"Do you know where she is?"

"No, I don't know where she is."

"Can you tell me when you saw her last?"

"Saw her last? I don't remember."

"Listen, this is important," Bobby said. "I've got to get in touch with her. Do you have any idea where I could reach her?"

"Hey!" the guy yelled furiously. "Get the fuck out of my life, will you? Asking me all these fucking questions! Am I asking you all these fucking questions? I don't even know who the fuck you are? So fuck off!"

Oscar came to work at a quarter of six. He came into the office and said hello to Bobby, but in a voice so low Bobby could barely hear him, and his face didn't look brown now but gray, and under the eyes it looked bruised and his eyes were misty. After he said hello he went back out and sat on some concrete blocks that had been piled up against the wall near the door of the garage and he seemed to have shrunk up like a wet dog inside his crisp khakis. Bobby stood in the doorway of the office and looked at Oscar. Jerry and Daryle came out of the garage, where they had been washing up and putting on their street clothes preparatory to going home. They both said hello to Oscar, and he nodded but didn't look at them. They came over to Bobby and Jerry gestured with his head back toward Oscar.

"He looks like he don't feel good, Bobby," he said.

"Yeah, I saw him," Bobby said.

Jerry and Daryle got into their cars and left, and Bobby went over to Oscar.

"*Qué tal, chico?*" he said.

Oscar shrugged.

"Are you okay?" Bobby said.

"Yeah, I'm okay, Bobby," Oscar said.

Bobby didn't know what to do, so he went back in the office and had another rum and Coke. Then a divorced guy who had been sent by a mutual friend arrived and Bobby spent over an hour trying to work out a deal for him. The guy had lost his job and his car and everything else because of the divorce and now his credit was so bad he couldn't even get financing for a junker. So Bobby sat there with him, smoking, talking to the guy, squinting in the glare of the overhead light, manipulating the figures over and over again, backwards and forwards, and always coming up with the same answer, no way, and with his stomach killing him because he knew that the net result of all this would probably be that one way or another it was going to cost him money, which was almost always the way it turned out when his friends sent him business, which was why he wished to Christ they wouldn't send him business.

He finally got rid of the guy by telling him that he would call a private party in the morning who might make him a loan on a car if he, Bobby, would guarantee it, which he said he would do as a favor to the mutual friend, so the guy went away, more or less happy, leaving Bobby with the pain in his stomach, thinking about Oscar again.

He went outside and looked around for Oscar, and saw him now over on the far side of the lot leaning against the front fender of Today's Special. It was dark now and the wind had shifted around to the northeast and it was turning cold after all.

Oscar had turned on the lights, and the bare white bulbs that hung from the wires crisscrossing the lot danced in the wind. This was always a favorite time of day for Bobby. Everything always looked so much better in the evening under the lights. The cars glistened. You couldn't see so clearly now all the dings and the scratches and the wrinkles and the rust and the peeling chrome and the recapped tires and the cheap paint jobs, and even the interiors of the cars looked plush and sexy the way they had looked when the cars had been new. Even the junkers improved—they looked devil-may-care, and the big striped umbrella in the middle of the front line of cars didn't show all the ripped seams and frayed edges in this light, and it wasn't so obvious that the two buildings on the lot, the office and the garage, were about ready for condemnation.

Bobby had always wanted to decorate the lot with colored lightbulbs and all the plastic propellers and windmills and streamers that he thought added so much excitement to the atmosphere of a used-car operation, but the trouble was that the minute a dealer went beyond plain white bulbs on the overhead wires the city said he was getting out of the realm of safety and into the realm of display, for which he had to get a special permit, and Bobby had never been able to persuade himself over the years that the razzle-dazzle would bring in enough business to justify all the extra expense—and now of course the whole idea was out of the question when he had to cut every corner just to keep his head above water. Still, sometimes be liked to think of how sharp the lot would look with the colored lights and the red and green and yellow propellers and windmills and streamers all spinning and fluttering.

He went over to Oscar.

"*Hombre*, I have to tell you something," he said. "I wasn't going to tell you but now I think I better. I was talking to a guy today. He says you're in a lot of trouble with some people he knows because of the things you've been saying about the FCU and Ramón Pache."

Oscar looked around. "What kind of a guy?" he said. "A Cuban?"

"No, a gringo," Bobby said. "He said they're getting ready to shut you up, permanently."

Oscar started wiping the back of his hand across his mouth, and he started sweating even in the cold wind. "Who's the guy?" he said.

"Mike Duran," Bobby said. "Does that mean anything to you?"

Oscar shook his head.

"I sold him a car once," Bobby said. "That's all I know about him. But I have a feeling he knows what he's talking about."

Oscar looked at the face on the billboard across the road. "They know how to get you," he said bitterly. He turned and started to walk away very quickly with his head down and then stopped abruptly and stood making futile gestures as if he had run into a cobweb.

"I want to close up," Bobby said across the distance between them.

Oscar looked back. "Close up?"

"Yeah," Bobby said. "Right now."

"Bobby, don't do that to me," Oscar said, returning, looking desperate. "See, I have to be here tonight. I've got a guy coming on the Dodge. He was here last night and said he would definitely come back tonight. Then I've got another guy coming tonight on the Galaxie, definitely. So I could write two deals tonight. And then I know a guy who likes the Rambler—"

"I want to close up," Bobby said. "If they want these cars bad enough they'll come back."

"You're afraid they're going to bomb this place, aren't you?" Oscar said, his voice quivering, spitting a little over his words. "Same at Dixie. That's what I mean when I say they know how to get you. See, I got fired at Dixie Ford today."

"Shit," Bobby said.

"They gave me two weeks' pay and told me not to come back. They said it was the economy, but I think they heard the same thing you did today. Now they're afraid of getting bombed, just like you. When I went home and told Maria she got sick. She told me you called her, what you said—and then all of a sudden, Bobby, I see the truth. The truth is I can't hurt Ramón Pache even a little bit no matter what I do, but he can hurt me plenty. I can't got nobody to march with me down 8th Street—they won't even listen to me when I try to tell them the truth about Pache and the FCU. And I know I can never get close enough to him to shoot him. But he can bomb Dixie Ford and bomb you and kill me and my wife and kids or do anything else he feels like doing. So you know what I do today? I make a very big decision—maybe the biggest decision of my whole life. This is what I decided, and this I promise my wife and now I promise you too—that I will never talk against Ramón Pache no more, never talk against the FCU no more. All of that I throw out of my mind, because what good does it do anyway? From now on, if you will allow me, I will just work hard and try to sell a lot of cars."

"Yeah," Bobby said, "but what if it's too late?"

Oscar frowned and then moved away and leaned against the

fender of a car with his arms folded tightly across his chest and his head lowered.

"Want a drink?" Bobby asked.

"Okay," Oscar said.

Bobby made them each a rum and Coke and they stood in front of the office door with their drinks, watching the cars going by on 8th Street. Three Cuban kids were having a game of tag between the cars at the far end of the lot, and somewhere off in the distance a radio was playing "Cuando salí de Cuba."

"How do you know Pache killed your friends?" Bobby asked.

"The Death Squad has killed twenty-eight people in the past three and a half months. They were all known enemies of Ramón Pache, like Juan and Ricardo Azuela. So?"

A car drove onto the lot.

"That's the guy on the Dodge," Oscar said.

Bobby nodded. "Go get him."

"And then?"

"Yeah, you can stay open tonight if you want to," Bobby said.

"*Muchísimas gracias,*" Oscar said.

"Are you afraid?"

Oscar hesitated. "Yes, I'm afraid," he said. "But I'm going to pray to God that I can get through tonight okay. And if I get through tonight I'm going to pray to God that they'll see I ain't talking against them no more and that maybe after a while they'll just forget about me."

"Call me if anything happens," Bobby said. "And stay in the office as much as you can. Watch TV, keep warm, okay?"

Bobby climbed into a 1967 Lincoln Continental convertible from his back line that had no paint, no seat covers, no muffler, no hubcaps, no top and no valid inspection sticker and drove it across the sidewalk and off the curb and headed east down 8th Street, in the wild Cuban traffic, between the sidewalks crowded with Cubans, past all the brightly lighted Cuban shops and restaurants.

Everywhere there were signs and posters and spray-painted graffiti saying *VIVA EL FCU!* and *EL FCU ES LA RESPUESTA!* and *PACHE! PACHE! PACHE!*

Then he was out of Little Havana, climbing the ramp to I-95, then gliding swiftly on the expressway past downtown Miami. The streets below the expressway, shimmering in the pink glow of the sodium vapor lights, were deserted. The people in the cars on the expressway looked down on an empty city flooded with pink light. The narrow river that wound through the city didn't look like a river from up there but a crack in the earth, into which, perhaps, all the people who were not down there on the streets had fallen. The wide bay in the distance, that separated Miami from Miami Beach, didn't look like a bay from up there either but a dark plain stretching away to the east.

Bobby took the first Miami Beach exit off I-95 and the ramp came down on the MacArthur Causeway. Then the skyline of Miami was behind him and he was racing along beside the main ship channel of the port of Miami, the cruise ships in a row across the channel at Dodge Island, flags whipping in the wind, searchlighted funnels, people strolling on the decks, colored lights and calypso bands playing on the stern, each ship a bright city of lights in itself. Out in the channel small fishing boats were plunging against the current in the darkness, their masthead lights bobbing resolutely toward the sea buoy miles away. The cars on the causeway hurtled dangerously close to the channel on the big curve where the seaplanes in the Bahama Islands service nested like shore birds by the water's edge.

At the Miami Beach end of the causeway there were two ways to go—north toward Lincoln Road, Bal Harbor, the colossal condominiums, the convention hotels, the tourists, the bellhops, the front desks, the rental cars, the big money, or south to South Beach, a ghetto that has fiercely resisted change for fifty years and is still resisting but now finally is beginning to lose the battle—where almost everything, the streets, the apartments, the stores, the hotels, is old and shabby, where almost everybody used to be old and Jewish but now there are beginning to be large numbers of Cubans, young and old, and the two cultures seem to stand and gaze at each other dubiously.

When people asked Bobby why he lived on South Beach, he said, "When I was a kid I used to go over to South Beach on the bus from Miami to go swimming because I loved the beach there. South Beach had the best beach on Miami Beach then and it still has the best beach on Miami Beach now. When I was a kid I always thought that when I grew up I would like to live in one of the hotels on South Beach that are right on the beach itself, and the one I thought I would most like to live in was the Seabreeze. So when my daughter Sara wanted to go off and live on her own down in the Grove a couple of years ago I sold my house in Miami and moved to South Beach, and now I'm living in the Seabreeze, and I'm happy there. The same hotels are there that were there when I was a kid, the same stores, the same movies, the same streets, even some of the same people. And I like the people. I feel at home with them. They have what's called a siege mentality. Everything's closing in on them, the big-time real-estate operators, the city and county politicians, the federal government, the department of this and the department of that, even the Cubans now, and they all wish all these old Jews would drop dead tomorrow so they could come in and bulldoze every building that stands on South Beach right into the bay and start all over again with the condominiums and the high-rises. But these people are tough. They'll never surrender. They give ground inch by inch, and they know how to vote and how to sue and how to picket and how to nag and how to kvetch and how to obstruct."

Bobby had trouble finding a place to park the Continental near the Seabreeze and finally had to squeeze it into an alley two blocks away. Walking back toward the hotel he passed a lot of old people who were moving along slowly and carefully, some of them clinging to each other as if they were on ice. All the little hotels that he passed had verandas, and people sat in rows on the verandas talking to each other and to people going by on the sidewalk, or played cards and dominoes. It was possible to look through the windows of the hotels into the ground-floor rooms, and they were bare, with hot plates on the bureaus, no pictures on the walls, ceiling lights burning, bathing suits hung up to dry on coat hangers in the windows.

The veranda at the Seabreeze was like all the others but the lights were brighter. Out there it was like daylight. The card players and the people sitting in the rows of chairs waved to Bobby as he came up the steps and he waved back to them and went on into the lobby, a garish, windswept room where a few chairs were arranged theater-style in front of a color TV. Two small old women sat in the chairs, as far apart from each other as possible, watching a police show. A terrific wind sailed through the lobby from a door at the far end of the main hallway that opened onto the beach. The wind blew ashes out of ashtrays, rolled up the rug, made newspapers fly out the door, fluttered the notices that were tacked up on the bulletin board next to the reception desk.

Bobby went to the desk and leaned over it to get a view of the geezer minding the switchboard, Lester Katz.

"Katz, any calls for me?" Bobby asked.

"No, Mead," Katz said, not bothering to look up from his *Miami News*.

"It's turning goddamn cold," Bobby said.

"Yeah," Katz said, still not looking up. "Next year I'm going south for the winter."

Bobby lived on the second floor, in one of the rooms that faced the sea. When he stepped out of the elevator the first thing he saw was a big black rat. The rat saw him too but didn't pay much attention. He was like a cop, going along the hall checking each door to see if it had been left open a crack. He kept right on checking nonchalantly until Bobby threw a shoe at him, and then he ducked into a utility room.

Bobby had to push against the wind when be opened his door and had to hold on to the door firmly to keep it from getting away from him and slamming shut after he got inside. His room was full of the wind, which blew in through a big hole in one of the glass doors that opened on his balcony. His room was much like the rooms he had passed on his way to the Seabreeze, small and bare and decrepit. The difference was that since he was an aristocrat with an oceanfront room he had a balcony where he could hang his bathing suit over the back of an aluminum chair to dry instead of on a coat hanger in a window, and he could lean on his railing and look at the ocean.

The glass doors were caked with salt and everything in the room was sticky with salt, and there was fine sand in all the corners and crevices. Bobby went out on the balcony and picked up his bathing suit from the sandy comer where it had blown after it had dried on the back of a chair. Then he went back into his room and took off his canary-yellow slacks and flowered shirt and hung them up carefully in the closet out of the wind.

He put on his bathing suit and sandals and took a towel and went down the back stairway to the beach. There was no moon and at first he couldn't see anything ahead of him but the white-caps out on the black ocean. He slogged through the soft sand toward the water, bent over against the wind and just trying to keep from running into any of the metal wastebaskets and scattered palm trees that he knew were in his way. He beard voices coming toward him and a pack of Cuban kids came out of the night, laughing and yelling, and ran past him, and he only saw them as white blurs for an instant before they were swallowed up in the night again and their voices went with them. Then his eyes got more used to the darkness and he saw the empty lifeguard's box off to his right and a few old people standing looking at the waves, holding on to their hair or their hats with one hand and with the other holding their coats closed at the throat. The combers rolled in and pounded the beach and rose up in the clouds of foam before falling back. But they were not the great waves of Atlantic City or Cape Fear. For one thing the water at this end of Miami Beach was quite shallow for a long way out, with long sand bars that kept big waves from building up, and besides, far away, past the Gulf Stream, the islands of the Bahamas took the full force of the Atlantic swells and broke them up on their countless reefs.

When Bobby reached the hard wet sand near the water's edge he stood for a moment looking around. To his left was the line of hotels and condominiums that formed a solid chain of lights along the shore all the way north to Palm Beach and beyond. To his right was South Beach, the ghetto, the old concrete fishing pier, that used to be covered over in the beginning and was the home of Minsky's Burlesque but now was just the place where mostly old Jews and old Cubans stood all day and maybe half the night trying to catch a fish so they wouldn't have to buy a fish, then the bright lights of the Miami Beach Kennel Club, and after that a long expanse of empty beach terminating in the jetties with their huge jumbled rocks, between which raced the deep, dark, silent current of the main ship channel.

Bobby threw himself into the waves and when he surfaced at the end of his dive he began swimming straight out to sea. He swam every night when he came home from work in all but the very roughest seas and on all but the coldest days. He knew it was dangerous to swim far out when there were no lifeguards on duty and with the water full of loose timber and orange crates and jellyfish and Portuguese men-of-war as well as raw sewage, but he was a strong swimmer and he was never afraid in the water.

He swam for about half an hour and when he returned to the beach he found that he had been pulled a long way north by the current and he had to trudge back along the beach to his hotel, where he took a shower in fresh water downstairs and dried off. Then, up in his room, he put on a T-shirt and a pair of pants and sat down on the bed and made a call.

"Hello?" A black guy.

"Listen, have you seen Sara Mead around?"

"Who is this?"

"A friend of hers."

"Well, I don't know anybody by that name."

"She said I could call this number."

"Did she say a lot about me?"

"She didn't say anything about you."

The black guy just breathed for a while.

"What's her name again?"

"Sara Mead."

"Okay, that one ain't around."

"Do you know where I could reach her? This is important."

"I heard she's in Nassau."

"Nassau?"

"Yeah, Nassau. Hey, and listen, if you happen to see her before I do, call me, hear? And I'll come right over and kick the shit out of her."

"Why?"

"Huh?"

"Why do you want to kick the shit out of her?"

"Don't worry about that. Just call me, hear?" The black guy hung up.

Bobby went downstairs and stood on the veranda, and saw Max Lorman wave to him. Max was seventy-six years old and had lost his wife two years before. He was a very formal man, always wearing a matching jacket and tie when he took the air on the veranda. Tonight he was wearing his plaid jacket and tie, with white duck pants and black-and-white shoes. He sat alone, as usual, apart from the rows of chairs and the card players and kibitzers, and Bobby went over and sat next to him.

"Bobby, something funny happened to me today," Max said. "I was talking to some newcomers and they refused to believe that trolley cars were still running on Miami Beach in 1938. They laughed at me. But you remember, don't you?"

"Sure, I remember," Bobby said.

Max chuckled. "'Newcomers,'" he said. "They think everything was always the same around here as it is right now. The trolley cars turned at Second Street and went past the Leonard Hotel and then circled back to Fifth Street and then from there went back on over the causeway to Miami."

"The County Causeway, of course," Bobby said.

Max grinned appreciatively. "Correct, the County Causeway," he said. "It wasn't renamed the MacArthur Causeway until the war. And in between trolleys there was the jitneys."

"That's right, in between trolleys there was the jitneys," Bobby said.

"Newcomers just refuse to take you seriously when you try to tell them anything about the way Miami Beach used to be," Max said. "They refuse to take you seriously when you try to tell them we used to be able to play the horses right there on the beach at First Street. Remember that board room they had right on the beach in the thirties, Bobby? You could come in there in your bathing suit and all covered with sand and everything and nobody said nothing. And there would be a guy up on a stepladder writing in the entries at the Fair Grounds or Aqueduct or wherever they happened to be running at the time, on this big blackboard. The minimum bet was fifty cents and there was a free lunch. No cops to worry about. They could care less in those days. You could just as well have been sitting around Bache & Company as far as those cops were concerned. But these newcomers just look at you when you tell them stuff like that. Tell them that up past Fortieth Street in 1939 there was still only private homes along the beach and see what kind of a reaction you get. Tell them that in 1942 Bal Harbor was just a great big Army camp and see what kind of a reaction you get. But you remember, don't you, Bobby?"

"Sure, I remember," Bobby said.

"All that stuff," Max said dreamily. Then he looked at Bobby.

"Say, how old were you in 1942, anyway? I'll bet you were just a little kid, weren't you?"

"Yeah, but I remember all that," Bobby said.

Suddenly Max stood up and excused himself, saying that he had to heed the call of nature. He had to heed the call of nature about every half hour or so, because of his kidneys, which was why he never could stray too far from the Seabreeze.

Bobby had dinner at a little restaurant on Washington Avenue that had a sign in the window saying, *The Best Arroz con Pollo on Miami Beach.* Then he went on down to the First Street pier. Halfway out on the pier was Senior Citizen Friendship Corner Number One, where about twenty seniors were sitting on the rows of wooden benches listening to a very old guy named Mr. Haber who was up on the stage singing into a dead microphone. The cold wind, which was turning colder all the time, was broken somewhat by the green concrete doghouse behind the stage where Officer Al Deutsch of the Miami Beach Police Department, who was in charge of the evening programs at Friendship Corner Number One, stored the microphone and the amplifiers and the flags when they were not in use. Officer Al, middle-aged, seriously overweight, sweating heavily in spite of the cold wind up there on the stage between the big American flag on the left and the small Israeli flag on the right, in his full uniform and harness, was trying frantically to get the microphone back into operation. But all he could seem to get out of it was an occasional piercing shriek. Mr. Haber, coming to the end of his Jerome Kern medley, either didn't know that he didn't have any mike or didn't care, but his thin voice could barely be heard over the pounding of the waves under the pier.

Just as Mr. Haber wound up, Officer Al finally fixed the microphone.

"All right, everybody," Officer Al said, "Let's really hear it for Mr. Haber, who had to work under extremely difficult conditions tonight but still turned in another fabulous performance!"

There was almost no applause but Mr. Haber bowed deeply and thanked everyone anyway. Then Officer Al introduced the next performer, Mrs. Feldman, who wore a long white summer dress embroidered with tiny pink flowers, and blue tennis shoes with white ankle socks. She sang a very short song in Yiddish and was followed by Mrs. Rimsky in a lime-green pantsuit who sang a very long song in Polish and tried to get everybody to come in on the chorus, with no success.

After that, Officer Al took over the microphone and wrapped up the program. "Okay, I guess that's all for tonight," he said. "Except to say that I think I can speak for us all when I say that we had an excellent time and certainly enjoyed all the fabulous entertainment. So everybody stay warm and keep out of trouble so I don't have to come around and arrest you, and, hopefully, we'll all see each other here again next Wednesday."

Al Deutsch and Bobby Mead had gone to Shenandoah Junior High together. Then Al had played center on the Miami High teams on which Bobby had played halfback. Now one was a cop who had never made it and the other was a used-car dealer who had never made it.

Bobby helped Al put away the microphone and the amplifiers and the flags and then they went out to the end of the pier, where the old Cubans and Jews were fishing, and leaned against the wall looking at the lights along the coast. Even on a filthy night like this the fishermen had total concentration. The fact that the wind was blowing half a gale and they were wet to the skin from the flying spray meant nothing to them. They kept on reeling in and squatting down in the lee of the wall to bait their hooks and then throwing out their lines again as if they were getting paid a hundred dollars an hour to do it.

There was a commotion when one of the fishermen suddenly got a big strike. The old guy was standing right under a pier light when the fish hit and his face looked white and scared and popeyed as if he was about to have a heart attack, but when anybody went near him to try to help him he snarled at them and yelled at them to keep away. He wore a plastic raincoat, regular brown leather street shoes with no socks, short pants that came down below his knees and looked as if they were really long pants that had been cut off and hemmed, a Miami Dolphins T-shirt with the number 12 and the name *GRIESE* on the back, and a black beret. The fish on his line must have been very big because it bent his pole almost double, but he was fighting it awkwardly and really didn't seem to know what he was doing, and then his line broke and his feet slipped out from under him on the slick concrete and he fell down on one knee. Still he wouldn't let anybody come near him to try to help him, and when people yelled at him that it had probably just been a shark anyway he yelled back at them, "Beat it! Beat it!"

"Big news, Bobby," Al said. "We took a vote tonight before you got here. We decided to make you an honorary Jew."

"It couldn't happen to a nicer guy," Bobby said.

"Yeah, I knew you'd be real pleased," Al said. "Well, you live on South Beach, so you should be one thing or the other, a Cuban or a Jew. Listen, would you rather be a Cuban?"

"No, I think I'll be a Jew," Bobby said.

"Beautiful," Al said. "Just think, from now on you can eat belly lox any time you want to, no questions asked. From now on you can dance the hora any time you want to, no questions asked. From now on you can kvetch about the goddamn goyim any time you want to, no questions asked. Is this a fabulous deal or isn't it?"

"It's a fabulous deal," Bobby said.

"Is that why you look so happy?" Al asked.

"Yeah, that's why I look so happy."

"Hey, you're not having second thoughts, are you? Are you sure you wouldn't rather be a Cuban? Get to eat *medianoches* any time you want to, no questions asked? Dance the rumba? Bitch about the goddamn Anglos?"

"No, I'll be a Jew," Bobby said.

"Hey, nice to have you aboard," Al said, sticking out his hand.

SATURDAY NIGHT SPECIAL

BY CHARLES WILLEFORD

Kendall

(Originally published in 1988)

I t started out as kind of a joke, and then it wasn't funny anymore because money became involved. Deep down, nothing
about money is funny.

There were four of us at the pool: Eddie Miller, Don Luchessi,
Hank Norton, and me—Larry Dolman. It was just beginning to
get dark, but the air was still hot and muggy and there was hardly
any breeze. We were sitting around the circular, aluminum table in
our wet trunks. Hank had brought down a plastic pitcher of vodka
martinis, a cupful of olives, and a half-dozen Dixie cups. That is
one of the few rules at Dade Towers: it's all right to eat and drink
around the pool so long as only plastic or paper cups and plates
are used.

Dade Towers is a singles-only apartment house, and it's only
one year old. What I mean by "singles-only" is that only single
men and women are allowed to rent here. This is a fairly recent
idea in Miami, but it has caught on fast, and a lot of new singles-
only apartments are springing up all over Dade County. Dade
Towers doesn't have any two- or three-bedroom apartments at all.
If a resident gets married, or even if a man wants to bring a woman
in to live with him, out he goes. They won't let two men share an
apartment, either. That's a fruitless effort to keep gays out. But
there are only two or three circumspect gays in the 120-apartment
complex, and they don't bother anyone in the building. The rents
are on the high side, and all apartments are rented unfurnished.

The rules are relaxed for women, and two women are allowed to share one apartment. That rule is reasonable, because women in Miami don't earn as much money as men. And by letting two women share a pad, the male/female ratio is evened out. So some of the one-bedrooms have two stewardesses, or two secretaries, living together. Other women, who have more money, like school teachers, young divorcées, and nurses, usually make do with efficiencies. If a man wanted to, he could get all of the women he wanted simply by hanging around the pool.

Under different circumstances, I don't think Don, Hank, Eddie and I would have become such good friends. But the four of us were all charter members, so to speak, the first four tenants to move into Dade Towers when it opened. And now, after a solid year together, we were tight. We swam in the pool, went to movies together, asked each other for advice on the broads we took out, played poker one or two nights a month, and had a good time, in general, without any major fights or arguments. In other words, we truly lived the good life in Miami.

Eddie Miller is an ex–Air Force pilot. After he got out of the service, he managed to get taken on as a 727 copilot. Flying is just about all Eddie cares about, and eventually he'll be a captain. In the meantime (he only flies twenty hours a week), Eddie studies at the University of Miami for his state real estate exam. That's what many of the airline pilots do in their spare time: they sell real estate. And some of them make more money selling real estate than they do as pilots, even though real estate is a cutthroat racket in Dade County.

Hank Norton has an AB in psychology from the University of Michigan. He has a beautiful job in Miami as a detail man, or salesman, for a national pharmaceutical firm. He only works about ten or fifteen hours a week, when he works at all, and he still has the best sales record in the US for his company. As the top detail man in the field the year before, his company gave him a two-week, all-expenses-paid vacation to Acapulco. He is a good-looking guy, with carefully barbered blond hair and dark, Prussian-blue eyes. He is the best cocksman of the four, too. Hank probably gets more strange in a single month than the rest of us get in a year. He has an aura of noisy self-confidence, and white flashing teeth. His disingenuous smile works as well on the doctors he talks with as it does on women. He makes about twenty-five thousand a year, and he has the free use of a Galaxie, which is exchanged for a new model every two years. His Christmas bonus has never been less than two thousand, he claims.

Don Luchessi makes the most money. He is the Florida rep for a British silverware firm, and he could make much more money than he does if the firm in Great Britain could keep up with his orders. They are always two or three months behind in production and shipping, and Don spends a lot of time apologizing about the delays to the various department and jewelry stores he sells to. What with the fantastic increase of the Miami Cuban population, and the prosperity of the Cubans in general, Don's business has practically doubled in the last four years. Every Cuban who marries off a daughter (as well as her friends and relatives, of course) wants the girl to start off her married life with an expensive silver service. Nevertheless, even though Don makes a lot more money than the rest of us, he is paying child support for his seven-year-old daughter and giving his wife a damned generous monthly allowance besides. As a Catholic he is merely legally separated, not divorced, and although he hates his wife, we all figure that Don will take her back one of these days because he misses his daughter so much. At any rate, because of the money he gives to his wife, by the end of the year he doesn't average out with much more dough than the rest of us.

Insofar as I am concerned, what I considered to be a bad break at the time turned out to be fortuitous. I had majored in police science at the University of Florida, and I had taken a job as a policeman, all gung-ho to go, in Florence City, Florida, two weeks after I graduated. Florence City isn't too far from Orlando, and the small city has tripled in population during the last few years because of Disney World. After two years on the force I was eligible to take the sergeant's exam, which I passed, the first time out, with a 98. They were just starting to build Disney World at the time, and I knew that I was in a growth situation. The force would grow along with Florence City, and because I had a college degree I knew that I would soon be a lieutenant, and then a captain, within a damned short period of patrolman apprenticeship.

So here I was, all set for a sergeancy after only two years on the force. None of the other three men who took the exam with me was even close to my score. But what happened, I got caught with the new ethnic policy. Joe Persons, a nice enough guy, but a semiliterate near-moron, who had failed the exam for five years in a row, finally made a minimum passing score of 75. So the Board made him a sergeant instead of me because he was black. I was bitter, of course, but I was still willing to live with the decision and wait another year. Joe had been on the Florence City force for ten years, and if you took seniority into account, why not let him have it? I could afford to wait another year. But what happened was incredible. The chief, a sharp cracker from Bainbridge, Georgia, called me in and told me that I would be assigned to Sergeant Persons full-time to do his paperwork for him. I got hot about it, and quit then and there, without taking the time to think the matter out. What the chief was doing, in a tacit way, was making it up to me. In other words, the chief hadn't liked the Board's decision to make Joe Persons a sergeant instead of me any more than I had. By giving me the opportunity to do the sergeant's actual work, which Persons was incapable of handling, he was telling me that the next vacancy was as good as mine, and laying the groundwork to get rid of Sergeant Persons for inefficiency at the same time.

I figured all this out later, but by that time it was too late. I had resigned, and I was too proud to go back and apologize to the chief after some of the angry things I had said to him.

To shorten the story, although it still makes me sore to think about the raw deal I was handed in Florence City, I came down to Miami and landed a job with National Security as a senior security officer. In fact, they could hardly hire me quickly enough. National has offices in every major city in the United States, and someday—in a much shorter period than it would have taken me to become the chief of police in Florence City—I'll be the director of one of these offices. Most of the security officers that National employs are ex-cops, retired detectives usually, but none of them can write very well. They have to dictate their reports, which are typed later by the girls in the pool. If any of these reports ever got out cold, without being edited and rewritten, we would lose the business of the department store industry receiving that report in five minutes flat. That is what I do: I put these field reports into some semblance of readability. My boss, The Colonel, likes the way I write, and often picks up phrases from my reports. Once, when I wrote to an operator in Jacksonville about a missing housewife, I told him to "exhaust all resources." For about a month after that, The Colonel was ending all of his phone conversations with, "Exhaust all resources, exhaust all resources."

So down at National Security, I am a fair-haired boy. Four years ago I started at $10,000, and now I'm making $15,000. I can also tell, now, from the meetings that they have been asking me to sit in on lately, "just to listen," The Colonel said, that they are grooming me for a much better job than I have already.

If this were a report for National Security I would consider this background information as much too sketchy, and I would bounce it back to the operator. But this isn't a report, it's a record, and a record is handy to keep in my lockbox at the bank.

Who knows? I might need it someday. In Florida, the guilty party who spills everything to the State's Attorney *first* gets immunity . . .

We were on the second round of martinis when we started to talk about picking up women. Hank, being the acknowledged authority on this subject, threw out a good question. "Where, in Miami," Hank said, "is the easiest place to pick up some strange? I'm not saying the best, I'm talking about the easiest place."

"Big Daddy's," Eddie said.

I didn't say so, but I agreed with Eddie in my mind. There are Big Daddy's lounges all over Miami. Billboards all around Dade County show a picture of a guy and a girl sitting close together at a bar, right next to the bearded photo of Big Daddy himself, with a caption beneath the picture in lower-case Art type: *Big Daddy's— where you're never alone* . . . The message is clear enough. Any man who can't score in a Big Daddy's lounge has got a major hang-up of some kind.

"No," Hank said, pursing his lips. "I admit you can pick up a woman in Big Daddy's, but you don't always score. Right? In fact, you might pick up a loser, lay out five bucks or so in drinks, and then find her missing when you come back from taking a piss."

This was true enough; it had happened to me once, although I had never mentioned it to anyone.

"Think, now," Hank said. "Give me one surefire place to pick up a woman, where you'll score, I'll say, at least nine times out of ten."

"Bullshit," Don said. "Nobody scores nine times out of ten, including you, Hank."

"I never said I did," Hank said. "But I know of one place where you *can* score nine times out of ten. Any one of us at this table."

"Let's go," I said, leaping to my feet.

They all laughed.

"Sit down, Fuzz," Hank said. "Just because there is such a place, it doesn't mean you'll want to go. Come on, you guys— think."

"Is this a trick question?" Eddie said.

"No," Hank said, without smiling, "it's legitimate. And I'm not talking about call girls either, that is, if there're any left in Miami."

"Coconut Grove is pretty good," Eddie said.

"The Grove's always good," Hank agreed, "but it's not a single place, it's a group of different places. Well, I'm going to tell you anyway, so I'll spare you the suspense. The easiest place to pick up a fast lay in Miami is at the VD clinic."

We all laughed.

"You're full of it, Hank," Don said. "A girl who's just picked up the clap is going to be turned off men and sex for a long time."

"That's what I would have thought," Hank said. "But apparently it doesn't work that way. It was in the *Herald* the other day. The health official at the clinic was bitching about it. I don't remember his name, but I cut out the piece and I've got it up in my apartment. He said that most of the girls at the clinic are from sixteen to twenty-two, and the guys and girls get together in the waiting room to exchange addresses and phone numbers because they know they're safe. They've all been treated recently, so they know there's no danger of catching anything. Anyway, according to the *Herald*, they've brought in a psychologist to study the problem. The health official wants to put in separate waiting rooms to keep the men and women apart."

"Would you pick up a girl in a VD clinic?" Don asked Hank.

Hank laughed. "Not unless I was pretty damned hard up, I wouldn't. Okay. I'll show you guys the clipping later. Here's a tougher question. Where's the *hardest* place in Miami to pick up a woman?"

"The University of Miami Student Union," Eddie said solemnly.

We all laughed.

"Come on, Eddie," Hank said. "Play the game. This *is* a serious question."

"When a man really needs a piece of ass," I said, "any place he tries is hard."

"That's right," Eddie said. "When you've got a woman waiting for you in the sack, and you stop off for a beer, there'll be five or six broads all over you. But when you're really out there digging, desperate, there's nothing out there, man. Nothing."

"That's why I keep my small black book," Hank said.

"We aren't talking about friends, Hank," I said. "We're supposed to be talking about strange pussy."

"That's right. So where's the hardest place to pick up strange?"

"At church—on a Sunday," Eddie said.

"How long's it been since you've been to church?" Hank asked. "Hell, at church, the minister'll even introduce you to a nice girl if you point one out to him."

"But who wants a nice girl?" Eddie said.

"I do," Hank said. "In my book, a nice girl is one who guides it in."

"If that's true," I said, "every girl I've ever slept with has been a nice girl. Thanks, Hank, for making my day. Why don't we give up this stupid game, get something to eat, and go down to the White Shark and play some pool?"

"Wait a minute," Eddie said, "I'm still interested in the question. I want to know the answer so I can avoid going there and wasting my time."

"A determined man," Don said, "can pick up a woman anywhere, even at the International Airport. And you can rent rooms by the hour at the Airport Hotel."

"It isn't the airport," Hank said. "As you say, Don, the airport's not a bad place for pick-ups. A lot of women, usually in pairs, hang around the Roof Lounge watching the planes take off."

"Well I give up, Hank," I said. "I've had my two martinis, and if I don't eat something pretty soon, I'm liable to drink another. And on my third martini I've been known to hit my best friend—just to see him fall."

"Eighty-six the Fuzz," Eddie said. "Tell us, Hank." Eddie poured the last drink into his Dixie cup.

"Drive-in movies," Hank said.

"I don't get it," Don said. "What's so hard about picking up a woman at a drive-in, for Christ's sake? Guys take women to drive-ins all the time—"

"That's right," Hank said. "They *take* them there, and they pay their way in. So what're you going to do? Start talking to some woman while she's in her boyfriend's car, while he's got one arm around her neck and his left hand on her snatch?"

Eddie laughed. "Yeah! Don't do it, Don. The guy might have a gun in his glove compartment."

"I guess I wasn't thinking," Don said.

I thought about the idea for a moment. "I've only been to a drive-in by myself two or three times in my whole life," I said. "It's a place you don't go alone, usually, unless you want to catch a flick you've missed. The last time I went alone was to see *Two-Lane Blacktop*. I read the script when it came out in *Esquire*, and I really wanted to see the movie."

"I saw that," Eddie said. "Except for Warren Oates in the GTO, none of the other people in the movie could act."

"That isn't the point, Eddie," I said. "I didn't think the movie was so hot either, although the script was good. The point I'm trying to make is that the only reason I went to the drive-in alone was to see *Two-Lane Blacktop*, and it didn't come on until 1:05 a.m. Where're you going to find anyone to go to the drive-in with you at one in the morning? And when I didn't like the movie either, I wanted to kick myself in the ass."

"I don't think I've ever been to a drive-in alone," Don said. "Not that I remember, anyway."

"Well, I have," Hank said, "just like Larry. Some movies only play drive-ins, and if you don't catch them there you'll miss them altogether."

"I've been a few times, I guess," Eddie said, "and you'll always see a few guys sitting alone in their cars. But I've never seen a woman alone in a car at a drive-in, unless her boyfriend was getting something at the snack bar."

"Let me tick it off," Hank said. "First, if a woman's there, she's either with her parents, her husband, or her boyfriend. Second, no woman ever goes to a drive-in alone. They're afraid to, for some reason, even though a drive-in movie's safer than anyplace I know for a woman alone. Because, third, a man would be stupid to look for a broad at a drive-in when there're a thousand better places to pick one up."

"That's the toughest place, all right," I said. "It's impossible to pick up a woman at a drive-in."

Hank laughed. "No, it isn't impossible, Larry. It's hard, but it's not impossible."

"I say it's impossible," I repeated.

"Better than that," Eddie said, "I'm willing to bet ten bucks it's impossible."

Hank, shaking his head, laughed. "Ten isn't enough."

"Add another ten from me," I said.

"I'll make it thirty," Don said.

"You guys aren't serious," Hank said.

"If you don't think thirty bucks is serious enough," Eddie said, "I'll raise my ten to twenty."

"Add another ten," I said.

"And mine," Don said.

"Sixty dollars is fairly serious money," Hank said. "That's twice as much dough as I'd win from you guys shooting pool at the White Shark."

"Bullshit," Eddie said. "We've offered to bet you sixty hard ones that you can't pick up a broad at the drive-in. And we pick the drive-in."

"You guys really love me, don't you?" Hank said, getting to his feet and rotating his meaty shoulders.

"Sure, we love you, Hank," I said. "We're trying to add to your income. But you don't have to take the bet. All you have to do is agree with us that it's impossible, that's all."

"What's my time limit, Eddie?" Hank said.

"An hour, let's say," Eddie said.

"An hour? Movies last at least an hour and a half," Hank said. "And I'll need some intermission time as well to talk to women at the snack bar. How about making it three hours?"

"How about two?" I said.

"Two hours is plenty," Don said. "You wouldn't hang around any other place in Miami for more'n two hours if you couldn't pick up a broad."

"Let's compromise," Hank said. "An hour and a half, so long as I get at least ten minutes intermission time. If the movie happens to run long, then I get more time to take advantage of the inter-mission, but two hours'll be the outside limit. Okay?"

"It's okay with me," I said.

"Then let's make the bet a little more interesting," Hank said. "For every five minutes under an hour, you add five bucks to the bet, and I'll match it."

Hank's self-confidence was irritating, but I considered it as unwarranted overconfidence. We took him up on his addition to the bet, and we agreed to meet in Hank's apartment in a half hour.

We all had identical one-bedroom apartments, but we fur-nished them so differently none of them looked the same. I don't have much furniture, but the stuff I've got is unique. On Saturday nights I often get the early Sunday edition of the *Miami Herald* and look for furniture bargains in the Personals. That's how I got my harpsichord. It was worth at least $850, but I paid only $150 for it. I can pluck out "Birmingham Jail," but I plan to take lessons if a harpsichord teacher ever moves to Miami. I'm not in any hurry to complete the furnishings; I'm willing to wait until I get the things I want to keep.

Eddie has a crummy place, a real mess, but his mother drives down from Fort Lauderdale every month to spend a couple of days with him, and that's the only time it's clean.

When Don left his wife, he took all of his den furniture, and his living room is furnished as a den. He's got two large comfort-able leather chairs, tall, old-fashioned, glass-door bookcases, and a half-dozen framed prints of *A Rake's Progress* on the walls. When we're watching football and drinking beer in Don's place, it's like being in some exclusive men's club.

Hank, because he doesn't have an office, has almost a third of his living room taken up with cardboard boxes full of drugs and samples of the other medical products his company manufactures. Hank serves as our "doctor." We get our painkillers, cold remedies, medicated soap, and even free toothbrushes from Hank. Before the strict accountability on drugs started, he could sometimes spare sleeping pills and a few uppers. But not any longer. His company counts them out to him now, in small quantities, and he has to account for the amphetamines he passes out free to the doctors he calls on.

Hank's apartment is overcrowded with possessions, too, in addition to the medical supplies. Once he has something, he can't bear to part with it, so his apartment is cluttered. On top of everything else, Hank has a mounted eight-foot sailfish over the couch. He caught it in Acapulco last year, had it mounted for $450 and shipped to Miami. Across the belly, in yellow chalk, he's written, *Hank's Folly*. He still can't understand how the boat captain talked him into having the sailfish mounted, except that he was so excited, at the time, about catching it. He's so genuinely unhappy now, about his stupidity in mounting a sailfish, we no longer kid him about it.

When I got to my apartment, I was feeling the effects of the two martinis, so before I took my shower, I put on some coffee to perk. After I showered, I put on a T-shirt, khaki shorts, and a pair of tennis shoes. I fixed a very weak Scotch and water in a plastic glass, and carried it with me down to Hank's apartment.

The other guys were already there. Don, wearing yellow linen slacks and a green knit shirt, was checking the movie pages in the *Herald*. Eddie wore his denim jacket and jeans with his black flight boots, and winked at me when I came in. He jerked his head toward the short hallway to the bedroom. Hank, of course, was still dressing, and a nose-tingling mixture of talcum powder, Right Guard, and Brut drifted in from the bedroom.

Eddie grinned, and jerked his head toward the bedroom. "An actor prepares," he said. "Stanislavski."

"Jesus," Don said, rattling the paper. "At the Tropical Drive-in they're showing *five* John Wayne movies! Who in hell could sit through five John Wayne's, for Christ's sake?"

"I could," I said.

"Me, too," Eddie said, "but only one at a time."

"If you go to the first one at seven thirty," Don said, "you don't get out till three a.m.!"

"I wouldn't mind," Eddie said, "if we all went and took along a couple of cases of beer. It's better than watching TV from seven thirty till three, and I've done that often enough."

"Yeah," I said, "but you can watch TV in air-conditioned comfort. You aren't fighting mosquitoes all night."

"They fog those places for mosquitoes," Eddie said.

"Sure they do," Don said, "and it makes them so mad they bite the shit out of you. Here's one. Listen to this. At the Southside Dixie. *Bucket of Blood, The Blood-Letters, The Bloody Vampires,* and *Barracuda!* There's a theater manager with a sense of humor. He put the barracuda last so they could get all that blood!"

We laughed.

Eddie got up and crossed to the kitchenette table, where Hank kept his liquor and a bucketful of ice. "What're you drinking, Fuzz-O?"

"I'm nursing this one," I said.

"Pour me a glass of wine, Eddie," Don said.

"Blood-red, or urine-yellow?"

"I don't care," Don said, "just so you put a couple of ice cubes in it."

Eddie fixed a Scotch over ice for himself, and brought Don a glass of Chianti, with ice cubes.

"The Southside's probably our best bet," I said. "There'll be fewer women at the horror program than at the John Wayne festival. And besides, there's a Burger Queen across the highway there on Dixie. We can eat something and watch for Hank when he comes out of the theater."

"Shouldn't one of us go with him?" Eddie said.

"It wouldn't be fair," Don said. "I don't think he'll be able to pick up any women there anyway, but it would be twice as hard to talk some woman into getting into a car with two guys. So we let him go in alone. As Larry says, we can watch the exit from across the Dixie Highway."

Hank came into the living room, looking and smelling like a jai-alai player on his night off. He wore white shoes with leather tassels, and a magenta slack suit with a silk blue-and-red paisley scarf tucked in around the collar. Hank had three other tailored suits like the magenta—wheat, blue and chocolate—but I hadn't seen the magenta before. The high-waisted pants, with an un-cuffed flare, were double-knits, and so tight in front his equipment looked like a money bag. The short-sleeved jacket was a beltless, modified version of a bush jacket, with huge bellows side pockets.

Don was the only one of us with long hair, that is, long *enough*, the way we all wanted to wear it. Because of our jobs, we couldn't get away with hair as long as Don's. Hank had fluffed his hair with an air-comb, and it looked much fuller than it did when he slicked it down with spray to call on doctors.

"Isn't that a new outfit?" Eddie said.

"I've had it awhile," Hank said, going to the table to build a drink. "It's the first time I've worn it, is all. I ordered the suit from a small swatch of material. Then when it was made into a suit, I saw that it was a little too much." He shrugged. "But it'll do for a drive-in, I think."

"There's nothing wrong with that color, Hank," Don said. "I like it."

Hank added two more ice cubes to his Scotch and soda. "It makes my face look red, is all."

"Your face *is* red," I said.

"But not as red as this magenta makes it look."

"When you pay us off tonight," Eddie said, "it'll match perfectly."

Hank looked at his wristwatch. "Suppose we synchronize our

watches. It is now, precisely . . . seven twenty-one. We'll see who ends up with the reddest faces."

We checked our watches. For the first time, I wondered if I had made a bad bet. If Hank lost, I consoled myself, at least his overconfidence would preclude my giving him any sympathy.

We decided then to meet Hank at the Burger Queen across from the Southside Drive-in. He would take his Galaxie, and the rest of us would ride down in Don's Mark IV.

Because we stopped at the 7-Eleven to buy two six-packs of beer, Hank beat us to the Burger Queen by about five minutes. Don gave Hank a can of beer, which he hid under the front seat, and then Hank drove across the highway. It was exactly seven forty-one.

We ordered Double Queens apiece, with fries, and then grabbed a tile table on the side patio to the left of the building. The Burger Queen didn't serve beer, and the manager couldn't see us fish our beers out of the paper sack around to the side. We could look directly across the highway and see the drive-in exit.

Unless you're going out to dinner somewhere, eating at eight p.m. in Miami is on the late side. We were all used to eating around six, and so we were ravenous as we wolfed down the double burgers. We didn't talk until we finished, and then I gathered up the trash and dumped it into the nearest garbage can. Don ripped the tops off three more beers.

Below Kendall, at this point on the Dixie Highway, there were six lanes, and the traffic was swift and noisy both ways. Eddie began to laugh and shake his head.

"What's so funny?" I said.

"The whole thing—what else? I know there isn't a hellova lot to do on a Thursday night, but if I ever told anyone I sat around at the Burger Queen for two hours waiting for my buddy to pick up a woman at a drive-in movie—"

"You'd better hope it's at least an hour and a half," Don said.

"I know, I know," Eddie said, "but you've got to admit the whole business is pretty stupid."

"Yes and no, Eddie," I said. "It isn't really money, either. You and Don both know that we'd all like to take Hank down a notch."

Don smiled. "I think you may be right, Larry."

"I'm not jealous of Hank," Eddie said.

"Neither am I," I said. "All I'm saying is that for once I'd like to see old Hank lose one. I like Hank, for Christ's sake, but I hate to see any man so damned overconfident all the time, that's all."

"Yeah," Eddie said. "I know what you mean."

Don snorted, and looked at his watch. "You'll have to wait until another time, I think. It's now eight twelve, and here comes our wandering overconfident boy."

Don had spotted Hank's Galaxie as it cleared the drive-in exit, and Hank, waiting to make a left turn, was hovering at the edge of the highway when I turned to look. He had to wait for some time, and we couldn't see whether there was a woman in the car with him or not. He finally made it across and parked in the Burger Queen lot. We met him about halfway as he came toward us—by himself.

"How about a beer?" Hank said.

"We drank it," Eddie said.

"Thanks for saving me one. Come on. I'll introduce you to Hildy."

We followed Hank to the Galaxie. When he opened the passenger door and the overhead light went on, we saw the girl clearly. She was about thirteen or fourteen, barefooted, wearing a tie-dyed T-shirt, and tight raggedy-cuffed blue jeans with a dozen or more different patches sewn onto them. On her crotch, right over the pudenda, there was a patch with a comic rooster flexing muscled wings. The embroidered letters, in white, below the chicken read: l'M A MEAN FIGHTING COCK. Her brownish hair fell down her back, well past her shoulders, straight but slightly tangled, and her pale face was smudged with dirt. She gave us a tentative smile, and tried to take us all in at once, but she had trouble focusing her eyes. She closed her eyes, and her head hobbled on her skinny neck.

"She's only a kid," Eddie said, glaring at Hank.

Hank shrugged. "I know. She looked older over in the drive-in, without any lights, but you guys didn't set any age limit. A girl's a girl, and I had enough trouble snagging this one."

"It's a cop-out, Hank," I said, "and you know it."

"Suit yourself, Fuzz-O," Hank said. "If you guys don't want to pay off, I'll cancel the debt."

"Nobody said he wouldn't pay," Don said. "But the idea was to pick up somebody old enough to screw. You wouldn't fuck a fourteen-year-old girl—"

"That wasn't one of the conditions," Hank said, "but if that's what you guys want, I'll take Hildy home, give her a shower, and slip it to her. I sure as hell wouldn't be getting any cherry—"

The girl—Hildy—whimpered like a puppy, coughed, choked slightly, and fell over sideways in the seat. "Nobody's going to hurt you, kid," Don said.

"She's stoned on something, Hank," I said. "You'd better get her out of there before she heaves all over the upholstery."

Hank bent down, leaned inside the car, and pushed up the girl's eyelids. He put a forefinger into her throat and then grabbed her thin right wrist to check her pulse. He slammed the passenger door, and leaned against it. His red, sunburned face was watermelon pink—about as pale as Hank was capable of getting.

"She's dead," Hank said. He took out his cigarettes, put one in his mouth, but couldn't get his lighter to work. I lighted a cigarette myself, and then held the match for Hank. His fingers trembled.

"Don't play around, Hank," Don said. "Shit like that isn't funny."

"She's dead, Don," Hank said.

"Are you sure?" Eddie said.

"Look, man—" Hank ran his fingers through his fluffy hair,

and then took a long drag on his cigarette. "Dead is *dead*, man!
I've seen too many . . . too fucking many—"

"Take it easy, Hank," I said.

"What do we do now, Larry?" Don said. Hank and Eddie
looked at me, too, waiting. At twenty-eight, I was the youngest
of the four. Hank was thirty-one, and Don and Eddie were both
thirty, but because of my police background they were dumping
the problem in my lap.

"We'll take her to Hank's apartment," I said. "I'll drive Hank's
car, and Hank'll go with me. You guys go on ahead in the Continental and unlock the fire door to the northwest stairway. Meet us
at the door, because it's closest to Hank's apartment. Then, while
you three take her upstairs to the apartment, I'll park Hank's car."

"Okay," Don said. "Let's go, Eddie."

"Don't run, for Christ's sake," I said.

They slowed to a walk. Hank gave me his car keys, and I circled the car and got in behind the wheel.

On the way back to Dade Towers I drove cautiously. Hank sat
in the passenger bucket seat beside me, and held the girl's shoulders. He had folded her legs, and she was in a kneeling position on
the floor with her face level with the dash glove compartment. He
held her steady, with both hands gripping her shoulders.

"How'd you happen to pick her up, Hank?" I said.

"Thursday's a slow night, apparently," Hank said. "There're
only about twenty-five cars in there. No one, hardly, was at the
snack bar. I got a paper cup from the counter, and went outside to
pour my beer into it. Sometimes, you know, there's a cop around,
and you're not supposed to drink beer at the drive-in, you know."

"I know."

The girl had voided, and the smell of ammonia and feces was
strong. Moving her about hadn't helped any either. I pushed the
button to lower the windows, and turned off the air-conditioning.

"That was a good idea," Hank said. "Anyway, I got rid of the
beer can in a trash basket, and circled around the snack bar to the

women's can. I thought some women might come out, and I could start talking to one, but none did. Then I walked on around the back of the building to the other side. Hildy, here, was standing out in the open, not too far from the men's room. She was just standing there, that's all, looking at the screen. The nearest car was about fifty feet away—I told you there were only about twenty-five cars, didn't I?"

"Yeah. A lot of people don't come until the second feature, which is usually the best flick."

"Maybe so. The point is, nobody was around us. 'Hi,' I said, 'are you waiting for me?' She just giggled and then she mumbled something.

"'Who?' I said, and then she said, 'The man in the yellow jumpsuit.'

"'Oh, sure,' I said, 'he sent me to get you. My name's Hank—what's yours?'

"'Hildy,' she said.

"'Right,' I said. "You're the one, all right. I hope you don't mind magenta instead of yellow.'

"Then she asked me for some of my Coke. She thought I had a Coke because of the red paper cup, you see. So I gave her a drink from the cup and she made a face. Then she took my hand, just like I was her father or something, and I led her over to my car. It was dark as hell in there, Larry, and I swear she looked older—around seventeen, anyway."

"That doesn't make any difference now," I said.

"I guess not. I wish to hell I had a drink."

"We can get one in your apartment."

The operation at Dade Towers worked as smoothly as if we had rehearsed it. I parked at the corner, ten feet from the door. Hank wrapped a beach towel around Hildy, an old towel he kept in the backseat, and Eddie opened the car door. The fire door to the stairway, which was rarely used, only opened from the inside. Don held the door partly open for Hank and Eddie, and they had carried her inside and up the stairs before I drove across the street and into the parking lot. After parking in Hank's slot and locking the car, I shoved Hildy's handbag under my T-shirt.

I knocked softly at Hank's door when I got upstairs. Don opened it a crack to check me out before he let me in. Hildy was on her back on the couch, with the beach towel beneath her. She was only about four eight, and the mounted sailfish on the wall above her looked almost twice as long as she did. The sail's name in yellow chalk, *Hank's Folly*, somehow seemed appropriate. When I joined the group, Hank handed me a straight Scotch over ice cubes.

The four of us, in a semicircle, stared down at the girl for a few moments. Her brown eyes were opened partially, and there were yellow "sleepies" in the corners. There was a scattering of pimples on her forehead, and a few freckles on her nose and cheeks. There was a yellow hickey on the left corner of her mouth, and she didn't have any lipstick on her pale lips. Her skin, beneath the smudges of dirt, was so white it was almost transparent, and a dark blue vein beneath her right temple was clearly visible. She wasn't wearing a bra beneath her T-shirt; with her adolescent chest bumps, she didn't need one.

"She looks," Eddie said, "like a first-year Brownie."

Don began to cry.

"For God's sake, Don—" Hank said.

"Leave him alone, Hank," I said. "I feel like crying myself."

Don sat in the Danish chair across from the TV, took out his handkerchief, wiped his eyes, and then blew his nose.

I emptied the purse—a blue-and-red patchwork leather bag, with a long braided leather shoulder strap—onto the coffee table. There were two plastic vials containing pills. One of them was filled with the orange heart-shaped pills I recognized as Dexies. The other pills were round and white, but larger than aspirins, and stamped *M-T*. There was a Mary Jane, a penny piece of candy wrapped in yellow paper, the kind kids buy at the 7-Eleven; a roll of bills held together by a rubber band; a used and wadded Kleenex; and a blunt, slightly bent aluminum comb.

As I started to count the money, I said to Eddie, "Search her body, Ed."

"No," he said, shaking his head.

"Let me fix you another drink, Ed." Hank took Eddie's glass, and they moved to the kitchenette table. Don, immobilized in the Danish chair, stared at the floor without blinking.

There were thirty-eight dollars in the roll; one was a five, the rest were ones. I emptied the girl's front pockets. This was hard to do because her jeans were so tight. There were two quarters and three pennies in the right pocket, and a slip of folded notebook paper in the left. It was a list of some kind, written with a blue felt pen. *30 ludes, 50 Bs, no gold.* There was only one hip pocket, and it was a patch that had been sewn on in an amateurish manner. The patch, in red denim, with white letters, read, *KISS MY PATCH.* The pocket was empty.

"There's no ID, Hank," I said.

"So what do we do now," Eddie said, "call the cops?"

"What's your flying schedule?" I said.

"I go to New York Saturday. Why?"

"How'd you like to be grounded, on suspension without pay, for about three months? Pending an investigation into the dope fiend death of a teenaged girl?"

"We didn't do anything," Eddie said.

"That's right," I said. "But that wouldn't keep your name out of the papers, or some pretty nasty interrogations at the station. And Hank's in a more sensitive position than you are with the airline, what with his access to drug samples and all. If—or when—he's investigated, and his company's name gets into the papers, as soon as he's cleared, the best he can hope for is a transfer to Yuma, Arizona."

Hank shuddered, and sat down at the coffee table beside me in a straight-backed cane chair. He opened the vial holding the pills that were stamped *M-T.*

"Methaqualone," Hank said. "But they're not from my company. We make them all right, but our brand's called 'Meltin.' There're twenty M-T's left in the vial, so she could've taken anywhere from one to a dozen—or more maybe. Four or five could suffocate and kill her." Hank shrugged, and looked at the girl's body on the couch. "The trouble is, these heads take mixtures sometimes of any and everything. She's about seventy-five pounds, I'd say, and if she was taking a combination of Dexies and M-T's, it's a miracle she was still on her feet when I picked her up." He tugged on his lower lip. "If any one of us guys took even three 'ludes, we'd sleep for at least ten hours straight. But if Hildy, here, was on the stuff for some time, she could've built up a tolerance, and—"

"Save it, Hank," I said. "The girl's dead, and we don't know who she is—that's what we need to know. The best thing for us to do, I think, is find the guy in the yellow jumpsuit and turn her over to him."

"What guy in what yellow jumpsuit?" Eddie said.

Hank told them what the girl had said, that she was waiting for a man in a yellow jumpsuit.

"Do you think it was her father, maybe?" Don said.

"Hell no," I said. "Whoever he is, she's his baby, not ours."

"How're we going to find him?" Eddie said.

"Back at the drive-in," I said. "I'm going to get my pistol from my apartment, and then we'll go back and look for him."

"D'you want me to take my pistol too, Larry?" Eddie asked.

"You'd better not," I said, "I've got a license, and you haven't. You and I and Hank'll go back. You'd better stay here with the girl, Don."

"I'd just as soon go along," Don said.

"No," I said. "Somebody'd better stay here with the girl. We'll go in your car, Hank." I handed him his keys. "I'll meet you guys down in the lot."

I went to my apartment, and changed into slacks. I put my pistol, a Colt Cobra .38, with a two-inch barrel, into its clip holster, and shoved the holstered gun inside the waistband of my trousers. To conceal the handle of the weapon, I put on a sand-colored lightweight golf jacket, and zipped up the front. Hank and Eddie were both in the Galaxie, Eddie in the backseat, and Hank in the driver's, when I got to the parking lot. I slid in beside Hank.

On our way to the drive-in I told them how we would work the search party. Hank could start with the first row of cars, going from one to the next, and Eddie could start from the back row. I'd start at the snack bar, checking the men's room first, and then look into any of the cars that were parked close to the snack bar. I would also be on the lookout for any new cars coming in, and I would mark the position of new arrivals, if any, so we could check them out when we finished with those already there.

"One other thing," I said. "If you spot the guy, don't do anything. We'll all meet in the men's room, and then we'll take him together. There aren't that many cars, and we should finish the search in about five minutes."

"What if he isn't there?" Eddie said.

"Then we wait. I think he'll show up, all right. My worry is, he might not be alone, which'll make it harder to pick him up. But there aren't that many guys wearing jumpsuits, especially yellow ones, so we should be able to spot him easily enough."

"Not necessarily," Hank said. "He might be a hallucination, a part of the girl's trip. Hell, she came with me without any persuasion to speak of, and she would've gone with anybody. She was really out of it, Larry."

"We don't have to look for the guy, Hank," I said. "If you think it's a waste of time, let's go back and get the girl and dump her body in a canal someplace."

"Jesus, Larry," Eddie said, "could you do that?"

"What else do you suggest?"

"Nothing," Eddie said. "But before we do anything drastic, I think we'd better look for her boyfriend in the jumpsuit."

"That's why we're going to the drive-in," Hank said.

I took a five and a one out of my wallet, and had the money ready to pass across Hank to the girl in the box office the moment Hank stopped the car. Hank had cut his lights, but I regretted, for a moment, not taking my Vega instead of returning in his Galaxie. The Galaxie, because it was leased by Hank's company, had an *E* prefix on the license plate. But because there were three of us in the car instead of only one, it was still unlikely that the girl would make an earlier connection with Hank.

We parked in the last row. The nearest car was three rows ahead of us. As we got out of the car, Eddie laughed abruptly. "What do we say," he said, "if someone asks what we're looking in their car for? Not everybody comes to this fingerbowl to watch the movie, you know."

"Don't make a production out of it," I said. "Just glance in and move on. If somebody does say something, ask for an extra book of matches. That's as good an excuse as any. But look into each car from the side or back, and you won't get into any hassles. Remember, though, if you do spot the guy, keep on going down the line of cars as before. Don't quit right then and head for the men's room. He might suspect something."

A few minutes later we met in the men's room. I lit a cigarette, and Eddie and Hank both shook their heads. I wasn't surprised. I hadn't expected to find any man in a yellow jumpsuit. In fact, I suspected that Hank had made up the story. And yet, it was wise to get all three of them involved. I had realized, from the beginning, that I would have to be the one who would have to get rid of the girl's body, but it would be better, later on, for these guys to think that they had done everything possible before the inevitable dumping of the kid in a canal.

"Okay," I said. "To make sure, let's start over. Only this time, you start with the first row, Eddie, and you, Hank, start with the back. It won't hurt anything to double-check."

"If you really think it's necessary," Hank said.

"We've got to wait around anyway," I said.

They took off again. It wasn't necessary, but I wanted to keep them busy. They didn't have my patience. These guys had never sat up all night for three nights in a row at a stake-out in a liquor store. But I had. I went around to the back of the snack bar, where it was darkest, and kept my eye on the box office entrance, some hundred yards away. Two more cars, both with their parking lights on, came in. The first car turned at the second row and squeezed into an empty slot. The second car, a convertible, drove all the way to the back, and parked about three spaces to the right of Hank's car. If you came to see the movie, it was a poor location, so far from the screen, and angled away from it. A man got out of the car, and started toward the snack bar.

I caught up with Hank, and pointed the man out as he came slowly in our direction, picking his way because his eyes weren't used to the darkness. "I think we've got him, Hank," I said. "Go straight up to him and ask for a match, and I'll circle around in back of him."

"What if he's got a gun?" Hank said.

"I've got a gun, too. Hurry up."

When Hank stopped the man, I was behind him about ten yards or so. He gave Hank a light from his cigarette lighter; then he heard me and turned around. I clicked the hammer back on my .38 as he turned.

"Let's go back to your car, friend," I said.

"A stick-up in the drive-in? You guys must be out of your fuckin' minds," he said.

"Stand away from him, Hank," I said. "If he doesn't move in about one second, I'll shoot his balls off."

"I'm moving, I'm moving," the man said. He put his arms above his head and waggled his fingers.

"Put your arms down, you bastard," I said. "Cross your arms across your chest."

When we reached his car, a dark blue Starfire, with the top down, I told him to get into the passenger' side of the front seat.

Eddie, breathing audibly through his mouth, joined us a moment later.

"Okay, Hank," I said, "the same as with the girl. You drive on ahead, get Don, and have the fire door open for us. Eddie'll drive this car, and I'll watch the son of a bitch from the backseat. Okay, friend, put one hand on top of the dash, and pass over your car keys with the other."

"No dice," he said. "If you guys want my dough, go ahead and take it, but I ain't leavin' the drive-in—"

He sat erect in the seat with his arms crossed, looking straight ahead. He was wearing a yellow jumpsuit, and from the cool way he was taking things I knew that he was the right man. I slapped the barrel of the pistol across his nose. His nose broke, and blood spurted. He squealed, and grabbed for his nose with his right hand.

"Cross your arms," I said.

He quickly recrossed his arms, but he turned his head and eyes to glare at me. "Now," I said, "slowly—with one hand, pass over your car keys to the driver." He kept his right forearm across his chest, and dug the keys out of his left front pocket. Eddie slid into the driver's seat, shut the door, and took the keys.

"Get going," I said to Hank, who was still standing there. "We'll be right behind you."

Hank walked over to his car. I climbed over the side of the Starfire, into the backseat, and Eddie started the engine.

"Wait till Hank clears the exit before you pull out," I said to Eddie.

"Where're you guys takin' me, anyway?" the man said. "I got friends, you know. You're gonna be sorry you broke my fuckin' nose, too. It hurts like a bastard." He touched his swollen nose with his right hand.

"Shut up," I said, "and keep your arms crossed. If you move either one of your arms again, I'm going to put a round through your shoulder."

Eddie moved out, handling the car skillfully. He drove to the extreme right of the row before turning onto the exit road, and without lights. There was a quarter-moon, the sky was cloudless, and we'd been in the drive-in so long by now that we could see easily.

When we reached the fire door at Dade Towers, Don and Hank were waiting for us. I ordered the man in the yellow jumpsuit to follow Don, and Hank followed me as we went up the stairs. Eddie parked the convertible in a visitor's slot across the street, and came up to Hank's apartment in the elevator.

While we were gone, Don had turned on the television, but not the sound. On the screen, Doris Day and Rock Hudson were standing beside a station wagon in a suburban neighborhood. She was waving her arms around.

The man in the yellow jumpsuit didn't react at all when he saw the dead girl. Instead of looking at her, he looked at the silent television screen. He was afraid, of course, and trembling visibly, but he wasn't terrified. He stood between the couch and the kitchen, with his back to the girl, and stared boldly at each of us, in turn, as though trying to memorize our faces.

He was about twenty-five or -six, with a glossy Prince Valiant helmet of dark auburn hair. His hair was lighter on top, because of the sun, probably, but it had been expensively styled. His thick auburn eyebrows met in the middle, above his swollen nose, as he scowled. His long sideburns came down at a sharp point, narrowing to a quarter-inch width, and they curved across his cheeks to meet his mustache, which had been carved into a narrow, half-inch strip. As a consequence, his mustache, linked in a curve across both cheeks to his sideburns, resembled a fancy, cursive lower-case *m*. His dark blue eyes watered slightly. There was blood drying on his mustache, on his chin, and there was a thin Jackson Pollock drip down the front of his lemon-yellow poplin jumpsuit. His nose had stopped bleeding.

Jumpsuits, as leisure wear, have been around for several years, but it's only been the last couple of years that men have worn them on the street, or away from home or the beach. There's a reason. They are comfortable, and great to lounge around in—until you get a good profile look at yourself in the mirror. If you have any gut at all—even two inches more than you should have—a jumpsuit, which is basically a pair of fancied-up coveralls, makes you look like you've got a pot-gut. I've got a short-sleeved blue terry-cloth jumpsuit I wear around the pool once in a while, but I would never wear it away from the apartment house. When I was on the force and weighed about 175, I could have worn it around town, but since I've been doing desk work at National, I've picked up more than twenty pounds. My waistline has gone from a thirty-two to a thirty-six, and the jumpsuit makes me look like I've got a paunch. It's the way they are made.

But this guy in the yellow jumpsuit was slim, maybe 165, and he was close to six feet in height. The poplin jumpsuit was skin-tight, bespoke, probably, and then cut down even more, and he wore it without the usual matching belt at the waist. It had short sleeves, and his sinewy forearms were hairy. Thick reddish chest hair curled out of the top of the suit where he had pulled the zipper down for about eight inches. He wore zippered cordovan boots, and they were highly polished.

"What's the girl's name?" I said.

"How should I know?" he said. "I never seen her before. What's the matter with her, anyway?"

"There's nothing the matter with her," Don said. "She's dead, now, and you killed her!" Don started for him, but Hank grabbed Don by the arms, at the biceps, and gently pushed him back.

"Take it easy, Don," Hank said. "Let Larry handle it." When Don nodded, Hank released him.

"Step forward a pace," I said, "and put your hands on top of your head." The man shuffled forward, and put his hands on his head. "Here, Don," I said, handing Don the pistol. "Cover me while I search him. If he tries anything, shoot him in the kneecap."

"Sure, Larry," Don said. His hand was steady as he aimed the .38 at the man's kneecap.

"I'll hold the pistol, Don," Hank said, "if you want me to."

Don shook his head, and Eddie grinned and winked at me as I went around behind the man in the jumpsuit to frisk him.

"Leave him alone, Hank," I said. "Why don't you fix us a drink?"

I tossed the man's ostrich-skin wallet, handkerchief, and silver ballpoint pen onto the coffee table from behind. He didn't have any weapons, and he had less than two dollars worth of change in his front pockets. He had a package of Iceberg cigarettes, with three cigarettes missing from the pack, and a gold Dunhill lighter.

At his waist, beneath the jumpsuit, I felt a leather belt. I came around in front of him, and caught the ring of the zipper. He jerked his hands down and grabbed my wrists. Don moved forward and jammed the muzzle of the gun against the man's left knee. The man quickly let go of my wrists.

"For God's sake, don't shoot!" he said. He put his hands on top of his head again.

"It's all right, Don," I said.

Don moved back. I pulled down the zipper, well below his waist. He wasn't wearing underwear, just the belt. It was a plain brown cowhide suit belt, about an inch and a half in width. I un-buckled it, jerked it loose from his body, and turned it over. It was a zippered money belt, the kind that is advertised in men's maga-zines every month. If he had been wearing the belt with a pair of trousers, no one would have ever suspected that it was a money belt. I unzipped the compartment. There were eight one-hun-dred-dollar bills and two fifties tightly folded lengthwise inside the narrow space. I unfolded the bills, and counted them onto the coffee table.

"That ain't my money!" the man in the yellow jumpsuit said.

"That's right," Eddie said, laughing. "Not anymore it isn't."

"I'm telling you, right now," the man said, "that dough don't belong to me. You take it, and you're in trouble. Big trouble!"

I sat down at the coffee table, and went through his wallet. Eddie sat beside me in another straight-backed chair. Hank set Scotches over ice in front of us. He held an empty glass up for Don, and raised his eyebrows. Don shook his head, but didn't take his eyes off the man in the yellow jumpsuit. Hank, with a fresh drink in his hand, leaned against the kitchenette archway, and stared at the man.

There were three gas credit cards in the billfold: Gulf, Exxon, and Standard Oil. The Gulf card was made out to A.H. Wexley, the Exxon to A. Franciscus, and the Standard card was in the name of L. Cohen. All three cards listed Miami Beach addresses. There was no other identification in the wallet. There was another eighty dollars in bills, plus a newspaper coupon that would entitle the man to a one-dollar discount on a bucket or a barrel of Colonel Sanders's fried chicken. There was a parking stub for the Dupont Plaza Hotel garage, an ivory toothpick in a tiny leather case, and a key to a two-bit locker. Bus station? Airport? Any public place that has rental lockers. And that was all.

"I've never seen a man's wallet this skimpy," I said to Eddie.

"Me either," Eddie said. "I can hardly fold mine, I got so much junk."

"Which one is you?" I said, reading the gas credit cards again. "Cohen, Franciscus, or Wexley?"

"I don't like to use the same gas all the time, man," he said, then he giggled.

I got up and kicked him in the shin with the side of my foot. Because I was wearing tennis shoes, it didn't hurt him half as much as he let on, but because he was surprised, he lost some of his poise.

"Look, you guys," he said, "why don't you just take the money and let me go. I haven't done anything—"

"What's the girl's name?" I said.

"I don't know her name. Honest."

"What's her name? She told us she was waiting for you, so there's no point lying about it."

"Her name's Hildy." He shrugged, yawned, and looked away from me.

"Hildy what?"

"I don't know, man. She worked for me some, but I never knew her last name."

"Doing what?" I said.

"She sold a little stuff for me now and then—at Bethune."

"Mary Bethune Junior High?"

"Yeah."

"Did you drop her off, earlier tonight, at the drive-in?"

"No. I was supposed to collect some dough from her there, that's all."

"Do you know how old she is?"

"She's in the eighth grade, she said, but I never asked how old she was. That's none of my business."

"So you turned her on to drugs without even caring how old she was?" Hank said. "You're the lowest son of a bitch I've ever met."

"I never turned her on to no drugs, man," the man said. "She was takin' shit long before I met her. What I was doing, I was doing her a favor. She lives with her mother, she said. Her mother works at night, over at the beach, she said. And her father split a couple of years back for Hawaii. So Hildy asked me if she could sell some for me. She was trying to save up enough money to go to her father in Hawaii. That's all. And the other kid, a black kid, who used to sell for me at Bethune, he took off for Jacksonville with fifty bucks he owed me. I needed someone at Bethune, and I told Hildy I'd give her a chance. She needed the bread, she said. She wanted to live with her father in Hawaii. So what I was doing, I was doing her a favor."

He ran down. We all stared at him. Beneath his heavy tan, his face was flushed, and he perspired heavily in the air-conditioned room.

"I ain't no worse'n you guys," the man in the yellow jumpsuit said. "What the hell, you guys picked her up to screw her, didn't you? Well, didn't you?"

"You mean you were screwing her, too?" Don said.

"No—I never touched her. She might've gone down on me a couple of times, but I never touched her."

"What do you mean, 'might have'?" Don said. "Did she or didn't she?"

"Yeah, I guess she did, a couple of times. But I never made her do it. She wanted to, she said."

Don fired the pistol. It was like a small explosion in the crowded room. Hank, standing in the kitchenette archway, dropped his glass on the floor. It didn't break. Eddie, sitting beside me, sucked in his breath. The man in the yellow jumpsuit clawed at his chest with both hands. He sank to his knees and his back arched as his head fell back. The back of his head hit the couch and his arms dropped loosely to his sides. He remained in that position, without toppling, his face in the air, looking up at nothing, on his knees, with his back arched and his head and neck supported by the couch. Don made a funny noise in his throat. There was a widening red circle on the man's hairy chest, as blood bubbled from a dark round hole. I stood up, took the pistol away from Don, and returned the gun to my belt holster. The man in the yellow jumpsuit had voided and the stench filled the room. I crossed to the TV and turned up the volume.

"I didn't—" Don said. "I didn't touch the trigger! It went off by itself!"

"Sit down, Don," Hank said. He crossed to Don, and gently pushed him down into the Danish chair. "We know it was an accident, Don."

"Eddie," I said, "open the windows, and turn the air-conditioning to fan."

Eddie nodded, and started toward the bedroom where the thermostat was on the wall. I opened the door to the outside hallway. Keeping my hand on the knob, I looked up and down the corridor. A gunshot sounds exactly like a gunshot and nothing else. But most people don't know that. I was prepared, in case someone stuck his head out, to ask him if he heard a car backfire. The sound from the TV, inside Hank's apartment, was loud enough to hear in the corridor. I waited outside for a moment longer, and when no heads appeared, I ducked back inside and put the night lock on the door.

"Larry," Hank said, "d'you think I should give Don a sedative?"

"Hell no," I said. "Let him lie down for a while on your bed, but we don't want him dopey on us, for Christ's sake."

Don was the color of old expensive parchment, as if his olive tan had been diluted with a powerful bleach. His eyes were glazed slightly, and he leaned on Hank heavily as Hank led him into the bedroom.

Eddie grinned, and shook his head. "What a night," he said. "When I opened the damned window behind the couch, I accidentally stepped on the guy's hand. One of his damned fingers broke." Eddie looked away from me; his mouth was twitching at the corners.

"Don't worry about it, Ed," I said. "You and I are going to have to get rid of him, you know—both of them."

"That figures. Any ideas?"

Hank came back from the bedroom. "I'm treating Don for shock," he said. "I've covered him with a blanket, and now I'm going to make him some hot tea."

"Never mind the fucking tea," I said. "I'm not worried about Don. We've got to get these bodies out of here."

"I know that," Hank said. "What do you suggest?"

"We'll put them into the backseat of the convertible, and then I'll drive his car over to the Japanese Garden on the MacArthur Causeway. I'll just park the car in the lot and leave it." I turned to Eddie. "You can follow me in my Vega, and pick me up."

"Okay," Eddie said. I gave him my car keys.

"I'll go with you, if you want," Hank said.

"There's no point, Hank. You can stay here after we load the bodies, and make some fucking tea for Don."

"Wait a minute," Hank said, "you don't have to—"

"I don't have to what?" I said.

"Cut it out, you guys," Eddie said. "Go ahead, Larry. Get the convertible and park it by the fire exit. I'll bring the girl down first, but it'll take all three of us to carry him down."

"All right," I said. "Except for the money, put the girl's bag and his wallet and all their other stuff into a paper sack." I pointed to the stuff on the coffee table. "And we'll need something to cover him up."

"I've got a GI blanket in the closet," Hank said.

Taking the car keys to the convertible from Eddie, I left the apartment.

While Eddie and I wedged the girl between the back and front seats on the floor of the convertible, Hank held the fire door open for us. We covered her with the beach towel, and I tucked the end under her head.

"Shouldn't one of us stay down here with the car?" Eddie asked.

"No," I said. "He's too heavy. It'll take all three of us to bring him down. It won't take us long. We'll just take a chance, that's all."

On the way back to Hank's apartment, we ran into Marge Brewer in the corridor. She was in her nurse's uniform, and had just come off duty at Jackson Memorial. She was coming toward us from the elevator.

"I'm beat," she said, looking at Hank. "A twelve-hour split shift. I'm going to whomp up a big batch of martinis. D'you all want to come down in ten minutes? I'll share."

"Give us a rain check, Marge," Hank said. "We're going down to the White Shark and shoot some pool."

"Sure," she said. "'Night."

We paused outside Hank's apartment. Hank fumbled with his keys at the door until she rounded the corner at the end of the corridor.

"Go inside," I said. "I'd better pull the emergency stop on the elevator. You can take it off after we leave, Hank."

They went inside. I hurried down the hall, opened the elevator door, and pulled out the red knob. There was an elevator on the other side of the building, and the residents who didn't want to climb the stairs could use that one.

Hank and I, being so much bigger than Eddie, supported the man in the yellow jumpsuit between us. We each draped an arm over our shoulders, and carried him, with his feet dragging, down the corridor. If someone saw us, it would look—at least from a distance—as if we were supporting a drunk. Eddie, a few feet in front of us, carried the folded army blanket and the sack of stuff. It was much easier going down the stairs. I went down first, carrying the feet, while Hank and Eddie supported him from behind. After we put him on top of the girl, in the back of the car, and covered him with the GI blanket, I got into the driver's seat. The fire door had closed and locked while we loaded him, so Hank started down the sidewalk toward the apartment entrance.

"Look, Eddie," I said. "Drive as close behind me as you can. If I'm stopped—for any reason—I'm going to leave the car and run like a striped-ass ape. And I'll need you behind me to pick me up. Okay?"

"No sweat, Larry," Eddie said. "If you want me to, I'll drive the convertible. I'm a better driver than you."

I shook my head. "That's why I want you behind me, in case we have to make a run for it in the Vega. Besides, I'm not going to drive over thirty, and when I cross the bridge, before the Goodyear landing pad, I'm going to throw my pistol over the side. It'll be a lot easier to throw it over the rail from the convertible."

"Move out, then. I'm right behind you."

I got rid of the gun, leaving it in the holster, when I passed over the bridge, and a few moments later I was parked in the Japanese Garden parking lot. There were no other cars. The Garden itself was closed at night, and fenced in to keep the hippies from sleeping in the tiny bamboo tearoom. But the parking lot was outside the fence. Sometimes lovers used the parking lot at night, but because most people knew that the Garden was closed at night, they didn't realize that the parking lot was still available. Eddie pulled in beside me and cut his lights.

I got some Kleenex out of the glove compartment of my Vega, and smudged the steering wheel and doors of the convertible. I did this for Eddie's benefit mostly; it's almost impossible to get decent prints from a car. Then I got the GI blanket and the beach towel and the paper sack of personal belongings. As we drove back toward Dade Towers, I folded the blanket and the towel in my lap.

Eddie said: "What do you think, Fuzz-0?"

"About what?"

"The whole thing. D'you think we'll get away with it?"

"I'm worried about Don."

"You don't have to worry about Don," Eddie said. "Don's all right."

"If I don't have to worry about Don," I said, "I don't have to worry about anything,"

"You don't have to worry about Don," Eddie said.

"Good. If you don't scratch a sore, it doesn't suppurate."

"Hey! That's poetry, Larry."

"That's a fact," I said. "When you hit Twenty-seventh, turn into the Food Fair lot. I'll throw all this stuff into the Dempsey dumpster."

When we got back to Hank's apartment, Don and Hank were watching television. The color was back in Don's face, and he was drinking red wine with ice cubes. Hank had found an old electric fan in his closet, and some Christmas tree spray left over from Christmas. The windows were still open, but the pungent spray, diffused by the noisy fan, made the room smell like a pine forest. I turned off the TV, fixed myself a light Scotch and water, without ice, and sat in front of the coffee table. I counted the money, and gave two one-hundred-dollar bills each to Eddie, Hank, and Don, and kept two of them for myself. I folded the remaining money, and put it into my jacket pocket.

"I'll need this extra money to buy a new pistol," I said. "I got rid of mine—and the holster."

"What did you do with it, Larry?" Don said.

"If you don't know, Don, you can't tell, can you?" I looked at him and smiled.

"What makes you think Don would ever say anything?" Hank said.

"I don't," I said. "But it's better for none of you guys to know. Okay? Now. If anybody's got anything to say, now's the time to say it. We'll talk about it now, and then we'll forget about it forever. What I mean, after tonight, none of us should ever mention this thing again. Okay?"

Hank cleared his throat. "While you and Eddie were gone, Don and I were wondering why you had us bring the girl here in the first place."

"I was waiting for that," I said. "What I wanted was a make on the girl. I figured that if I could find out her address, I could call her father, and have him come and get her. Either that, or we could take her to him after I talked to him. That way, he could've put her to bed and called his family doctor. That way, he could've covered up the fact that she died from an OD, if that's what it was."

"That wouldn't have worked," Hank said.

"Maybe not. But that was the idea in the back of my mind. You asked me why I brought her here, and that's the reason."

"It would've worked with me," Don said. "I wouldn't've wanted it in the papers, if my daughter died from an overdose of drugs."

"Okay, Larry," Hank said. "You never explained it to us before, is all. I just wonder, now, who those people were."

"The papers will tell you." Eddie laughed. "Look in the *Miami News* tomorrow night. Section C—Lifestyle. "

"Don?" I said.

"One thing," Don said, looking into his glass. "I didn't mean to pull the trigger. I'm sorry about getting you guys into this mess."

"You didn't get us into anything, Don," Eddie said. "We were all in it together anyway."

"Just the same," Don said, "I made it worse, and I'm sorry."

"We're all sorry," I said. "But what's done is done. Tomorrow, I'm going to report it at the office that my pistol was stolen out of the glove compartment of my car. They may raise a little hell with me, but these things happen in Miami. So I'm telling you guys about it now. Some dirty son of a bitch stole my .38 out of my glove compartment."

No one said anything for a few moments. Don stared at the diluted wine in his glass. Eddie lit a cigarette. I finished my drink. Hank, frowning, and looking at the floor, rubbed his knees with the palms of his hands.

"Eddie," I said, "do you want to add anything?"

Eddie shrugged, and then he laughed. "Yeah. Who wants to go down to the White Shark for a little pool?"

Hank and Don both smiled.

"If we needed an alibi, it wouldn't be a bad idea," I said. "But we don't need an alibi. If there's nothing else, I think we should all hit our respective sacks."

Eddie and I stood up. "You going to be okay, Don?" Eddie asked.

"Sure." Don stood up, and we started toward the door.

"Just a minute," Hank stopped us. "I picked up the girl in the drive-in, and bets were made! You guys owe me *money*!"

We all laughed then, and the tension dissolved. We paid Hank off, of course, and then we went to bed. But as far as I was concerned, we were still well ahead of the game: four lucky young guys in Miami, sitting on top of a big pile of vanilla ice cream.

THE WORKS

BY T.J. MacGregor

South Beach

(Originally published in 1990)

I know how it is down here on the beach for the old ones now, what with rising prices and traffic and crime. They're afraid to go out at night. Their Social Security checks barely cover a month of meals at Wolfie's. They feel like Miami Beach's postscript.

The Art Deco craze did it, you know. Ever since folks decided Deco was in again, those little hotels over on Ocean Drive are booming with business, charging prices like I can't believe, and yeah, people pay them. I mean, seventy bucks for a room no larger than a closet, five bucks for a hard-boiled egg and a slice of bread that's hardly toasted, two bucks for coffee. The old ones can remember when coffee in these places cost a dime.

There's a haughty look to the hotels that really gets me too. They stand so prim and proper at the edge of the sea, all spiffed up in pastels, windows so clean they gleam like jewels. The old ones feel like they can't afford to even walk there, and when they do, shuffling in their tired bones, under the weight of eighty or ninety years of memories, they're nearly trampled by the youthful crowds rushing to this hotel or that bar.

So I keep my prices low and do what I can. When an old one is troubled or sad, sick or too drunk to stand, I take him or her in. Word has gotten around that Millie's Place is where you go when it's gotten bad.

Like tonight, for instance.

Toby wandered in off Washington Avenue a few minutes ago,

out of the thick night heat, looking about as bad as a man can look and still be alive. He's ninety-four years old, with a spine so bent he can hardly lift his head, glasses thicker than his arm, a heart that just won't quit.

He's counting one-dollar bills from a tattered envelope with SOCIAL SECURITY ADMINISTRATION in bold black letters across the top. If I remember correctly, he worked nearly half a century for an auto parts plant that merged with another plant, and most of his pension got lost in the transition. His Social Security check amounts to about three hundred dollars a month, and we all know what that buys you in Miami Beach.

"The room's only six bucks, Toby," I tell him when he keeps counting out the bills.

"Want a meal, too," he mumbles, moving his dentures around in his mouth because they hurt his gums.

"Eight bucks, then."

"And the Works. I think I want the Works, Millie."

"You'd better be sure. It's a bit more expensive."

His head bobs slowly. It reminds me of a beach ball, rising, falling, riding a wave, and I want to stroke it, embrace it, kiss this old, beautiful head. It's as hairless as a Chihuahua, with a mass of wrinkles that seems to quiver and dance to the back of the skull. Not so long ago, on a rainy afternoon down at the Ace Club, some of the old ones and I gathered around Toby's head to see if we could read our fortunes in the wrinkles, like they were creases in a palm.

"I'm sure," he says softly, depositing an old canvas bag on the counter, straining to look up. "How much?" His eyes behind those thick glasses are alarmingly small, almost transparent. I feel like they might disappear at any second.

"Twenty-five. I guess you know what all the fee includes."

His smile creases his mouth and, like a widening ripple in a pond, touches all the other wrinkles in his face. For a moment or two, his features shift and slide, rearranging themselves. "Sure. I came with Mink, remember?"

Mink: right. She was close to a hundred, small as a toy doll with white hair that had fallen out in spots, exposing soft pink patches of scalp. She had cancer and the radiation or chemo or whatever it was they'd used on her had rotted her from the inside out, but her heart ticked on. She took baby steps, I remember, like a toddler learning to walk, and drooled a little when she talked.

It's true that decades stretch between infancy and old age, but children and old ones aren't all that different. Both are afraid. Both have special needs. Both require love. I understand that and they know it.

"There. Twenty-five." He taps the stack of bills against the counter, straightening them, then slides the pile toward me.

"Sure?"

"Positive."

"Okay, let's go take a look at the menu."

I ring for Sammy to man the desk and he shuffles in, big as a truck and all muscle. He's not an old one, but he was living on the streets until I took him in and now I don't know how I'd run this place without him. I've never heard him speak. I don't know if it's because he can't or just that he chooses not to.

I come out from behind the counter and Toby hooks his old, tired arm in mine. The kitchen is in the back and while it's not as grand as the ones in the fancy hotels on Ocean Drive, it feels like home to me. The fridge is always filled with everyone's favorites— home-baked pies, drumsticks, potato salad, coleslaw, cookies by the dozens.

When I was doing private-duty nursing a long time ago, I made a point of cooking for my patients. They appreciated it. A lot of them were old ones too, and I learned to prepare the food to accommodate dentures, taste buds that had gone as smooth and dull as river stones, noses that no longer worked right. It taught me the importance of spices, sauces, garnishes that dressed the food good enough to make your mouth water.

Toby's mouth is watering now as we peer into the fridge together, I can tell. He points at what he wants. One of those, one of these, this, that. His finger is curved into a permanent claw from arthritis; just looking at it hurts me. That's how it is with me and them. That's how it always is when someone I care for is in pain. It becomes my pain.

"And cookies," he finishes. "Chocolate chip cookies."

"They've got nuts in them."

"Soft nuts?"

"Not really."

"Aw, so what. Nuts are fine."

Together, we remove the items from the fridge and set them out on the counter. Before I begin preparing the meal, though, I show him to the best room in the house. It's on the top floor, in back. There's a skylight over the huge bed, a color TV and VCR, forty or fifty videocassettes for him to choose from, and an adjoining bath with a sunken tub that swirls and bubbles like a Jacuzzi, where fluffy towels, a silk robe, and matching pajamas are laid out. He sighs as his feet sink into the thick carpeting on the floor and sighs again as he eases his tired bones onto the bed and peers up, up into a sky strewn with stars.

"You'll tell me when dinner's ready?" he asks, frowning as though he doesn't quite trust me now.

"I'll bring it up here. Feathers is going to smell that chicken. You mind if she comes up too?"

"No, no, of course not," he says, hooking his hands under his head, lost in the stars. He doesn't hear me leave, but Feathers hears me enter the kitchen.

She's a white Persian who has a definite fondness for chicken and old ones. She likes to curl up on their chests and knead their soft bones with her gentle paws. I toss her tidbits as I prepare the meal and explain the situation to her. She blinks those sweet amber eyes as if to say she understands perfectly and follows me upstairs when I take Toby his meal. He's perched on the wicker couch in the black silk pajamas and robe, squinting at the TV, watching

Cocoon. It's a favorite with all the old ones. I set his tray down on the table and pull up the other chair.

Feathers flops across Toby's feet, covering them like a rug, and he looks down at her and laughs. I can't remember the last time I heard him laugh and I've known Toby for ten or twelve years, since he moved down here after his wife died. I don't know if he has kids. He's never spoken of them if he does. But that's how it is with a lot of the old ones. When they get too old for their kids to deal with them, when there's talk of nursing homes, of confinement, they get scared and run away. Who can blame them?

"Watch this, Millie," he says excitedly, stabbing a gnarled finger at the screen. "This is where they swim in the rejuvenation pool."

I divide my attention between the screen and the chicken, which I cut up into small, manageable bites for him. I pass him a napkin, which he tucks under his throat like a bib, and pass him his plate. He sets it carefully on his lap, impales a chunk of meat, and dips it into a scoop of dressing. His hand trembles as it rises to his mouth. A dab of dressing rests on his chin, but he doesn't seem to notice it. He chews slowly, thoughtfully, eyes glued to the screen.

"Will it hurt?" he asks, not looking at me.

"Of course not."

"Are you sure?"

"You were here with Mink," I remind him. "Did she look like she hurt?"

Mouth puckering around a cranberry: "She always hurt. From the cancer. Or the radiation. From something."

Physical pain or psychic pain—the difference isn't that great. Shift your focus and one becomes the other. Mink knew that. "She's okay now, though."

"You talked to her?"

"Sure. I talk to her pretty often."

"And she's okay?"

"A lot better."

This is the game we play, Toby and I. We both pretend we don't know the truth.

"She's finished with the beach, Toby."

He mulls this over, nods, dips his fork into the steaming squash. "Can you do me a favor, Millie?"

"Sure, anything."

He reaches into the pocket of his robe and brings out a sheet of notebook paper. The words on it are printed, almost illegible. I can imagine Toby hunched over at the Ace Club, where some of the old ones hang out, moving a pen up and down against the paper, putting his thoughts in order. I get the point. "Okay," I tell him, and slip the sheet inside the old canvas bag, which slumps on the floor beside the bed like an aged and faithful pet.

"Can I watch another movie after this one?"

"Whatever you want. When you get tired, just pick up the phone and ring the desk. I'll be up to tuck you in."

"Don't go," he says quickly. "Stay here with me, Millie."

I pat his hand. "Let me get a pitcher of iced tea and your slice of pie and I'll be right back. Was it pumpkin or apple that you wanted, Toby?"

"Both." He grins mischievously, dark spaces in his mouth where there should be teeth. He's removed part of his denture.

"Both it is."

Feathers doesn't move as I get up; she knows the routine.

From the kitchen, I fetch iced tea for myself and two slices of pie for Toby and some treats for Feathers. In my bedroom, I bring out the Works, running my hands over the smooth, cool leather, remembering. I change into more comfortable clothes, cotton that breathes, that's the color of pearls. Makeup next. A touch of eye shadow, mascara, blush, lipstick. The way I look is part of the Works. Sometimes the old ones ask me to hold them, stroke them, caress them, make love to them. Other times they just want to listen to Frank Sinatra and dance or they ask me to walk on the beach with them in the moonlight. Their requests are as different as they are, and I always comply. But with all of them, there's a need for a special memory, an event that perhaps reminds them of something else. It's as if this memory will accompany them, comfort them somehow, like a friend.

Toby is still watching the movie when I return. His supper plate is clean. His eyes widen when he sees the pieces of pie, and he attacks the apple first, devouring it with childlike exuberance, then polishes off the pumpkin as well. We watch the rest of the movie together, Feathers purring between us on the couch. Now and then, his chin drops to his chest as he nods off, but he comes quickly awake, blinking fast as if to make sure he hasn't missed anything.

While the movie rewinds, I fold back the sheets on the bed. They're sea blue, decorated with shells and seahorses, the same ones Mink slept in. "Can we listen to music?" he asks, crouching in front of the stereo on the other side of the room.

"Sure. Whatever you want. Choose an album."

Harry Belafonte.

Toby gets up from the chair and holds out his arms and I move into them. I'm taller than he is, but it doesn't matter. We sway, his silk robe rustling. I rest my chin on his head and feel all those wrinkles quivering, shifting, warm as sand against my skin. He presses his cheek to my chest, eyes shut. The lemon scent of his skin haunts me a little, reminds of all the old ones who have come here for the Works. I've loved each of them and love them still.

When the record ends, Toby and I stretch out on the king-size bed, holding each other, talking softly, the moon smack in the heart of the skylight now. He falls asleep with his head on my shoulder, and for a long time I lie there just listening to him breathe, watching stars against the black dome of sky above us.

The window is partially open, admitting a taste of wind, the scent of stars, the whispering sea. I imagine that death is like this window, opening onto a pastel world where everything is what you will it to be. Yellow skies, if that's what you want. Silver seas. A youthful body. A sound mind. A family who cares. A state of grace.

And that's my gift to the old ones.

I untangle my arms and rise, drawing the covers over Toby. His wrinkled head sinks into the pillow. I bring out the leather case. New York. My old life. The business with the nursing board. Such unpleasantness, really. Like the old ones, I have my secrets. I take the syringe from my leather case and fill it. I have trouble finding a vein in his arm. They're lost in the folds of skin, collapsed beneath tissue, and I have to inject the morphine into his neck, just below his ear.

And then I wait.

Always, in the final moment, there's something that seems to escape from the old shell of bones and flesh, an almost visible thing, a puff of air, a kind of fragrance, the soul released. It leaves Toby when he sighs, fluttering from his mouth like a bird, and sweeps through the crack in the window, free at last.

Funny, but the wrinkles on top of his skull don't seen quite as deep now. His spine doesn't look as hunched. If I tried, I know I could straighten out his fingers. But the most I do is kiss him goodbye.

I get rid of the syringe. Sammy will take care of getting Toby's body to the pauper cemetery. There won't be a headstone, of course. I do have to make some concessions. But the burial will be proper, with an old pine box and all.

I unzip his canvas bag for the sheet of paper I slipped in here earlier and read it over. The list of who gets what is simple; all the names are old ones who hang out at the Ace Club. His belongings are in the bag. I sling it over my shoulder and walk downstairs, where Sammy is still at the desk. He looks up and I nod. He reaches under the desk and switches on the VACANCY sign outside. I take his place at the desk and he leaves to tend to Toby.

Most of the old ones will know about Toby before they hear it from me. They'll know because the only time the VACANCY sign goes on is when the Works are finished.

Tomorrow when I go down to the Ace, I'll also pass out my card to newcomers. After all, I've got to drum up business just like anyone else. *MILLIE'S PLACE. CHEAPEST RENT ON THE BEACH. GOOD FOOD. SPACIOUS ROOMS. THE WORKS.*

SMALL TIMES

BY James Carlos Blake

Flagler Dog Track

(Originally published in 1991)

The Loss

There was this guy I knew down in Miami, worked as a ticket seller at the dog track for a short time. Gordon. He had a routine for boosting his take-home. Strictly legit. (Tax-free, too. *You* tell the IRS everything? Not in this life.) Anyway, what Gordon did was, every time a guy at the window'd ask him what number to play, he'd tell him. Every race there's guys asking him for the winning number. They figure he's selling the tickets, he's gotta know the winners. Only he'd give each guy a different number. Some races he got asked by so many guys, he'd go through all the entries nine, ten times before the windows closed. He was handing out that many winners some races. Sure, a lot of those guys were stiffs; they'd grab their winnings and split without even a thank you. But plenty of them were sports. They'd come back grinning, give him a wink, cut him a percent—anything from a fin to a C-note. End of the night, it added up. Told me he was taking it home in a wheelbarrow. The problem was with some of those guys he gave a bum number. He'd get some hard looks the next time *they* came to the window, sometimes some hard words. He'd give a tough-luck shrug and try not to make eye contact. Then one night a coupla apes who lost big on the number he gave them laid for him in the parking lot. *Real* sore losers. Took him off to the last nickel, then stomped him damn near to death. Both legs busted, most his ribs, face all mashed, you name it. He was a mess for months. Went broke on the hospital bills. I hear he's in Orlando now. Sells insurance.

The Roust

Every man's got reasons to be bitter, but you can't give in to them any old time. There Hollis and me were, killing a pint under the overpass and wishing we had another, and this cop car comes screeching right into the lot—damn near runs us over. Shook me so bad I dropped and broke the bottle. There's just one cop. He jumps out yelling "Spread 'em!" and yanks out his gun and it goes flying out of his hand and bounces smack at my feet. Hollis yells "Get it!" and I do. I hadn't held a gun since the army. Up go the cop's hands. I'm shaking and wondering what I'm doing. "Easy now," the cop says. Hollis tells him shut up. The cop says he's looking for two white guys just hit the McDonald's on Third, he can see now we're not them, give him his gun and we can scram. I'm saying let's *go* man, but Hollis is *pissed*. He grabs a chunk of cinder block and POW!—he spiderwebs the cop's windshield. He yells "*Sicka* getting rousted!" Takes another chunk of block and busts the headlights. Pow!—Pow! Yells "Fuck it *all!*" He's smashing the car's party lights, going "Goddam *cops!* Goddam *people!* Goddam *Terry*, you whore!" Terry's his ex. Now sirens are closing in from all sides like walls, but Hollis keeps pounding the car and cussing a blue streak. Forget running. I hand the cop the gun and we just watch the backups come tearing in. Hollis went down swinging and swearing. I drew ninety days in the county stockade. Hollis got a year and a day at Raiford. Probably spending it brooding on all the goddam things he's sick of.

The Holdup

We hit this convenience store last Thursday night nearly did us in. The routine went just fine at first. Rankin braced the redhead chick at the register while I watched the doors and kept the others covered. Rankin worked smooth and quiet as always. Red went big-eyed but quick started sticking it in a paper bag. The two guys holding hands by the ice cream freezer were freaked out but they stood fast and kept their mouths shut. So did the big Cuban momma holding her little girl against her legs. They couldn't keep their eyes off the gun. That's why I use the .44—they remember the cannon better than my face. But this guy in a Dolphins shirt's got his head in the deli cooler and doesn't know what's going down. He's already chomping on a sandwich when he turns around and catches the scene. Next thing you know he's on the floor, choking and turning blue—and all I can think is how in Florida if somebody dies for any reason in a felony it's murder. Rankin sees what's happening, says "Damn," and drops down to work on the guy. Who's now *purple*. Eyes rolled up, tongue bulging out. Rankin hugs him from behind and gives one hard squeeze after another. Everybody's watching like it's TV. I'm about to wet my pants. Suddenly this glob of sandwich flies out and splats on a Fritos bag. The guy starts sucking breath like an air brake. We split fast. And come to find out we scored sixty-two bucks. Jesus, this business. I usually have me two beers every night. *That* night I put down a dozen.

THE ODYSSEY

BY Elmore Leonard

Miami Beach

(Originally published in 1995)

J oe Sereno caught the Odyssey night clerk as he was going off:
prissy guy, had his lunch box under his arm.

"I saw it this morning on TV," Joe said. "So there was a lot of
excitement, huh? I thought the cops'd still be here, at least the
crime scene guys. I guess they've all cleared out. You hear the
shots? You must've."

"I was in the office," the night guy said.

Joe wondered how this twink knew he was in the office at the
exact time the shots were fired. What'd he think, it was sound-
proof in there? But the cops no doubt had asked him that, so Joe
let it pass and said, "It was the two guys in one-oh-five, wasn't it?"

"I think so."

"You're not sure?"

The night guy rolled his eyes and then pretended to yawn. He
did things like that, had different poses.

"Fairly respectable-looking guys," Joe said, "but no luggage.
What're they doing, shacking up? Maybe, maybe not. But I remember thinking at the time, they're up to something. The TV
news didn't mention their names, so there must not've been any
ID on the bodies and the cops didn't think the names they used to
register were really theirs. Am I right?"

The night guy said, "I wouldn't know," acting bored.

"Soon as I saw those guys yesterday—they checked in as I was
getting ready to go off—I said to Mel, 'Let me see the registration

cards, see what names they gave.' He wouldn't show me. He goes, 'Registering guests is not a security matter, if you don't mind.'" Mel, the day guy, sounding a lot like Kenneth, the night guy.

"I didn't have time to hang around, keep an eye on them," Joe went on. "I had to go to another job, a function at the Biltmore. They put on extra security for this bunch of Cuban hotshots meeting there. I mean *Cuban* Cubans, said to be Castro sympathizers, and there was a rumor Fidel himself was gonna show up. You believe it? I wore a suit instead of this Mickey Mouse uniform, brown and friggin' orange; I get home I can't wait to take it off. Those functions, you stand like this holding your hands in front of you, like you're protecting yourself from getting a hernia, and you keep your eyes moving. So"—he gestured toward the entrance—"I saw the truck out there, the tan van, no writing on the sides? That's the cleanup company, right?"

"I wouldn't know," the night guy said.

Little curly-haired twink, walked with his knees together.

"Well, listen, I'll let you go," Joe said, "and thanks for sharing that information with me, it was interesting. I'll go check on the cleanup people, see how they're doing. What room was that again, one-oh-five?"

It sure was.

There was furniture in the hall by the open door and a nasty smell in the air. As Joe approached, a big black guy in a white plastic jumpsuit, latex gloves, what looked like a shower cap, goggles up on his head, blue plastic covering his shoes, came out carrying a floor lamp.

Joe said, "Joe Sereno, security officer."

"I'm Franklin, with Baneful Clean-Up."

"*Baneful?*"

"The boss named it. He tried Pernicious Clean-Up in the Yellow Pages? Didn't get any calls."

Joe said, "Hmmmm, how about Death Squad?"

"That's catchy," Franklin said, "but people might get the wrong idea. You know, that we doing the job 'stead of cleaning up after. This is my partner, Marlis," Franklin said, and Joe turned to see a cute young black woman approaching in her plastic coveralls, hip-hop coming out of the jam box she was carrying.

"Joe Sereno, security officer."

"Serene, yeah," Marlis said, "that's a cool name, Joe," her body doing subtle, funky things like it was plugged into the beat. She said to Franklin, "Diggable Planets doing 'Rebirth of Slick.' 'It's cool like dat.'"

"'It's chill like dat,'" Franklin said. "Yeah, 'it's chill like dat.'"

Franklin bopping now, going back into the room.

Joe followed him in, stopped dead at the sight, and said, "Oh, my God," at the spectacle of blood: on the carpet, on two walls, part of the ceiling, a trail of blood going from this room into the bathroom. Joe looked in there and said it again, with feeling, "Oh, my God."

"Like they was skinnin' game in here," Franklin said. "Shotgun done one of them at close range. The other one, nine-millimeter pistol, they believe. Man got shot four times through and through—see the holes in the wall there? They dug out the bullets. Made it to the bathroom, got three more pumped into him and bled out in the shower. Thank you, Jesus. We still have to clean it, though, with the green stuff, get in between the tiles with a toothbrush. We thankful the man came in here, didn't go flop on the bed to expire."

Joe said, "Man, the smell."

"Yeah, it's what your insides get like exposed to the air too long, you know what I'm saying? Your viscera, it's called. It ain't too bad yet. But if you gonna stay in here and watch," Franklin said, "better breathe through your mouth."

Joe said, "I think I'll step out to the patio for a minute."

The two secretaries from Dayton, Ohio, their bra straps hanging loose, were out by the pool already, this early in the morning, to catch some rays, working at it, not wasting a minute of their vacation. Joe took a few deep breaths inhaling the morning air to get that smell out of his nose. On the other side of the pool, still in shade, a guy sat in a plastic patio chair smoking a cigar as he watched the girls. Guy in his sixties—he'd be tall with a heavy frame: his body hadn't seen much sun, but his face was weathered. Joe believed the guy was wearing a rug. Black hair that had belonged to a Korean woman at one time. A retired wigmaker had told him they used a lot of Korean hair. This one looked too dark for a guy in his sixties. Joe had never noticed the guy before—he must've checked in yesterday or last night—but for some reason he looked familiar. Joe went back in the unit, ducked into the bedroom and picked up the phone.

"Sereno, security. Who's in one-twenty?"

The day guy's voice said, "Why do you want to know?"

I'm doing something wrong, Joe thought. I'm failing to communicate. "Listen, it's important. The guy, there's something about him isn't right."

"Like what?"

"I think he's using the Odyssey as a hideout."

"Is this the guy with the Steven Seagal hairpiece?"

"You got it."

"Just a minute."

The twink was gone at least five minutes while Joe waited, trying to breathe through his mouth. Finally he came back on.

"His name's Garcia."

Franklin was working on the ceiling with a sponge mop; he would come down off his metal ladder and squeeze into a pail, then take the pail into the bathroom and dump it in the toilet. Marlis was scrubbing a wall with what looked like a big scouring pad, moving in time to the beat coming from the jam box, kind of spastic, Joe thought, but sexy all the same.

The two looked like they were dressed up in moon suits they'd made for Halloween: the white plastic coveralls, goggles, respiratory masks, covered head to toe. The smell of the chemicals they were using was even stronger now than the other smell. Joe got a whiff and started coughing as he asked Marlis what it was they cleaned with.

She said, "The green stuff for a lot of heavy, dried blood; the pink stuff when it isn't too old and hard to get off."

"Girl," Franklin said, "your head keeps touching the wall and I see some hair sticking out."

"I'll fix it in a minute."

Marlis had on rubber gloves that came up her arms. She said to Joe Sereno, "See these little specks here in the wall? They from the man's skull, little tiny fragments of bone. Sometime I have to use pliers to pull them out. This dark stuff is the dude's hair. See these other holes? They from the shotgun." She funked around, doing steps to the music as she said to Franklin, "Coolio, for your pleasure."

Franklin listened and said, "Ain't Coolio." Listened some more, said, "You got your Cools confused. It's LL Cool J, no other, 'cause that's 'Hey Lover.'" He paused, looking past Marlis to a framed print on the wall. "Girl, is that like modern art on there or something else?"

Marlis went up to the picture for a close look and said, "It's something else."

Joe looked at it and said, "Oh, my God."

He watched Marlis remove the print and drop it into a red bag. "Ain't worth cleaning. Anything has body fluids, tissue, poo-poo, you know, anything biohazardous, goes in these bags. We give them to a company takes care of medical waste to get rid of."

"You missed a speck there," Franklin said, pointing at the wall.

"I'm still working on it, baby." Lowering her voice, she said to Joe, "He don't like to see me talking to other men."

"Are you and him married?"

"You'd think so to hear him."

"I was wondering, is there any money in cleanup work? You don't mind my asking."

"We quoted this job at fifteen hundred. Hey, how many people can you find to do it? Another reason it's a good business, recessions don't bother it none. This one here looks worse'n it is. Doesn't smell too bad. You work where a body's been decomposing awhile, now you talking about smell. Like old roadkill up close? You go home and take a shower, you have to wash out your nostrils good. The smell like sticks to the hairs in your nose."

"What's the worst one you ever had to clean up?"

"The worst one. Hmmmm." She said, "You mean the very worst one? Like an advanced state of decomp has set in? The body's in a dark, damp place and dung beetles have found it?"

Franklin said, "Girl?"

"I'm coming," Marlis said. She got a scraper, like a big putty knife, from a box of tools and went back to work. She said to Joe, "It dries on here it's hard to get off."

"What is that?"

She was scraping at something crusted on there. "Little piece of what the dude used to use to think with. His brain, honey. He maybe should've thought better about coming here, huh? Two dudes die and nobody even knows who they are. Least it's what I heard." She looked over at Joe Sereno standing by the closet door, staring at the knob. "Don't touch that, baby."

"It looks like candle wax," Joe said, "but I don't see any candles in the room."

"It ain't wax," Marlis said, "it's some more the dude's gray matter. Gets waxy like that outside the head. See how the wood's splintered right above it? That's from skull fragments shot in there. This one dude, I swear, is all over the room."

"You just do murders?"

"Homicides, suicides, and decompositions."

"How about animals?"

"Once in a while. We cleaned up after a woman poisoned her dogs, fifteen of 'em she couldn't feed no more. It smelled worse'n a dead manatee laying in the sun too long."

Joe perked up. "There's a manatee over on the bay was shot. You hear about it?"

Joe thought he saw a look pass between Marlis and Franklin on the ladder as she said no, she didn't think so.

"A pretty friendly creature," Joe said, "used to play with that old woman who was killed. Marion something?"

"McAlister Williams," Marlis said. "Yeah, I've heard of her. Hundred and two years old and still swimmin' in the bay."

Joe said, "And there was that guy tried to jump the drawbridge and didn't make it."

"Name was Victor," Franklin said, down from the ladder, heading for the john with his pail. "Actually was a scuba tank I understand flew out of a truck, hit the man's car and blew him up. Totaled 'em both. Yeah, we heard about that. 'Cool like dat.'" He said, "So-Lo Jam," and right away said, "I take that back."

"You better," Marlis said.

"That's from *Cold Chillin'*, so it has to be Kool G. Rap. Yeah."

Joe had to wait, not having any idea what they were talking about, before saying, "How about that disaster at Club Hell? I was working there that night. It was horrible."

"Nobody had to clean that one up," Franklin said, coming out of the john, "the sharks took care of it."

"Come here for a minute, will you?" Joe motioned them over to the sliding glass door that led to the patio. "See that guy sitting by the pool? Over on the other side. Who does he look like?"

"I can't see him good," Franklin said.

"Take your goggles off."

Franklin squinted now, eyes uncovered. He said, "I don't know. Who?"

Marlis came over and right away said, "The dude with the cigar? He looks like Castro. Either Castro or that dude goes around thinking he looks like Castro. You know what I'm saying? Mickey Something-or-other's his name. Yeah, Mickey Schwartz."

"Wait a minute," Franklin said, still squinting. "What Castro you talking about?"

"Castro, the one from Cuba."

"They *all* from Cuba."

"What's his name—Fidel," Marlis said. "Fidel Castro. Shaved off his beard." She paused and hunched in a little closer to Joe and Franklin. "Shaved his beard and must've shaved his head, too, 'cause the man's wearing a rug."

"That's what I thought too," Joe said. "But whose hair does the rug look like?"

Now Marlis squinted till she had it and said, "Yeah, that high-waisted cat kung-fus everybody he don't shoot."

Franklin said, "I know who you mean. That kung-fu cat with the big butt. Doesn't take shuck and jive from nobody. But listen to me now. If that's *the* Fidel we talking about here, there's a man will pay a million dollars to see him dead. Man name of Reyes. It would be easy as pie to cap him sitting there, wouldn't it?" He looked at Joe Sereno. "I mean if it was your trade."

"Tempting," Marlis said, "but safer to clean up after. Celebrity, be nothing wrong with doubling the fee."

Joe was thinking. He said, "You suppose a hit man killed these two in here?"

"Hit men as a rule," Franklin said, "don't make this kind of mess. One on the back of the head, use a twenty-two High Standard Field King with a suppressor on it. We've followed up after hit men, haven't we, precious?"

"We sure have," Marlis said. "Lot of that kind of work around here."

Joe Sereno said, "You don't suppose . . ." and stopped, narrowing his eyes then to make what he wanted to say come out right. "In the past few days I've run into three homicides, counting these two, and a fourth one they're calling an accident looks more like a homicide to me. I have a hunch they're related. Don't pin me down for the motive, 'cause I don't see a nexus. At least not yet I don't. But I got a creepy feeling that once these two are identified, it will explain the others. I'm talking about the old woman, and a guy named Phil. And, unless I miss my guess, it all has something to do with that man sitting over there smoking a cigar."

"Unless," Marlis said, "the dude over there is the Fidel impersonator, Mickey Schwartz."

"Either way," Joe Sereno said, "ID these two and this whole mess will become clear."

A look passed between Franklin and Marlis.

Joe caught it and thought, Hmmmm.

PART III

MIAMI'S VICES

TO GO

BY LYNNE BARRETT

Hialeah

(Originally published in 1996)

So I insist that we stop and at least I'll get something to go, even if B.K. won't come in, won't eat, his stomach nervous, he's in such a rush to make Clewiston by noon. He stays in the cool car

while I pass through bright heat into one of those places, lunch counter/souvenir store, where the air has the sweet mustiness of pecans and orange wine. I wait while they zap the sausage biscuits and when I come out with iced teas on a tray and hop into the Chrysler

he's dead. Hunched over the wheel with the same glare he had when he drove a two-lane and some old-timer in an Airstream got ahead of him and nothing, not flashing the high beams, not honking, not gunning up to ride three inches from the guy's bumper, nothing would make the slow poke speed up. B.K. looks just like that now, aggravated

and dead, clutching the wheel. His cheeks are slippery with tears and there's a faint bad smell. The air conditioner is blasting. The motor runs ragged. I stick my foot over and press his shoe down on the gas, and the idle richens. I want to charge inside and howl for help, but I know for once in my life I ought to stop and think. I look out through purple-tinted windows at the parking lot—nobody in sight but some family at a picnic table under the sign for *LIVE BABY ALLIGATORS* and *GOAT'S MILK FUDGE*. If I go inside I'll have to say,

Excuse me, Mr. Brian Kittery is out there, dead. It must have been his heart. His stomach bothered him last night, but it always did. He used to say, "Nobody dies of indigestion." And it never slowed him down. Sure, we did it this morning in that motel on South Dixie he liked to stay in whenever he visited the Home Office, me leaning on the table, looking out the window at the sunlit swimming pool, him with his pants around his ankles as if when he finished he would yank them up and dash—but that was his favorite way and it was his idea, don't blame me,

he wouldn't, he wasn't that kind of guy. Impatient, sure, with inept cashiers, Zavala Junior at the Home Office, but basically fair. He groused about phoning his wife in Arcadia every evening at seven, but he did it on the dot, I noticed. When I first rode with him, six weeks ago, he was so jumpy I thought he could be one of those guys like they show on TV, Mr. Normal Church Choir Wife and Two Kids in Little League, who is socking it away the whole time, stealing everyone's investments, and then takes off—but no, I got to see he was just in a rush, horny, in hock, buying scratch-off lottery tickets, pressing to make time on the road, driving

up and down Florida stopping in every I Love Jesus Beauty Parlor & Auto Repair to sell his line of beauty products—Seagrape Scrub and Alligator Mask and Key Lime Conditioner, with me as his demo. It was his great idea, my fake ID saying I'm forty-two years old and look thirty, when really I'm twenty-six looking thirty, which is an achievement if you ask me because I've been through enough to look forty-two. We like to say life is short

but it's a long, long time when you're sitting in it. When I met him, I was in Cocoa, doing a Miller Lite promotion, giving out free hats in a sports lounge during *Monday Night Football*, wearing short-shorts and high heels. "Nice wheels," he said, meaning my legs. I told him I taught aerobics in the daytime, was saving for a move to Miami, where you can get work as a dancer, and he said, "Why wait?" Big man, seventeen-inch neck, eating chicken fingers. That night we got as far as Briny Breezes, Palm Beach County, and next morning, just for me, he took the slow route down the A1A past the oceanfront millionaire houses, to Miami. While he was at the Home Office, Señora Zavala's storefront in Coconut Grove, I checked out the rents and decided to say yes to a swing around the state with him, zigzagging: Naples–Fort Pierce–Tampa-Orlando-Daytona-Jacksonville and then the long glide out the Panhandle where I saw my granny. And then back down, opening up new territory in Ocala and Port St. Lucie. Amazing how fast the state changes, new cutteries in strip malls and vanished salons. Florida is motion

even on this part of 27, the old tourist trail from Miami on up to Tallahassee. After we'd gotten through bumper-to-bumper Hialeah, the road was stretching out toward empty wetlands and sugar country when I made him stop. It's almost eleven and the parking lot is beginning to fill up. Nobody gives us a glance, but I think it will look better if we seem to be eating, so I stick my straw in my tea and suck its sweetness, then chew the warm fat of my sausage biscuit while I try to figure out my situation. I keep looking at his eyes, dark blue with the long lashes of a lover boy. Reassuring shoulders. I liked him. He'd say,

"Make your own luck," he believed in hard work and drive, but who's gonna stand up at the funeral and say, At least he made those last three calls. Honestly, what'll happen if I go, Excuse me, this man is dead. No, I had no warning, Sheriff—

they have sheriffs, places like this, elected for their swagger and intolerance of strangers—

Well, I didn't really know him and um. Can't say my boyfriend. My employer, and please call his dear wife. She must suspect he was out here with someone like me, though women, my God, women can not-know whatever they put their minds to. Turn him into a shadow and concentrate on the kids. Then she'll be here, and Zavala Junior will say B.K. was supposed to do his demo on a local girl each time, and when they check the motel records they'll know we slept together if you can call it sleep, him always on the side nearest the door, grinding his teeth. Something was chasing him, and I guess it's caught him now. He won't be resting any easier if there's a fuss. Excuse me, I noticed this man in a parked car, he hasn't moved, I think he's dead. How did I get here, though? Excuse me, I was just hitchhiking. Excuse me, Sheriff—and then I better not have ID for Carrie Hull, forty-two. B.K. got her birth certificate, a little girl he went to school with who died, leukemia. He must've liked her all those years ago. He said it was like we were giving her another chance, but that driver's license with my picture, my granny's address, is fraud, probably a felony. How simple it was when I used to be

Ruth Ann Reedy, just a little cracker girl from Paxton, highest point in Florida, 345 feet, right near the Alabama line. And then Ruth Ann Wheeler, when I married at nineteen. Jeep Wheeler threatened me into it and I was fool enough to think if I gave in he'd be reassured and uncrazy. On our honeymoon weekend in St. Pete he punched me out so, duh, I wised up. Back in Paxton I went to a lawyer and said, "You'll think I'm weird, I've been married five days and I want a divorce," and the lawyer said, "Happens all the time." When I was hiding out, then, Jeep beat his mother up, and she got me word to come sign the papers to commit him for observation, which I did. Before he could get loose

I took off, went back to Reedy, made it Reed, and cocktail waitressed and studied dance in Tampa, where they started calling me Ginger in tap class. It's Ginger Reed with the record for disturbing the peace, 'cause when I drank rum I liked to do the time step, *flap shuffle flap shuffle flap ball change,* on the roof of my apartment building. And it's Ginger Reed who got pulled in when they raided the exotic dance club in Daytona where I was shaking it for the college boys. Charges dropped but those sheriffs can still get in to where it's on record, and Now then, little lady, you've got quite a past, they say while they're checking out your boobs. Which makes me think this leotard, fine for demonstrating Avocado Bosom Cream, shows too much for any decent Excuse me, so I recline the passenger seat and slither through to crouch under B.K.'s suits and shirts hanging from the rack across the backseat. I wriggle into a long cotton skirt and T-shirt and switch my silver sandals for my Keds. I take down the two dresses I'd hung up and stuff everything into my big soft bag. Check to make sure my money's in my tampon box, the place I figure no thief will look. I guess I can't take the big sample case, so I just snag some Orange Mint Restorer, Señora Zavala's original recipe, 'cause I really think it's done my skin a lot of good. I toss my bag up front, and when I get in the seat and slowly crank it up I see

an old school bus, painted blue, has pulled into the lot. Home-made script proclaims, *Christ's Canaries, Choir of the First Church of Our Savior Sanctified.* Out come round-faced women with virtuous perms. They look like home to me. Excuse me, but some sinning fellow ditched me here and could you please give me a lift? Excuse me, I'm working my way to my granny's in Sebring, Leesburg, wherever you're going. I'll mingle with them in the bathroom line. I'm a second soprano, Carrie Hull, age forty-two—why, thank you, if I look good it must be living clean. B.K. will get found on his own. They'll shut down for the night and there he'll be, car stalled, heart attack, warm tea, and no one will even know I was here. I gather our food wraps and get out, soft bag across my shoulder, purse in hand. At the trash basket I turn,

look at him across the parking lot. He stares into the tinted windshield like any man left waiting for a woman. He must hate being stuck. He used to take right turns on red just to keep moving. We'd twine through a new town not yet on the map, and he'd grin when I worried and say, "We may be lost, but we're making good time."

LEMONADE AND PARIS BUNS

BY JOHN DUFRESNE

Aventura

(Originally published in 1996)

I called the clinic and made an appointment for a cholesterol test. I ticked that off my list. I called Dentaland at the Aventura Mall. They told me Dr. Shimkoski was no longer affiliated with their practice. Well, what was I supposed to do then? I've got this temporary crown here. I thought I heard someone outside talking to Spot. We can set you up with Dr. Perez. Fine, I said. Wednesday, noon. I dumped the whites into the washer, poured in the Tide, set the timer. I walked to the window to check on the voice.

Four children sat on the ground near Spot patting him, talking to him. Spot, I could tell, was loving the attention. I went out to the deck and introduced myself. I said, I'm the dog's—and I was going to say *master* until I heard the word in my head and realized how absurd it was—I'm the dog's dad, I said. I take care of him.

"What you dog name?" the oldest-looking child said.

"Spot. And yours?"

They were brothers, I learned, named Smith. The oldest, Trayvien, probably ten, introduced me to Demetrius, Everett, and Kendrick.

Spot rolled on his back with his legs in the air like quotation marks. Everett stroked Spot's belly. I asked them where they lived. Trayvien pointed across the backyard. I asked them if they'd like a snack. They would. So we had brunch on the deck.

Trayvien helped me set the table and led us in Grace before

we ate—his idea. We had lemonade and Paris buns. That's what I called them for the occasion. They were crescent rolls, actually, from Pastry Lane. Kendrick, the tiny one, sat on my lap and rubbed the hair on my arm back and forth. Trayvien was like the father. He poured lemonade for his brothers, wiped their faces with napkins. He asked me what I did for a job. I told him I write stories. He said that's what he did too. I asked him to tell me a story. Trayvien told me the one he called "The Wolf, the Bear, the Lion, and the Man." The four characters are friends, and they don't have enough money to buy ice cream. The lion wants to eat the bank to get some. The man says they should go to work and earn the money. The bear is sure they can find some dollars in the street. The wolf says we could just ask nice. And the wolf is right.

As I scooped out the chocolate ice cream, I asked Trayvien did he have any stories with vegetables in them. No, he didn't. I told them all they should come by more often. Spot and I would enjoy their company. Trayvien said where they were living—he pointed across the yard again—was a frosted home, and they didn't know how long they'd be here. Foster home? I said. That's it, Trayvien said. Everett asked me, Where you daddy?

Louisiana, I said. Way far away.

I found out that their mama lived with a man named Walter. Their granny took care of them for a while. Now they're here. What are your foster parents' names? I said. Trayvien said, We don't know yet. You think they might be worried where you are? Trayvien shrugged. I said, Well, let's go find them, okay? We all washed up at the kitchen sink. We put Spot on his leash and paraded down the street. We waved to Mr. Lesperence next door. Everett walked beside Spot. Spot kept licking Everett's face. Demetrius held the leash. Trayvien held Kendrick's hand. I held Trayvien's. Trayvien was sure it was a blue house. We made a couple of lefts and rights, but nothing looked familiar. Demetrius told me that Spot pees a lot.

Here it is, Trayvien said.

258 // Miami Noir: The Classics

I wanted to ring the bell, let the people know we were back, but Trayvien wouldn't let me. They napping, he said.

The boys hugged Spot. They stood in the driveway and waved goodbye until we turned the corner. This all happened a year and a half ago. I've never seen them again.

For a while, Spot and I took our walks by the blue house. One evening a man in a T-shirt and shorts stood there in the front yard, watering a Manila palm. He must have thought I was crazy. No kids ever lived here, he said. I looked around. This was the house. Spot slurped water from the hose. The man said, Shoo. Spot woofed at him. So you're not a foster parent? I said. He made a face. Spot sniffed around the sidewalk. Evidently, the children's volatile molecules lingered here, though the children did not. I called the Welfare. No one there would tell me anything— confidentiality, the woman said. I said, What kind of world is this? Four babies wandering the streets. You shouldn't worry, she said.

My cholesterol is in the stratosphere it turns out. So I drink red wine now with my Paris buns. I brunch on the deck with Spot, imagine Trayvien telling me a story with a happy ending. Like maybe he says, The lion wants his friends back, but the man says forget about it. The bear is sure it was all a dream anyway. But the wolf says what he believes is you meet everyone twice before you die.

THE RED SHOES

by Edna Buchanan

Downtown

(Originally published in 1999)

H e stared from the shadows until the lights went out. He knew which apartment was hers, had conducted several recon missions to scout the layout of the building after following her home a week ago. She had been wearing narrow red sandals with little straps that night. The heels had to be four inches high. She wore them bare-legged, soles arched, each delicious digit of her toes spread like some exotic bird clinging to her elevated perch. Harvey's knees felt weak as he remembered, picturing the voluptuous curve of her instep, and the right heel, slightly smudged, from driving. She should carpet the floor of her car, he thought, it would be a shame to ruin those shoes. Their sharp stiletto heels had pounded across the pavement and up the stairs, piercing his heart. Had to be at least four and a half inches high, he thought.

Suddenly her second-floor door swung open and someone emerged, taking Harvey by surprise as he gazed up, lost in fantasy. A big man trotted down the stairs, stared for a moment, then brushed by, ignoring him. Though husky, the fellow was light on his feet, in running shoes, jeans, and a hooded yellow sweatshirt. Must be the boyfriend, Harvey thought, turning away as the stranger strode toward the parking lot. Harvey took the opposite direction, the breezeway to the mailboxes, his head down, pretending to be a tenant coming home late.

His first instinct was to abort, to go home and watch another old movie, but instead he lingered. Nobody could know all the neighbors in a complex this size, he assured himself, aware that he was not a man most people would notice, or remember, anyway. A car door slammed and a big engine sprang quickly to life. Harvey relaxed as headlights swung out of the parking lot and melted into the night.

A close call, he thought, loitering behind the dumpsters. From his vantage point he continued to watch her apartment. The lights were still out. He had read that the deepest sleep comes soon after the first hour. He was too excited to give up now. The wait would be worth it, he thought, and settled down.

Harvey had always liked women's feet. The roots of his obsession dated back to the moment he realized that he was the only one in his high school art-appreciation class turned on by the bare feet of the Virgin Mary.

Women's feet became even more alluring after he stopped drinking. He had worked the steps, had a sponsor, and saw the truth behind an AA counselor's comment that "you often replace one addiction with another." How true.

Unfortunately, his recent expeditions had made the newspapers, forcing him to exercise more caution. But this one was worth the risk, more exciting than all of the others he had followed home.

Two of his encounters had apparently never been reported. That had perplexed him. He wondered if they had been too afraid or too embarrassed, or too lacking in faith in the local police? Perhaps they had liked it and hoped he'd be back. He pondered that possibility until, consulting the luminous dial of his watch, he decided it was time to make his move.

He silently ascended the open staircase. Glittery stars winked from above and Mars burned like an ember to the east. The rudimentary hardware on the sliding glass door was laughable. The high school summer he worked for a local locksmith had been well spent. These people should know how little protection they have, he thought righteously, then slid the door open just enough to slip in sideways. The darkened dining room smelled of lemon furniture polish on wood and the fruity aroma of fresh oranges arranged in a ceramic bowl.

A pendulum clock's rhythmic tick was the only sound. It followed him to her bedroom, keeping time with his stealthy footsteps. His body quaked with anticipation. He knew the right room, always the last light out at night. Her faint form was barely distinguishable, a dim outline on the bed as he paused in the doorway. A jumbo jet roared overhead in ascent from Miami International Airport, but she never stirred. He waited until the airliner's thunder faded, replaced by the faint hum of the ceiling fan above her bed.

He did not need his penlight to find what he had come for. The stiletto heels, side by side, stood at rigid attention next to her closet door. She had slipped them off carelessly, without unfastening the tiny metal buckles and the skinny straps. That's how you ruin an excellent pair of shoes, he thought indignantly, then shivered with delight at her rash and wanton behavior.

In the beginning, during his early forays, he simply seized his prize and fled, pilfering their shoes, sometimes from the floor next to the very bed where they slumbered. Sometimes he snatched a bonus, a worn sock or nylon stocking from the dirty-clothes hamper on the way out. But one breezy and memorable night, his inhibitions had crumbled, along with his resistance. She was a shapely little waitress from Hooters, red-haired with a ponytail. Creeping in a window left open to the breeze, he had found her running shoes. They radiated a delightful, intoxicating aroma, a mixture of musky sweat, rubber, and Odor-Eaters. He was about to depart with them, when the blossoming full moon silvered the room, the sweet, alluring scent of night-blooming jasmine filled the air, and she stirred, murmuring in her sleep, and kicked off the flowered sheet. He stood frozen, the enticing arch of her bare foot beckoning, just inches away. Lord knows, he wasn't made of stone. Who could resist? He planted a passionate wet kiss on her metatarsal.

She woke up screaming, of course, and he beat feet out of there, but the shared terror, the adrenaline, the flight were irresistible. He was hooked.

Since then, local papers and television newscasters had reported the unknown intruder's fondness for feet, announcing that police wanted him for eight to ten such escapades. The notoriety made it a more risky business. Couldn't they see how harmless it was? Nobody hurt. And no matter how many valuables, jewelry, cash, even drugs that he found scattered across dresser tops, all he ever took was footwear. He had his pride. Actually, he was doing them a favor, demonstrating their lack of security before some truly dangerous stranger paid a visit. This might be out of the norm, but it was certainly safer than driving drunk or ruining his liver. And it was so much more stimulating—and satisfying. Nobody could deny that.

Excited now, he heard her breathing, or was that his own? This one slept naked, sprawled on her back, her feet apart at the foot of the bed. His heart thudded as he stepped closer, hoping she hadn't showered. The polish on her bloodred toenails gleamed in the eerie green light from her bedside clock as he focused on the seductively plump curve of her big toe. He licked his lips in anticipation, the pleasure centers of his midbrain slipping into overdrive as he touched her, stroking her feet gently with his thumbs and index fingers, then leaned forward. The toes were cool beneath his warm lips. He could almost feel them stiffening.

The scream came as expected, but it was his own, as the moon broke free from clouds and he saw her clearly in the light spilling between the blinds. Eyes wide open and protruding, the twisted stocking grotesquely embedded in an impossibly deep groove around her throat. He gasped, stumbled back in horror, and tried not to gag. Instinctively he fled, then hesitated in the dining room and turned back, wasting precious moments.

He snatched the red stiletto heels off the floor near the closet, shoved them under his shirt without looking at the bed, and scrambled for the exit. The bulge beneath his shirt forced him to push the sliding glass door open even farther to escape. What if someone had heard his cry? The door shrieked unexpectedly, metal rasping on metal, resounding through the night. In his haste, he stumbled against a plastic recycling bin outside her neighbor's door. It tipped over, spilling aluminum cans that clattered everywhere. He righted the receptacle with both hands and stood quietly for a moment, breathing deeply, his pulse pounding like a racehorse at the gate. A few feet away someone opened a window.

"Who's out there?" a deep voice demanded.

Harvey fled blindly, in panic, descending two and three steps at a time. Another window cranked open.

"What's going on?"

"There he goes!" someone else shouted.

He plunged headlong from the landing, stumbled, scrambled painfully to his feet, and hobbled across the parking lot, right ankle throbbing.

Lights bloomed, a concert of light behind him, as he glanced over his shoulder. Miamians are notoriously well armed and primed to shoot. He could not chance an encounter with some trigger-happy crime stopper. The cold metal of the dead woman's stiletto heel jabbed him in the belly as he flung himself into his Geo Metro. He winced at the pain as it broke the skin, fumbling frantically to fit the key into the ignition. His hands shook so uncontrollably that it seemed to take forever. Finally the engine caught. He tore out of the parking lot, burning rubber, lights out.

He took deep breaths, the car all over the road, his eyes glued to the rearview mirror. No one in pursuit. He forced himself to slow down, assume control, and switch on his lights, just in time. He saw the blue flasher of an approaching patrol car. It roared past at a high rate of speed, westbound, no siren, probably responding to the prowler call. Harvey whimpered, turned onto US 1, and merged with other late-night traffic. How could that vibrant young girl be dead? Murdered. Her killer had to be that bastard, the man he saw leave, the man in the yellow sweatshirt. But the police wouldn't know that, they'd think he did it. His prize, the coveted strappy red sandals now resting uneasily against his heart, could send him to the electric chair.

Fear iced his blood and he shuddered involuntarily as he wrenched them from beneath his shirt, tearing it as a heel caught the fabric. He rolled down the window to hurl the incriminating evidence out by the side of the road, but could not bring himself to do it. It was not only because another motorist or some late-night jogger might see. He felt suddenly emotional about the final mementos of that lovely woman, so vivacious and full of life. The sort of lovely, lively woman who never would have given him a second look. He tried to think.

How could he explain? What would he say if they arrested him? "I'm not a murderer, I'm only a pervert." He said it out loud and didn't like the way it sounded.

How good a defense was that? Nobody would believe him. His favorite fantasies occasionally involved handcuffs, but their image now horrified him. Yet he could not bring himself to throw away her shoes like so much garbage, like someone had left her lifeless body, naked and exposed. He needed a drink, really needed a drink. Mouth dry, his tongue parched, he eased into the parking lot of the Last Chance Bar, but changed his mind before he cut the engine. Drinking was no answer, backsliding wouldn't help his situation. He needed to think clearly. He drove back out onto the street, toward Garden Avenue. The AA meetings there were attended in large part by restaurant workers and airport employees whose shifts ended at midnight or later.

The big room radiated light, fellowship, and the smell of fresh coffee. He was glad to see Phil, his sponsor, in the crowd.

Harvey sat and listened, sweating despite the cool evening and the laboring air conditioner. He wondered why nobody ever bothers to turn them off in Florida, even when the weather is comfortable. He sailed through the preliminaries when his turn came, then began, "You don't know how close I just came." He shook his head and ran his fingers through his hair, already thinning at twenty-six. "Something happened tonight." The shrewd eyes of a member named Ira lingered speculatively on Harvey's torn shirt.

"Old bad habits almost got me in big trouble." Harvey licked his lips. His mouth felt dry again despite the coffee he'd had. "You know how they always tend to come back and cause you problems." He looked around. Several people he didn't know were present. "Tonight, I was only trying . . ." Harvey's eyes continued to roam to the back of the room, to the coffee urn, where the man in the yellow sweatshirt stood watching him.

Harvey nearly strangled on his own words. "I have to go," he mumbled. His sponsor called his name, but he was out the door.

The Dew Drop Inn was quiet, a few regulars at the knotty-pine bar, an old martial arts movie on TV, and some guys and girls playing pool in the back room. Harvey swallowed his first drink in a single scalding gulp, quickly followed by another, then sat nursing the third, trying to focus on the taste, avoiding all other thoughts. The double doors opened, admitting fresh air and street sounds along with a new arrival. A dozen empty stools stood at the bar, but the newcomer chose the one next to his. Harvey knew who it was before he looked up.

"Fancy seeing you here." The man in the yellow sweatshirt grinned.

Harvey squirmed, trying to look casual, his stomach churning. "Just testing the waters again."

"Me too." The man paused and lit a cigarette. "I can only take so much culture before I have to roll in the shit." He looked at Harvey. "They say it's the first drink that gets you drunk."

"I'm on number three."

The barkeep hovered expectantly. "J.D. neat," said the newcomer. "And hit my friend here again." He studied Harvey's glass, then raised hooded eyes as cold-blooded and hard as a snake's. "What is that?"

"Stoly'tini, twelve to one."

"I like talkin' to a man who speaks my language." The big man in the yellow sweatshirt flipped a twenty onto the bar as their drinks arrived.

Harvey wondered if he could make it out the door if he decided to run for it. He might make it out the door, but not into his car. Was the killer armed? Would he pause to pick up his change before he came charging after him? If Harvey did make it to his car, the man would surely see what he drove, and his tag number—if he didn't already have them. Had he been followed? Or had the big man methodically checked every bar in the neighborhood? At this hour, Harvey's little Geo could easily be forced off the road with no witnesses. He could call the police, but how would he explain why he was at the murder scene? He would probably rot behind bars longer than the killer.

The big man sighed aloud in gratification after knocking back half his drink. "The program really tends to ruin your drinking, you know?"

Harvey did not answer, his mind racing. The man half turned to him. "You were starting to share back at the meeting," he said carefully, "think you said something happened tonight, then you bolted like a deer who just saw Bigfoot. What the hell happened?" He waited for an answer.

"Nothing," Harvey said weakly. "Nothing that a few more of these won't cure." The man wasn't as handsome up close, he realized, raising his glass. His skin was rough and craggy, a small scar bisected one eyebrow, and there was a mean curl to his thin upper lip.

"A woman," the man persisted, a knowing undertone to his voice. "Has to be. I bet that's it."

Yeah, Harvey thought. It's a woman. The problem is, her lips are blue, she's dead, and you killed her. He nodded, unable to trust his voice. He felt his eyes tear and looked away.

"They drive us all nuts. Yeah," the man continued philosophically, "we all have our addictions, our weaknesses, that's why it's lucky that we all understand and support each other." He took another gulp of his drink, then peered closely at Harvey. "Haven't I seen you somewhere, other than a meeting? I'm sure we've crossed paths, I just can't place it."

"I don't know," Harvey croaked. "I'm not good at faces." He cleared his throat and got to his feet.

"You live somewhere around here?" the man persisted. "Hey, where ya going?"

"Gotta go drain the lizard, be right back. Order us a coupla more. I shall return."

Leaving his change on the bar, Harvey strolled past the rowdy pool players to the men's room, trying to look casual and nonchalant.

He had remembered correctly. There was a pay phone in the men's room and it worked. He punched in the familiar number, willing his sponsor to be home, willing him to answer.

"Thank you for your call," the machine's robotic message began.

"Phil, pick up, pick up, for God's sake!" Harvey muttered, glancing at the door behind him.

"Harv, that you? What happened at—"

"Thank God you're there, Phil. No time to talk, I need your help."

"Where are you?"

"Never mind, Phil. That tall guy in the back tonight, by the coffee urn, the one in the yellow sweatshirt. Do you know him? Who is he?"

"Sure," Phil said slowly. "Quiet, intense type o' guy, shows up sporadically at the Garden Avenue meetings and the group over at St. John's. Left right after you did."

"What's his name? What's he do?"

Harvey gasped as the door opened, nearly dropping the phone, but it was only one of the pool players, a bone-thin Oriental with dyed-blond hair and a nose ring. The man went to a urinal, ignoring him.

"Where the hell are you, Harv?"

"Who is he?" Harvey hissed, his voice frantic.

"Calm down, calm down, son. Some kinda general contractor, he builds houses. Name is Ray, drives one o' them pickups, big blue one, a Cherokee, I think, with the company name on the doors. Can't think of it off the top of my head."

"Ray. A contractor. Thanks, Phil. Later."

"Wait a minute, Harv. Where—"

Harvey hung up. When the pool player left, he unlocked the narrow window and struggled to open it. His hands were sweaty and slippery. It had been painted shut and wouldn't budge. Panic-stricken, expecting his drinking companion to burst in at any moment, he upended a wastepaper basket and, ankle throbbing, climbed atop it to gain better leverage. With a desperate wrench he threw open the window, grasped the sides, pushed off with his good leg, and managed to half drag and half hoist himself through. He tumbled forward and landed on his hands and knees in the alley.

He lurched to his feet, wincing at the pain from his ankle, and tried to catch his bearings. The blanket of stars overhead earlier had vanished, and the night looked as murky and unpromising as Harvey's future. How had an evening he had looked forward to so much ever come to this? Tears flooded his eyes, but no time for regrets. The big man had to be wondering where he was. He would check the men's room any minute now. He would see the open window.

Harvey half ran, half limped to the parking lot behind the building. There it was. A blue Cherokee, RAYMOND KARP CONSTRUCTION lettered on the side. A built-in toolbox rested in the bed of the truck, double locked, then secured by a padlocked chain. Harvey memorized the tag number and the wording on the door, then scrambled into his Geo. As he looked back he saw no one.

He drove aimlessly, focused on the rearview mirror. Not until certain he was not being followed did Harvey head home. He knew the big man could track him down, but it would probably take him a day or two. Harvey parked two blocks from his own place anyway, then walked cautiously to his apartment, scanning the darkness. Safely inside, he felt weak with relief.

His locks were the best—he had installed them himself—but straining and grunting, he pushed his mother's old china cabinet against his front door, just in case. He then lined up his coffee mugs and mismatched jelly-jar drinking glasses along the window-sills, and balanced saucers on a kitchen chair placed against the back door. He took a ball peen hammer from his tool shelf to bed with him, then tried to sleep, his throbbing ankle elevated on a pillow. But he was still wide awake as the sun rose, staring at the ceiling, waiting for the sounds of breaking glass or china crashing to the floor.

Before brewing his morning cup of English breakfast tea, Harvey channel-surfed the early-morning news. They all had the story. The murder was apparently the most newsworthy of that day's three Miami homicides. Channel 7 aired footage of the shrouded corpse being taken away. Harvey shuddered, the remote in his hand, watching as they wheeled her out and down the stairs on a gurney, an inanimate form beneath a blanket. He remembered her energy, her spirited and distinctive walk, and heard her name for the first time: Sandra Dollinger, twenty-four years old, receptionist at a South Beach photo studio. Somebody's daughter, somebody's child. Harvey wanted to weep, overwhelmed by mixed emotions. Why did he ever go there? Why hadn't he gone sooner? Had he been first, she would have been cautious, frightened, more security-conscious. Perhaps the killer never would have gotten to her. Never again, Harvey swore, if somehow he got through this, he would never again risk his life, his freedom, everything. Nothing was worth this.

"I can't believe it," a woman neighbor was saying in the Channel 10 report. She looked pale and near tears. "We've lived in this building for five and a half years, and nothing like this ever happened before. We didn't know her well. But she seemed nice, always said hello, always friendly."

She and her husband heard the killer flee, the reporter said. "I looked out, almost got a look at him," said the husband, a chunky fellow wearing a mustache and a gold chain, "but he ran, and by the time I pulled some pants on and got out there, he was driving off. We didn't know yet it was a murder." They rapped on their neighbor's door but there was no answer. Her sliding glass door stood ajar. They alerted the manager who found the body, they said.

The victim's sister and best friend were assisting detectives in determining what was missing from the murder scene, a police spokesman said on camera. Harvey felt a thrill of fear at his words. Asked if robbery was the motive, the spokesman hinted that certain items might be missing, but he was not free to divulge what they were since it was crucial to the investigation.

"Do you think this could be linked to other cases?" a reporter asked. The spokesman lifted a meaningful eyebrow. "No comment at this time."

Harvey knew then what he had to do.

He limped into the kitchen first, to prepare his usual breakfast—two poached eggs, whole wheat toast, orange juice, and tea. He had no appetite for anything, not even the high-heeled red sandals. He looked at them and felt only sadness. He forced himself to nibble at his meal the best he could. Maintain regular habits, he told himself, do not become overwhelmed by stress and fear. This was no time to go haywire. He stacked the breakfast plates in the dishwasher, then called in sick to his job as inventory clerk at Federated department stores. He had injured his ankle in a fall, he told them. No lie there.

Raymond Karp Construction was listed in the yellow pages without a street address. The man must work out of a home office,

Harvey thought. He tried the number, carefully preceding it with star sixty-seven to block caller ID.

"You have reached the office of Karp Construction, please leave a message at the sound of the tone."

It was the big man's voice. Harvey hung up.

He stopped at a drugstore to buy an elastic bandage for his ankle and at 10 a.m. walked into the building department at city hall. He wore sunglasses, a baseball cap, and carried a notebook. His elderly mother was planning renovations, he explained, and he wanted to check out a potential contractor. A smart move, said the friendly clerk who confirmed it was all a matter of public record and helped him access the computer database.

By noon he cruised his newly rented Ford Taurus past the modest ranch-style home of Raymond Karp Construction. The blue truck wasn't there. He found it at the second of three permitted projects Karp had underway, a two-story corner house on Northeast Ninety-third Street. The next forty-eight hours became a recon mission, as Harvey observed Karp from a distance, day and night, recording in his notebook where the contractor parked at each stop, and for how long. Karp seemed preoccupied during the day. He looked guilty, it seemed to Harvey, but, he reasoned, Miami contractors were notorious for their shoddy work and greedy post-hurricane rip-offs of helpless homeowners. They probably all looked guilty, or should.

Karp attended AA meetings at night, though, Harvey noted, he never stayed long and went from one to another, as if looking for someone.

Harvey arrived home late. Headachy and hungry, he popped a Lean Cuisine in the microwave, then checked his message machine.

"Where ya been, Harv?" Phil's friendly voice sounded concerned. *"Is everything okay? That fellow you mentioned, Ray, the contractor, he's been asking around about you. What's going on?"*

The clock was ticking down, no time left for further recon. Harvey set his alarm for 3:00 a.m. Somebody once wrote that it is always 3:00 a.m. in the dark night of the soul. He tried to remember who it was, before napping fitfully, anticipating the alarm.

When it sounded, he arose and reluctantly began to gather his collection. He cleaned out his closets, removing other souvenirs from beneath his bed, touching them longingly, reliving the special moments evoked by each one. The Salvatore Ferragamo slingbacks that had hugged the long narrow feet of that tall blonde with the swanlike neck and high cheekbones. He had trailed her from Saks Fifth Avenue all the way home to Coconut Grove. The soft suede loafers had been well worn by that long-haired young woman he had followed home from the library, and the black and white mules with their pointed toes and open heels unleashed a rush of memories. He had shadowed them all the way down Lincoln Road as she strolled, window-shopped, and chatted with friends. She seemed demure, so shy, so quiet, but screamed loud enough to wake the dead when she woke up as he fondled her feet.

He included the anklets, stockings, peds, and house slippers, all the little bonuses picked up along the way. He nearly forgot the silvery thong sandals tucked between his mattress and his box spring and had to go back for them. Finally he had dropped them all—the battered running shoes, the bejeweled evening slippers, the rubber flip-flops—into the maw of a big, black plastic garbage bag.

Each was a part of his life, he would miss them, but never again. The AA counselor was right, it was easy to replace one addiction with another, but now it was over. He wasn't going back to booze either. If he got out of this, it was time to exert some control over his life. His firm resolve felt good. He pulled the rental car up to his front door, checked the street, then carried the bag to the car. This would be his final caper.

The brisk Miami winter night was splendid, the temperature sixty-five, a star-studded sky, and the moon nearly full. The blue Cherokee was exactly where he expected to find it, parked in the driveway of the modest rancher. The house was dark. He stopped on the street near the foot of the driveway and wondered if the sleep of the man inside was as troubled as his had been.

Harvey sat in the car, watching, listening. He thought about prowlers gunned down by irate homeowners and trigger-happy cops on patrol. Even fifteen-year-olds had been shot for stealing hubcaps.

He wondered what this town was coming to.

As high-flying clouds obliterated the bright face of the moon, he made his move, melting like a shadow into the bed of the truck. There was an alarm on the cab but nothing in back. His penlight clenched between his teeth, he worked methodically on the padlock, then on the toolbox. It didn't take long. He cautiously lifted the creaky lid, then stopped to listen. A dog barked in the distance, but the house remained quiet and dark. The box was half full of tools, with rolled sets of plans on top. Harvey removed the plans and the tools, then replaced them with the shoes and other intimate items of footwear. He kept only a single red high-heeled sandal. He replaced the plans, closed the box, chained and padlocked it, sighing with relief as the lock snapped shut. He wrapped the tools in the empty garbage bag, scanned the street, then carried them back to the rental. He was about to start the car when he saw approaching headlights and crouched, holding his breath.

A Miami prowl car, two officers in the front seat. Harvey whimpered, some neighbor must have made a prowler call.

He thought he would faint when he heard the two cops talking companionably as their car pulled abreast of his, then rolled by, ever so slowly. He fought the urge to jump out, hands in the air, to surrender before they pulled their guns. But they kept moving and turned right at the end of the block. He must have a strong heart, Harvey thought, unlike his father. If ever he was to succumb to a heart attack, it would have been now.

He continued to crouch, body limp, heart pounding, until he was convinced they were gone, that no SWAT team was surrounding the block, then started the car, rolled a few hundred feet, switched into second gear, and turned on the lights.

He went to an all-night Denny's, suddenly ravenous, and ate a hearty breakfast. He read the morning paper as he devoured a stack of pancakes, syrup, and bacon, food he usually never ate. There was nothing more in the paper about the murder except a short paragraph and a telephone number, asking that anyone with information call Crime Stoppers.

At precisely 7:28 a.m. he was parked near the expressway entrance ramp three blocks from Karp's rancher. Karp passed by behind the wheel of the blue Cherokee at 7:31 a.m., on the way to his first jobsite stop of the day.

Harvey's next step was more tricky. Neighbors were up and about, getting their children off to school. He approached on foot from the block behind the house and pushed through a thick hedge into the backyard. The back door lock was a good one, an inch-long solid steel dead bolt that would take a lot of tedious time and work. He skirted the house and was thrilled to find the kitchen entrance, an old-fashioned jalousie door. It takes no smarts or training at all to simply remove a jalousie, reach in, and turn the knob. The kitchen was a mess. Dishes in the sink, a cardboard pizza box, empty except for a few gnawed crusts, a nearly empty Jack Daniel's bottle on a counter. The garbage can was overflowing. The living room was no neater. Neither was the bedroom. Harvey took the remaining high-heeled red sandal from inside his shirt, tucked it between the rumpled sheets of Raymond Karp's unmade bed, then left the way he had come, replacing the jalousie on the way out. He left Karp's tools just inside the door, still wrapped in plastic.

He called Crime Stoppers from a roadside pay phone.

"I believe I have some information," he began. He told the volunteer he had overheard a stranger in a bar brag to a companion about the murder. The stranger also commented that he had to get rid of some evidence he had hidden in his vehicle. Later, he saw the man drive off in a truck. Just this morning he had spotted the same man, in the same truck, at a construction site. Harvey gave the address and a description of the truck and its driver. He was only a good citizen doing the right thing, he said, and was uninterested in any reward. Being a family man, he was reluctant to become further involved. Harvey hung up and went home.

As he heated some tomato soup for lunch, the Channel 7 news on the tube, a bulletin announced a breaking story, a police chase in progress. Harvey stepped away from the stove to watch. Police were in hot pursuit of a man they had approached at a building site that morning. The newsman said the suspect had given police permission to examine the contents of his truck, but when they found something suspicious, he had struggled with them, broken away, leaped into his truck, and fled. The station's eye-in-the-sky chopper crew was bringing live coverage from Interstate 95, where it was now reported that the fleeing driver was the suspect in a homicide.

Harvey turned off the burner under the soup and watched. How lucky, he thought, that Karp had made a run for it. How incriminating.

The chase was frightening. Other motorists were being forced off the road. Harvey's heart was in his throat. It looked to him as though the fleeing driver was headed home. Sure enough, the Cherokee sailed down the exit ramp into his neighborhood, trailed by wailing police cruisers. More were waiting. Karp's Cherokee skidded into a patrol car, then sideswiped a cement truck.

Harvey couldn't stay away, he had to see for himself that it was over. Galvanized into action, he dashed out to the rental.

The scene was chaotic, traffic was jammed. News choppers throbbed overhead, on the ground were sirens, camera crews, and a growing crowd. Just like an action movie, but this was real life.

Thrilled, he watched from a distance as Karp, dazed and bleeding from a gash on his head, was led away in handcuffs, Justice had triumphed, Harvey thought, justice for Sandra Dollinger. The police spokesman had convened a press conference and was addressing reporters. Microphones bristled, cameras zoomed in. Harvey edged up front, into the crowd.

The man arrested, the spokesman said, was the chief suspect in the murder of Sandra Dollinger. Physical evidence had been discovered that detectives believed would not only link him to the homicide but to a frightening rash of assaults on women—and identify him as the notorious serial shoe thief. Reporters gasped.

"Another classic case," the public-information officer said wisely, "of a deviate whose sex crimes continue to escalate in violence until culminating in murder."

Puleeze, Harvey thought as he walked away. Whatever. He was free, he thought jubilantly. It had all worked. He smiled, safe at last, no cops, no killer on his trail. No drinking in his future, no more women's feet. This experience had turned him off both for good. He was free at last.

His smile lingered and caught the eye of a passing police officer. She smiled back. "Helluva story, ain't it?"

"It sure is," he said. "What a town."

She turned to direct traffic away from the scene. She wore the crisp dark-blue uniform of the department and was attractive, in an athletic sort of way, her sandy hair pulled tightly back from her fresh scrubbed face. But that was not what caught his attention. Harvey's eyes were focused on her thick, shiny leather gun belt and holster. He heard it creak faintly as she walked. He breathed deeply and imagined how it smelled. Clipped to one side were an intriguing pair of black leather gloves, probably for manhandling suspects when necessary, he thought, and little leather compartments probably full of shiny metal bullets.

Harvey followed, longing to stroke the smooth leather and bury his face in her belly to inhale its aroma mingled with her perspiration. His face flushed, his knees felt weak. She turned, still smiling, and motioned the vehicles forward with a broad wave, raising her right arm, giving him the perfect opportunity to read her name off the metal tag pinned to her shirt pocket.

TAHITI JUNK SHOP

BY LES STANDIFORD

North Miami Beach

(Originally published in 1999)

"It's bad news, isn't it?"

Guerin didn't have to look up to see who was speaking. It was a favorite trick of Adele's, shadowing him down to the mailboxes. He stood in a peeling little alcove off the shabby main lobby of their Hallandale building—a testament to the better intentions of another South Florida era. He studied the wall cracks that radiated out from the bank of brass boxes in the pattern of a giant spiderweb. In a moment, she'd deliver one of the incessant invitations to her apartment, for coffee, for cake, for a "little chat," as if they'd just happened to bump into one another.

He folded the letter and put it in the breast pocket of his coat, a smoking jacket he'd salvaged from the effects of his father decades ago. Adele watched him, practically gloating. Maybe she'd been reading over his shoulder.

"Investments," he said, affecting a philosophical tone. "One accepts the bad with the good." In truth, his heart had turned to lead.

"Sinking good money into a snow pea farm in the desert is not an investment," she said.

So she *had* been looking. He glanced about the tiny mailroom. Adele, no giant, nonetheless blocked his way to the door.

"You look a little gray," she said in a softened voice. "How about some chicken soup?"

"I have business," he said.

"There's always time to file bankruptcy," she sniffed. "Besides, I wanted to tell you. The Centurion Village representative is coming to talk today." She produced a colorful brochure from behind her back. He'd seen it before, littering the tables of the common rooms. It was full of pictures of oldsters biking, swimming, dancing, and shuffleboarding, cavorting in the Florida sun and enjoying the "golden years." Just looking at all the activity made him feel tired.

He took the brochure and pointed at the immense condominium building that was featured in almost every shot. "They ought to put some bars over all these windows," he told her. "Because none of these people will ever get out."

She snatched the brochure back. "That's ridiculous," she said. "This is a place where you could put what you've got left. It'll do you some good."

Guerin saw that her eyes were starting to water. He knew what she wanted. They should pledge all their assets, turn over everything to this coven of the dead and dying, and move in together. Wait hand in hand in a wallboard cave for the inevitable. He had to admit, they were clever, these Centurions. Just give up everything you have and they guarantee you peace of mind for as long as you live, and pray that it's not too long.

"That Centurion thing's a scam." It was a new voice echoing about the gloomy mailroom. Guerin and Adele spun about. A shambling man, who might have been in his fifties—wearing a checked sport coat and white shoes and belt—had appeared in the doorway.

He indicated the brochure in Adele's hand. "You give 'em everything, including your Social Security, and sign a blanket power of attorney. They got you by the *cajones* for the rest of your life, which probably ain't too long given the quality of the food I hear they put out."

A white ring of fury had come to outline Adele's lips. "Who *are* you," she demanded. "How did you get in here?"

The man tipped an imaginary hat and smiled grandly. "Jack

Squires, ma'am." He glanced at Guerin. "With Astral Invest-ments." He broke off to consult a well-worn spiral notepad. "Came to see a Mister Gunderson who answered one of our ads: *a little risk, a lotta return . . .*"

"Oh, my God," Adele breathed.

Squires glanced up. "Something wrong?"

Guerin spoke up. "It's me," he said. "I'm Gunderson."

Squires grinned and snatched up Guerin's hand. "Imagine that," he said, pumping it vigorously. "Running into you right here."

"Not so strange," Guerin said, looking at Adele.

"Let go of his hand," Adele said.

"It took me awhile to get back to you," Squires said, still pumping, "but now that I'm here, we're gonna roll."

"I'm calling the police," Adele said, making a tentative move for the door.

Guerin felt a warmth growing in the hand that Squires held. It was probably just the exercise. He couldn't remember a more vigorous handshake. Yet there seemed to be something more that coursed up his arm from Squires's big paw.

Guerin felt Adele's gaze burning upon him. "I'm a man of . . . some years," he said. "I need something solid."

Squires nodded, finally releasing his hand. "I couldn't agree more." He glanced at his notebook and shook his head. "Chinchil-las, zoysia plantations, Mojave snow peas." He clucked his tongue in sympathy. "That's a tough run of luck."

"That's idiocy," Adele said.

"I need to be certain of my future. Take the downside into account for a change."

Squires nodded. "I know just what you mean. I've got a place for your cash."

"You don't give him a cent!" Adele's voice had risen to a shriek.

Squires put his hand on Guerin's shoulder. "Now, tell me.

What kind of property is it you're most interested in? What is it you really want?"

Adele tried to jockey herself in front of Squires. "He wants some peace of mind. Not jackals trying to steal his money."

"Adele." Guerin tried to restrain her, but Squires was unfazed. He had not taken his eyes from Guerin.

"What is it that you really want, Mr. G?"

Guerin's eyes locked in on Squires's. He looked down the man's gaze until his head was swimming. He was on the staircase of their once-grand building, his legs limber, his flesh glowing, ascending the steps toward a glorious field of light. At every landing, well-wishers whooped and urged him on: forty-niners with panning kits slung to their backs, men holding strange machines and hopeless patent applications, little girls in ballet dresses, a huge rabbit with a replica of a human foot hung around its neck for luck, thumping him with its paw . . .

Guerin pulled his glance away at last. Adele stared at him in concern. He nodded reassurance to her, then gathered himself to speak.

"Well, Mr. Jack, I'll tell you. Forty years I work, no union, no pension, but I put what I can aside, and I make investments . . ."

"*Investments?*" Adele cried.

". . . so that someday, I don't have to work for somebody anymore, and maybe, if things work out, I could retire," he looked sheepish, "in Tahiti, I think." He cleared his throat then and his face fell. "But, things, they don't work out so well." He threw up his hands.

Adele seemed relieved. She turned to Squires, vindicated.

"If you'll pardon us," Adele took Guerin's arm.

Guerin held back, looking at Squires in appeal. "So, to answer your question, if I had just one more chance to make it happen, I'd want a little carryout market, maybe. Nothing fancy, but on a good corner. Enough business so in a year or two, I sell out and go to Tahiti, unless you know someplace better."

Adele turned, astonished. Guerin avoided her, and shrugged at Squires, who had, after all, asked.

Squires did not hesitate. "I can do it for you."

"Throw this crook out," Adele wailed.

"I don't need your money, Mr. G. This is one man of vision to another." Squires bent to jot a note on a slip of his pad. He stood and stuffed it into Guerin's pocket. "I'll be at this address at four. You think about it."

He slipped his pad into his pocket, nodded a goodbye to Adele and clapped Guerin on the shoulder as he left. "You got a spirit I like."

Guerin pulled out the paper and took a look at the address. Adele stared up at him, anxious. Finally, Guerin turned to her.

"An honest face he had, don't you think?"

"Oh, my God," she wailed, as she ran out the door. "Oh, my God."

As he moved farther and farther inland from his building and far from anyplace he knew, Guerin reassured himself that finding opportunity was, for one in his position, a matter of trusting one's intuitions over what others might call logic. There was the known path, and the other path. And he was destined to be an adventurer.

He was passing now through an area of ramshackle shops, including a laundry so filthy he wondered how anything could be cleaned there, then a liquor store with a row of swarthy men hunkered in a row beneath its front window. The proprietor stood near the barred doorway with a pistol in his hand and glared at Guerin as he passed.

In the next block, all the shops seemed closed, except for a balloon and message service from whose entry issued a blare of music he could not begin to identify. Outside, a van with gay balloons stenciled on its side sagged at the curb, its two right tires gone flat. Guerin peeked inside the shop and saw a young man with the made-up face of a woman standing bare-chested behind a counter. He was staring into a mirror and was sawing intently at his front teeth with a heavy file. Guerin staggered back into the street and hurried on, thinking that there were perhaps limits to adventure.

Soon, he had passed into a district of warehouses and storage yards interspersed with vacant lots. It was there that he heard the first sound behind him. He spun about to check, but there was nothing but empty street to be seen. He paused, then forced himself onward. When he heard the sound again, he did not turn but walked more quickly to a corner ahead and ducked around the edge of a shuttered moving and storage building to wait.

As the footsteps neared, he thought of various assaults upon the unwary he might copy from his nights of television viewing, but then he thought of his dry and brittle bones snapping as he struck, and there was nothing to do but wait.

Shortly, his pursuer was upon him. He took a deep breath, stepped forward boldly . . . and caused Adele to shout her violent surprise into the calm of the deserted street.

They stood staring at each other for a moment, searching for words, two people met accidentally in hell. Finally, Adele surveyed their surroundings and sniffed, "This is not a neighborhood for decent people."

While Guerin considered what to say, a bag man pushing a grocery cart laden down with things that looked furry and once-alive jostled past them. Adele fell toward Guerin with a yelp. Shaken himself, he offered her his arm, and they hurried on.

The shadows had begun to lengthen when they reached the last possible block, another assemblage of broken buildings on a street that died against the high wall of an abandoned factory. At the corner, Guerin checked the address once more and shook his head. They stood in front of a grimy storefront where a sign dangled from a single bolt: *ROGOVIN'S TRASH AND TREA-SURES*, it read, rocking slightly in a breeze that skirted dust and yellowed newsprint pages at their feet. A wino snoozed in the shop's entryway.

Guerin turned glumly to Adele. "Let's go home," she said, quietly, and tugged at his arm.

Behind them came the tap of a car horn. They turned as a black limousine, its windows heavily smoked, purred up to the curb and Jack Squires danced nimbly out from the rear.

"You folks made the right decision," he said, extending his hand to Guerin. Adele huffed. Guerin studied the impressive car for a moment, then turned back to the junk shop, where the wino stirred, annoyed at this interruption of his nap.

"I thought we were talking a market," Guerin said.

Squires threw up his hands. "I'll be honest with you, Mr. G. The only market I had in your price range was in a bad neighborhood."

Ignoring Adele's gasp, Squires took Guerin by the arm and steered him toward the entrance of the shop, shooing the wino off with a wave of his hand.

"Market, *schmarket* . . ." Squires said.

He unlocked the door and led the way into the place, flipping on a light switch. He turned, radiant with anticipation as Guerin and Adele followed him in, blinking in the dim light.

"*This*, Mr. G," he said, sweeping his arm about, "is the answer to your dreams."

Guerin stared. Instead of the vacant shop he expected, he found before him a rabbit warren of aisles toppling toward one another, jammed with junk store flotsam and jetsam. Here was a pile of army helmets, there a stack of 78 records. One aisle was a tunnel through thick walls of magazines and newspapers. Nearby lay an ancient Coca-Cola tray atop a tumult of faded clothing. Adele glanced about distastefully, running her finger through a thick layer of dust on the front counter.

Guerin found himself drawn into the dim recesses of the shop, past banks of battered toasters, mixers, and blenders, beyond shelves full of cracked and mismatched china. At a twist in an aisle that seemed to dive off the face of the earth, he stumbled over a cobbler's anvil and found himself face to face with an Indian in war paint and headdress, a tomahawk raised to brain him. Guerin staggered backward and a hand fell upon his shoulder.

"You're a very lucky man," Squires said. "The place has been tied up in probate for months. You get first crack."

Guerin stared, recovering from his fright. "But the price. Surely the three thousand I have is not sufficient."

Squires waved his concern away. "The old boy who ran the place croaked awhile ago, and his heirs are back east. They don't know junk. I told 'em it'll cost two grand just to haul the stuff away and they begged me, 'Sell. Sell the junk?'"

He patted the wooden Indian on the cheek and took Guerin back toward the front. "So you get all this," he continued, "and ten more years on the original lease."

They emerged into the light where Adele waited impatiently by the door. Squires ran his hand over an old brass cash register as he moved behind the counter to sweep aside a curtain there. He pointed in at a small room, where the corner of a single bed was visible. "There's even a living quarters here in the back."

Adele's mouth fell open. "What? Live in this rat's nest?" She hurried to Guerin's side. "You don't know what's going to crawl out of there in the night . . . and who's going to cook for you?"

Guerin patted her hand, then moved forward to peer into the tiny room which contained, besides the bed, a kitchenette, a small table, and a battered easy chair with a reading lamp beside it. He stepped inside and turned a knob on the stove. A jet of blue flame leaped up from a burner. He tried the sink faucet, and a stream of clear water gushed out. He turned to face Adele and Squires.

"This is a come-back neighborhood," Squires said. "It's a steal for a man of vision."

Guerin found himself nodding. "I used to have vision," he said, softly.

"Guerin!" Adele cried.

Squires nodded, waving his notepad. "I know, Mr. G. We checked you out."

"This place has a nice feeling," Guerin said, warming.

"It's where you belong," Squires said.

Guerin nodded thoughtfully. "A market probably *is* a great deal of trouble."

Adele's eyes had begun to glaze. "He's lost his mind," she wailed.

"I took your best interest to heart," Squires said, stepping forward, his hand outstretched.

Guerin hesitated. His gaze went upward, to a shelf where a dusty candelabra stood, its cups cast in the shape of cherubs, which seemed to dance in the glint of the stove's blue flame.

"I'll take it," he said, and felt Squires's large hand envelop his. Adele stood weeping in the doorway.

Guerin stood outside his shop in the balmy air of a fine spring morning, nodding approval as the sign painter he had engaged leaned from his ladder for one last stroke. *TAHITI JUNK SHOP*, it read, with Guerin's name in script just to the side and the replica of a tiny island with a palm tree added for a logo.

Guerin motioned the man down and handed him some bills, then went back inside his shop. Caruso opera issued scratchily from an ancient Victrola placed beside the front counter. Behind the counter he had hung a thermometer-like sales chart with the legend *$10,000—Off for the Islands* scrawled at the top. He smiled and moved to lift the needle as the music stopped.

Behind him the doorbell of the shop tinkled and he turned to greet his first customer . . . only to find Adele advancing upon him, her face gray and sunken.

"Adele," he said, hopefully, "you've come for a little shopping."

She patted at her cheeks with a handkerchief. "I came to talk sense to you. Did you sign anything yet? Tell me it's not too late."

Though he felt impatience, her despair was disarming. He took her hand reassuringly. "Adele, a little less gloom, if you please. I am a *proprietor* now."

A thump sounded at the front window then and they turned to see the wino glowering in at them. Adele banged her purse against the glass and the man slunk away. She turned back.

"Wonderful. A roomful of junk, in the middle of hell. That's what you've got."

Guerin took a deep breath, determined not to argue. While he understood the necessity of risk, he could not expect Adele to sympathize. He took her arm and drew her down the aisle.

"Let me show you something," he said, taking her around a dark turn and snapping on a light. They were now in a room larger than the first, and even more crowded with aged merchandise.

"Look," he said, waving his arms. "Anything you want, you could find it here."

She stared about at piles of old coats, at paintings in bad colors in splintered frames, at shaky stacks of ancient saucers, and her lower lip began to quiver. "What are you talking about? These are things people threw out because they *didn't* want them."

She stared plaintively at him, but his attention had been drawn by a sled with wooden runners that leaned against the nearest wall. He shook his head—he had not noticed it before. Adele came to pull him back down the aisle.

"Listen, I had my nephew Myron, the attorney, do some checking. He found out the previous owner, God rest his soul, just disappeared last year, without a trace."

Guerin looked over his shoulder toward the sled. "Maybe he had something better to do," he said, turning to her with a smile. "A trip to the islands maybe."

She huffed on toward the front, unamused. Guerin stopped to stare down at a wooden chest, another thing he had missed in all the clutter. A satin gown, glittering with sequins, trailed out of the partly opened lid. He found himself wondering if Adele had ever worn such a thing. Then she was back, pulling him impatiently along.

"I see these bums around here with their fires going and their cooking in the vacant lots. They probably took his money and his clothes and then they *ate* him."

At the counter, she turned to face him. She took a deep breath, her gaze faltering for a moment. "Guerin, come away from here. I want you to come with me to the Centurion place Myron found. I can cook for you. I'll take care of you. I have enough money for both of us."

She glanced away as she finished, and Guerin felt something knot in his throat. After a moment, he moved forward and took her shoulders gently.

"Adele, please. Try to understand. All my life I work for somebody else and try to get ahead and it never works out. Now I got this place that is mine. A market it isn't, but it's okay." He broke off and managed his broadest smile. "And God willing, I'll save my money and someday I'll go off to Tahiti."

She opened her mouth to protest, but he held up his hand to stop her. "It's a nice dream, Adele, and I don't want you should give me such a hard time about it, okay?"

She stared at him, her face falling into inestimable sadness. "I knew you wouldn't listen," she said. "Oh, it's so awful to get old." Her eyes had begun to fill, and she turned quickly for the door. When he tried to follow, she pushed him away.

"Stay here, then. Stay with your junk."

The door slammed behind her and Guerin stood staring uncertainly after her. Finally, he moved back behind the counter and sank glumly into the easy chair he had dragged out for better light, staring up at his bulletin board and his thermometer for success. He picked up an edition of Gaugin prints he'd found in the stacks and began to flip listlessly through the pages.

Shortly, his hands lay atop his favorite of the painter's illustrations, innocent natives awaiting a ship's arrival on their unspoiled beach. In this version, however, it was Guerin himself who stood at the prow of the vessel that was bound for the island port, the salt spray cool in his face and his eyes fixed upon a lovely maiden tying up her hair at the shore. Though it seemed impossible, and she was certainly younger and more carefree here, it was unmistakably Adele in the colorful sarong who awaited him. Even more astonishing than that was the happiness he felt as the ship moved inexorably toward the shore.

The doorbell of the shop sounded then, interrupting the snores of dreaming Guerin. He started awake, the book slipping to the floor, his gloom swooping back upon him as he stood to assume the role of proprietor.

It was a blond woman wearing large-lensed sunglasses who came through the door, urging along her husband, a balding man in walking shorts and golf shirt, sporting around his neck a gold chain the thickness of Guerin's little finger.

"Oh, we're soooo glad to see you're open again, Mr. Rogovin. We just love your place," she cooed, already heading for the stacks.

The woman's husband came to clap him heartily on the shoulder. "Been out buying, have you? You must have scads of new things." He gave Guerin a wink and dove into the aisles after his wife, who had already begun squealing at some find.

As Guerin stared into the depths of the shop in befuddlement, there came the sounds of something heavy being dragged across the planked floor toward the front of the shop. Finally, the couple emerged, wrestling with a fortune-telling booth from a carnival arcade. The thing, the size of a phone booth, held a dummy gypsy wobbling over a cloudy crystal ball. Guerin clutched hold of the counter for support.

The wife motioned her husband forward with an unspoken command. The man affected unconcern as he approached Guerin. "Say, we've found something we *might* be interested in."

Guerin shook his head in wonder. "I've never seen that before . . ."

The man turned to his wife, who frowned and lifted her chin in a commanding motion.

"So, we'd be willing to go . . . say, a hundred and a half."

"Charles!" his wife whispered.

Charles shrugged. "I meant to say two hundred."

"Two hundred dollars?" Guerin repeated, dumbfounded.

The woman drew her husband aside. "I *want* it," she hissed. Charles turned back to Guerin and slapped some bills into his palm. "Look, we'll go four hundred dollars, and not a penny more."

Guerin stared at the hundred-dollar bills in his hand, wondering if he was still dreaming. The woman motioned to her husband, and they began wrestling the thing toward the door. "We just love it," she smiled, with a sidelong hateful glance at Charles. "You'd have to shoot us to stop us now."

"Shoot?" Guerin repeated. "Four hundred dollars?"

"Ciao!" she said, heaving the booth on out the door toward her husband.

He followed the pair outside and watched as they lifted the booth into the back of a Cadillac converted to a short-bed pickup, then returned the couple's wave as they sped off into the evening shadows.

He checked his watch and walked back into the shop, turning the window sign over and shooting the door bolt home. Through the glass he thought he saw the wino watching him from a storefront opposite, but when he blinked to clear his eyes, the vision was gone. He went quickly to the counter, certain that the cash too would have vanished, but it was still there, four crisp bills that marked the first notch upon his sales thermometer.

That night, though he did not dream, he awoke once with a start, certain he'd heard the sounds of thunderous surf about to crash down upon him. When he leaped from his small bed to investigate, he found that one of the paddle fans was rustling a grass skirt atop one of the stacks of papers. Guerin moved the skirt, then staggered back to bed and lay for hours, unable to sleep.

At eight the next morning, an insistent knocking roused him. He swung out of bed and drew on a satin dressing gown he'd scavenged from the stacks—it seemed like something his father would have fancied. If it *were* Adele come to pester him again, he'd offer her a gift, a gesture of peace, perhaps the sequined dress from the wooden chest.

When he opened up, he found instead two youths in ragged tennis shoes and jeans staring up at him warily. The taller youth stepped forward.

"We been looking for a basketball," he said, peering over Guerin's shoulder.

Guerin hesitated, doubtfully following the boy's glance. The shorter boy tried to pull his partner away. "I told you this ain't no place for a basketball."

The tall one restrained him, and looked impatiently at Guerin. "Well, you got a basketball?"

"I don't think so," Guerin said, stepping back. "But you're welcome to look."

The tall boy nodded and started inside, pulling his reluctant partner along toward the stacks. Guerin rubbed his face and stared out into the brilliant morning. He was about to step out for a breath of air when he heard the unmistakable *thump, thump, thump* of a ball being dribbled along the wooden floor behind him.

They had found the ball atop a wooden chest, they said, and professed no knowledge of a big man named Squires who wore white shoes and rode in a limousine: "A *limo* in this neighborhood, man?"

Though they offered fifty cents, Guerin would take only a quarter. He watched the two leave, passing the battered basketball back and forth on the pavement, then turned back into the shop.

As he entered, he heard once more the unmistakable sounds of crashing surf. He hesitated, then drew his robe tightly around him and moved steadfastly into the shadows.

When he reached the wooden chest where Adele's dress had been, he froze. On the floor nearby lay a child's beach pail and shovel, and next to those, a battered beach chair with sailcloth seat and wooden frame. The sounds of the surf had died away.

Uncertain, he extended his hand toward the chest. The lid was locked, or swelled shut, and the sequined dress was nowhere in sight. He grasped one of the heavy brass handles on the chest, to pull it toward the front, but the thing would not budge. He straightened and looked warily about the darkened aisles. "Mr. Jack . . . ?" he called, but there was no answer. And then the door-bell began to ring in earnest.

It was nearly closing time when Adele did show up, her nephew Myron in tow. The pair had to stand aside at the doorway to let a stream of customers past. One man carried a huge moose head over his shoulder, followed by a couple toting an intricately molded brass bed. Next came a cigar-chewing man carrying a bar-ber's pole, then a stylishly dressed couple pushing a jukebox out atop a dolly. The man winked at Adele, patting the jukebox with one hand: "Everything Ella ever did is right in here."

Guerin waved at Adele and Myron from his place in the can-vas beach chair. He'd found an old-fashioned, knee-length bathing suit with a striped top and was basking in the glow of a battered sun lamp.

"I thought you said the place was belly up," Myron said.

Adele bit her lip and turned upon Guerin. "So this is how you wait on customers?"

Guerin rose amiably from his chair and snapped off the light. "I had an inspiration." He gestured at his trunks. "Goes with the name of the shop, don't you think?"

Myron nodded. "Business is looking up, I take it."

"Plenty of traffic. But I don't drive a very hard bargain, I'm afraid." Guerin swept his arm toward the dark aisles. "Have a look around. Maybe there's something you need."

Adele stepped impatiently between them. "Myron has come here to help you. He can get your money back."

Guerin looked at her in disbelief.

Myron cleared his throat. "I put together a group looking for a public housing site; now I find out this whole block's available.

You sign over your lease, I'll get you three thousand up front. Once the buildings go up, you get an override. In the long run you could clear some real coin."

"Clear some coin?" Guerin repeated. He gave Adele an exasperated look, then turned back to Myron. "I'm sorry you went to this trouble, Mr . . ."

"Myron's fine."

Guerin nodded. "Well, Myron, do I look to you like a man concerned with the long run?"

Myron smiled tolerantly. "I heard you were tough. Tell you what. Being as you are a friend of the family, so to speak, I think we could go five thousand up front."

Guerin felt very tired. "I'm sorry. I don't want to sell."

Myron shot an inquiring glance at Adele, who silently urged him on. "Uh, yes," Myron continued, looking at the toe of one soft leather loafer. "Well, my people have authorized me to offer ten thousand dollars."

Guerin took Adele by the arm and began to guide her sadly toward the door. "Take your nephew and go home," he said.

She stared at him, speechless.

"This is a rare opportunity," Myron protested.

"Take him home, Adele." Guerin ushered her out the door.

Myron hesitated at the threshold. "I don't get it. You could go to Tahiti the long way for ten thou."

Guerin stared at him steadily. Finally, Myron's gaze faltered. Guerin put a hand on his shoulder. "Come back someday on your own. We have nice things here." He smiled and closed the door.

It was dark and he was finishing a can of soup at his tiny kitchen table when he heard the tapping at the outer door.

"Please. I'm afraid out here." Adele's voice was muffled by the glass, but her fear kept its edge. He sighed and opened up.

"I thought you'd take the money," she said, sinking with exhaustion into the canvas beach chair.

Guerin turned over the beach pail and sat down stiffly on it. "You shouldn't have come here this late by yourself."

"You could have gone to Tahiti, if that's what you wanted." She shook her head sadly.

Guerin reached for her hand. "That was a very generous thing you did, Adele. A very kind and noble thing."

She looked at him tearfully. "Did you know it was my money Myron was talking about? Is that why you wouldn't take it?"

He shook his head. "Maybe I don't want to go anywhere after all."

She gave him an uncertain glance.

"You see, I am making some people very happy with the 'junk' they find here."

"But what about Tahiti?" Hope had entered her voice.

He paused, his gaze faltering for a moment. Finally, he rose and walked to the bulletin board. He turned to Adele with a wan smile and reached to take down the sales thermometer. Quickly, he tore it in half and dropped it into a trash bin.

"Tahiti was a dream, Adele. A dream like you need to get you through the days when other things are not the way you want them." He drifted off for a moment but caught himself and turned back to her, gesturing. "I'm very lucky to have found this place. I'm becoming important to my neighborhood."

She stared back at him, dumbfounded. "You really do want to stay here, don't you? I'd rather have you go off to that idiot island." She fumbled in her purse for a handkerchief and began to dab at her eyes.

Guerin came to take her by the shoulders. She stared up at him, uncertain. "Tell me, Adele, are you happy?"

She swallowed, drawing back from his touch. "Happy? I'm as happy as you can be at my age."

"And what does that mean?"

Her mouth drew grim. "It means that I'm old, and I'm going to die soon, and nobody is going to give a damn, that's what it means." She tried to meet his gaze defiantly, but turned away suddenly. Her shoulders began to heave, and then she was sobbing.

Guerin stared down, gauging the depth of her despair. He put his hand on her shoulder. "It's that bad for you, isn't it?"

She nodded as she blew her nose into her hanky, and Guerin sat down beside her, brushing his hand at her tears. "You know, Adele, if you'd just learn to dream a little, maybe you and I . . ."

She looked up as he faltered. "Maybe you and I what?"

He felt his impatience growing and sighed. "Nothing. You don't understand. If a man can't go out and make something decent, what does he have to offer?"

"Is that it?" Her voice rose. "You think you have to be rich to make me happy?" She reached for his hand.

He drew back. "It's not rich I'm talking about, it's something else, it's . . ." As he struggled for the right words, the door swung open behind her and the wino from the streets entered, his hand shakily outstretched, waving something in the dim light.

Guerin stood. "Can I help you . . . ?" His voice trailed off as he caught sight of the pistol that the man held, at the wild glint in his bloodshot eyes.

"Hit the register, old man. You had a great day. Now it's my turn."

Adele did not hesitate. "You march right out of here . . ." She rose, swinging at him with her purse. The man ducked, then backhanded her into the beach chair.

Guerin made a dive for the pistol. The man stumbled back, clubbing Guerin to his knees, and the gun went off with a tremendous roar.

A mounted hawk above the counter exploded in a flurry of feathers and stuffing. The man trained his pistol on Guerin. "I won't ask again."

"For God's sake, give him the money." Adele wiped at her bloody lip and scrambled for the cash box that lay near the deck chair.

The man's eyes glittered as he snatched the box from her frightened hand. He riffled through the thin stack of bills, then turned upon Guerin with menace. "I saw what walked out of here today. Where's the rest of the cash?"

Guerin shook his head helplessly. "It's all I asked for," he said.

The man didn't bother to argue. He swung his aim to Adele. "It's your last chance, Pops. I'll blow her away in a heartbeat."

Adele whimpered. Guerin scanned the shop, searching for a weapon, a miracle, a policeman . . . and froze when he beheld it.

Not ten feet away, at the mouth of an aisle, sat the chest he had tried to drag forward earlier. He could swear he heard the faint sounds of pounding surf, and if he were not mistaken, the heavy box swayed slightly with the rhythm of the waves.

As Guerin pulled his gaze away, he found the man smiling slyly at him. "So open it up, old man."

Guerin shook his head in protest. "You don't understand. There's no money there."

He broke off as the man snatched Adele roughly by the hair, holding the pistol to her face.

Guerin, growing dizzy, found himself at the top of an endless staircase, winded, beaten, facing a doorway that opened upon an empty room. All the former well wishers stood below on a vast landing, breathless, waiting for his move. Inside the room, a figure stirred in a darkened corner—a woman, he saw, as she came toward him, her hand outstretched, her face a mask of anguish. "Adele?" he said . . .

. . . and stepped forward to the chest. The top swung easily open at his touch, and Guerin stared down in disbelief at stacks and stacks of cash that neatly stuffed the box.

The man gave him a murderous smile and pushed Adele roughly aside. "You old son of a bitch," he said, amazed. He plunged his hand toward a stack of bills, keeping his pistol trained on Guerin. "You found a fortune." He riffled through a thick packet of cash and shrugged. "Too bad for you."

And indeed, Guerin thought, it was too bad, but then what good thing had he ever had that hadn't been taken away?

The man trained the pistol on Adele, who stirred groggily on the floor.

"Just take the box," Guerin cried. "It has everything you want."

The man sneered. "Nice of you to offer," he said, and cocked his pistol.

As the cylinders of the gun fell into place, Guerin beheld the instantaneous, sorry history of his hopeful life: withered fields of once-grand snow peas, zoysia sod farms that had started out strong but found the wilt, sullen cages full of molting chinchilla with no interest whatever in sex, a panorama of exotic failure, of promise gone wrong, capped by this last swell joke, a shop full of magic that would lead him to his death. And not, incidentally, lacking company for the trip.

He stole a glance at devastated Adele, felt his heart give, and, with nothing of his own to lose, took fate into his own hands. He ducked under the swiveling aim of the thief and drove him backward into the chest. The man's legs folded up as his knees caught the edge of the box, and he pitched over backward into the maw full of cash.

A great cloud of dust billowed up from the chest, driving Guerin away. The thief coughed wildly inside the pall and wilder still as the dust grew thicker, obliterating him finally from sight.

"What? Hey . . . HEY!" The disembodied screams lingered for a moment, and then there was a thud as the pistol fell to the floor and skittered to Guerin's feet, followed by another thump, which was the lid of the chest slamming down.

As quickly as it had sprung up, the cloud of dust drifted off, and Guerin and Adele were left to stare wonderingly at each other in a silent, vacant shop.

A muffled whining sound came from the chest and Guerin edged cautiously toward it, the pistol wavering in his hand. Adele clutched his arm as he tried the lid. He gave her a look, then flipped the top all the way up. Inside, where a fortune had momentarily gathered and where there should have been a man, was now a skinny mongrel in an otherwise empty box. The thing cowered at their gaze, its tail curled through its legs in terror.

Still groggy, Adele stared down in surprise. "Why, the poor thing. How did he get in there? Do you suppose he scared that man away?"

Guerin stared into the depths of the shop. There were the far-off strains of Polynesian music sounding in his ears, but Adele seemed to hear none of it. "Something like that," he said. He ignored her perplexed stare to bend and pet the dog. The mutt whimpered and licked wildly at his hand.

"Do you think he's gone?" Adele peered anxiously into the dim recesses.

Guerin stared at the terrified animal. "Yes," he said finally, lifting the dog from the chest. "I'm sure of it.

She took his arm. "You saved my life," she began, and Guerin had started an embarrassed shuffling when there was a sudden crash of surf roaring at them out of the depths of the shop and Adele screeched, clutching him in terror.

Guerin's mouth fell open as a wave of golden sunlight burst upon them, washing out of the aisle, and the glitter of light reflected from the water began to dance across their faces.

They stood transfixed as the shimmering landscape lay itself open before them, paradise where once aisles of stacked junk had lain.

Adele's lip trembled. "He shot us after all. This is how you die."

Guerin shook his head. "I don't think so . . ." He stepped forward, feeling his foot sink into sand. He held his face up to the sun and felt the warmth soak his ancient cheeks. Though the brightness blinded him, he could sense that the beach stretched endlessly, and he could hear the rustle of the tall palms just above his head. He whistled, and the dog bounded in after him.

He smiled and turned back. "It's been here all this time, Adele."

He felt the old promise stirring within him, in the tang of the air that filled his lungs. And yet there was this one last, important thing, without which intuition and persistence and even dreams did not matter, without which he could not go forward. He held out his hand, which glowed with the beach's gleam.

"Come, Adele, don't be afraid," he said, warmed by the tropic sun. "Don't be afraid of your dreams."

She hesitated, glancing over her shoulder at the dark shop and the dark street that stretched beyond. She turned back. She met Guerin's hopeful eyes. Finally, she took his hand and stepped forward.

Outside the shop, Jack Squires stood, listening with satisfaction to the faint sounds of crashing surf and the shrieks and whoops and yaps of creatures frolicking somewhere on a happy beach.

He passed his hand before the entrance glass in greeting, perhaps, or was it bon voyage? *CLOSED FOR VACATION*, read the sign that appeared there, just below the rendering of a little island and its palm tree that Guerin, in his perpetual hopefulness, had sketched beside his name.

GHOSTS

BY DAVID BEATY

South Miami

(Originally published in 1999)

I t was just before sunset in Biscayne Estates, and the Armstrongs were safe at home. Darryl paced around his study, sipped Scotch, and listened on his cordless telephone as a client screamed threats at him in broken English. Finally, he said, "Narciso, old buddy, stay calm. This is a temporary setback." He kept his voice reasonable but firm. "You've been going on about killing me all week. What good would that do you?"

Darryl cleared his throat. He said, "And believe me, I understand your anger. Nobody likes to lose money. But you wanted to play with the big boys, remember? Then the market went limit down three days in a row." He paused, not certain of what he'd just heard. "What? Simultaneous buy and sell orders? Who told you that? That's a lie. I don't care who told you. I've never dumped a bad trade in your account. That one? You gave me a direct order. Well, no, I can't play it back for you because your order came over my untaped line." He winced and said, "Hey, c'mon, you're calling me at *home*."

He took a greedy swallow of Scotch and said, "Stop it. That's enough. I need a vacation from hearing about how I'm going to die. I'll hang up now, okay? But call me if you get any more crazy ideas. Don't sit there obsessing. We're going to work this out. You have my word on that, okay? Bye-bye." He lowered the telephone into its cradle.

While Darryl talked in his study, his wife Caroline drifted

among the racks of clothes and shoes in her walk-in closet, searching for a simple blouse to wear. She wondered at the forces in herself that had driven her to buy so many bright, costly things. Who was the woman who'd chosen them? Where was the exhilaration and hope they'd represented? She couldn't visualize herself in them now. The sight of them embarrassed her. When she looked around the closet, she imagined an aviary of tropical birds.

Caroline had recently turned thirty-three, and now, with a rueful laugh, she told friends that she was quickly closing the gaps: next year she'd be eighty-eight! Last week she'd resigned from her civic committees, her charities, her mothers' groups: places where she'd been spinning her wheels. She felt herself changing. She was tired of people who thought about money and not much else—and that included herself. She yearned for a more spiritual life. She wanted to break free.

At the moment, however, she felt blocked. A free-floating gloom seemed to hang over her life.

The telephone was driving her crazy. It started ringing as soon as Darryl came home from the office. When she answered it, the caller hung up, but he stayed on if Darryl took the call. Then Darryl would hurry into his study and shut the door. He pretended that everything was fine, but she knew better. Worrying about it—and how could she not?—kept her under the thumb of depression. Caroline turned again in her closet, sorrowing over the constant losses, the daily disconnections from hope, that seemed to define her life now.

Darryl, forced out of his study by the need for more Scotch, signaled his availability to Kyle, age nine, and Courtney, age eleven, by cracking open a tray of ice in the bar. They appeared behind him in the doorway, energetic and needy.

He wondered when Narciso would call again. Silence was a danger signal. Silence meant: *Grab your wallet and go out the window!* Darryl poured Scotch over the smoking ice in his glass. He had to keep Narciso talking, had to draw off his anger, like draining pus from a wound, or God only knew what that maniac might do. He wondered, But what if my luck has deserted me?

He fled onto the patio with the children chattering at his heels like dwarfish furies. He sagged into a white plastic chair and tried to quiet Courtney and Kyle with the promise that if they ate all the food on their plates and didn't give Mrs. Hernandez a hard time, they'd get a big surprise after dinner.

"Oh, what surprise?" Kyle said. Feeling full of the idea of surprise, he danced around the patio. Courtney, who liked to mimic adults, folded her arms on her chest, struck a pose, and said, "Daddy, what on *earth* are you talking about?"

"Something of interest to you, my little madam." He talked to distract them, afraid that they could hear the voice of Narciso raging and threatening in his head. His children circled him—his fragile offspring, driven by such blatant needs. He felt the spinning pressure of their love. What have I done to them? he wondered, and abruptly closed his mind against that thought. He offered them a face all-knowing and confident. "If I tell you, it won't be a surprise. Wait until after dark." He drank deeply.

"After dark!" Kyle shouted. "Wow!" Making airplane noises, he skimmed away. He ignored a barrage of furious looks from Courtney and settled into a holding pattern around the patio table. Courtney said, "But Daddy, you didn't answer me."

Daddy's attention, however, had been captured by the sapphire beauty of his swimming pool, and by his trim green lawn, where sprinklers whispered *chuck, chuck, chuck* and tossed quick rainbows in the evening light, and by the *Lay-Z-Girl*, his sixty-foot Bertram yacht, which seemed to bob in polite greeting from its mooring on the canal. It was a typical view in Biscayne Estates, just south of Miami, and fragrant with the odors of damp earth and thrusting vegetation and the faint coppery tang of the ocean, but this evening its beauty and the achievement it proclaimed seemed like a trap to Darryl. Like one of those insect-eating flowers, but on a huge scale.

At one time, this life was all Darryl had hoped for. Now the prospect of working to sustain it made him think of a photograph he'd seen in *National Geographic,* of Irish pilgrims crawling on their knees over a stony road in the rain.

He felt, on his eardrums, the light percussion of rock music from next door, where Mr. Dominguez, a successful importer of flowers, fruits, and vegetables from Colombia, lived with his young wife, Mercedes, and a son Kyle's age, a sweet boy named Brandon. There was another son, from his first marriage, Jorge, a seventeen-year-old monster with shocking acne, who lived there too. Jorge was forever wounding Darryl's sense of neighborliness with his sleek red Donzi speedboat, his roaring Corvette, his end-of-the-world music, and his endless succession of guests, who used Darryl's lawn to drink and drug and screw and then left their detritus for Courtney and Kyle to puzzle over. Whenever Darryl trotted next door to complain, Mr. Dominguez laid a manicured hand over his heart and said, "I sorry, I sorry," and somehow managed to imply that he was apologizing for Darryl's bad manners, not Jorge's.

Jorge was a painful reminder that there were millions of teenagers out there having a high old time with their parents' money. Meanwhile, Darryl's resources dwindled away. If only he could get a tiny slice of what those parents were wasting on their kids. The idea of offering an Armstrong Education Fund shimmered in his mind, then faded. The word *slice* had turned his thoughts back to Narciso and his death threats.

Darryl didn't want to think about Narciso, so he let himself get angry with Jorge Dominguez. A door cracked open in Darryl's mind, and Darryl scampered down the rough stone steps to the dark arena where he played his special version of Dungeons & Dragons with his enemies. There, in his imagination, he passed a few delightful moments clanking around, teaching Jorge Dominguez to howl out his new understanding of the word *neighbor*.

And then, from somewhere close by, Darryl heard the sounds he'd been dreading. He raced up from his mental dungeon to see the water empty from his swimming pool, and the swimming pool float into the sky and join the other clouds turning pink in the evening light. After that, the noises of a chain saw and a wood chipper came growling toward him and his gardenia bushes, hibiscus, sea grape, the low hedge of Surinam cherry that separated him from the Dominguezes, and all of his palms fell over, crumbled into mulch, and blew away. His lawn burst into flame and burned with the fierceness of tissue paper, exposing earth the color of an elephant's hide, dusty and crazed with cracks. The *Lay-Z-Girl* popped her lines and fled down the canal into Biscayne Bay. Behind him, Darryl heard glass shattering and sounds of collapse and rushing wind, and he knew that if he turned around he'd find empty space where his house had once stood. His world had vanished. Ashes filled his heart.

Then it was over. His vision cleared. He lifted his shaking hand and glanced at his watch and guessed that no more than half a minute had passed. He took a swallow of Scotch and saw, with gratitude, Kyle circling the table and Courtney staring at him.

He looked away from them and regarded the *Lay-Z-Girl*. Another broken-down dream. At first, Darryl had retained a full-time captain, but when that became too expensive, he'd found someone less competent who was willing to work part-time. Now he couldn't even afford that. A week ago, without telling Caroline, he'd fired the man. Yesterday he'd called a yacht broker and put the *Lay-Z-Girl* on the market.

Tonight, however, he dreamed of sailing away with his family to a new life. Tortola. The Turks and Caicos. A home on the ocean wave. Yes. He said to Courtney, "Mommy knows I'm here?"

"Mommy knows," a voice behind them said. Caroline, barefoot, dressed in designer jeans and a white linen blouse, closed the sliding glass door on the greenish talking face of the television news announcer and stepped onto the patio, darting shy, uncertain glances at Darryl.

He said, "Baby, you look great."

She brightened and gave him a smile and a kiss.

He sniffed the air between them. "Love the perfume too."

The children cut across their current, clamoring for attention. A moment of plea bargaining with their mother ensued, after which Kyle and Courtney trudged away toward the kitchen, where Mrs. Hernandez, a smiling Nicaraguan who was going to apply for her green card any day now, stood ready to dish out their supper before she began her trek out past the guardhouse and estate gates to the bus stop, and her night off.

"Any better today, sweetness?" Caroline asked, sitting down and taking a joint from her jeans pocket and lighting up.

The phone rang inside the house. Darryl lurched to his feet, saying, "I did okay in coffee. Made a buck or two. But I got hammered again in currencies. Big time." He stepped into the house, carefully closing the sliding glass door behind him.

"I'm sorry to hear it," Caroline muttered, watching him pick up the phone in the television room. She took a hit off her joint. When she exhaled, it sounded like a sigh.

She smoked and watched Darryl waving a hand and talking. Behind him, the colors on the television screen changed into electric blues, greens, and reds, and became a map of Israel, Jordan, and Syria, which was replaced by the image of a handsome young man in a safari jacket talking into a microphone in a desert. Caroline wondered, Would he find me attractive? The correspondent's eyes narrowed, as if he were thinking it over. Then his hair lifted, like the wing of a bird, revealing a bald spot the size of Jordan. Caroline shouted with laughter.

Darryl paced around the television room: tall, red-haired, muscular, dressed in chinos and a blue Izod shirt, moving his right arm as if he were conducting the conversation. Still handsome, Caroline thought. She'd fallen in love with him when she was sixteen years old and he was twenty. He desired her still. She was as certain of that as she was of anything else in this darkening world. Lately, though, he had been making love to her with such a blind, nuzzling intensity that she felt herself recoiling from him. His need frightened her. At the same time, her response left her feeling inadequate and guilty.

Well, she would get him a nice safari jacket for his birthday. She watched the frown on his face and drifted into a fantasy: Darryl was talking to the correspondent in the desert. Together they were solving a knotty international problem. *I told Arafat that he better cut the crap.* Something like that.

Darryl slid open the door and returned to slump into the chair next to her.

Caroline glanced at him. "What's happening, Mr. A?"

His face looked drained. "That client keeps calling to say that he's going to kill me."

Dread thumped on Caroline's heart. She blinked and fingered a button on her blouse. "Have you called the police?"

"It's under control."

"Control?" She sat up and flicked away her joint. "Whose control? He's calling you at home?"

"Well, he's upset."

"And you're not? He should be locked up."

"I've got to keep him talking. Calm him down."

"So, are we in danger? And damn you, Darryl, don't you lie to me."

"He'll calm down. And there's a guard on the gate and police on tap. We're safe."

"I don't feel safe. I mean—you're going to do nothing?"

"I've just got to live with it for a while. It'll blow over. Someday I'll kick his ass. He's a jerk. The market turned against him and he started hollering that I'd robbed him."

Caroline asked where this client was from, and Darryl said that, as far as he could make out, he'd begun in Ecuador but had ended up in Panama. Darryl shrugged. "He uses a Panamanian passport. But who knows? He hangs out on Key Biscayne when he's not in Panama."

"He's the only one complaining?"

Darryl looked darkly at her. "In a down market, everybody complains."

"But he says you clipped him? Why would he think that?"

Darryl shrugged. It wasn't what she thought. This guy loved playing the commodities market. Darryl had made a lot of money for him in the past. Last week, however, he'd lost big time—stopped out, three days in a row. Darryl had told him, "Cool off." But he was hot to jump in again. Well, he'd lost again, big time. Now he claimed it was Darryl's fault. He wanted his money back.

"And the threats?"

"You want his actual words?"

She looked away. She didn't want to hear the threats. "Well, anyway, this isn't Ecuador, or wherever he's from."

"Oh, no. Thank God we live in little old Miami, where everybody fears God and pays their taxes." Darryl nodded over his shoulder. "Like that nice Mr. Dominguez."

"This is not a sane way to live."

"Well, my choices are limited at the moment."

Caroline asked if maybe, just maybe, Darryl was getting too old for the commodities game?

Darryl bristled. "You don't like the style of life we have down here? I do it for you and the children. You want to go back to Chunchula, Alabama?"

She gave him a troubled smile. She told him that she surely loved him more alive than dead. And his children did too.

"Lover," he said, calming down. He took her hand and kissed it and admitted that maybe his life was a little too exciting now. That happened in his business. It was part of the adventure. As soon as he was clear of this little problem, they would think about changing things. Right now, he had to sit tight and roll with the punches.

Darryl told her a story about how Napoleon interviewed officers slated for high rank. The last question Napoleon asked was:

Are you lucky? If they hesitated, or said no, he didn't promote them. Darryl grinned. "I damn well know what I would've told him."

Caroline had heard the story before. Tonight, it lacked its old magic. An aggressive attitude to luck might help on a battlefield. But in business? She worried that Darryl bragged about luck just to keep himself moving through the scary scenarios he seemed bent on creating for himself these days. Maybe bragging was a fuel. Or a mantra. Or a charm. He'd always been addicted to danger, to the edge, to the thrill of winning big. A little impromptu craziness had made life interesting for him. It used to refresh him. Now it seemed to her as if something else was going on.

She worried about Darryl's attitude toward other people's money. She used to love hearing him romance a client: his voice had carried a weird and beautiful music, rich and deep and sexy—a "brown velvet" voice, somebody had once called it. But over the years she had identified new sounds, less beautiful. Now when the check changed hands, the music suffered a modulation too. She heard dry notes of contempt in Darryl's voice. Darryl acted as if the client had signed away his rights over his own money, and Darryl resisted with bewilderment and outrage any client's attempts to withdraw his account. He acted as if the client were trying to weasel away his, Darryl's, property.

Caroline worried that Darryl was growing addicted to the stronger jolt, the darker thrill, of losing big. She had been trying to identify the signs. Was she seeing another example tonight? She wasn't sure. He'd deny it, of course. Could she tell before it was too late? The fragility of their life worried Caroline, but it seemed to excite something in Darryl.

"Lover?" he said. "Didn't you hear me? I said I'm thinking of making some big changes."

"When?"

"Well, as soon as I get clear of these problems."

They looked at each other, and then away, toward the canal,

where the *Lay-Z-Girl* gently chafed at its moorings in the evening breeze.

Courtney and Kyle returned to the patio just as the telephone rang again. Their father went into the television room and returned immediately, shaking his head at their mother.

"So, Daddy," Kyle said, "what's the big surprise?"

His remark startled his parents. They stared at him.

"Surprise?" Caroline said, reaching up to finger the button at her throat.

"Daddy," Courtney said, "you promised a surprise."

"Oh, that surprise." Their father put his face in his hands and choked with laughter, and his neck flushed bright pink. When he didn't stop laughing, the children grew uneasy. They looked to their mother for guidance and saw her staring at the top of their father's balding head, as if there were something wrong with its color or shape. The phone rang and both parents moved, but their father was faster. His absence left everybody on the patio wordless and uneasy.

He was back in a moment. As he came out onto the patio, Darryl breathed out sharply, clapped his hands, and shouted, "Ghost!" That got everybody's attention. He said, "We're playing Ghost tonight. That's the surprise." He waited for the confusion to subside. They'd played it once before: after their dinner, Mommy and Daddy had turned out all the lights and come searching for Courtney and Kyle.

Caroline said, "Not tonight."

Courtney said, "I hate that game."

Kyle said, "What's the prize?"

"Something really nice," Darryl said. "Now listen up."

They'd play for only an hour. Kyle giggled and said, "I'll hide at Brandon's house." No, Darryl told him, nobody could leave the house. Whoever remained free, or was the last to get caught, won the game.

"What's the prize?" Kyle said.

"It's a *su*-prize," Darryl said. The children examined this statement and rejected it as adult nonsense.

Kyle gasped, "We're staying up late," and his mother said, "Not too late. School tomorrow. Tonight's special." Why was it special? the children wanted to know, and their mother directed them to their father for their answer. He winked and said that it was a secret. "Why is everything a surprise or a secret?" Courtney said.

"Is this necessary?" Caroline said. She sensed her evening sliding toward a dark corner. But she knew that marijuana stoked her paranoid tendencies, and she was confused about what she really felt, so she went out of her way to enunciate her doubts in reasonable tones. "Do we really need this tonight, honey?" They were eating on the patio. The children had been banished to the television room. Caroline served the food that Mrs. Hernandez had prepared—pork chops and rice, a salad of crispy greens, and a bottle of Chilean cabernet—and then she brought out the portable television so she could keep an eye on a rerun of *Star Trek* while she ate.

Darryl had drunk himself into a mood where he found life piquant. "C'mon," he said, "I need a little lighthearted fun. It's just a game." He laughed. "It reminds me of what my daddy said to me at his own daddy's funeral: 'These are the jokes, so start laughing.'"

"Stop." Caroline put down her fork.

The image of Mr. Spock came on the television screen and said, "Irritation. Ah, yes. One of your earth emotions."

"Darryl, this just doesn't sound right."

He shrugged. "Isn't it like life? You're in your house and it feels safe, but suddenly it's dark as Hades, and out there are people who are coming to get you."

"I forbid you to talk like that." Caroline blinked at the pale light coming down over the canal and felt a heavy downward drop in her emotions. "Let's just take the kids to Dairy Queen, okay?"

They wrangled quietly. "I was joking," Darryl said. "The kids were bugging me. We'll play for an hour."

Caroline, unhappy and distrustful, looked over at the portable television. Mr. Spock, wearing earphones, said, "This must be garbled. The tapes are badly burned. I get the captain giving the order to destroy his own ship."

Caroline told Darryl that she'd think about it. She busied herself with her dinner, even through she wasn't hungry now, and pretended to concentrate on *Star Trek*. Captain Kirk was ordering a twenty-four-hour watch on the sick bay.

And then she thought, Maybe I'm not being fair to him. Maybe I'm not being helpful. He's so edgy tonight. He needs to play more than the kids do. She wavered and then gave in. "Okay. Okay. But only for an hour." He brightened immediately. She looked away, feeling slightly creepy.

"Let's do it right this time," Darryl said. They discussed ways to turn themselves into ghosts.

"We need sheets," Darryl said.

"You're not cutting my good sheets," she said.

"I'm talking about old sheets," Darryl said.

Caroline said that all their sheets were new. She said, "Everything in this house is new."

"But what's a ghost without a sheet?" Darryl said.

From the television, Mr. Spock shouted, "We're entering a force field of some kind! Sensor beam on!"

"Hold it!" Caroline shouted. "We're almost ready. But not yet, so you can't come in." Courtney and Kyle wouldn't stop tapping on the locked bedroom door, so their mother, whose hair had suddenly turned white and who was wearing the palest makeup she could find, burst out of the bathroom in her bra and panties, trotted across the bedroom, and shouted through the door for them to knock it off. The telephone rang and she picked up the receiver and said, "Hello?" She waited, and when nobody spoke she muttered, "Oh, fuck you," and dropped the receiver into the cradle and walked to her dressing table and looked at the image of herself with white hair. She shook her head, closed her eyes, and sighed. She felt exhausted.

She reached into a drawer and retrieved a small vial. She dipped her finger, applied it to each nostril and inhaled, rubbed the finger around her gums, and then replaced the vial and went back into the bathroom, where Darryl waited nude in the shower stall singing an old Pink Floyd number about money, and she finished powdering his hair with flour.

She wiped the flour off his shoulder with a towel, kissed him on the lips, tweaked his nipples, and fondled his penis. She stepped back, her eyes hard and sparkling, and considered her handiwork. From the shower stall, Darryl, smiling, red-faced, and drunk, blew kisses at her.

"Hmmmnnn," she said.

"Hmmmnnn what, baby?" he said.

She said, "I just wanted to see how you'd look as an old white-haired cracker with a hard-on."

The children rushed through the doorway and halted just inside the bedroom and almost fell over with fright. In front of them, holding hands side by side on the bed, sat two laughing ghosts with pale, shiny faces, chalky white heads, and bloodshot eyes. They wore flowing white sheets. The ghosts raised their hands in the air, flopped them around and wailed, "Whoooooooo!" and Kyle turned and ran into the doorframe.

A ghost jumped up and took Kyle's face in its white-dusted hands and said, "Honey, you all right?"

Kyle looked up with one of his eyes shut and said, "Mom?"

The ghost nodded.

Kyle said, "You scared me."

The ghost bent back Kyle's head to examine the bump over his eye and asked, "You sure you're all right?"

Kyle nodded.

"You want to play the game?"

Kyle nodded again. "I guess so."

"It's only for an hour," the other ghost said, and Courtney said, "Kyle's so spastic."

"So, if we're all okay . . ." Darryl said. He reminded them that no lights or flashlights were allowed during the game.

"And Kyle better find his own hiding place," Courtney said.

Darryl told them that the ghosts would wait in this bedroom, then come out and search for the children, *ha ha ha.*

Courtney pressed her hand to her forehead and said, "Dad, you're weird."

Darryl, noticing a look on Kyle's face, said, "And you can't just give up. If you're caught you'll have to wait in the TV room—with the TV off. Under no circumstances can you go outside the house. Okay?"

Kyle nodded and touched the bump on his forehead and said, "But what's the prize?"

"A Peanut Buster Parfait at Dairy Queen," Darryl said.

"Tonight?" Kyle said, in a rising voice.

Darryl nodded.

"Wow!" Kyle said, and even Courtney forgot herself enough to show enthusiasm.

"So, we're ready?" Darryl asked.

From where the children waited in the TV room, they caught glimpses of the ghosts floating around the house, turning off lights. They heard, in the gathering darkness, one ghost remind the other about the alarm system. Then the ghosts returned to the doorway of their bedroom, their sheets billowing behind them.

Darryl called out, "Children, can you hear me? Can you hear me?"

"Yes!" the children shouted.

They had ten minutes to hide themselves, he announced. "From *now.*" He slammed shut the bedroom door, and he and the other ghost groped toward the bed and lay down side by side in the darkness.

He said, "Lordy, think of them creeping around out there like mice." Caroline said she didn't know if she had the energy to spend an hour chasing the kids around a dark house, and Darryl reached over and touched her nipple and said, "Who says you have to do that? I've got a great idea. Want to hear?"

"Hmmmmnnn—probably not," she said. "But tell me anyhow."

As he began to speak she sat up, moved off the bed, and found her way over to her dresser. She quietly opened the drawer, found her little vial, and applied some of its contents to her nostrils and gums, and when her husband paused to ask what on earth she was doing at her dressing table, she sniffed and told him that she was looking for her eye drops, because flour from her hair was irritating her eyes.

"I'll take some," Darryl said.

"Some what?" she said.

"Eye drops," he said, and she said, "Coming right up!"

A moment later she started swearing because, she said, she'd just dropped the container on the shag carpet and now she couldn't find it.

Kyle couldn't find a place to hide. Every spot he chose turned out to be too obvious, or it bothered Courtney, who seemed to be playing a game of her own, popping up behind him in every room he went into and hissing at him to *go away*. He finally returned to the living room and squeezed himself under the sofa. Kosmo the cat came over to keep him company and interpreted all of Kyle's efforts to shoo him off as invitations to play, and just when Kyle realized that he'd picked another stupid place to hide, he heard his parents' bedroom door open. His father's voice called out, "Ten minutes is up. This is now officially a *ghost house*. Only *ghosts* live here. Watch out, heeeeeerrrre we come!"

From under the sofa, Kyle looked over and saw the two ghosts standing in the doorway of his parents' bedroom. He whimpered when they laughed like those jungle animals from Africa he had seen on TV. As they began searching through the house, flapping their sheets and making terrible noises, Kosmo finally ran away, and Kyle squeezed himself into the tiniest ball he could imagine and tried not to think about the throbbing bump on his forehead, or about all places on his body that itched, or the fact that he badly needed to clear his throat, at least once. An hour seemed like forever.

The game glided over Caroline's imagination with the sinister smoothness of a dream bird. She felt more energetic now, and she put her best effort into it. Action kept her paranoia—the panic feeling that she was wavering like an old quarter around the edge of a bottomless pit—far enough away to be bearable.

They swept through the house making ghostly noises, and the first place they looked for Kyle was under the living room sofa, because they both remembered that when Kyle was a little younger he loved to crawl under this sofa and declare himself invisible. Caroline spotted one of his feet and pointed it out to Darryl, who nodded. They circled the sofa, moaning and flapping their sheets, and went on in search of Courtney.

Caroline's senses twitched when they passed the broom closet just off the kitchen, and they stopped and flapped their sheets outside that. While she was dancing around and tapping on the freezer next to it, Caroline felt a stronger twitch of intuition, and she led Darryl to the linen closet by the laundry room. She had remembered that Courtney loved the floral smell of the sachets slipped between the laundered sheets and towels to keep out the smell of mildew. The ghosts wept out her name, and Caroline rattled the linen closet doorknob and felt a sudden pull from the other side. She pulled harder, but the door wouldn't budge. She pictured Courtney obstinately hanging on to the doorknob, and a wave of irritation rose up in her, and she felt a wild urge to yank open the door and strike terror into her daughter's heart, and then she felt ashamed. She loved Courtney. Why should she want to terrorize her? Caroline was appalled at herself. This game had gone too far. She turned away and signaled urgently to Darryl. They made one last sweep through the house, then silently departed through the sliding glass door to the patio and fled across the lawn.

Courtney sat on a pile of towels in the linen closet and hung on to the doorknob with both hands. She wept as silently as she knew how. She had felt, through the door, the force of her mother's anger, and it had shocked her. What had she done to deserve it? She knew she was overweight and unlovely, but she couldn't help it. Her father was acting so weird too. She cried harder now, because she wanted to love him but he wouldn't let her, and she felt so alone.

Kyle strained until he thought his ears were going to pop, but he only heard the thumping of his own blood. He waited and waited and *waited* for the ghosts to make a noise, and finally he just had to move his legs, and then he had to scratch all his itches, and after that he couldn't stop himself and he cleared his throat. Time dragged by. He couldn't remember the house being this quiet, ever.

Caroline and Darryl threw cushions down on the dew-dampened afterdeck of the *Lay-Z-Girl* and tore off each other's sheets, T-shirts, shorts, and underwear, and made love in the silvery light of an almost full moon, as if they were young again and back in a field outside Chunchula, Alabama. Ah, it was sweet and powerful, the best ever, they told each other afterward. Sweaty and relaxed, they dozed for a while, until the crisp growl of twin outboard engines, approaching in the canal from the direction of Biscayne Bay, awakened them. The outboard engines shut off close by, and they looked at each other and shook their heads.

"Jorge?"

"Jorge."

Both of them had thought the same thing: young Jorge Dominguez was returning home. Darryl got up into a crouch, looked over the railing, and glimpsed two figures moving across the Dominguezes' lawn. He lay back down again next to Caroline. They decided that Jorge had taken his girlfriend out in his boat, to smoke a joint or fuck in the moonlight.

"Someday," Darryl murmured, lying on his back and tracking the blinking lights of a passing airplane, "I'll get me a sweet little .357 Magnum and take Jorge's heart for a spin over the red line. I surely will. I swear it on the grave of my Aunt Alice, who always had a strap handy for uppity children—I'm not joking," he said, turning toward Caroline.

"You're my big strong hero," she said, fondling him. "Sure you are."

Kyle flitted from room to room, growing more and more upset. He was alone, all alone in this dark house. They'd gone away and left him. Even the cat was gone.

Or maybe they were playing a joke on him? Yes, that was it, he thought with a burst of blistering hatred, because Courtney was a bully and she always got what she wanted and she loved to gang up on him, and now they'd taken her side. Now they were all together someplace, laughing at him. They were waiting for him to act like a baby. Well, he wouldn't. He wouldn't call out or turn on any lights.

But what was he supposed to do? Where was everybody? He'd checked everywhere—now he was coming out of his parents' bathroom, leaving a safe zone of damp towels and reassuring smells, the scent of his mother's perfumed powder, his father's cologne. He walked through a house now unfamiliar, pretending not to notice how the walls bulged out at him. It was hard not to shout with fear when he saw the dark hairy animals that had taken the place of the chairs and sofas he had known. He pretended he didn't see them, and the animals stopped breathing and watched with glowing eyes as he passed. He heard their hearts beating; they gave off a rank, rotten smell as they inched nearer in the darkness, on every side. He knew that they longed to touch him.

He slipped into the kitchen, quietly closing the door behind him, sniffing the air and finding faint traces of the pork chop and rice Mrs. Hernandez had served him for supper. He missed her and her kindly, rough hands. He felt so alone. He fetched up in front of the refrigerator, pondering his father's last words: *This is now officially a ghost house.* Was that a secret message which Courtney had understood, but which he, Kyle, had missed? Would it be a ghost house forever? Did they have to abandon it? As Kyle repeated his father's words in his mind, they became alien and threatening. He opened the refrigerator door. The light was wonderfully bright and warm. He reached in, grabbed four slices of bologna, shut the refrigerator door, and stuffed the bologna into his mouth. He stood there in the dark, chewing.

The more Kyle thought about it, the more he grew convinced that they were all someplace together, Mom, Dad, and Courtney. Well, if they weren't inside, they weren't playing fair.

They were together outside. That had to be it. He pictured them sitting together on the back terrace, near the pool, waiting to see how long it would take dumb Kyle to figure out their big joke, and because this picture was the brightest thing in his world at the moment, Kyle accepted it as the truth. Courtney had gotten hold of his mom and dad. Now they were on her side.

So now he'd leave the house too. He'd sneak around to the terrace, where they were sitting around playing their big joke on him, and he'd leap out of the bushes and give them the fright of their lives. *Ha ha ha!* he'd yell. He'd beat up Courtney. He'd wipe everyone out, *pow pow pow.* Then they'd be sorry. Boy, would everybody be sorry when Kyle the Avenger jumped onto that terrace. They'd see how Courtney had lied to them and they'd never ever play a stupid joke on Kyle again.

He grinned as he opened the kitchen door, slipped into the night, and began trotting toward the back of the house and the terrace. He was playing that scene over again in his mind, the one where Kyle the Avenger jumps onto the terrace and frightens the willies out of everybody, when he heard a noise behind him. He dropped down on the ground and froze against the side of the house. He looked back and saw two figures in dark clothes detach themselves from the Surinam cherry hedge. They had come from the Dominguezes' yard. They walked directly over to the kitchen door and opened it, silently entered the house, and just as silently closed the door behind them. Kyle stared at where they'd been. They'd moved so smoothly, so quickly, so quietly. Like ghosts. For a moment, Kyle found it hard to breathe. He felt dizzy and light-headed; he wanted to clear his throat, but he fought against it, and then he began to gag.

He jumped up and plunged through the Surinam cherry hedge and landed on his hands and knees in the Dominguezes' yard, where he quietly vomited up the bologna. He wiped his mouth with his hand and flopped onto his back in the grass and lay shaking in the darkness. Music poured from the Dominguezes' house, and it felt soothing and familiar to him. Dad hadn't told him there were other people playing the game. Where'd they come from? Why were they wearing dark clothes?

Lying in the Dominguezes' yard, Kyle looked up at the moon and thought of the ghosts in dark clothes. Boy, were they scary. He never wanted to play this game again. He closed his eyes and saw stars and felt dizzy, so he opened his eyes and stared up at the sky and wondered how long he'd have to wait until the game was finally over and he could go home and fall asleep in his own bed.

"Christ Almighty, would you listen to that racket?" Darryl said when the heavy metal rock music started up at the Dominguez house. Darryl and Caroline had dozed off again; the music had awakened them.

"I'm going to the head," Caroline muttered, "and then let's collect the kids. Don't forget we've got to take them to Dairy Queen." She kissed him, then groaned as she got off the deck. "I'm getting old, sweetness," she said, descending the stairs. "Old."

Darryl moved to a chair moist with dew. He looked up at the stars and over at the lurid night sky above downtown Miami. He felt better than he had in a long while. Getting out of the house and away from the telephone and making love to Caroline in the moonlight had brought him to a place of balance between the ever-tightening inner craziness of the last few weeks and a sense of future possibilities. He felt refreshed. Hopeful. He loved his wife and he loved his children. He stretched, feeling sexy and content and not at all drunk. He knew he could solve his problems. He was ready to fight the fight. "Fucking rock music," he muttered, staring at his neighbor's house. How could old Dominguez stand that shit? Was he deaf?

"That client—the one who's been threatening you?" Caroline was coming back up onto the deck.

Darryl sighed.

She peered up at the sky and began to pick up her clothes. "What are you going to do?"

"Make a deal."

"What kind of deal?"

"I'll make them happy. I'm thinking of a way to pay them back."

She stopped dressing and stared at him. "*Them?*"

"Yes." He looked at her. "I told you that."

"You did?" She began crying.

He touched her, but she moved away. He opened his mouth but didn't know what to say. He pulled on his shorts and T-shirt.

She zipped up her shorts, weeping. "What are we going to do?"

"I borrowed some of their money."

"Borrowed?"

"Something like that."

"Well, for God's sake, give it back." Her head emerged from her T-shirt.

"I don't have it right now."

"What have you done with it?"

"It's gone." He opened his hands. "I'm in a deep hole."

She wept again. "Oh, tell them—anything."

"I've been doing that."

She hugged herself. "This is too much."

"It's business. I can't panic, or they'll be on me like sharks."

"Aren't we talking about your life—our lives? Is it all some kind of a game to you?"

"No." He felt her receding from him and he wanted to set things right between them. He told her that he loved her, and he embraced her, breathing in her smell, waiting to feel her soften. She didn't, so he stepped back and willed a smile onto his face. "Look," he said, "I screwed up, but I *know* a way to get out of it."

"How?"

"My luck's got to hold out a day or so, and then I'm clear. I want a different life. I can't go on like this. And that's a definite promise. We'll sit down and you'll tell me what you want and we'll make a plan."

She stared at him. "You're never going to change, are you?"

He remembered the flour in his hair and felt self-conscious. He must look absurd. "I'm changing," he said. "You'll see."

"I don't believe it."

"My biggest worry at the moment," he went on, rubbing his head, "is how I'm going to get this gunk out of my hair. Go back to the house and round up the kids and we'll go out to Dairy Queen. I'll use the boat dock hose and be right there."

She climbed down onto the concrete edge of the canal, and then looked toward their house. It was dark and silent. Compared to the Dominguezes', so bright, throbbing with music and energy, her house seemed like the negative of a house. The children, she thought, were being unusually patient and quiet. She looked up at

Darryl. She was angry at him and disappointed. "Oh, hurry up," she said.

"I love you," he said.

She gazed up at him, then turned and started into the darkness. Darryl tried, and failed, to find something reassuring to call after her.

He stepped into the cockpit, groped around, found a key, fitted it into the ignition, and tried to start the twin diesel engines.

The *Lay-Z-Girl* was Darryl's province, one in which Caroline was not interested. She hated fishing, and she complained about sunburn and seasickness.

The *Lay-Z-Girl* badly needed repairs. Now the main engines wouldn't start. He couldn't work the radio. The gauges for the three fuel tanks were hovering near empty. He gave out a deep sigh. How he had loved this boat. And what a mess his life had become. He had told Caroline the truth. He wanted to change. But what was he going to do about Narciso? A solution seemed impossible but at the same time close, very close.

On his way back to the railing, he almost tripped over the sheets that Caroline and he had shed on the deck. He threw them over his shoulder, climbed down onto the concrete dock, turned on the hose, then changed his mind and turned it off.

He'd seen the Dominguezes' lawn explode into low fountains of water. Their automatic sprinklers had come on. In the light from their porch, Darryl saw droplets sparkling on their grass. It was a strange and beautiful sight. His own lawn was dark. So was the house. Caroline hadn't turned on the lights. He halted, uneasy, and stared at his house and around his backyard. He felt that something was wrong with it all, but he didn't know what it was.

His house was perfectly quiet. Darkness seemed to flow out of it toward him in dense waves. He felt a spurt of anxiety and fought to control it. Where was Caroline? Where were the kids?

"Caroline?" he called. There was no answer. He thought that he glimpsed a dark movement behind the sliding glass door to the living room. "Caroline?" he called again. Why didn't she answer?

Darryl studied his house. For some reason, it didn't look like his home. It seemed alien. He didn't like it. He glanced with irritation at all the bright lights illuminating the Dominguezes' house, and he wrestled down his anxiety.

He made up his mind: he'd had enough paranoia for one day. He was tired and he wanted this game to be over. There was, he decided, only one reason for the silence in his house. His family was waiting inside in the darkness to surprise him. Well, he'd play along, even though the notion of moving into that darkness gave him the creeps.

He wanted to be greeted by warmth and light and happy children. He had a vision of them standing just inside the door, holding their breath, waiting to switch on the lights and yell, "Boo!" That vision propelled him forward, smiling.

Perhaps, he thought, as he walked up the lawn, rubbing the flour from his hair, perhaps when they got back from Dairy Queen, he'd switch on his porch lights and turn on his sprinklers and show the kids how beautiful water can be, even at night.

PART IV

GATORS & GHOULS

GATORS

BY VICKI HENDRICKS

The Everglades

(Originally published in 2000)

It was a goddamned one-armed alligator put me over the line. After that I was looking for trouble. Carl and me had been married for two years, second marriage for both, and the situation was drastic—hateful most times—but I could tell he didn't realize there was anything better in the world. It made me feel bad that he never learned how to love—grew up with nothing but cruelty. I kept trying way too long to show him there was something else.

I was on my last straw when I suggested a road trip for Labor Day weekend—stupidly thinking that I could amuse him and wouldn't have to listen to his bitching about me and the vile universe on all my days off work. I figured at a motel he'd get that vacation feeling, lighten up, and stick me good, and I could get by for the few waking hours I had to see him the rest of the week.

We headed out to the Everglades for our little trip. Being recent transplants from Texas, we hadn't seen the natural wonders in Florida. Carl started griping by midafternoon about how I told him there were so many alligators and we couldn't find a fucking one. I didn't dare say that there would've been plenty if he hadn't taken two hours to read the paper and sit on the john. We could've made it before the usual thunderstorms and had time to take a tour. As it was, he didn't want to pay the bucks to ride the tram in the rain—even though the cars were covered. We were pretty much stuck with what we could see driving, billboards for

Seminole gambling and airboats, and lots of soggy grassland under heavy black-and-blue-layered skies. True, it had a bleak, haunting kind of beauty.

Carl refused to put on the air conditioner because he said it sapped the power of the engine, so all day we suffocated. We could only crack the truck windows because of the rain. By late afternoon my back was soaked with sweat and I could smell my armpits. And, get this—he was smoking cigarettes. Like I said, I was plain stupid coming up with the idea—or maybe blinded by the fact that he had a nice piece of well-working equipment that seemed worth saving.

At that point, I started to wonder if I could make us swerve into a canal and end the suffering. I was studying the landscape, looking ahead for deep water, when I spotted a couple vehicles pulled off the road.

"Carl, look. I bet you they see gators."

"Fuckin' A," he bellowed.

He was driving twenty over the limit, as always—in a hurry to get to hell—but he nailed the brakes and managed to turn onto a gravel road that ran a few hundred yards off the side of a small lake. One car pulled out past us, but a couple and a little girl were still standing near the edge of the water.

It was only drizzling by then, and Carl pulled next to their pickup and shut off the ignition. My side of the truck was over a puddle about four inches deep. I opened the door and plodded through in my sandals, while Carl stood grimacing at the horizon, rubbing his dark unshaved chin.

We walked toward the people. The woman was brown-haired, wearing a loose print dress—the kind my grandma would've called a housedress—and I felt how sweet and old-fashioned she was next to me in short-shorts and halter top, with my white-blond hair and black roots haystack style. The man was a wiry, muscular type in tight jeans and a white T-shirt—tattoos on both biceps, like Carl, but arms half the size. He was bending down by some rocks a little farther along. The little girl, maybe four years old, and her mother were holding hands by the edge.

"That guy reminds me of my asshole brother-in-law," Carl said in a low tone, as we got closer. I nodded, thinking how true it was—the guy reminded me of Carl too, all the same kind of assholes. Carl boomed out, "Hey, there!" in his usual megaphone, overly friendly voice. The mother and child glanced up with a kind of mousy suspiciousness I sometimes felt in my own face. It was almost like they had him pegged instantly.

We stopped near them. The guy came walking over. He had his hands cupped together in front of him and motioned with his arms toward the water. I looked into the short water weeds and sticks and saw two small eyes and nose holes rising above the ripples a few yards out. It was a baby gator, maybe four feet long, judging by the closeness of his parts.

"There he is!" Carl yelled.

"Just you watch this," the guy said. He tossed something into the water in front of the nose and I caught the scrambling of tiny legs just before the gator lurched and snapped it up. "They just love them lizards," the man said.

Carl started laughing, "Ho, ho, ho," like it was the funniest thing he ever seen, and the guy joined in because he'd made such a big hit.

Us women looked at each other and kind of smiled with our lips tight. The mother had her arm around the little girl's shoulder holding her against her hip. The girl squirmed away. "Daddy, can I help you catch another one?"

"Sure, darlin', come right over here." He led her toward the rocks and I saw the mother cast him a look as he went by. He laughed and took his daughter's hand.

The whole thing was plenty creepy, but Carl was still chuckling. It seemed like maybe he was having a good time for a change.

"Reptiles eating reptiles," he said. "Yup." He did that eh-eh-eh laugh in the back of his throat. It made me wince. He took my hand and leered toward my face. "It's a scrawny one, Virginia—not like a Texas gator—but I guess I have to say you weren't lyin. Florida has one." He put his arm across my shoulder and leaned on me, still laughing at his own sense of humor. I widened my legs, to keep from falling over, and chuckled so he wouldn't demand to know what was the matter, then insist I spoiled the day by telling him.

We stood there watching the gator float in place hoping for another snack, and in a few minutes, the squeals of the little girl told us that it wouldn't be long. They came shuffling over slowly, the father bent, cupping his hands over the girl's.

"This is the last one now, okay, sweetheart?" the mother said as they stopped beside her. She was talking to the little girl. "We need to get home in time to make supper." From her voice it sounded like they'd been sacrificing lizards for a while.

The two flung the prey into the water. It fell short, but there was no place for the lizard to go. It floundered in the direction it was pointed, the only high ground, the gator's waiting snout. He snapped it up. This time he'd pushed farther out of the water and I saw that he was missing one of his limbs.

"Look, Carl, the gator only has one arm. I wonder what got him?"

"Probably a Texas gator," he said. "It figures, the one gator you find me is a cripple." Carl had an answer for everything.

"No," I said. "Why would one gator tear off another one's arm?"

"Leg. One big chomp without thinkin. Probably got his leg in between his mother and some tasty tidbit—a small dog or kid. Life is cruel, babycakes—survival of the fittest." He stopped talking to light a cigarette. He waved it near my face to make his point. "You gotta protect yourself—be cruel first. That's why you got me—to do it for you." He gave me one of his grins with all the teeth showing.

"Oh, is *that* why?" I laughed, like it was a joke. Yeah, Carl would take care of his own all right—it was like having a mad dog at my side, never knowing when he might turn. He wouldn't hesitate to rip anybody's arm off, mine included, if it got in his way.

The mother called to her husband, "Can we get going, honey? I have fish to clean."

The guy didn't look up. "Good job," he said to his daughter. He reached down and gave her a pat on the butt. "Let's get another one."

It started to rain a little harder, thank God, and Carl motioned with his head toward the car and started walking. I looked at the woman still standing there. "Bye," I called.

She nodded at me, her face empty of life. "Goodbye, honey." It was then she turned enough for me to see that the sleeve on the far side of the dress was empty, pinned up—her arm was gone. Jesus. I felt my eyes bulge. She couldn't have missed what I said. I burned through ten shades of red in a split second. I turned and sprinted to catch up with Carl.

He glanced at me. "What's your hurry, sugar? You ain't gonna melt. Think I'd leave without ya?"

"Nope," I said. I swallowed and tried to lighten up. I didn't want to share with him what I saw.

He looked at me odd and I knew he wasn't fooled. "What's with you?"

"Hungry," I said.

"I told you you should've had a ham sandwich before we left. You never listen to me. I won't be ready to eat for a couple more hours."

"I have to pee too. We passed a restaurant a quarter mile back."

He pointed across the road. "There's the bushes. I'm not stopping anywhere else till the motel."

We crossed the state and got a cheap room in Naples for the night. Carl ordered a pepperoni pizza from Domino's, no mushrooms for me. The room was clean and the air and remote worked, but it was far from the beach. We sat in bed and ate the pizza. I was trying to stick with the plan for having fun and I suggested we could get up early and drive to the beach to find shells.

"To look for fucking seashells? No."

His volume warned me. I decided to drop it. I gave him all my pepperonis and finished up my piece. I had a murder book to curl up with. He found a football game on TV.

I was in the grip of a juicy scene when Carl started working his hands under the covers. It was halftime. He found my thigh and stroked inward. I read fast to get to the end of the chapter. He grabbed the book and flung it across the room onto the other bed.

"I'm tryin to make love to you, and you have your nose stuck in a book. What's the problem? You gettin it somewhere else and don't need it from me? Huh?"

I shook my head violently. His tone and volume had me scared. "No, for Chrissakes." His face was an inch from mine. Rather than say anything else, I took his shoulders and pulled myself to him for a kiss. He was stiff, so I started sucking his lower lip and moving my tongue around. His shoulders relaxed.

Pretty soon he yanked down the covers, pulled up my nightie, and climbed on top. I couldn't feel him inside me—I was numb. Nothing new. I smelled his breath.

I moaned like he expected, and after a few long minutes of pumping and grabbing at my tits, he got that strained look on his face. "I love you to death," he rasped. "Love you to death." I felt him get rigid and come hard inside me, and a chill ran all the way from his cock to my head. He groaned deep and let himself down on my chest. "It's supernatural what you do to me, dollface, supernatural."

"Mmm."

He lit up a cigarette and puffed a few breaths in my face. "I couldn't live without you. Know that? You know that, don't you? You ever left me, I'd have to kill myself."

"No. Don't say that."

"Why? You thinkin of leaving? I *would* kill myself. I would. And knowin me, I'd take you along." He rolled on his side, laughing eh-eh-eh to himself. My arm was pinned, and for a second I panicked. I yanked it out from under him. He shifted and in seconds started snoring. Son of a bitch. He had me afraid to speak.

The woman and the gator came into my head, and I knew her life without having to live it, the casual cruelty and a sudden swift slice that changed her whole future. I could land in her place easy, trapped with a kid, no job, and a bastard of a husband who thought he was God. Carl said he was God at least three times a week. I shuddered—more like the devil. First, he'd take an arm, then go for my soul, just a matter of time. He'd rather see me dead than gone.

There was no thought of a road trip the next weekend, so we both slept late that Saturday. By then, the fear and hatred in my heart had taken over my brain. I was frying eggs, the bathroom door was open, and Carl was on the toilet—his place of serious thinking—when he used the words that struck me with the juicy, seedy, sweet fantasy of getting rid of him.

"I ought to kill my asshole brother-in-law!" he yelled. The words were followed by grunts of pleasure and plunking noises I could hear from the kitchen.

Uh-huh, I said to myself. I pretended to be half hearing—as if that were possible—and splashed the eggs with bacon grease like he wanted them. I didn't say anything. He was building up rage on the sound of his own voice.

"The fuck went out on Labor Day and left Penny and the kids home. She didn't say anything about him drinkin, but I could hear it in her voice when I called last night. I can't keep ignoring this. I oughta get a flight over there and take ol' Raymond out."

"How's he doing after his knife wound?"

"Son of a bitch is finally back to work. I should just take him out. Penny and the kids would be fine with the insurance she'd get from GM."

"Oh?"

"Those slimy titty bars he hangs out in—like Babydoe's—I could just fly into Dallas, do him, and fly back. Nobody would think a thing unusual."

I heard the flush and then his continued pulling of toilet paper. He always flushed before he wiped. I knew if I went in there after him I would see streaky wads of paper still floating. He came striding into the kitchen with a towel wrapped around him, his gut hanging over. He seemed to rock back as he walked to keep from falling forward. He turned and poured his eighth cup of coffee, added milk, held it over the sink, and stirred wildly. Half of it slopped over the sides of the cup. His face was mottled with red and he growled to himself.

I looked away. I remembered that at seventeen he had thrown his father out of the house—for beating his mother. He found out later they snuck around for years to see each other behind his back—they were that scared of him.

I knew going opposite whatever he said would push him. I pointed to the phone. "Calm down and call your sister. Her and the kids might want to keep Ray around."

"Yeah? Uh-uh. She's too nice. She'll give that son of a bitch chance after chance while he spends all their money on ass and booze. If anybody's gonna take advantage of somebody, it's gonna be me."

I handed him his plate of eggs and turned away to take my shower and let him spew. I heard him pick up the paper again and started with how all the "assholes in the news" should be killed.

Before this, it didn't occur to me as an asset that he was always a hair's breadth from violence. I'd tried for peace. I didn't want to know about the trouble he'd been in before we met, his being in jail for violating a restraining order. He'd broken down a door—I heard that from his sister because she thought I should know. I figured he deserved another chance in life. He had a lousy childhood with the drunk old man and all. But now I realized how foolish I was to think that if I treated him nice enough—turned the other cheek—he would be nice back. Thought that was human nature. Wrong. I was a goddamned angelic savior for over a year and not a speck of it rubbed off. He took me for a sucker to use and abuse. It was a lesson I'd never forget, learned too late.

This sounds crazy—but something about the alligator incident made me know Carl's true capabilities, and I was fucking scared. That alligator told me that a ticket for Carl to Dallas was my only ticket out. It was a harsh thought, but Penny's husband wasn't God's gift either, and if Carl didn't get him, it was just a matter of time till some other motherfucker did.

At first, I felt scared of the wicked thoughts in my heart. But after a few days, each time Carl hawked up a big gob and spit it out the car window or screamed at me because the elevator at the apartment complex was too slow, the idea became less sinful. He was always saying how he used to break guys' legs for a living, collecting, and he might decide to find some employment of that kind in Florida since the pay was so lousy for construction. Besides that, there was his drunk driving—if I could get him behind bars, it would be an asset to the whole state. Or maybe I'd only have to threaten.

One morning he woke up and bit my nipple hard before I was even awake. "Ouch!" I yelled. It drew blood and made my eyes fill up.

"The world's a hard place," he told me.

"You make it that way."

He laughed. "You lived your little pussy life long enough. It's time you find out what it's all about." He covered my mouth with his booze-and-cigarette breath, and I knew that was the day I'd make a call to his sister. He wasn't going to go away on his own.

Penny did mail-outs at home in the morning, so I called her from work. I could hear her stuffing envelopes while we talked. I asked about the kids and things. "So how's your husband?" I added. "Carl said he went back to work."

"Yeah. We're getting along much better. He's cut back on the drinking and brings home his paycheck. Doesn't go to the bar half as much."

"He's still going to that bar where he got hurt?"

"Oh, no, a new one, Cactus Jack's, a nicer place—no nude dancers, and it's only a couple miles from here, so he can take a cab if he needs to. He promised he wouldn't go back over to Babydoe's."

Done. It was smooth. I didn't even have to ask where he hung out. "Yeah," I said. "He gets to the job in the morning. That's what I keep telling Carl."

"He only goes out Fridays and maybe one or two other days. I can handle that. I'm not complaining."

She was a good woman. I felt tears well in my eyes. "You're a saint, honey. I have to get back to work now—the truckers are coming in for their checks. Carl would like to hear from you one night soon. He worries."

I had all I needed to know—likely she'd wanted to tell somebody and didn't care to stir Carl up and listen to all his godly orders. She wasn't complaining—goddamn. It was amazing that her and my husband were of the same blood. And, yeah, she was being taken advantage of—I could hear it. Now I had to tell Carl when and where to go without him realizing it was my plan.

That night I started to move him along. "I talked to your sister Penny this morning," I told him at the dinner table.

"Oh yeah?" He was shoveling in chicken-fried steak, mashed potatoes with sawmill gravy, and corn, one of his favorite meals.

I ate with one hand behind my back, protecting my arm from any quick snaps. "She's a trouper," I said. "Wow."

"Huh?"

"I never heard of anybody with such a big heart. You told me she adopted Ray's son, right?

"Yeah. Unbelievable." He chewed a mouthful. "Him and Penny already had one kid, and he was fuckin around on her. I'd've killed the motherfucker, if I'd known at the time. I was in

Alaska—workin the pipeline. Penny kept it all from me till after the adoption." He shook his head and wiped the last gravy from his plate with a roll. "Lumps in the mashed potatoes, hon."

"She works hard too—all those jobs—and doesn't say a thing about him having boys' night out at some new bar whenever he wants. I couldn't handle it." I paused and took a drink of my beer to let the thought sink in. "He's a damn good-looking guy. Bet he has no trouble screwing around on her."

Carl looked up and wiped his mouth on his hand. "You mean now? Where'd you get that idea?"

I shrugged. "Just her tone. Shit. If anybody's going to heaven, she will."

"You think he's hot, don't ya? I'll kill the son of a bitch. What new bar?"

"Cactus Jack's. I bet you he's doing it. She'd be the last to say anything. Why else would he stay out half the night?"

Carl threw his silverware on the plate. "I ought to kill the son of a bitch."

"I don't like to hear that stuff."

"It's the real world, and he's a fuckin asshole. He needs to be fucked."

"I hate to hear a woman being beat down, thinking she's doing the right thing for the kids. Course, you never know what's the glue between two people."

"My sister's done the right thing all her life, and it's never gotten her anywhere." He was seething.

"She's one of a kind, a saint really." I tucked my hand under my leg—feeling protective of my arm—took a bite of fried steak, and chewed.

Carl rocked back on the legs of the chair. His eyes were focused up near the ceiling. "Hmm," he said. "Hmm."

"Don't think about getting involved. We have enough problems."

"You don't have a thing to do with this. It's family."

I gathered up the dishes and went to the sink feeling smug,

even though I was a little freaked by the feeling that the plan might just work. I was wiping the stove when the phone rang.

"Got it!" Carl yelled.

It was Penny. She'd followed my suggestion to call. I could hear him trying to draw her out. He went on and on, and it didn't sound like he made any progress. By the time he slammed down the receiver, he had himself more angry at her than he was at her husband. He went raging into the bathroom and slammed the door shut. It was so hard I was surprised the mirror didn't fall off.

I finished up in the kitchen and was watching *Wheel of Fortune* by the time he came out, their special Labor Week show.

He sat down on the couch next to me and put his hand on my thigh, squeezed it. "You got some room on your Visa, don't you? How 'bout making me a reservation to Dallas? I'll pay you back. I need to talk to that asshole Raymond face to face."

I stared at the TV, trying to control my breathing. "He's not going to listen to you. He thinks you're a moron."

"A moron, huh? I think not. Make a reservation for me—"

I was shaking my head. "You can't go out there. What about work?"

"Do it—get me a flight after work on Friday, back home Saturday."

"Not much of a visit."

He squinted and ran his tongue from cheek to cheek inside his mouth. "I'm just gonna talk to the motherfucker."

I'd never seen murder in anybody's eyes, but it was hard to miss. I took a deep, rattling breath. It was too goddamned easy—bloodcurdling easy. I reminded myself it was for my own survival. I needed both goddamned arms.

That night I called for a reservation. I had to make it three weeks in advance to get a decent fare. I'd saved up some Christmas money, so that way I didn't have to put the ticket on my charge. I could only hope nobody ripped Raymond before Carl got his chance. The guy that stuck Ray the first time was out on probation. It would be just my luck.

The days dragged. The hope that I would soon be free made Carl's behavior unbearable. I got myself a half-dozen detective novels and kept my nose stuck inside one when I could. I cooked the rest of the time, lots of his favorite foods, and pie, trying to keep his mouth full so I wouldn't have to listen to it—and throw him off if he was the least bit suspicious of what I had in mind. It was tough to put on the act in bed, but he was in a hurry most of the time, so he slathered on the aloe and poked me from behind. Tight and fast was fine with him. His ego made him blind—thinking he was smarter than everybody else, especially me, and that I could possibly still love him.

Thursday morning, the day before Carl was supposed to leave, he walked into the bedroom before work. I smelled his coffee breath and kept my eyes shut. A tap came on my shoulder. "I don't know where that new bar is," he said. "What was it? Cactus Bob's? Near their place?"

"Jack's. Cactus Jack's. I'll get directions at work—off the computer. No problem—Mapquest."

"Get the shortest route from the airport to Babydoe's and from there to the cactus place. He's probably lying to Penny, still going back to Doe's for the tits and ass."

I printed out the route during lunch. It was a little complicated. When I came in the door that evening, I handed Carl three pages of directions and maps. He flipped through them. "Write these on one sheet—bigger. I can't be shuffling this shit in the dark while I'm driving a rental around Arlington."

"Sure," I said. A pain in the ass to the end, I thought. I reminded myself it was almost over. I copied the directions on a legal sheet and added, *Love ya, your babycakes.* Between his ego and my eagerness to please, I hoped he didn't suspect a thing. I couldn't wait to show him the real world when I gave him my ultimatum.

I got up in the morning and packed him a few clothes and set the bag by the door. I called to him in the bathroom. "Your ticket receipt is in the side pocket. Don't forget to give Penny my love." I knew he really hadn't told her a thing.

He came out and took a hard look down my body. His eyes glinted and I could see satisfaction in the upturn of his lips, despite their being pressed together hard. I knew there was some macho thing mixed in with the caretaking for his sister. In a twisted way, he was doing this for me too, proving how he could protect a poor, weak woman from men like himself.

I thought he was going to kiss me, so I brought on a coughing fit and waved him away. He thumped me on the back a few times, gave up, and went on out. He paused a second at the bottom of the steps, turned back, and grinned, showing all those white teeth. For a second, I thought he was reading my mind. Instead he said softly, "You're my right arm, dollface." He went on.

I shivered. I watched his car all the way down the street. I was scared, even though I was sure he had every intention of doing the deed, and I was betting on success. He was smarter and stronger than Ray, and had surprise on his side. Then I would hold the cards— with his record, a simple tip to the cops could put his ass in a sling.

I was tense all day at the office, wondering what he was thinking with that grin. Too, I hoped he'd remembered his knife. I went straight to his bureau when I got home and took everything out of the sock drawer. The boot knife was gone. I pictured him splashed with blood, standing over Ray's body in a dark alley. I felt relieved. He was set up good.

I went to the grocery and got myself a six-pack, a bag of mesquite-grilled potato chips, and a pint of fudge royale ice cream. I rented three videos so I wouldn't have to think. I started to crack up laughing in the car. I was between joy and hysteria. I couldn't stop worrying, but the thought of peace to come was delicious.

Carl was due home around noon on Saturday, and I realized I

didn't want to be there. I got a few hours sleep and woke up early. I did his dirty laundry and packed all his clothes and personal stuff into garbage bags and set them by the door. I put his bicycle and tools there. I wrote a note on the legal pad and propped it against one of the bags. Basically it said to leave Fort Lauderdale that afternoon and never come back—if he did, I'd turn him in. I wrote that I didn't care if we ever got a divorce or not, and he could take the stereo and TV—everything. I just wanted to be left alone.

I packed a bathing suit, a book, and my overnight stuff, and drove down to Key Largo. Carl was obsessed with me in his lurid, controlling way. The farther away I was when he read the note, the safer I'd feel.

I stayed at a little motel and read and swam most of Saturday, got a pizza with mushrooms, like Carl hated. On Sunday morning I went out by the pool and caught a few more rays before heading home. I stopped for a grouper sandwich on the drive back, to congratulate myself on how well I was doing, but I could barely eat it. Jesus, was I nervous. I got home around four, pulled into the parking lot, and saw Carl's empty space. I sighed with relief. I looked up at the apartment window. I'd move out when the lease was up. I unlocked the door and stepped inside. The clothes and tools were gone. I shut the door behind me, locked it, and set down my bag.

The toilet flushed. "Eh-eh-eh-eh."

I jumped. My chest turned to water.

The toilet paper rolled. Carl came swaggering out of the bathroom. "Eh-eh-eh-eh," he laughed. The sound was deafening.

"Where's your car?" I asked him. "What are you doing here?"

"Car's around back. I wanted to surprise my babycakes."

I looked around wildly. "Didn't you get my note? You're supposed to be gone—I'm calling—" I moved toward the phone.

He stepped in front of me. "No. You don't wanna make any calls—and I'm not going anywhere. I love you. We're a team. Two of a kind."

"You didn't do it." I spat the words in his face. "You chickened out."

He came closer, a cloud of alcohol seeping from his skin and breath, a sick, fermented odor mixed with the bite of cigarettes. "Oh, I did it, babe, right behind Doe's. Stuck that seven-inch blade below his rib cage and gave it a mighty twist. I left that bastard in a puddle of blood the size Texas could be proud of." He winked. "I let Ol' Ray know why he was getting it too."

He took my hair and yanked me close against him. He stuck his tongue in my mouth. I gagged but he kept forcing it down my throat. Finally, he drew back and stared into my eyes. "I did some thinkin on the flight over," he said, "about you and me, and how your attitude isn't always the best. I figured I could use some insurance on our marriage. You know? Penny'll remember you askin her about the bars if she's questioned, and she wouldn't lie to the cops. Also, the directions are in your handwriting, hon. I rubbed the prints off against my stomach, balled up the sheet, and dropped it right between his legs. Cool, huh?" He licked his lower lip from one side to the other. "Oh, yeah, I found one of your hairs on my T-shirt and put that in for extra measure."

My skin went to ice and I froze clear through.

"A nice little threat in the works, if I needed it to keep you around. Guess I saved myself a lot of trouble at the same time." His eyebrows went up. "Where I go, you go, baby girl. Together forever, sweetheart."

He grabbed my T-shirt and twisted it tight around the chest. All the air wheezed out of my lungs, and he rubbed his palm across my nipples till they burned. He lifted my hand to his mouth, kissed it, and grinned with all his teeth showing. He slobbered kisses along my arm, while I stood limp. "Eh-eh."

Like the snap of a bone, his laugh shot chills up my spine and the sorry truth to my brain. I was the same as Carl, only he'd been desperate all his life. My damned arm would be second to go—I'd already handed Satan my soul.

WASHINGTON AVENUE

BY CAROLINA GARCIA-AGUILERA

Washington Avenue

(Originally published in 2001)

One

Tommy MacDonald and I were sitting at a terrace table at Oceana—one of the outdoor restaurants that line Ocean Drive on Miami Beach. We were sipping mojitos and enjoying the sunset on the horizon. It was a wondrous sight, the fiery red ball going down over the palm trees and bathing the wide stretch of sand across from us with a golden orange glow as it made its final journey into the deep waters of the Atlantic Ocean.

It was late summer, my favorite season in Miami, when the town was deserted. Only the bravest Miamians stayed in town during the hellish three months of summer. Locals who could escaped to cooler climates, and the season was too risky for tourists who feared they would lose their vacation deposits if a hurricane hit. For me, it was perfect. I don't believe there's such a thing as too much heat and humidity. Maybe it's my Cuban blood, maybe it's my contrarian nature.

Tommy and I were trying to ignore our discomfort and make the most of the dismal, pathetic breeze that was struggling to break through the ninety-plus-degree, eight p.m. heat. Our bodies were sticking to the repellent cream-colored canvas that covered our chairs. I was wearing a white linen sleeveless dress, so I was a little cooler than Tommy, who was in his tan poplin suit. I had had the luxury of going home to shower and change after work. Tommy had come straight from a court appearance.

Of the twenty tables on the terrace, only three others were occupied. That was about right for August. Tommy and I sipped our drinks and looked over the menu—although we had eaten at Oceana so often recently we practically knew it by heart.

That night we were at Oceana for a different reason than the food and the ambiance, though. Leonardo—my cousin, office manager, and supervisor of my professional, personal, and spiritual life—had asked me to go there. Manny Mendoza, Leonardo's longtime friend and Oceana's manager, had some sort of problem that he wanted to discuss with me. Apparently the phone wouldn't do, and Manny wanted to see me in person. I had no problem complying with Leonardo's request, since Tommy and I had planned to go out anyway.

Tommy MacDonald was my friend, occasional employer, and sometime lover. He was also the most successful criminal-defense attorney in Miami—no small accomplishment in a city full of people who need legal representation for their criminal matters, and who often have plenty of money to pay for the best. At any given time an inordinate percentage of Miami's population is being investigated, is under scrutiny by a grand jury, is facing indictment, incarceration, deportation, or is headed straight for the witness protection program. It's that kind of town.

I had known Tommy for seven years, when he was just a few years out of law school and I was starting as an investigator. He had been pinch-hitting for one of his partners in a personal-injury case, and I was the investigator of record. As soon as I saw him walk into a conference room for a deposition, the run-of-the-mill case turned very interesting—at least as far as I was concerned. Our relationship, both personal and professional, took off quickly. Aside from our personal chemistry, we've worked on some of the more interesting criminal cases in the recent history of Dade County.

Physically we're different as night and day, but we complement each other. Tommy is light-skinned and Irish; I'm Cuban and olive-colored. At six feet, Tommy is a full foot taller than me. He's thin in contrast to my voluptuousness, and he has light-blue eyes and sandy hair to set off my hazel eyes and waist-length, wavy black hair that I've worn in a braid since I was a child. For some inexplicable reason I have freckles on my face, little black dots clustered around my nose and spreading across my cheeks.

Tommy knew about the subtext to our dinner that night. Leonardo hadn't shared any details with me, so I didn't have any idea what was about to happen. It wasn't really possible to blindside Tommy, though; he was as unflappable as a Zen master.

"It's getting cooler," Tommy said as he sipped his mojito.

I nodded my assent. At least an oversized blue-canvas umbrella was protecting us from the still-scorching sun. And we had a good view of Ocean Drive. South Beach isn't the place for anyone with an inferiority complex about their age or physical appearance. Only the most self-assured can handle the sight of so many seminaked perfect bodies without contemplating suicide or self-mutilation. Tonight's parade included the usual rollerbladers, young men and women, models and wannabe, all dressed in the most minimal of clothing and showing impossibly tanned and taut bodies with body-fat indexes that could be tallied with the fingers of one hand. And there were the designer pets, the exotic dogs and even a couple of birds. South Beach is nothing if not competitive, from the shape of one's body, to the quality of drugs one consumes, to who can get past the velvet ropes at the VIP section of the trendiest clubs.

Tommy and I were into our second mojito when Manny Mendoza came outside. He was small and wiry, in his late twenties, dressed in black from head to toe. He seemed nervous when he came over and, in a discreet voice, asked if I had time to speak with him.

"Of course," I said. "Please. Sit with us."

I introduced Tommy and scooted over my chair so that Manny could sit between us, facing the water.

"Ms. Solano—" Manny began.

"Please, call me Lupe."

Manny looked around anxiously, making sure no one was close enough to overhear. I wondered what could be so troubling to the manager of one of South Beach's most successful restaurants. Could it be that supermodels were going to boycott over the fat content of the sushi? Or were the rock stars heading for another place down the road?

Manny lit up a cigarette and tilted his head toward me.

"Young gay men are dying on South Beach," he said in a dramatic whisper. "It's like an epidemic."

Tommy and I looked at each other. Then Tommy voiced what we were both thinking—it was no secret that South Beach was predominantly gay. "AIDS?" he asked.

Manny shook his head slowly. "No, that's pretty much under control these days. It's not the death sentence that it used to be. No, I'm talking about GHB."

GHB. I tried to remember what I knew about that particular drug. I thought it was something like Ecstasy and Special K— which gave users a euphoric high and heightened sexual energy.

"People don't usually die from taking GHB," I said.

"That's right—usually." Manny took a deep drag on his smoke. "If it's taken correctly: on its own, and without any alcohol. But something's happening. This stuff is killing people. I'm almost positive it's because they're drinking alcohol with it, but that doesn't make sense. Everyone on South Beach knows not to combine drinks with GHB."

"I haven't heard anything about this," I said.

"Me either," Tommy concurred.

"I asked around," Manny said. "The guys who died were drinking in the clubs. And their deaths seemed like bad GHB reactions. Word gets around, you know."

"I see."

"You wouldn't have read about it in the paper or seen anything on TV," Manny said. "But we've had six deaths over the last two Saturday nights."

I blinked, and Tommy and I sat in stunned silence. Our food arrived just then, but neither of us started eating.

Manny perked up a little, seeming satisfied that we understood the seriousness of what brought us there. He crushed out his cigarette so hard that I thought he might break the glass ashtray on the table. Then he took out another one and lit up.

"The police are keeping quiet," Manny said. "It's really bad for tourism. Labor Day is just a couple of weeks away, and South Beach is booked solid then. Summer's slow, and businesses here need all the money they can make in the fall. A lot of jobs are on the line, and no one wants to endanger that. Six drug-related deaths in two weekends would be a real party pooper, if you know what I mean."

Manny looked at me expectantly. He had made his point. If people were scared to come to South Beach, then people like Manny would be out of their high-paying jobs.

"Me and a couple other restaurant managers have put some money aside to hire you," he explained. "If you'll take the case."

Sure, why not? I was a straight Cuban woman from Coral Gables who was supposed to investigate the drug-related deaths of six gay men on South Beach. It made as much sense as anything did.

Two

Thinking about what Manny Mendoza had told me kept me from sleeping much that night. Around dawn I got tired of tossing and turning. I got up, showered and dressed, and put on my usual work outfit of jeans and a T-shirt.

The drive from my family's home in Cocoplum—an enclave of the tony Coral Gables section of Miami—to my Coconut Grove office took only about fifteen minutes at that early hour. I drove on autopilot and thought about my conversation with Manny. It was going to be hard to investigate the deaths—whether they were accidental or, I had to consider, murders. The authorities were staying silent, so I'd have to be careful to keep a low profile. I hoped that Manny's obvious fervent trust in me was justified. Leonardo had apparently portrayed me to him as the Cuban Sherlock Holmes, with dashes of Agatha Christie and Hercule Poirot thrown into the mix.

I was so preoccupied by the case that I narrowly missed two bicyclists in brilliantly colored latex outfits pedaling north on Main Highway. I also came a little close to two rollerbladers, who cursed me and gave me the finger. So it was going to be *that* kind of morning.

Solano Investigations operated out of a three-bedroom cottage in the heart of the Grove, which Leonardo and I had converted into two offices and a gym. We'd been happily ensconced there for the past seven years. I slowed down and parked my Mercedes in its usual spot under the frangipani tree. Once inside, I went straight to the kitchen and brewed up an extra-strong café con leche, then headed for my office. I got out a fresh yellow legal pad.

After a while I heard the outer door to the reception area open, and I called out to my cousin.

"Leo, I need to talk to you," I said. I heard Leo drop his keys on his desk and rummage in the kitchen for his own cup of coffee.

Close as we were, this wasn't going to be an easy conversation. I was dreading it, in fact, but it was necessary if I was going to get anywhere on the GHB case. Leo poked his head in my office door, took one look at my serious expression, and backed out again.

"Just a minute," he said, going back to the kitchen. "I think I'd better make this café con leche a double."

I had no problem with Leonardo fortifying himself with Cuban coffee before our conversation. I could have used another myself. Because in all the years we'd worked together, I'd never really asked Leo a direct question about his personal affairs. I was more than happy to listen whenever he wanted to talk, but I'd never initiated an inquiry into the specific details of his life.

I had my suspicions about his tastes and inclinations, but I never felt that I had the right to intrude. Now, because of Manny Mendoza and the deaths on the Beach, I was going to have to ask some probing questions.

"*Hola*, Lupe," Leo said. He took his steaming mug of coffee to the couch across from my desk and sat down.

I tried not to wince, now that I had a good look at his outfit. Solano Investigations had a pretty loose policy about office attire, but Leonardo sometimes went overboard even by our standards. A couple of years ago, I'd been forced to implement an "eight-ounce" rule: anything he wore had to weigh more than half a pound. I had a postal scale out in the reception area if I ever needed to check.

This morning, Leonardo was pushing the envelope. He was wearing a fluorescent-pink tankini over fuchsia bicycle pants. The ensemble was grounded by orange high-tops. I resisted the impulse to put on my sunglasses to cut the glare.

Leo made himself comfortable, then looked at me with an expression of wary apprehension.

"So," he asked slowly. "*Qué pasa?*"

"I went to see Manny Mendoza last night at Oceana," I said. Leo nodded and blew on his coffee to cool it. "Do you know what he wanted to talk to me about?"

Leo looked out the window as though suddenly mesmerized by the family of parrots who lived in the avocado tree. "Sort of," he said.

I was willing to bet that Leonardo knew more than he was allowing, but I played along and told him everything. Finally I got to the part where I needed his help.

"Leo, I've been a PI here for seven years," I said, trying to find a way to get to the subject I needed to reach.

Leo nodded. "I know. I've been here the whole time."

"Right." I nodded too vigorously. "I've worked all kinds of cases, criminal and civil. And I've worked cases for gay clients, and cases that had gay components, but I've never—"

I stalled out. Leo's eyes widened.

"I've never worked a case that dealt so centrally with the gay subculture in Miami."

Leonardo's body language changed completely; he had figured out where this conversation was heading. He sat up straight, very much the deer in the headlights. I felt like dashing over there and hugging him, but I told myself that we had to press on.

"If I'm going to help Manny, then I have to understand gay club life on South Beach," I told my cousin. "I need someone I trust who has connections to the clubs to help me out, tell me things that I couldn't possibly know about."

I exhaled deeply. This was exhausting.

"Okay, Lupe, I know what you're asking me—even though you're not coming out and directly asking me." Leo pursed his lips impatiently.

Well, I wanted to say, *coming out* was an interesting choice of words at that particular moment.

"You want me to be the person who tells you about gay life in Miami," he concluded.

"That's right, Leo. That's what I'm asking you." I was relieved the topic was on the table. Without going into details, I had finally found out that Leo was gay. I supposed that everyone in the family knew it, or suspected it, but we had all respected Leo's privacy.

Leo seemed to realize that the worst was over, and that I wasn't asking to delve into his personal life. Suddenly I realized that he and Manny might have had some sort of relationship.

"No problem." Leo smiled, leaned back, and sipped his coffee. "What exactly do you need from me?"

"First, I need to know about the designer drugs that are being taken in the clubs," I said. "I know a little about the drug scene, but not what's going on in South Beach. Specifically GHB."

I didn't want to get into how I knew anything about drugs, and I wasn't going to ask Leo how he might know about the drugs in the gay clubs. Our mutual don't-ask-don't-tell policy was stronger than ever.

"GHB is different from Ecstasy and Special K and Ruffies because it's not a controlled substance," Leo explained.

"What do you mean?"

"Well, that means that anyone can manufacture it—not just trained scientists or chemists," Leo said. "There's even a website that tells you how to make GHB."

"Like the sites that tell you how to make a nuclear bomb?" I shouldn't have been at all surprised.

"Right," Leo said. "GHB is taken in liquid form. It's a clear liquid that people buy in little vials. Depending on how much you take, it can last as long as twenty-four hours—and it's an upper, so that's a day without sleep. And the sexual energy it gives is really awesome."

Leo seemed to catch himself when he saw me looking at him. He took on a more serious expression. "Anyway—" he said.

"Manny said something about GHB being lethal in combination with alcohol."

"That's right, and that's what I heard happened." Leonardo shook his head, and I could see how deeply he felt the senseless loss of those six men. "They went into a G hole."

"A G *hole?*" I repeated. Now I really felt out of the loop, having to ask questions like that.

Leonardo looked me over for a moment, as though trying to gauge just how naive and uninformed I really was.

"A G hole is when someone has a bad reaction to GHB." Leo visibly shuddered. "I've seen it happen. Guys get seizures; they vomit. I heard about one guy who went into a G hole and aspirated on his own vomit. And other people are supposed to have choked on their own tongues. It's really nasty."

"What causes this G hole?" I wondered aloud. "I mean, GHB is sold in individual vials, so that's probably pretty effective in keeping people from overdosing."

"It had to be alcohol," Leonardo said. "Everyone knows not to mix GHB with alcohol. It leads to a very bad trip and can kill you."

"'But why risk it?" I asked. "These guys took GHB; they knew they were going to get high. Why try to get drunk on top of it, if everyone knows this is the one rule not to break?"

"I'm not sure," Leonardo admitted. "Maybe—"

As he spoke, my voice joined in: "—they didn't know they'd taken GHB."

I got up and started to pace, which always helped me think. Leo was sitting up very straight, watching me.

"What if they thought they were taking something else?" I asked.

"Remember Ruffies, Lupe?"

"That was the date-rape drug," I said. "Guys were slipping them into girls' drinks, or else telling them they were something a lot weaker."

"It was awful," Leo said. "Guys were prosecuted and sent to jail—and they deserved it."

"What if something similar is going on here?" I stopped pacing when I reached the big picture window. "I'd love to see the autopsy reports on those guys, but I know that's not going to happen. We're not even supposed to know the deaths occurred in the first place."

I walked over to my chair and slumped down heavily. Leonardo seemed lost in thought; I didn't usually involve him so closely in my investigations, and he was giving the moment his undivided attention.

"And what if there were no autopsies conducted?" I said, thinking aloud. "If the authorities are bent on keeping this under wraps, it's possible they kept autopsies from being performed."

"You can't search public records, like in other cases," Leonardo said. "This is like a lot of other things in the gay world: underground."

I paused and considered what he had said. He was right. This case was murky, hidden from public view.

And what was hidden was a killer. I was sure of it. If everyone knew that alcohol combined with GHB resulted in a lethal body chemistry, then those six young men didn't know they were consuming GHB. Two and two made four. They had been tricked or manipulated into consuming a deadly cocktail.

I looked up at Leonardo. He had finished his coffee and gotten up from the sofa.

"You're going to have to be creative on this one," he said. Which was, of course, quite an understatement.

Three

"So how do you decide who to let in and who to keep out?" I asked the burly, balding man sitting across from me. I noticed he was sporting a couple of new tattoos since the last time I'd seen him.

I was drinking a double-latte-extra-espresso shot at Starbucks on Lincoln Road. Jimmy de la Vega was having a black coffee. Jimmy was a private investigator who'd become a security guard. I knew Jimmy well enough to confide in him, and I'd told him the bare outlines of my new case. It was no surprise that he'd already heard about the deaths.

Jimmy worked for me a few years back, on a contract basis, first as a moving-surveillance specialist and then as a bodyguard when one of my clients needed protection. Jimmy liked being a security guy, and in a couple of years he had set up his own business, which was now one of the most successful in South Florida. We kept in touch and referred clients to one another. If we weren't friends, we stayed friendly.

I knew that the South Beach clubs had security guys stationed at the front door, where they checked IDs. According to Jimmy, there were guards inside as well.

"We don't let anyone inside who looks drunk or stoned on drugs," Jimmy said. "Or anyone who seems like they're looking for trouble. People are there to have a good time. We're in charge of making sure things don't get weird or heavy."

Jimmy was on the fast track in Miami, and his clients were trendy clubs and stars who needed someone to watch their backs. In spite of the company he was keeping, though, Jimmy was a serious, laid-back family man. Those characteristics were probably why he survived and prospered in such a tough business, while so many others had crashed and burned.

"And you should see the fake IDs," Jimmy said with a chortle. "I have a stack of them back at my office. I mean, I've seen a little five-foot blond kid with hay sticking out of his ears hand me a green card saying his name is Pedro Flores and that he's six foot one and lives in the Bronx!"

"Ridiculous," I agreed.

Jimmy's smile turned rueful. "Well, now there's an outfit in Calle Ocho that's selling green cards! Can you believe that? Green cards for IDs so that kids can party. No respect for anything!"

Jimmy was first-generation Cuban-American. For him, the United States could do no wrong. The idea that someone was selling coveted resident alien cards was abhorrent and borderline sacrilegious.

I liked Jimmy, but now I was remembering that his conversation tended to go off on tangents. I tried to gently steer him back to the subject at hand.

"What about the security in the clubs?" I reminded him.

"Right. Security." Jimmy looked faintly embarrassed. "Well, the first step is at the door. If a person looks suspicious, then we pat him down for drugs."

"What kind of drugs are they taking these days?" I asked.

"The usual club drugs," Jimmy said with a shrug. "Ruffies, GHB, Ecstasy, Special K. There's probably even some new ones I don't know about. These bathtub chemists are always trying to come up with the next big thing."

"What do you know about GHB?" I asked. I already knew that GHB—gamma hydroxybutyrate—was sometimes referred to as 'liquid Ecstasy' and sometimes mistaken for E in cases of overdoses. It's broken down quickly in the body, which makes it very difficult to recognize through autopsy. And, as Manny and Leonardo had told me, it could be lethal when mixed with alcohol.

"It comes in little vials—like those perfume samples they give out at department stores," Jimmy told me. "Most of the time they take it with cranberry juice. You probably know how nasty it can be when it reacts with alcohol."

"That's my theory for what's going on," I said. "And it doesn't make sense that all six men would make the same stupid mistake in such a short period of time."

"You're saying someone slipped it to them?"

"Or else they thought they were taking something else." I paused. "People can drink on Ecstasy, can't they?"

"Yeah." Jimmy rubbed his chin. "Are you saying you think there's a killer working the clubs in South Beach?"

"That's what I'm saying."

Jimmy made a sour face. Part of his job was keeping the peace in the clubs, and I knew he would take this personally. "You let me know if there's anything I can do to help," he said gravely. "And I mean anything."

"Which clubs do you handle security for?" I asked.

"Almost all the ones on Washington Avenue." Jimmy rattled off the names of ten clubs. I recognized some as exclusively gay, some as mixed. Among the clubs were the three where young men had died.

"Look, Lupe, to be honest with you, this is reflecting badly on me and my company," Jimmy said.

"I understand." I rubbed my eyes, trying to mine a new idea. "What about when you find drugs on someone, Jimmy?"

He sighed and rolled his eyes. "Listen, this is between you and me. The club owners say there's a zero-tolerance policy on drug use in the clubs, all right? Well, that's bullshit. If they cracked down too hard on drugs, then people would stop coming to the clubs. A lot of the time when I find drugs on someone, I just tell them to be careful and stay out of trouble that night. Sometimes I confiscate the stuff, but then there's a hassle turning it in to the police."

I thought about this. "So what's the point of patting them down?"

Jimmy looked at me as though I were a little child. "Appearances, Lupe. There are some city commissioners who want to shut down the clubs completely. They think the clubs bring the wrong element to Miami Beach." He finished off his coffee.

"But South Beach is famous for the clubs," I said. "Take away the clubs and you take away the top industry on the Beach."

I hadn't considered a political/economic angle to this case, but the possibility was too strong to ignore.

"You don't know the whole story." Jimmy looked around to make sure no one was listening, then moved closer to me. His voice had lowered to a whisper.

"What do you mean?"

"Whenever there's an overdose or a bad reaction in one of the clubs, our orders are to take the person out back and dump him in the alley," Jimmy told me. "In other words, get him out and get him away. And we're supposed to search him, make sure he doesn't have a matchbook or anything linking him to the club."

"What then?" I asked. "Call an ambulance?"

Jimmy paused, seeming almost sad for an instant. "Police and ambulances get noticed. That brings publicity and investigations. Keep things quiet, and the clubs stay in business. If a guy takes too many drugs and dies, well, I guess it wasn't his lucky day."

Even though it was about a hundred degrees outside, I had to suppress a shiver. I couldn't believe that it had come to this. And I didn't like knowing that Jimmy was a part of it. "You don't agree with this, do you?" I asked him. "Leaving guys in the alley like they're sick dogs?"

Jimmy looked at me long and hard. "Lupe, someone *did* call the police about the six guys," he said, very slowly. "And that guy isn't surprised that nothing came of it. You know what I'm saying?"

With that, Jimmy got up, said goodbye, and left. I hadn't learned enough to know how to proceed on this case, I realized. And Jimmy didn't know what to tell me. If anything, he was more frustrated than me. It was shaping up to be that kind of case.

Four

After Jimmy left, I finished my latte and walked back to my car, which I had parked on 17th Street. I planned on returning to my office as I turned off the alarm and unlocked the door.

I began weighing the possibilities, and decided that I needed to talk again with Manny Mendoza. Instead of driving back to the Grove by way of Alton Road, I decided to take Washington Avenue, the street that's home to most of the South Beach clubs. It had been awhile since I'd been there, and I wanted to get the lay of the land.

The three clubs were within four blocks of each other—definitely close enough for someone to cover the area on foot in a short period of time. I saw an empty space in front of the Miami Beach post office and parked the Mercedes there. From where I was parked, I could see most of the relevant stretch of Washington Avenue.

The blocks weren't very long, and they were jammed with small storefronts—mostly an odd assortment of shops that sold cheap, glittery clothes, along with a few fast-food joints and delicatessens. The outfits in the windows of the clothes shops catered mostly to cross-dressers, from what I could tell. It wasn't exactly a high-rent district. In the cold light of day, the neighborhood looked run-down and in need of a face-lift. By night, though, I knew it was a different story. The place would be pulsing with activity and energy.

The clubs' entrances were marked with small, nondescript signs, looking as though they were almost an afterthought. I as-

356 // Miami Noir: The Classics

sumed this was intended to convey a cachet of exclusivity. If a visitor hadn't known this was the place to find the clubs, they would have been easy to miss. At night it would be easy to find them; usually there were crowds outside on the sidewalks, hoping they would be among the chosen ones allowed entry into the hallowed ground.

I left my motor running to supply me with life-giving air-conditioning, and sat there for a good fifteen minutes trying to figure out why someone would murder six young men in such a nasty manner. No answers came to me, no matter how long I stared, so I grabbed my purse from the floor of the car—where I usually kept it to avoid tempting a smash-and-grab artist. I looked up Manny's number at the Oceana from the case file and punched it in.

I was in luck. Despite the early hour, Manny answered on the second ring.

"Any luck?" he asked hopefully.

"We'll see," I said. "Look, I'm parked a couple of blocks away. Is it all right if I come by to talk to you?"

"Sure," Manny said, a note of cautious curiosity in his voice.

I turned off the car, put some quarters in the meter, and crossed Washington Avenue headed toward Ocean Drive. Manny was waiting for me on the Oceana's terrace. He was again dressed all in black, with a cigarette dangling from his lips and a fresh pack clutched in his hand. He was staring out at Ocean Drive and obviously waiting for me.

He called out my name when he saw me, then bounded down the half-dozen steps to street level to greet me. He kissed me on the cheek, surprising me a little, and escorted me back to the table where we'd talked with Tommy a couple of nights before. I declined Manny's offer of a drink and got down to business.

"Manny, you told me these guys died from a combination of GHB and alcohol," I said. "You're sure about that?"

We were the only people on the terrace, but Manny leaned close to me and whispered, "Whatever I tell you is confidential?"

"Of course," I said.

"Promise me?"

"I promise you."

Manny put out his half-smoked cigarette and took a fresh one from the pack. As he lit it, I was willing to bet that smokes were one of the primary expenses in his budget. I didn't want to even think about the condition of his lungs.

"I found out about the deaths from my boyfriend," Manny said, his voice almost inaudible. "He's the one who gave me all the inside information. He's worried sick about what happened, and how it's all been kept quiet. He's really afraid of what's going to happen this weekend."

Manny took a long drag on his cigarette. "He's been a mess since this happened," he continued. "He can't eat, can't sleep."

I knew this might be delicate ground, but I had to ask: "Manny, who is your boyfriend?"

He flinched back from me. He thought for a moment, wrestling with some unvoiced question.

"All right," he said. "My boyfriend is an officer in the Miami Beach Police Department."

That made sense. It explained how Manny had access to so much information that was being hidden from the public.

"I don't need to know his name," I said, eliciting a look of relief on Manny's face. "But I need to know more details about the deaths."

"Sure, ask away. But I don't have all the answers."

"What about the police investigation?" I asked. Manny nodded slowly; I could tell that he was worried about getting his lover in trouble. "Was there anything to tie the six victims together, any common links that might explain why they were killed?"

"No." Manny smiled without pleasure. "You know, that was the first question I asked. But my boyfriend said that it seems to be random. Six guys over two weekends. Like a serial killer."

Sounded right. But I had no proof of anything.

"So apart from the fact that they were all partying in gay clubs, there's nothing to link them? You're sure about that?"

"That's what Jake told me." A second after he realized what he had said, Manny gasped.

I pretended not to have heard anything. "Were there autopsies conducted?"

"Yes. The results were sealed, but my boyfriend found out that they had mixed GHB with alcohol." Manny paused. "The victims' families were told that their boys had died as a result of drug overdoses." He lit a new cigarette off the burning end of the one he had just finished. "I guess the families didn't ask too many questions. They were probably embarrassed their sons died in gay nightclubs, high on drugs."

Through a cloud of smoke, Manny looked at me. "You know, Lupe, we may live in a free and easy place here, where anything goes and all kinds of lifestyles are accepted, but that's not the way it is in the rest of the country."

"And that's why the guys come to South Beach," I said.

Manny smiled, glad that I understood what he was telling me. "Because they can be themselves here. And not have to put up with any bullshit about who they are and how they lead their lives. A lot of these guys have families who don't want to know anything about their sons' lives—as long as they're in the dark, they don't have to confront the fact that their sons are gay. It's an old story, everyone in denial. And that's how the police got away with giving the families so few details about how these boys died. The families really didn't want to know. And then the police can say that they didn't disclose detailed information out of respect for the families."

I considered what Manny was saying. Keeping the deaths quiet served more than one purpose. The families didn't have to confront too much information about their sons' lifestyles, and the police didn't have to admit that they weren't solving a case that involved the serial murders of six young gay men.

"Is the investigation still ongoing?" I asked. If it was, I had to be very careful. There were strict rules for private investigators in such cases.

"Nothing much is happening right now," Manny said. "The police are hoping that there are no more deaths and that the whole thing just goes away. Starting a high-profile investigation right now would kill tourism. It would be nothing but bad publicity. There might be a few ghouls—like those tourists who have their pictures taken on the spot where Gianni Versace was murdered—but most people would be scared off."

I knew what Manny was talking about. On more than one occasion I had seen tourists milling around the wrought-iron gates outside the Versace home, trying to get close to the cordoned-off area where the designer had been shot and killed in broad daylight. It was gruesome.

Manny shook his head with a touch of disgust. "The police figure there'll always be deaths from bad drugs on South Beach and that this situation is really no different. They're playing the whole thing down."

"But your boyfriend doesn't agree," I said. "And that's why he thought of the idea of hiring a private investigator."

Manny nodded. "You got it."

"And you knew about me through Leonardo," I said, almost adding the word *relationship* but stopping short.

"Leonardo always bragged about what a great detective you were, Lupe," Manny smiled. "He said that if anyone was going to find out what happened to those six guys, it was going to be you."

I felt myself blushing at the compliment. I was a little surprised to hear that Leonardo had spoken so highly of me to his friend.

A few customers were starting to arrive; they were looking around expectantly for a maître d' to show them to a table. It was clear that things were going to get busy soon, so I stood up to leave.

Before I did, though, I had one question for Manny: "If it had been six straight men who had been killed, does your boyfriend think the police would have handled the situation differently?"

Manny's silence told me everything I needed to know.

Five

After I left Manny, I decided to check out the alleys behind the clubs, which run parallel between Collins Drive and Washington Avenue, so I could have a look at where Jimmy had told me the bodies of the young men were dragged out and left.

Each club was about half a block wide and occupied the space from Washington Avenue to the alley directly behind it. I began walking the alley behind the Neptune, the most northern club. The back door was unmarked steel secured by three prominent dead bolts. There were no markers to indicate where the door led. There were trash cans outside the back door and there was no one in the alley at that time of early afternoon, unless I wanted to count the mangy cats who were pawing through the garbage.

The smell in the alley was almost overwhelming and grew stronger the longer I stood there. It smelled like rotten fruit, animal waste, vomit, and other fluids that I didn't much want to contemplate. The heat was baking it all to the point at which I felt like gagging.

Looking around, I was filled with sadness for those six young men who had been unceremoniously dumped back there like so much refuse. And if what Manny had told me was true, nothing much was being done to investigate the deaths. If I had access to active police sources, I might have had leads to follow and facts to pursue, but for now I had little more than instinct.

The alley behind the Neptune was yielding no secrets, so I moved on to the next one. The Zenith was also in the middle of its block, with a dumpster next to the back door. It smelled a little better back there—a little. The Zenith's back door was also protected by big dead bolts, along with a sign next to the doorknob

warning that the area was protected by twenty-four-hour surveil-
lance. I looked around for a camera but didn't find one, not even a
phony one to frighten away amateur thieves. As far as I could tell,
the sign was nothing more than a bluff.

The third club, the Majestic, was on a street corner a block
away from the Zenith. Unlike the other two clubs, its back door
opened onto a side street. That meant, in order to dump a body,
someone would have to carry it around the corner in full view of
passersby. That wouldn't be easy, with the door in plain sight. I
knew that South Beach was crawling with police on a Saturday
night. They were out in force, setting up roadblocks and stopping
drivers who might be impaired. Washington Avenue was typically
well patrolled, with cops busting underage drinkers and arresting
anyone who got drunk and disorderly.

South Beach came alive after dark. Most clubs didn't even
open until eleven at night and closed around five in the morning. And then the after-hours places opened, from five to eight
o'clock, sometimes even until ten. So whoever carried the bodies
out of the Majestic would have had little opportunity to wait for
the crowds on the street to thin out.

I decided to drive back to the office without making any more
detours. I had something that I wanted to look into.

Back at Solano Investigations, I went straight to my office and
turned on the computer at my desk. Leonardo had left for the day,
probably heading home before going clubbing that night. I waited
for my computer to boot up and banished from my thoughts what
he might be wearing for such an evening.

I was pretty much computer illiterate, but I was able to find a
few drug-related websites. I struck out on the first two, but the last
one confirmed my suspicions about GHB.

I was almost sure the guys who died didn't know they were
taking GHB. The last website I visited said that it was possible
to boil down GHB to a point at which it cooled, became a pow-

der, and then resembled Special K—which could be taken with alcohol without any deadly consequences. What if someone substituted GHB for the victims' powdered Special K without their knowing about it, or sold them GHB while saying it was Special K?

And how could that be done? However it happened, the killer had gotten away with it. The question was: would the killer be satisfied with taking six lives, or would there be more to come?

I sat and stared at the parrots outside my window. If they knew the answer, they sure weren't saying. I was going to have to come up with an individual who would have the opportunity to commit the murders. And in the clubs in South Beach, that might be anyone. I knew that when someone went clubbing on South Beach, the pattern was often to start off at one club and visit two or three others before the night was finished. So the killer—who committed his crimes at three different clubs over the course of two Saturdays—wouldn't have been unusual in moving about from place to place in a relatively short period of time.

I figured I could dismiss club owners as suspects—from what I knew, they tended not to go to clubs other than the ones they owned, and they would have been spotted if they visited the competition. Besides, it didn't make sense that one of them would knock off his or her own customers.

Another possibility would be people who worked at the clubs, maybe a disgruntled employee. But that would be self-destructive. If the clubs were eventually closed as a result of the deaths, then they would be out of work. Plus, why run the risk of going to other clubs to commit the crime? It didn't fit.

Then there were the city commissioners who wanted the clubs shut down on moral grounds. They weren't likely suspects, since they were older and ostensibly straight and would stand out in the clubs. And from the sound of it, they wouldn't be caught dead in such dens of sin.

I looked down at my notes. There was only one place left for me to go. I picked up the phone to call Leonardo. I hoped he would be free that night. I needed an escort for my night of clubbing.

Six

Leonardo and I agreed to go clubbing together in one car; he was going to pick me up at home at midnight. I didn't want him to ring the doorbell and wake everyone up, so I was waiting by the window when he arrived. When he got out of his car, I was pleasantly surprised to see him dressed in conservative clothes—matching black polyester body-hugging pants and shirt, and boots that John Travolta might have sported in *Saturday Night Fever*. I was also in black satin jeans and a sheer Lurex T-shirt. We headed off for South Beach together, looking as if we were headed for a seventies funeral.

Traffic was relatively light at that hour, and we got there in about thirty minutes. Fate blessed us, and we found a parking spot on Collins Avenue, just a couple of blocks from Washington. Instead of going into the first club—Neptune—I took Leonardo's arm and stopped us across the street, in the shadows, where we could watch the entrance.

"What are we looking for?" Leo asked me, staring across the street in a visibly anxious attempt to look calm and relaxed.

"Anything," I said. "We're just watching."

I took my miniature binoculars out of my purse and focused on the Neptune. The first thing I noticed was the fact that, by night, Washington Avenue looked a lot more glamorous and sophisticated than it did by day.

There were about thirty men outside the Neptune, most dressed in blue jeans and white "wife-beater" T-shirts. Two red-velvet ropes cordoned off the in-crowd from the wannabes. I knew the first set of ropes was for normal customers, out-of-towners and the like. Even though the club might be empty inside, those poor souls would be made to wait outside for half an hour anyway. The second rope was for VIP clients, who were let in immediately and without a cover charge.

"That's the door-god," Leo said. "The big black guy in the yellow jacket."

Non-VIP patrons were subject to the whims of the door-god, a big guy with a shaved head who decided who was let in and who had to wait. Next to him were a few men in dark suits—not particularly nice ones—who were checking IDs. I refocused my binoculars when I saw another man move out of the shadows. It was Jimmy de la Vega.

"Jimmy's here," I said in a low voice. "I sure found him quick."

Jimmy had been dressed pretty conservatively earlier that day at Starbucks, but now he was wearing a tailored Italian-cut black suit that made him look like chief undertaker at a Mafia funeral home. I watched him pat down a couple of customers after they had been given the nod to pass through the velvet rope. Jimmy took them aside by the door, as their final obstacle before they could enter the hallowed halls of the club.

I knew Jimmy's pat-down was for drugs and weapons, although I knew from what he told me that the clubs' drug policies were basically to wink and look the other way. Leonardo leaned back against the wall and sighed. I knew this wasn't his idea of an exciting start to our evening.

I watched Jimmy pat down a couple of young guys. Something seemed strange to me. I couldn't be sure, so I handed over the binoculars to Leonardo.

"Watch Jimmy, over there by the door," I told him.

Leo focused the binoculars. "Oh, yeah. I remember him. Jimmy de la Vega." He paused for a second. "Um, he really seems to be getting into his job."

"You see what I'm seeing?" I asked him.

"I don't know," Leo said. "But when he patted those guys down, it looked almost like he was feeling them up."

I watched Jimmy perform the next pat-down. His hands were all over a young guy in a black T-shirt and jeans. I didn't know, but there seemed something inappropriate about it. Jimmy was a family man, though, married to his high school sweetheart. I figured I was just overreacting. I saw Jimmy's hands reach deep into the guy's front shirt pocket and pause for a second. Jimmy said something to him, then clapped him on the shoulder and waved him in.

None of the other security men or the door-god seemed to notice what Jimmy was doing, but then, none of them were paying attention to much of anything outside their direct line of responsibility. I watched the next pat-down. I wasn't sure, but I thought I saw the young man Jimmy was touching react with a flinch of surprise.

"Let's go inside," I said to Leo.

"Finally," my cousin replied.

Leonardo and I darted across Washington Avenue, and approached the club. Jimmy spotted us and waved us over to the VIP rope.

"Lupe!" he said in a welcoming voice. "You should have called ahead, like you said you would."

I recalled saying nothing of the kind, but I smiled at him anyway. "Hey, Jimmy," I said, "You remember Leo?"

Jimmy gave Leo a nod and an awkward smile. Leo blinked in the bright light outside the club, taking Jimmy in.

"We wanted to check out the clubs," I said to Jimmy. "It's been awhile since I've been out in South Beach."

Jimmy took two tickets from a stack the door-god was holding in his hand. He handed them both to me. "Have a good time," he said. "So how are things going on the matter we talked about this morning?"

"Nothing major," I said. "That's why I'm having a look around."

Jimmy nodded. We were holding up the line. Jimmy held up his hand in the call-me gesture and waved us in. He began searching the next patron in line.

We reached a window in a tiny vestibule, where our tickets

were exchanged for drink vouchers. I saw that, had we not been comped by Jimmy, the charge for coming in would have been twenty dollars each. And that didn't include drinks.

As soon as we stepped inside, the music was too loud to talk over. It was a sort of tribal rock, part electronic, instrumental with no lyrics. It was so dark in the entryway that Leonardo and I had to grope our way upstairs while our eyes were adjusting.

We hadn't even reached the main room yet when my head began to pound to the same beat as the music. I didn't think I was going to last long at the Neptune. If possible, it was even darker upstairs in the main room. I saw clusters of light in the dark as my eyes struggled to focus. The only lights in the place came from strategically placed high hats on the ceiling.

"God'd get the day!" Leo yelled at me, his mouth close to my ear. The music was far too loud to know what he was saying.

"What?" I yelled back.

"Gunner diss a drake!" he screamed.

"What?"

Then I got it: he was offering to get us some drinks. I gave him the thumbs-up. Leo left me standing against the wall, watching the scene in front of me. The main room was cavernous, filled with young men mostly in their twenties and thirties. Some wore T-shirts, others were bare-chested. Most wore jeans. All looked amazingly toned and physically fit. I noticed that a few had drinks in their hands, although far more common was the sight of water bottles tucked into the jeans' back pockets.

I was the only woman in the whole place, as far as I could tell, but no one looked at me strangely or made me feel unwelcome. I was pretty much ignored, in fact, which was fine with me.

Just about all the men in the room were dancing—some alone, some with partners. The place was freezing cold from air-conditioning, but they were all sweating copiously. I hadn't seen any bullets or vials, but I saw on many faces the spaced-out, blissed-out expression of someone on drugs. Those looks—not to mention the excessive sweating and the water bottles—were pretty broad clues to indicate what was going on.

I watched these young, attractive men, swaying to the tribal beat of the music, and couldn't help but wonder what the future held for them, what would follow after the allure of the clubbing lifestyle wore off. But then I told myself that I was sounding like an old lady.

Leo returned with our drinks: a Manhattan for him and a red wine for me. Both were served in identical plastic cups. I felt as though I were at a frat party. We crossed the room and found a smaller room off the main dance floor, where mercifully there was an empty table by the north wall. Once we were seated, I had a look around at the tables nearest us. Although I spotted some makeup and cleavage, I was still pretty sure that I was the only biological female in the place.

There were three bars in the Neptune. Each one was three deep with young men waiting to buy drinks—bottles of water, it turned out, were as popular as alcoholic beverages.

Because these young men knew better than to mix booze with GHB. They dissolved it in juice to get high. The guys who were drinking hadn't had any GHB.

At least, they'd better hope they hadn't.

We had been there less than fifteen minutes, but I had seen what I needed.

"What do you think?" Leo yelled at me, straining his vocal cords.

"We can skip the next two clubs, Leo," I told him. "I just realized something. I think I have an idea what happened."

"So what'd you think about the Neptune?" Jimmy asked me. He had come to Solano Investigations in the early afternoon the next day, as I'd requested. "You really should have told me you were coming. I could have arranged the real VIP treatment for you and Leo."

"That's all right," I said. "We had a nice time."

Jimmy was back to his regular casual mode of dress, in dark pants and a white, open-necked polo shirt stitched on the shoulder with *de la Vega Security*. Unlike me, he looked none the worse for the late hours he was keeping. One night on the Beach, and I was ready for a week off.

I escorted Jimmy from the reception area toward my office. Leonardo was at his desk, looking over a report before sending it out with a bill. He didn't glance up from his work, nor did he offer to make coffee for the first time in my memory. Once inside my office, I motioned toward the chair in front of my desk.

"You want to close the door?" Jimmy said.

"No, I keep no secrets from my cousin."

Jimmy peered over his shoulder, then back at me. His chair was arranged perfectly so that he couldn't look out the open doorway without turning in his seat. I gave him an *are you comfortable?* look, then hit him with it.

"So, Jimmy, tell me something. Why'd you do it?"

"Do what?" he said, his eyes widening. "What are you talking about?"

I waited a long moment; we stared into each other's eyes, each waiting for the other to break.

"All I want to know is why," I said.

Jimmy looked at me as though I were a lunatic. For an instant, one tiny moment, I doubted myself. But no, it all fit together too well.

"When you patted down customers at the door searching for drugs, you substituted their bullets of Special K with GHB that you had boiled down into a powder," I told him.

"You're crazy," Jimmy said.

But I saw a look in his eyes—a look that told me I was right.

"You had access to GHB—you confiscated it from a few club-goers," I told him. "And as door security, no one was going to say much if you were rummaging around in their pockets long enough to switch vials. They're carrying an illegal substance, and they're not in a position to complain."

Jimmy shook his head. "I don't have to listen to—"

"You worked security at a few clubs that night, right?" I said. "You had plenty of opportunity to make your mark at three different places."

Jimmy's lip curled into a sneer, but he didn't get up and leave. I knew that he wasn't going to, either.

"You found six guys who had already been drinking," I said. "You got close enough to smell their breath when you were patting them down. Even if they didn't continue drinking that night, the amount of alcohol in their system would make sure they went into a G hole when they took the GHB."

"Maybe you're the one who's been taking junk," Jimmy said, trying to laugh. "It's made you lose your mind."

"As security chief, you had full access to the clubs at any time. No one would suspect you had anything to do with the deaths," I said. "You took them out into the alley and no one suspected a thing. Even at the Majestic—where you had to take a body out in view of people—your clout and position on the Beach probably made people think you were just taking a drunk guy to a taxicab. And then, like you said, you went through the guys' pockets to take away anything that might link them to the clubs. How perfect was that?"

"I guess I'm a real criminal mastermind," Jimmy said sarcastically.

"And, to top it all off, you were the one who called for help," I went on. "And you certainly wanted me to think you were cooperating with my investigation."

Jimmy put his hands on the chair arms, as though to leave. "Why would I do something like that, Lupe? Why?"

I walked to the side of my desk and perched on the edge. "Jimmy, I know you. Something's wrong. I saw you the other night patting down those guys. Leonardo saw it too. And after he saw you at the club he said you were setting off his 'gaydar.'"

Jimmy sputtered. "He said what?"

"You're in the middle of all this, Jimmy," I said. "And you're giving off signals. Why'd you do it, Jimmy? Please, tell me."

Jimmy amazed me just then by getting up and closing the door. Before he could turn around to face me again, I pressed the open intercom button on my speakerphone.

"Can I really talk to you?" Jimmy asked me. I could see that he had started sweating, and there was a haunted look in his eyes.

"It's just us here," I said. "I want to know how you thought of it, and why. I just want my curiosity satisfied. You know as well as I do that I don't have any fingerprints or witnesses."

Jimmy looked out the window at the parrots, who were squawking and fighting. I could see the wheels spinning. My heart was beating so hard that I was afraid Jimmy would hear it and not speak.

"You're right, Lupe," he finally said. "I did it. Does that make you happy?"

"No, Jimmy," I said. "It really doesn't."

"It's a goddamned mess," he said. "And when I found out you were investigating it, I got worried. I didn't know how to handle you, and I was worried it might come to this."

"Why, Jimmy?" I whispered.

"Is my secret safe with you?" Jimmy said, his voice suddenly hoarse.

I nodded.

"I want those clubs closed down. I wanted to do something to get the clubs shut down and out of my life."

"But they employ you, Jimmy," I pointed out.

"That's just it," he said. "Don't you see? I have to be there at those damned clubs all the time."

"So?"

Jimmy hung his head down. He was standing in the middle of my office, his arms limp at his sides. I glanced over and saw that the office intercom channel was still open.

"I was beginning to like it too much." Jimmy raised his hands to his eyes and stifled a sob. "All those young, half-naked kids. Sweating and dancing all around me. I was inside those clubs too much, seeing too much. I don't need the temptation, Lupe. I have a family."

I was speechless. Before last night, I would never have considered Jimmy capable of any crime, much less murder. But after talking to Leo about Jimmy's "vibe," as my cousin called it, I began to realize that my old friend Jimmy was in the throes of a sexual conflict.

"What would people say if they found out I liked the boys on the Beach, Lupe?" Jimmy said, his voice breaking.

"I don't know, Jimmy. I guess they'd say you were gay. Or bi. Or somewhere in between."

"Don't *say* that," Jimmy hissed. He took a step toward me but stopped, his face constricted with self-loathing.

"There were better ways to eliminate temptation," I said to him. "There are plenty of other places you could work."

"Thought of that. Doesn't matter," Jimmy said. "As long as the clubs are there, I'm going to want to be there. The only way out for me is to shut down the clubs. And I found a way to make that happen."

Nowhere in Jimmy's worldview was a thought of remorse for his six victims. I was beginning to see that Jimmy was one sick puppy.

"But the cops were keeping it all quiet," I offered.

"I know. I hadn't counted on that happening," Jimmy said with genuine amazement. "Still, sooner or later word's going to get out. Right?"

Jimmy was still in his moment, still thinking he had options. I was chilled to realize that he was contemplating committing more murders.

"Gotta get rid of those clubs," Jimmy said. He looked at me strangely. "Are you with me or against me, Lupe?"

At that, I whistled sharply. Jimmy started when the door burst open and a man with a gun shouted at him to hit the floor. It was Miami Homicide Detective Anderson, whom I'd worked with once or twice before.

"Get it on tape?" I asked him.

"No problem," Anderson replied. "That intercom worked perfectly."

Leonardo poked his head around the corner with a look of mixed alarm and satisfaction. The South Beach killer was caught. All the evidence against Jimmy was circumstantial, but the taped confession wouldn't hurt matters.

"You lied to me! *Puta!*" Jimmy shouted in disbelief as he sank to the floor, his fingers instinctively interlacing behind his head. "You said it was just you and me!"

"You need help, Jimmy," I said.

"That's an understatement," Leo called from the doorway.

Detective Anderson started reading Jimmy his Miranda rights. Jimmy's worst fear was about to be realized. Everyone in Miami was going to find out that Jimmy de la Vega, husband of Maria and father of three, had killed six young men because he was tempted by their youth and beauty.

With Detective Anderson on the case, every detail of Jimmy's crimes was going to become public knowledge very quickly. Jimmy had just been outed. In a big way.

SUPERHEROES

BY PRESTON L. ALLEN

Opa-Locka

(Originally published in 2006)

The Sister

The sister has the moon in her hair and the wind at her feet. The brother has the wind at his heels. He wants to be a football star when he grows tall.

She wants to run fast and catch medals of gold, but she has the moon in her hair. She is fair. All men stare. She has the moon in her hair.

He has the wind at his heels. He has thunder and lightning in his hands. He hits hard. He steals fast. He runs fast.

His sister. She has the moon in her hair.

His little sister.

They live in the house in Opa-Locka their mother does not own, the house of the man with the snake in his eyes. In the summer, when there is no school, and the mother goes to work, the man with the snake in his eyes locks himself in the room with the sister with the moon in her hair because she is fair.

And the brother?

He hits. He hits hard. He hits fences and cars with baseball bats. He hits walls with clenched fists. He hits classmates, hits teachers, and screams at his mother, who will not listen. He wants to be a superhero when he grows taller than the man who owns the house. He is tall now, for fourteen. He wants to be Batman.

His friend says, "I want to be Superman."

The brother says, "I still want to be Batman."

His friend says, "Sometimes I want to be Batman too. Sometimes I want to be Superman, but no one can be so perfect. I mean, he's got no real weaknesses."

"Kryptonite," the brother points out.

"But there's no such thing."

"Magic. Magic can kill Superman," the brother of the moon child suggests.

"There's no such thing as magic," the friend says. Then he asks, "What's in the bag?" as he observes the bag the brother has brought to the roof.

Up on the roof, they lie staring up into earth's yellow sun. They pass the joint back and forth. They take sips from the pint of Mad Dog 20/20. They are getting fucked up, which is what they like to do on sunny summer days when there is no school to skip. They are getting so fucked up.

"Magic is real," the brother contends. "I went to a magic show to see a woman get sawed in half. She waved at us while she was in half, and she moved her toes. Magic like that can kill Superman."

"I don't think so. Before he could even get close to him with that saw, Superman would zap the magician with his X-ray vision eyes. Plus, it's fake. It's a trick."

"I saw magic in church. A man was sick in a wheelchair. The preacher laid hands on him and he jumped up out the wheelchair."

"Man, that's not magic. That's Jesus. Pass me that Mad Dog again, homeboy. Jesus ain't going to waste His time fighting no comic book hero," the friend says, trading the joint for the sweet bottle of wine they swiped from the Cuban man's store.

The friend is stouter than the brother, but with a leaner, more handsome face. The brother has a leaner body, but with musculature that is better defined, and he is taller by at least an inch. Six of one, half a dozen of another—they are both big boys. They are only in junior high, but they will grow up to be football stars, or criminals, or maybe even superheroes.

It all depends.

The friend gulps a good one from the bottle he has been handed and says again, "What's in the bag?"

The brother of the moon child says, "Too bad he won't fight him, though. 'Cause Jesus the only one be able to kick Superman's ass—" taking a hit off that joint after each syllable, his eyes glinting with malice, the demon smile curling his lips.

It's the bag. It's a plain brown paper bag, the kind they put groceries in. It has to be about the bag, thinks the friend.

"I want to know what's in the bag, homeboy."

"I bet you do, homes."

"Don't make me have to kick your ass off this roof, homeboy."

"I am Batman, homes."

"It's a long way to the ground, and Batman can't fly."

Something crazy in his head, something evil in his eyes, the brother says, "Wanna see something better than what's in the bag?"

The friend shrugs. "Yeah."

"Gonna see some real magic now."

"Yeah."

They are both nodding their heads, laughing and slurring "yeah" drunkenly, but only the brother knows what about.

They smoke the last of the joint. They drain the MD 20/20. They climb down and catch the wind at their heels and they run.

They are big boys. They are fourteen and still growing. They are fast. They are running fast. They are Batman and Superman. Batman and Plastic Man. Batman and the Flash. Batman and Little fucking Lulu. The friend is so fucked up, the fucked-up friend can't remember who he is—but the brother is always Batman. The Dark Knight.

The Bag

When they get to the brother's house, the brother is coaching the friend shhhh, don't say nothing, climb more quiet, shhhh, look inside the window, look inside, what you see?

The friend on the ladder looks inside the window, but not for long. He climbs down the ladder more quietly than he went up.

The brother says, "What you see?"

The friend kneels at the foot of the ladder and vomits. The friend is no superhero.

When the friend lifts his head again, there is a chunk of vomit on his chin and a little in his throat that he chokes on when he says, "I saw your dad on top of your little sister."

Then bowing, the friend vomits on the backyard lawn again. When he looks up this time, the brother is pulling the handgun from the brown paper bag. It is a nine millimeter, the kind street thugs use.

"Oh no," the friend says. He feels light-headed. He feels like he wants to puke again, but there is nothing left inside.

"He ain't my dad. He ain't her dad neither," the brother with the gun in his fist says.

The friend pleads, "Just tell your mom—"

"Slapped my mouth. Called me a liar. Told me stop making trouble where there ain't no trouble. She don't wanna believe."

"Maybe your sister likes it."

Thumb under, four fingers above—gangster style—the brother touches the friend's face with the cold steel barrel of the gun.

"Want me shoot you too, homes? She's only twelve."

The big gun is weightless in the brother's hand. He knows how to handle the gun. The brother reaches for the knob on the back door of the house. The friend raises a hand to stop him from going through that back door with that gun.

"Wait!"

The friend still feels like puking. There is something in him that would like to see the brother shoot the stepdad. There is something in him that longs to see the bad guy dead. It is the dream of every boy who wants to be a superhero.

Blam. Good riddance, bad guy. You got what you deserved. But there is the superhero's code. No killing. Even bad guys. And this bad guy is a stepdad. And a cop. He's the one gets them out of all the trouble they get into. He's the one taught them to fish and throw a football and drive a car and smoke cigarettes. The best porn in the whole wide world, he gave them. So this thing here the friend saw through the window with the naked stepdad on the naked twelve-year-old girl, well this is bad, this is real bad, but no matter how fucked up they are, you just can't go around shooting your role models.

"Wait." The friend is on his feet now, hand on the brother's arm, stopping him from going through the back door with that gun.

"Wait," he says to the brother, prying the gun from his hand, dropping it carefully back in the bag. "Listen to me, homeboy. Here is what we do."

The friend has a plan.

The Children

The plan worked like this.

They did it like superheroes. They did it with masks. What they needed was handcuffs and a Magic Marker.

And iron and wood to beat him with.

They also needed two more guys because the friend said the brother couldn't be in on it. The stepdad might recognize him even with the mask. So they got two more guys, two more big guys. A boy from another school who smoked weed with them from time to time and who was down for anything. And the big scary white guy with the hunch on his back who smoked weed with them from time to time and who was strong as a motherfuck.

What they did was, they put on their masks, they snuck in there real quiet, and they bum-rushed him while he was watching *All My Children*. The scary hunchback guy grabbed him while the friend and the big boy from the other school slapped the handcuffs on. The friend pushed the gun against his teeth and told him to shut up, keep still, quit moving around so much, while the big guy and the hunchback guy ripped the shirt off his back and dragged off his pants.

It was a shock to them and kind of embarrassing because he wasn't wearing any drawers, and the condom was still on. They didn't know what to do after that. They kind of backed off after that, when it hit them what he really was. They were just kids after all.

The big kid from the other school was the oldest at fifteen, and he freaked and ran out of the house and never came back.

If the stepdad were not cuffed he might have gotten away, they were all so freaked out. He sat naked on the couch with the condom on his dick and his hands cuffed behind him and a police officer's shield tattooed over his heart in black.

"You boys better just go home."

The boy with the hunch on his back didn't know what to do, so he looked to the friend.

The friend was shaking. He still had the gun in his hand, but he was hiding it behind his leg now. He didn't know what to do either.

"Uncuff me and go home. I'll forget about this," the stepdad told them. "Where's the damned key?"

The boy with the hunch on his back had a two-by-two maple wood scantling in his hand that he had brought to beat the stepdad with. The hard piece of wood was just trembling in his hand. There was the steel pipe lying on the ground that the big coward from the other school had left when he ran out. The friend had the key to the cuffs in his pocket, but he was so scared he was about ready to run out of the house too.

Then the brother came into the room.

He brought the sister in with him.

He wanted her to see it go down.

Holding his hand, she didn't seem scared at all.

She had the moon in her hair. She was so fair.

The hunchback guy fell in love with her and was ashamed he

lacked the courage for vengeance. The friend saw her innocence and swore always to defend a beauty so fair.

The brother picked up the steel pipe the big coward from the other school had left behind. He swung it above his head.

"Let's get this party started!"

They beat him until he rolled off the couch. They beat him until *All My Children* went off. Then they beat him some more.

When it came time to write, the brother wouldn't let anyone else hold the Magic Marker. He wrote all over the stepdad's naked body. *PERVERT STOP RAPING MY SISTER LEAVE HER ALONE!*

Then they all went over to the friend's house and raided his mom's refrigerator.

The boys and the hunchback guy ate all the pudding and chips and Kool-Aid while the sister quietly supped a small cup of vanilla ice cream. They watched for a long time to see if she would say something about it, or maybe cry, but she just kept holding her brother's hand like he was her hero. She kept looking up at him and smiling.

Then everybody went home.

The Roof

When the friend finally sees the brother again, he has two black eyes.

It has been a whole month since the friend has seen him.

He has to get the ladder out of the shed so the brother can climb up on the roof with him. The brother can't just do a pull-up to the low roof like before because his arm is in a cast.

The friend passes him the Mad Dog and whistles through his teeth. "What he do to you, homeboy?"

The brother swallows slowly from the pint. "You better watch your back, homes. He might come after you."

"Me?"

"Watch out for cops too," the brother says. "He called them and they came over and got him out of the cuffs while we were at your house. Washed off all the Magic Marker stuff I wrote. They're probably out to get you too. Thump you up a little bit so you won't tell on him. But maybe you're all right. Maybe you shouldn't worry about it too much. They had most of their fun with me already. I took one for the team."

With his good hand, the brother digs the joint out of the pocket of his jeans and passes it to the friend, who pushes it between his lips and lights it.

"Nothing happened for a couple days," the brother explains. "Then I was at the Cuban man's store and two of them showed up, told the Cuban man they had caught me shoplifting, go check the camera. What camera? You know the Cuban man ain't got no camera in that store much as we swipe stuff off him."

The friend inhales the sweet essence from the joint. His cheeks puff, and he coughs it out, fanning. "Yeah. I know."

"I didn't argue. I figured I was dead anyway. They beat me up and threw me in the trunk. I could hear them talking loud about the scary stuff they was gonna do to me. I was in there for like two hours with my heart pumping out my chest. But I focused on what we had did and that got me through. Then they brought me home and told my mom I had shoplifted and gotten hurt trying to run, but because of who my stepdad is they took care of it and got me off with no charges."

The friend ponders something he does not share with the brother. There are things you don't share even with your best friend. Things you have to keep to yourself. Things that make you sound crazy. Not crazy in a hard-core *I ain't scared, I'll do anything dangerous* kind of way. But crazy like in a real smart way.

Behind all these walls in all these houses. How many snakes in how many eyes? The baddest crime you've committed in all of your fourteen years is not as bad as this. The baddest crime you shall ever commit is not as bad. Six of one. Half a dozen of another. You shall grow up to be a preacher, or a criminal, or maybe even a superhero. It all depends.

The friend pinches the lit joint between two fingers but he does not smoke it. His breath smells like Mad Dog 20/20 when he says, "What about your sister?"

The brother shakes his head. "He don't mess with my sister no more."

"Yeah!"

"He better not. He know I'll kill him next time."

"Yeah, man."

They high-five, and the brother signals for the joint, which the friend passes to him.

He emphasizes each phrase with a hit off the joint. "I am fast as the wind. I got lightning in my hands. I got thunder in my hands. I am a superhero. I will kill you if you mess with those I love."

"Yeah, man," the friend says.

The friend stretches out on the roof and stares up into the earth's yellow sun. The sun is so beautiful, better than Krypton's red sun any old day.

THE MONKEY'S FIST

BY CHRISTINE KLING

Straits of Florida

(Originally published in 2006)

They had been married twenty-two years when he came home early one afternoon and announced he had bought himself a boat. She sat at the kitchen table grading papers, and she looked up at him, trying to break her focus away from Reynaldo's interpretation of Crane's "The Open Boat."

"What did you say?" She thought she hadn't heard him right, had somehow confused his spoken words with Reynaldo's written words. He'd probably bought himself a new coat.

He lifted her heavy gray braid and kissed her on the back of the neck. "It's an Irwin fifty-seven. I know that's pretty big for a first boat, but I wanted something we would be comfortable on when we go to the Bahamas." He slipped off the windbreaker with the company name stenciled across the back and draped it over an empty chair. "No crappy little shower in the head or doing without air. And ice, gotta have ice. This boat's got it all. Tons of electronics, radar, GPS, chart plotter. A ten-KW generator, nice big Ford Lehman diesel. Ketch-rigged too," he said. He'd been staring out the windows as he'd listed the boat's amenities, but now he glanced down at her for a brief moment. "That means it has two masts, honey."

"Right," she said.

He'd dropped his briefcase on the kitchen counter, and he took a highball glass out of the dishwasher, filled it with ice at the refrigerator door, and walked into the living room, headed for the bar cabinet and his bourbon. She heard the sound of the television as he clicked it on, and she knew he would be sitting in there in his chair with the television blaring—and reading.

He'd started buying sailing books about a year earlier. First, there were the adventure tales of couples who had crossed the oceans and cruised the South Seas. He stacked those on the end table next to his BarcaLounger. Then he got into the how-tos, and lately she noticed he had purchased a cruising guide to the Bahamas.

She kept her books shelved neatly by subject with separate sections for poetry, novels, short story collections or anthologies, and critical works. He had reshelved her poetry, stacking the slender paperbacks on top of her *Oxford English Dictionary* and *Riverside Shakespeare* to make room for his sailing books. He now had enough to require a shelf of his own.

She bent her head over the stack of essays from her eleventh-grade AP English students and went back to work. After deciding Reynaldo was parroting someone else's thoughts, she gave him a C and moved on. The kitchen table was her favorite spot to work; the light was good thanks to the corner windows that overlooked the backyard, the pool, and the canal beyond. She could get away without having to wear those damn reading glasses as long as the light was good enough. She could also watch the birds from here, the blue jays and mockingbirds who frequented the feeder she'd hung in the old oak, the only tree he'd saved on the lot.

They'd moved in about five years ago when he had finally started doing really well and branched out on his own, building spec houses and small groups of town houses. She often missed the simple, cinder-block, two-bedroom home with a white barrel tile roof they'd sold for almost three times what they'd paid for it. She had invested time there in painting bookshelves, polishing terrazzo, and potting orchids, and she'd reaped the good memories of their early years together.

What had happened to real estate values in South Florida in

the same time period was practically obscene, and no matter how ugly or opulent the homes he built seemed to her, there were always more nouveau riche types who could not wait to have him tear down the little fifty-year-old cottages here in Victoria Park or over in Rio Vista so he could build them another McMansion. This lot where they now lived had been unusually small, and he'd decided after the spec house had been on the market for six months that rather than take a beating on the price, they would move in and call it their home. After all, as the president and owner of a construction company in Fort Lauderdale, he deserved a classy address, a nice place to entertain clients, he'd told her.

At dinner that night, he chewed a large forkful of her chicken and rice and announced, "You're gonna have to learn how to sail." Little bits of rice escaped and flew out of his mouth. They landed back on his plate.

She nodded at that.

"It'll be a tight fit," he said, "but we're gonna bring the boat up to the dock here at the house. She's over at Bahia Mar right now. I told the broker I'd have her out of there by Saturday. That gives us about a month to get ready. I invited Gator and his wife to go with us to Nassau next month—when you're off on spring break. Should be a nice way to break in the boat."

Gator was his best friend from high school who had made a fortune in the dot-com glory days and had been smart enough to get out before the bubble burst. He'd recently married for the third time.

"What's her name?"

"Gator's wife?"

"No, your boat."

"She's called the *Verity*. Don't know if I like that, especially because it's in some foreign language, but I hear it's bad luck to change a boat's name."

"Verity means truth."

"I know that."

* * *

Saturday morning he told her they would take her Lexus to the marina, bring the boat to the house, and then they'd go back to get her car. When they walked into the broker's office, a thin white-haired man got up from behind his desk, buttoning his blazer and putting on his smile. "You must be the missus," he said in a pronounced British accent. She couldn't believe he had really called her that. "Congratulations. It's a lovely boat." His breath smelled of stale cigarettes.

It was quite clear her husband wanted to get rid of the broker as soon as possible. From the moment the man had suggested that they might want to hire a captain to help them motor to their dock, her husband had shut down. He wanted the broker off his boat. It didn't happen too often anymore, but her husband could be rude when he wanted to be.

With the broker gone, he had taken her on a tour down below. She was surprised by the amount of space and all the comforts that had been squeezed into that compact environment. It reminded her of a dollhouse. He showed her the galley first with the electric stove and the top-loading refrigerator and freezer. When she lifted the lid of the freezer, the dark hole smelled musty. She would need to do lots of cleaning, she thought, and wondered when she would find the time.

The aft cabin would be theirs, he said as he opened the small round door and stepped through.

She poked her head past his shoulder and remarked that the queen-size bed nearly took up all the space in the cabin.

"It's called a berth, honey."

Back on deck he began to explain to her about directions on the boat, fore and aft, port and starboard. The dock they were tied to was shaped like a letter T and they were tied at the end. It looked as though it would be quite easy to motor out, she thought. Just untie the ropes and off they would go. He explained to her over and over what he would do, and what he expected her to do.

He took her up onto the front of the boat and picked up a white rope with a small, knotted rope ball on the end. This rope looked newer than the others on the boat.

"This is called a heaving line," he said. "I was surprised they didn't have one on the boat. According to the *Marlinspike Sailor,* it's a necessity. See, on this end?" He held up the knotted ball. "This is called a monkey's fist. The weight of it makes it easier to throw the line."

It was almost more square than round, and she liked the look of it. Decorative, that's what she'd call it. She'd seen jewelry in that shape before, little gold versions that sold for hundreds of dollars in the shops on Las Olas.

"When we get up to the house, Gator's gonna be there. I asked him to come over to help us dock." He held the coiled rope in one hand and swung the loose end with the monkey's fist. "You're gonna take this line and when we get to within about ten feet of the dock you're gonna throw this to Gator like this." He tossed the monkey's fist back at the mast and released the coils he held in his left hand. The rope arced up through the air and landed past the mast on the plastic windshield of the boat. "You've always got to remember to let go of the line in this hand, see," he held up his left hand, "or the fist end isn't gonna go but about five feet and fall in the water. Okay, you try it."

He coiled up the line, stood behind her, and placed the coils in her left hand, the throwing end in her right. "Now swing this end back like this," he said, and pulled her right hand back, "then swing forward and let go."

She released the rope and the fist flew about ten feet and landed at the base of the mast. The coils dropped at her feet a second later.

"All right. That's good enough, honey. You keep practicing."

Gator was standing on their seawall, waving as they rounded the corner into the canal. Her husband was wearing his cell phone on his belt with a black wire that snaked up into his ear. He'd kept a running dialogue going with his friend throughout the trip from the marina.

"Okay, you ready up there, honey? Don't throw it until I say when, okay?" He was shouting so loud, she looked around to see if any of their neighbors were outside. All the windows were closed tight to keep the cold air inside, and the only people she saw were the gardeners in front of her neighbors' cottage.

It wasn't difficult to see which home was theirs. It was the only two-story house built out to within what seemed like inches of the property line on either side. The home was painted gray with a silvery tin roof and an imitation widow's walk. It would have looked more at home in New England than South Florida.

She glanced back at him standing in the cockpit. She thought the boat seemed to be going too fast. His hands gripped the massive stainless steel wheel at two o'clock and ten o'clock. His legs were braced shoulder-length apart. He was not a large man, and the size of the steering wheel made him appear even smaller. Ahead, their dock was coming up fast. She passed the monkey's fist into the hand holding the coiled line and shaded her eyes looking back at him.

"Get ready, honey. You ready?"

She heard a change in the sound of the engine. It revved louder, and she decided he had shifted into reverse. The boat speed slowed only slightly and the back of the boat began to twist away from the dock, pointing the bow toward the seawall beyond their wood dock.

"What the hell are you doing? Throw Gator the line, goddamnit!"

She swung the fist back and threw, and the white rope flew nearly straight up, then dropped down only inches from the dock. Gator cartwheeled his arms trying to grab the line before it splashed into the water. He missed.

Her husband pushed her aside, ran forward, and shoved the

boat off the dark wood piling with his shoulder. The sound of wood, fiberglass, and metal crunching together as the tons of boat rammed the dock made her smile.

Later, he assured her it wasn't all her fault, and besides, there wasn't really all that much damage to the boat. It was mostly cosmetic, just some scratches in the fiberglass, and he could easily get the kinks taken out of that stainless steel railing on the bow. His *Verity* could take a beating, he said. He'd known she'd be a strong, sound boat.

"You're just gonna need to spend some time practicing before we take off for the Bahamas. It'll be good for you. Get you back in shape. And I'll teach you everything you need to know."

She had met him when she'd taken a job as a secretary at the construction company when she'd finally decided it was time to get serious about finishing her college degree. She was twenty-eight years old, and she had been dropping in and out of college for almost ten years. Her parents kept insisting that she simply needed to lose a few pounds, and then she'd finally get married and wouldn't have to worry about school anymore. The project was a condominium complex down on the beach, and he was the foreman on the job. They'd dated less than a year before they got married, but she often wondered if it was the fact that they'd dated less than a week before she slept with him that had made him stop listening to her so early in their marriage. His face was badly scarred from teenage acne and his rounded shoulders did little to increase his small stature. Perhaps he figured that a girl who would sleep with him so quickly couldn't be all that bright.

Teaching surprised her. She had always been a bookworm as a kid, and she found that sharing this love of books with classrooms full of reluctant teenagers satisfied her in a way that nothing else ever had. And she was good at it. She was not a strong and assertive teacher, but her students admired her quiet nature. She could not remember how many times through the years she had heard one of her students yell at another to "shut up and let the lady talk." And they listened to her. They cared about what she had to say.

Gator and Cindy, his new wife, came over for dinner the night before they were to leave for their week in the Bahamas. The young woman could not have been more than thirty years old, and she was wearing a pink tank top with a push-up bra that reminded her of the waitresses in Hooters, one of her husband's favorite lunch spots.

"I've never been sailing before," Cindy gushed when she came into the kitchen and offered to help. "Gator says that if we like it, we're gonna get ourselves a boat even bigger than yours."

"That would be nice," she said, and handed the woman a large wooden salad bowl heaped high with greens to take out to the dining room.

She was tired. Her students had been wild the day before spring break, bursting with energy and not the least bit willing to discuss Zora Neale Hurston. She had thought that the scenes of the hurricane's devastation would touch these Florida kids, but they were all too young to remember Andrew, the last hurricane to hit the area. All her time outside school lately had been spent getting the boat ready for their trip and practicing with the heaving line as he'd told her to do.

After dinner, her husband took Gator and Cindy out to the boat to show them around, teach them how to use the marine head, and to help them settle their bags in their cabin. There were two guest cabins forward with double berths and her husband laughed loudly and winked when he told Gator that there wasn't much room up there in those berths, that it was a good thing he had a skinny wife.

She was glad when they'd gone out the back door, glad when she clicked off the stereo and the house grew quiet. She almost thought she could begin to like this house, if only it could be quiet more often. When she had finished loading the dishwasher, she pulled the full bag out of the plastic bin under the sink and tied the red ties in a neat bow. She opened the back door and stepped around to put the bag in the can on the side of the house. When she came back around the house, she saw the three of them standing on the pool deck, pausing to talk in lowered voices before going back into the house. Her hand stopped on the doorknob and she stepped back into the shadows of the narrow passage between their house and the wood fence along the property line.

Cindy reached for the sliding glass door. "I've got to go to the little girl's room. See you inside."

The two men watched her go in. Her husband shook his head.

"Gator, I don't know how you do it. What I wouldn't give for something like that."

"You just say the word, brother man. Cindy's friend Kiki, she's gonna be staying over on Paradise Island. She would love to go sailing with us. With you."

"You don't know how much I'd like that too," her husband said. "The thing is, I know she'll hate it." He jerked his head toward the house. "Sailing. Especially if it's rough. I'm pretty sure that by the time we get to Nassau, it would be easy enough to convince her to hop a plane for home."

"Then it's a plan."

"I don't know," he said.

"Man, I don't get you," Gator said. "You could have your pick of women. That one," he said, and nodded toward the French doors that led into the kitchen. "Look at her." He spread his hands wide. "And she didn't say a word all through dinner. Why the hell do you stay married to her?"

"What? Gator, how can you ask me that after what your ex's have taken from you? I'll take the monkey on my back before I'll give her half of what's mine."

* * *

The next morning they were motoring out through Port Everglades channel when the gray light in the east started to turn pink and soon the gray woolly clouds were tinged with crimson. She came up the ladder balancing two mugs of hot coffee, wearing her sweats to ward off the March chill air. Her husband was stowing the last of the dock lines in the cockpit locker under the seat. She handed him a steaming mug and turned to look at the spectacle in the east.

"You know what they say," she said to no one in particular. Gator and Cindy had shown up wearing shorts and tank tops, and they were cuddling under a blanket in the back of the cockpit. *Red sky at night, sailor's delight. Red sky at morning, sailor take warning.*

Her husband squinted ahead. "Where'd you pick that up?"

"Read it in one of your books," she said.

He laughed. "Ran out of your own books? Yeah, well, cold front came through overnight, but it should be clearing up later." He took a sip of the hot coffee. "Think you can handle a little rough weather, honey?"

She shrugged. "Are you sure it's wise to go if we know the weather's going to be bad?" The bow plunged into the first of the seas and spray splattered across the deck, peppering the clear plastic windows across the front of the cockpit.

"Damn," he said when the deck seemed to drop out from under them in the next trough, and he spilled his coffee down the front of his Dockers. "Clean that up, will you?"

She struggled down the ladder and grabbed a dish towel hanging on the front of the stove. As she mopped up the brown liquid, more seawater splashed aboard. "Don't you think it would be wiser to turn back?" she asked. "Wait a few days for this weather to settle down?"

"Honey, this boat can take it. Should take us about thirty hours to get to Nassau. We'll get in late tomorrow morning. The *Verity* can take whatever nature can dish up."

Gator took over the wheel while her husband got the sails set. The *Verity* had roller furling and electric winches, so the men were able to unfurl the sails without leaving the shelter of the cockpit. She watched them push buttons to pull the sails out, and wondered that this is what sailing had come to now. Gator had to let go of the wheel twice to heave over the side. Her husband teased him about the amount of beer he'd drunk the night before, but his friend wasn't laughing when he hunched back under the blanket with his new wife. Cindy's eyes had great dark circles under them where the salt spray has caused her mascara to run, and she was soaked through, her teeth chattering. Gator groaned and dry heaved a couple more times, then mumbled that he was going below and disappeared down the ladder with Cindy right behind him.

The sails steadied the motion of the boat somewhat, and made the seas appear less frightening. Her husband set the boat to run on autopilot and went below to change out of his wet clothes and put on his foul-weather gear. He told her to call him if she saw any other boats or ships.

It was as though they owned the sea that day. There were no other boats or ships as far as she could see in any direction. She was surprised at how quickly the buildings of Fort Lauderdale were shrinking off their stern. They would soon be surrounded by nothing but angry gray water. Occasionally, one of the seas broke at its peak and made a rushing noise like a wheezy monster exhaling, and when one of those breaking seas hit them, the autopilot groaned and ground its gears in protest as it attempted to right their course.

She heard her husband rummaging around in the galley below, opening the refrigerator, clanking pottery. He went a few steps up the ladder and threw an empty quart milk carton over the side. She stared open-mouthed, startled by the flagrant littering.

"It can handle it," he said. "It's a big ocean."

She turned away from him and watched the white carton rise

up on the face of a swell and disappear into the next trough. She saw the white flash only one more time on the peak of a swell before it was lost in the sea of gray. In less than a minute, it was gone.

When her husband came back up the ladder, he was outfitted from top to bottom in a plastic yellow suit. On his feet, he wore shiny new black sea boots. He settled on the cockpit seat and looked around the horizon. A few minutes later he checked the sails, then he checked his watch.

"Only about twenty-eight more hours to go," he said.

By late morning the seas had grown worse. The boat heeled at a constant twenty-degree angle. She tried going below, but she felt the nausea begin, so she grabbed a paperback novel and found she could read tucked up under the canvas shelter he called a dodger. There, most of the spray missed her. When noon came around, none of them felt like eating, and the only time she saw Cindy was when she came out to fetch the plastic trash can from the galley to use as a puke bucket in their cabin.

Her husband went up and down the ladder all afternoon. The boredom of sailing was something he had not reckoned with. He played with the radio below trying to raise other vessels, then came out into the cockpit and pushed buttons on the electric winches, taking in lines and letting them out again. She'd read over two hundred pages of the espionage thriller, but she was having a difficult time following the plot. The boat was groaning and below, whenever they rose on an extra-large swell, the contents of the cabinets rattled and shook. She imagined broken ketchup bottles and spilled vinegar. The *Verity* was a very high-sided boat, but when the wires on the low side started dipping underwater as the stronger gusts hit them, she decided she should say something.

"Don't you think we have too much sail up? Surely we're going fast enough." She'd read enough in those books of his to know that when the wind got stronger, you were supposed to put up smaller sails or take them in altogether.

A blast of spray hit the dodger, and it sounded like a round of BBs hitting the plastic window. Her husband had his yellow hood cinched tight around his pinched face. "This boat can take it, honey, don't you worry. Why don't you go down and fix me something hot to eat."

She looked at her watch and was surprised to see it was after five. It would be getting dark soon with the gloom of the heavy overcast and the patch of even darker clouds on the horizon ahead. They hadn't seen much rain this day, but judging from the look of those black clouds, they would shortly. The sun, though they wouldn't see it, would set just before six. She tucked a bookmark in her novel and made her way down the ladder, holding tight and determined to keep the nausea at bay.

She decided a can of Campbell's Chunky soup was the best she could do, and by the time she'd found a can opener and emptied the brown muck into the pot on the gimbaled stove, she was nearly sick. She braced herself on the seat of the navigation table as the cabin grew darker and the soup did its best to prove the adage about a watched pot. She cut off a thick slice of sourdough bread and a chunk of cheddar cheese, wrapped them in a paper towel, and tucked them into her sweatshirt pocket. She poured the soup into a large bowl and made her way to the ladder. The motion was even worse and the degree of heel had increased. She had to walk on the side of the ladder, and she knew she was going to spill the soup. He would be furious.

She'd just made it to the top of the ladder and was reaching out trying to pass him the bowl of soup, when he said, "Canned soup? Is that the best you can do?" Then the boat shuddered from the pounding of a huge wave, and she started to go over. She saw his face turn up, away from her, and in the next second a wall of green water dropped from the sky and enveloped him. Gallons poured down the hatch, bowing her head under the force of it, nearly knocking her off the ladder. The soup bowl was gone from her hand, and she wasn't even aware of having dropped it, only that she was holding on with both hands as the boat went completely over on her side. She was choking, gagging and spitting up salt water, and when she raised her head, he was gone.

She scrambled into the cockpit as the boat righted herself and looked off the low side. She turned, peering forward and aft, and saw no splash of yellow. The lifelines were still intact, but he was gone.

"Man overboard!" she hollered as loud as she could. "Man overboard!"

She hit at the buttons that should wind up the sails and looked up to see the mainsail gone, some fuzzy tatters blowing in the wind. She reached down and tried to remember the steps he'd taken when he'd started the engine. She pushed the heater and counted to ten as Gator's colorless face appeared in the companionway.

"What happened?"

She pointed over her shoulder. "He's back there somewhere. Got to start the engine."

Gator called over his shoulder, "Cindy, get on the radio and start calling mayday! Try to raise the Coast Guard!"

He climbed out just as the diesel roared to life. She lifted the cockpit locker and grabbed the heaving line. "Circle around this way," she said. "Look for his yellow jacket."

Clutching the line, she crawled forward slowly, moving from handhold to handhold, keeping her body low to the deck, her heart pounding and her teeth chattering as much from the cold as from fear. She was surprised that she did not feel particularly frightened. The waves were still huge, and she was rolling from one side to the other, the mast swinging in a wide arc through the black sky. She squinted into misty darkness, scanning the sea slowly, remembering the milk carton, giving him time to rise between the troughs. What she did feel was anger. Why hadn't he listened to her?

It was Cindy who spotted him. "Over there!" she cried. "See him? Over there!"

She thought she saw a speck of yellow, then it was gone. Night was on them. Gator was turning the boat back into the wind. The spray stung her cheeks and burned her eyes. There. She thought she saw something yellow. She arranged the coils of the heaving line in her left hand and transferred the monkey's fist to her right, swinging the weight of it comfortably off her hand.

"I don't want to get too close! I'm afraid I'll run him down!" Gator yelled into the wind. "Do you see him?" He was dashing from one side of the cockpit to the other, his voice high-pitched with panic. "Can you see him?"

One minute she couldn't find him anywhere, and then he was there, about twenty feet downwind, and they were going to pass him moving at a pretty good speed. She swung the fist back and shouted at him, "Here!" Just before she let go, she saw his face, saw his lips moving. He was talking—he wasn't listening to her. She let the monkey's fist fly, and a fraction of a second later she released the coils in her left hand. The line fell short, splashed into the sea. As they steamed on past the yellow dot bobbing in the trough, she felt the corner of her lip twitch.

"Goddamnit!" Gator yelled. "I'll come around again. Cindy, try to keep your eyes on him!"

"Where is he?" Cindy shouted. She raced to the stern and threw the yellow horseshoe life preserver into the night. It skittered across the surface as the wind caught it, then it disappeared in a trough.

A strong gust caught the headsail and Gator fought to bring the boat around. When they came around again Gator kept screaming, "Can you see him? He's got to be here! Can you see him out there?"

The Coast Guard told them via radio to keep circling in the area, to keep searching. Cindy and Gator clutched each other wrapped in a blanket, standing at the helm as they circled round and round. Occasionally, Cindy ducked below to read their position off the

GPS for the Coast Guard radioman. The two of them were cried out by the time a Coast Guard cutter reached them four hours later.

Her eyes were red too, mostly from the salt sting of squinting into the misty night. After an hour on deck, she had retreated to the corner of the cockpit where she sat huddled under the dodger, staring into the blackness. When the cutter appeared at last, they launched a fast black inflatable speedboat with four men aboard wearing orange rainsuits. She climbed out of the cockpit, still clutching the heaving line. Their boat was about twenty feet off when she let fly the monkey's fist, and it landed squarely in the hands of the yeoman in the bow of the boat.

"Nice shot," Cindy said.

"Yeah," she said, "I've been practicing."

ABOUT THE CONTRIBUTORS

Preston L. Allen

Preston L. Allen is a recipient of a State of Florida Individual Artist Fellowship, and has authored the novels *All or Nothing, Jesus Boy*, and the allegorical *Every Boy Should Have a Man* (a finalist for the Hurston/Wright Legacy Award). The *New York Times* has called him "a cartographer of autodegradation," placing his work on a continuum with that of Dostoevsky, William S. Burroughs, and Charles Bukowski. Allen is associate professor of English and creative writing at Miami Dade College.

J. Tomás Lopez

Lynne Barrett has received the Edgar Award for best mystery story and, for her collection *Magpies*, the Florida Book Awards' fiction gold medal. Some of her recent work has appeared in *Mystery Tribune*, the *Hong Kong Review, Necessary Fiction*, and *Just to Watch Them Die: Crime Fiction Inspired by the Songs of Johnny Cash*. Jai-Alai Books has just released her anthology *Making Good Time: True Stories of How We Do, and Don't, Get Around in South Florida*.

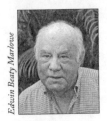

Edwin Beaty Marlowe

David Beaty was born in Brazil of American parents. A graduate of Columbia University, he earned an MFA in creative writing from Florida International University. He has lived in Greece, England, and Brazil, and currently resides in Miami. His story "Ghosts" was selected for *Best American Mystery Stories 2000*, and his story "The Last of Lord Jitters," originally published in *Miami Noir*, received an honorable mention for *Best American Mystery Stories 2007*, edited by Carl Hiaasen.

Maura Anne Wahl

James Carlos Blake was born in Tampico, Mexico, and raised in Brownsville, Texas, and Miami, Florida. After service in the US Army Airborne and a stint as a properties officer in a county jail, he earned an MA degree and taught literature at various colleges and universities before devoting himself to writing full-time. He venerates the music of Jelly Roll Morton and Philip Glass.

Jim Virga

Edna Buchanan won a Pulitzer Prize and a George Polk Award for her work on the Miami police beat. She reported more than five thousand violent deaths, and lived through the Cocaine Cowboys, the Mariel boatlift, and major riots. When editors insisted she cover only the "major murder" of the day, she resisted. How does one choose? Every murder is major to the victim. So she covered them all. Then she wrote novels. Lots of them.

LESTER DENT (1904–1959) is best remembered for Doc Savage, but he was distinguished beyond that series. He wrote only two stories for *Black Mask* magazine, both featuring Miami detective Oscar Sail. Dent's first stab at the character resulted in "Luck," the story in this volume, which stars a different version of Sail. In the 1930s, Dent lived on his schooner, *Albatross*, which led to creating Sail, and which may have also influenced John D. MacDonald's houseboat-dwelling Miami sleuth, Travis McGee.

MARJORY STONEMAN DOUGLAS (1890–1998), best known for her 1947 book *The Everglades: River of Grass*, was a conservationist, author, journalist, and women's suffrage advocate. Initially a reporter for the *Miami Herald*, Douglas became an outspoken advocate for preserving the Everglades, earning her the nickname "Grand Dame of the Everglades," and was instrumental in its gaining status as a national park. Douglas was awarded the Presidential Medal of Freedom by Bill Clinton.

JOHN DUFRESNE has written two story collections and six novels, including *Louisiana Power & Light* and *Love Warps the Mind a Little,* both *New York Times* Notable Books of the Year. He has also written four books on writing, two plays (*Liv & Di* and *Trailerville*), and has cowritten two feature films. His stories have twice been selected for *Best American Mystery Stories*. He is a Guggenheim Fellow and teaches creative writing at Florida International University in Miami.

DOUGLAS FAIRBAIRN (1926–1997) was an American author from Elmira, New York. Aside from his memoir, *Down and Out in Cambridge*, Fairbairn's books, including *A Squirrel Forever*, *A Squirrel of One's Own*, and *Street 8: A Novel*, focus on South Florida, where he lived for the greater part of his years until his death in 1997. His novel *Shoot* was developed into a movie starring Cliff Robertson in 1976.

Antonia Wright

CAROLINA GARCIA-AGUILERA is the Cuba-born, Miami Beach–based, award-winning author of ten books, as well as a contributor to many anthologies. She is best known for her Lupe Solano mystery series. Her books have been translated into twelve languages. Garcia-Aguilera became a private investigator—a profession she has practiced for over thirty years—so she could credibly write the novels featuring a PI as a protagonist.

BRETT HALLIDAY (1904–1977) was the primary pen name of Davis Dresser, under which he wrote and later commissioned installments of the popular Michael Shayne series. Dresser wrote numerous mysteries, westerns, and romances as Halliday, cofounded the Halliday and McCloy literary agency, and established the Torquil Publishing Company. Dresser was a founding member of the Mystery Writers of America in 1945, and received an Edgar Award from the organization in 1954.

Garry Kravit

VICKI HENDRICKS is the author of the noir novels *Miami Purity, Iguana Love, Voluntary Madness, Sky Blues,* and *Cruel Poetry,* which was an Edgar Award finalist in 2008. Her short stories are collected in *Florida Gothic Stories.* She currently lives in central Florida, the rural locale of her most recent novel, *Fur People.*

Courtesy of Barbara Hurston Lewis, Faye Hurston, and Lois Gaston

ZORA NEALE HURSTON (1891–1960) was a novelist, folklorist, dramatist, ethnographer, and cultural anthropologist. She is the author of four novels, including *Their Eyes Were Watching God*; two books of folklore; an autobiography; and over fifty short stories, essays, and plays. She attended Howard University, Barnard College, and Columbia University. She was born in Notasulga, Alabama, and grew up in Eatonville, Florida.

CHRISTINE KLING is an avid sailor as well as the author of eight nautical thrillers. Her first series of five novels is set in Florida and features a female tug and salvage captain, Seychelle Sullivan. The Shipwreck Adventures, her second series, are international thrillers based on real historical shipwrecks. Currently, Kling and her husband live in Antalya, Turkey, where they are building their next boat, an all-aluminum expedition passage maker designed for exploring the high latitudes.

No
Author
Photo

ELMORE LEONARD (1925–2013), once called the "Dickens of Detroit" by *Time* magazine, first began writing fiction in the fifth grade. Although he initially gained notoriety through his westerns, Leonard later became an extremely prolific author of crime novels, short stories, and screenplays, all distinct in their focus on characters and realistic, Detroit slang–ridden dialogue. During his career, Leonard was the recipient of the Edgar, Peabody, and National Book awards, among others.

T.J. MacGregor (a.k.a. Trish MacGregor, Alison Drake, and several other names) is the author of forty-two novels and several dozen nonfiction books on synchronicity, astrology, tarot, and dreams. Her most recent novel is *Skin Shifters*, and she won the Edgar Award in 2003 for her novel *Out of Sight*.

Damon Runyon (1880–1946) was a well-known journalist and author of short stories, many of which were collected into his popular 1931 book, and later Broadway show, *Guys and Dolls*, which is now considered a classic of musical theater. Although he gained notoriety through political and sports journalism, Runyon's trademark was his interest in people over facts. This led to his exaggerated caricatures of Broadway locals, cementing his career as one of New York's most sought-after writers.

Les Standiford, who edited 2006's *Miami Noir*, is the author of twenty-four books and novels, including the award-winning John Deal thriller series and the works of narrative nonfiction *Last Train to Paradise*, the One Read choice of a dozen public library systems, and *Bringing Adam Home*, a *Wall Street Journal* number one true crime best seller. He is director of the MFA program in creative writing at Florida International University in Miami.

Garry Kravit

Charles Willeford (1919–1988), who wrote seventeen novels including the popular Hoke Moseley series, was described by the *Atlantic* as "the unlikely father of Miami crime fiction." His books have been published in twenty languages. Four of them—*Cockfighter, Miami Blues, The Woman Chaser,* and *The Burnt Orange Heresy*—have been made into movies. A decorated World War II tank commander, Willeford is buried in the Arlington National Cemetery.

David Poller

Acknowledgments

I am indebted to a number of individuals who were of great assistance to me in assembling the stories found in this volume. For their help in identifying materials from the golden age of the pulps and for their interest in this enterprise, my most sincere thanks go to Otto Penzler, editor in chief and publisher of Mysterious Press, and to Will Murray, long-time pulp historian and expert on matters related to Doc Savage and Lester Dent. I am also greatly indebted to Betsy Willeford, Charles's widow, for her aid and unflagging encouragement. Thanks as well to my FIU colleague Lynne Barrett, herself an Edgar Award winner, for her many adroit suggestions: "Oh but there *must* be something out there by Damon Runyon!" And last but certainly not least, thanks to all my fellow ink-stained wretches who have so generously shared their most excellent work for this collection. Drawing us all together once again has reminded me what a great blessing it has been to spend a career working and playing among so many great talents—I believe that as a group we are second to none, here in our lovely literary Casablanca.

Permissions

Also available from the Akashic Noir Series

MIAMI NOIR
edited by Les Standiford
332 pages, trade paperback original, $15.95

BRAND-NEW STORIES BY: James W. Hall, Barbara Parker, John Dufresne, Paul Levine, Carolina Garcia-Aguilera, Tom Corcoran, Christine Kling, George Tucker, Kevin Allen, Anthony Dale Gagliano, David Beaty, Vicki Hendricks, John Bond, Preston L. Allen, Lynne Barrett, and Jeffrey Wehr.

"For different reasons these stories cultivate a little something special, a radiance, a humanity, even a grace, in the midst of the noir gloom, and thereby set themselves apart. Variety, familiarity, mood and tone, and the occasional gem of a story make *Miami Noir* a collection to savor." —*Miami Herald*

"For such a sun-stoked place, Miami sure is shady. Shadowy, too. Even at highest noon. Maybe it's the heat. Maybe it's the humidity. And maybe, just maybe, it's our destiny." —*Sun Post*

"Murder is nothing new in Miami—or any other big city, for that matter. But seldom has it been so entertaining as it is in the sixteen short stories included in *Miami Noir*." —*Palm Beach Daily News*

TAMPA BAY NOIR
edited by Colette Bancroft
304 pages, trade paperback original, $16.95

BRAND-NEW STORIES BY: Michael Connelly, Lori Roy, Ace Atkins, Karen Brown, Tim Dorsey, Lisa Unger, Sterling Watson, Luis Castillo, Sarah Gerard, Danny López, Ladee Hubbard, Gale Massey, Yuly Restrepo Garcés, Eliot Schrefer, and Colette Bancroft.

"Every classic mystery-fiction theme is represented here—murder, fraud, love, sex, money—and, overall, the writing is top quality. Lovers of short crime fiction should eat this one up." —*Booklist*

HAVANA NOIR
edited by Achy Obejas
322 pages, trade paperback original, $16.95

BRAND-NEW STORIES BY: Leonardo Padura, Pablo Medina, Alex Abella, Arturo Arango, Lea Aschkenas, Moisés Asís, Arnaldo Correa, Mabel Cuesta, Yohamna Depestre, Michel Encinosa Fú, Mylene Fernández Pintado, Carolina García-Aguilera, Miguel Mejides, Achy Obejas, Oscar F. Ortíz, Ena Lucía Portela, Mariela Varona Roque, and Yoss.

"[A] remarkable collection . . . Throughout these eighteen stories, current and former residents of Havana—some well-known, some previously undiscovered—deliver gritty tales of depravation, depravity, heroic perseverance, revolution, and longing in a city mythical and widely misunderstood." —*Miami Herald*

NEW ORLEANS NOIR
edited by Julie Smith
288 pages, trade paperback original, $15.95

BRAND-NEW STORIES BY: Ace Atkins, Laura Lippman, Patty Friedmann, Barbara Hambly, Tim McLoughlin, Olympia Vernon, David Fulmer, Jervey Tervalon, James Nolan, Kalamu ya Salaam, Maureen Tan, Thomas Adcock, Jeri Cain Rossi, Christine Wiltz, Greg Herren, Julie Smith, Eric Overmyer, and Ted O'Brien.

"*New Orleans Noir* explores the dark corners of our city in eighteen stories, set both pre- and post-Katrina . . . In Julie Smith, Temple found a perfect editor for the New Orleans volume, for she is one who knows and loves the city and its writers and knows how to bring out the best in both . . . It's harrowing reading, to be sure, but it's pure page-turning pleasure, too." —*Times-Picayune*

NEW ORLEANS NOIR: THE CLASSICS
edited by Julie Smith
320 pages, trade paperback original, $15.95

CLASSIC REPRINTS FROM: James Lee Burke, Armand Lanusse, Grace King, Kate Chopin, O. Henry, Eudora Welty, Tennessee Williams, Shirley Ann Grau, John William Corrington, Tom Dent, Ellen Gilchrist, Valerie Martin, O'Neil De Noux, John Biguenet, Poppy Z. Brite, Nevada Barr, Ace Atkins, and Maurice Carlos Ruffin.

"[An] irresistible sequel to Smith's *New Orleans Noir* . . . Anyone who knows New Orleans even slightly will relish revisiting the city in story after story. For anyone who has never been to New Orleans, this is a great introduction to its neighborhoods and history." —*Publishers Weekly*, starred review

ATLANTA NOIR
edited by Tayari Jones
256 pages, trade paperback original, $15.95

BRAND-NEW STORIES BY: Tananarive Due, Kenji Jasper, Tayari Jones, Dallas Hudgens, Jim Grimsley, Brandon Massey, Jennifer Harlow, Sheri Joseph, Alesia Parker, Gillian Royes, Anthony Grooms, John Holman, Daniel Black, and David James Poissant.

"Jones, author of *Leaving Atlanta*, returns to the South via Akashic's ever-growing city anthology series. The collection features stories from an impressive roster of talent including Jim Grimsley, Sheri Joseph, Gillian Royes, Anthony Grooms and David James Poissant. The fourteen selections each take place in different Atlanta neighborhoods." —*Atlanta Journal-Constitution*